Rold Simms and his sister Tyler are caught between the warring Scientist and Industrialist factions when Tyler is accused of a terrorist act which will have shocking consequences for the frontier planet of Caljunna. Only the mysterious Teton woman and the alien cloud haven she can enter at will can stave off the total annihilation of their galaxy.

About the author

M. Lee Locke is the author of *The Nestucca Retreat*, a novel. Born in Liberty, Texas, where he grew up, he then moved to California as an adult. He has been a philosophy student, a mathematics teacher, an artist, a software engineer, a singer-songwriter, a rock musician, a newspaper reporter, and a Fortune 500 corporate manager. Pursuing the dream of being an ex-pat in Europe, he is now living in The Hague, The Netherlands, where he is working on his third novel.

Reviews:

"A remarkable novel. A blend of science fiction, mythology and suspense thriller, it surprises the reader with every page. With a fascinating cast of characters, Mr. Locke has created a remarkable world which the reader cannot fail to become entranced by. This is a deeply emotionally satisfying novel which cannot leave any reader unmoved."

Evelyn Trimborn, *Forbidden Fantasy*

"Outstanding. Gripping, suspenseful, and situated in a compelling world both bizarre and familiar, the novel deals with social issues on a meaningful level, whilst at never letting up its pace. Rold and his sister Tyler can easily be identified with as they struggle to hold their world together, but the supporting cast of characters are enthralling as well. Highly entertaining, but with a strong philosophical underpinning, this novel confirms Mr. Locke as an up and coming novelist to watch out for."
Sorcha MacMurrough

Cloud Haven

M. Lee Locke

Domhan Books

ISBN: 1-58345-921-9 hardcover
1-58345-922-7 paperback

Published by Domhan Books
9511 Shore Road, Suite 514
Brooklyn New York 11209
www.domhanbooks.com

Printed by Lightning Source
Distributed by Ingram Book Group

CHAPTER 1

The wind carries her now as the machines once flew
From distant stars unseen to the secluded Beldine sun
The lone rider as brother, blessed Margona as sister
As in the ancient stories
They came to our earth as saviors.

From the epic poem "The Song of Margona"
by *Pitallela-Sim*

Rold Simms felt that typical panic born of being late. He rushed through the spaceport, plowing through the mass of travelers as best he could. He found the experience oppressive. Along with the acrid human odors and piercing noise level from machinery, shouts, and competing public address systems, the terminal assaulted his senses with color.

Among the crushing crowd he was surprised to see Gordon Johnnie and Thomas Renton. They were dressed for outbound travel, wearing Commonwealth robes of synth signifying their status as Scientists, which looked out of place amid the cotton tunics of the local desert dwellers and the lavish bejeweled suits of the Industrial colonists. Recognizing Rold, they nodded, smiling as they stood beneath circular display panels announcing the arrivals and departures.

The spiral pattern of symbols used by the Caljunnese was too far away for Rold to decipher, so he shouted his question: "Thomas! Has the O. E. Express made it in?"

Thomas tilted his head to look at the display. Gordon simply shouted an affirmative. Rold waved his thanks and resumed his charge through the crowds.

He tried to ignore the echoing roar in the voluminous bubble of a building surrounding him. His mind was on other things. He had eyes only for the arriving passenger he was to meet, the reason he had subjected himself to the spaceport on such a busy holiday.

"Rold!"

There she was, waving a hand high above her head. Her mouth was drawn back in an open smile. Her golden hair was cut short, to just below her jaw line. He was not sure he would have recognized her if she had not seen him first. But those lapis eyes sparkled and drew him to her. She wore a formal Old Earth robe and carried a barrel-shaped bag with a shoulder strap.

They crashed into each other, and Rold realized she had grown a lot taller. She was a young woman now, no longer the awkward, lanky girl he had known a couple of years ago, but a budding beauty. He saw himself in a mirrored wall beside them: his face darkened by several days' growth of beard, his long brown hair bleached by desert sun, and his peanut butter eyes staring back. *My sister. But we look so different,* he thought. *How had that happened?*

"I missed you," she said. Her voice was muffled against his chest, but Rold understood the words.

"What are you doing here?" he said in a stern monotone.

She drew back. "Aren't you glad to see me?"

"Of course, Tyler. I missed you, too. But what the hell are you doing here?"

"You must have gotten my message?"

"Cute. I knew it was you, of course, with your ancient codex signature. Who were you trying to fool?"

She shrugged. "I sneaked out. I'm supposed to be visiting Father. I know this isn't exactly *on the way*, but I just had to see you — and see the frontier. Rold, you understand, don't you? I'm bored with university life. Something drew me here — I don't know what. My life is so routine I could scream. You'll help me talk to Father?"

She had looked around the port as she spoke, then returned her attention to Rold. She gripped two wadded knots of his tunic. They stood silently for a moment, Rold absently rubbing her back and looking into her dark blue eyes.

"That's ridiculous, Tyler. You don't know what you're talking about."

"I thought you'd understand."

Rold took her head into his hands as he looked deeply into her eyes.

"Let's get out of here," he said, looking at the mass of people around them.

"Still can't stand crowds, eh? All right. I've got everything I need in this."

As she lifted the bag, the spaceport rumbled and the floor shook. People lost their balance. Rold and Tyler clutched each other to keep from falling. The shaking seemed to go on forever to the terrified crowd.

At last the trembling stopped, and emergency sirens blasted in a domino chain along the length of the port. Fortunately, few in the heaving mass of bodies panicked. Most of the travelers had become inured to the frequent transport mishaps and the increasing terrorist attacks.

But Rold did not like it, not with Tyler here. He took her by the wrist and began pulling her as quickly as he could toward the terminal exit.

A bright light washed through the port, coming from the observation windows along the concourse. The crowd was now bunching up in the bottle-neck at the exit.

"Police are here," they heard someone complain. "This is going to take forever."

"Feeling claustrophobic?" Tyler said.

Rold gritted his teeth and gave her another stern look. She maintained a grin, but her eyebrows wrinkled.

"Winter solstice," he said.

"What?"

"A traditional holiday. Ten days of festivities. People visiting family. You came at a very busy time for the port."

"Oh. Sorry. I didn't know. I just had to get away to see my big brother."

They had to shout their conversation over the ever-increasing buzz of the crowd.

From behind a group of police managed to swim through the mass of travelers and catch Rold's attention.

"Damn!" he hissed.

"What a mess," Tyler said as she clung to Rold's arm. "Why are the police here?"

"Tyler, just let me do the talking. Be quiet and we'll get out of here just fine. You understand?"

Tyler nodded, her smile disappearing abruptly at his sharp tone.

Rold looked at her worried expression and shook his head. He pulled her face close to his and spoke so that she could hear above the din.

"Sorry, Tyler. It's just . . . you don't know what you've walked into here. This is the frontier. It can be barbarous, not the romantic idea I'm sure you've been dreaming of. The law here is . . . harsh, precise. That was a terrorist bomb if ever I've heard one. And we're Scientists. This is an Industrialist world, a boom world. And we've got ourselves bottled up here. Do you understand now?"

"Not really."

He wanted to shake her, as if that would start her brain working. Tyler's naiveté was frustrating, especially in this situation. *She just shouldn't be here*, he thought. And he kept saying that to himself over and over.

Two police peeled off from the group and approached Rold. One was a street cop with a holstered weapon. The other was an investigator; a personal force field crackled about him. The energy field buffeted Rold like a hot desert gust.

"Scientists?" the officer said. He spoke in Ameranglo, but with a thick Caljunnese accent. "Yes? Your relation? Married perhaps?"

"She's my sister," Rold said.

Tyler moved closer to him as she stared at the policeman.

"Simms, is it?" The man was scanning him, retrieving data keyed on his emanation matrix. "Weather expert, working for Hoffman Enterprises. And your sister. We have no records. She hasn't presented her passport?"

"She's just arrived. Is there a problem?"

"There has been an accident, and we're to hold you for questioning, sir. I know this is an imposition, but we'll try to keep it as brief as possible."

Rold was hastily thinking of all the possibilities. He did not want Tyler involved. That was his first concern. Damn it! Why did she have to come? Now of all times!

"You won't need my sister," he said in his most commanding voice. He hoped his status would intimidate the inspector. "I would like her to go ahead to my apartment, and I'll be glad to stay with you for as long as you need. I certainly want to cooperate."

"Actually, sir, it's this young lady we wish to question."

"I said I'll do whatever…."

"I'm sorry, Mr. Simms. We must question you both. You'll see the importance presently. Now please, follow me to the Pilot's Club. We've cleared it for our inquiries."

Tyler hugged Rold's arm and looked up into his eyes.

"Frontier justice?" she whispered.

"It can be quite subjective. But don't worry. Everything'll be okay. I promise. I'll just offer a little token of my appreciation for keeping things short, and they'll cooperate. And if that doesn't work, I'll use Father. I don't like doing that. Draws attention to who we are, but I will if I have to. Of course, there are other alternatives."

If he were alone in this troubled situation, he would manage to be glib with these provincial police. His confidence was a towering attribute that at times brought him close to real danger. But with Tyler here he was consumed with worry. He could not let his risk-taking tendencies surface now and endanger his sister. She was too precious. At least he was mature enough to recognize that. He could laugh about this later. For the moment he had to gain control as quickly as possible.

They waded through the throng until they reached a wide glass door. There was still a commotion down the corridor: lights flashed, sirens sounded, people rushed about. They entered slowly. An attendant, dressed in gray synth, stood just inside the circular room, his eyebrows raised in anticipation.

Rold took a long look at the small crowd of VIPs, and instantly felt out of place. He looked down his long body, clothed in canvas trousers and cotton tunic, and rubbed his rough beard.

The little man gestured toward a server then retreated to the entrance. The police pushed Rold and Tyler forward, then stood motionless at the door. A server approached Rold, unconcerned about the strange goings-on.

"A drink, sir? Something to eat?"

The server was an ape, an Artificial Personality Emulator. It seemed human amid the confusion of people, but lacked the necessary details, upon close inspection, to pass. It emulated an attractive woman in sex-object attire, but its skin had no visible pores, no odor, no sweat, no wrinkles. Mechanical humming and clicking was audible from the movement of arms or neck or even eyes and eyelids as Rold moved his head in close to give a verbal dismissal.

"Simms!"

Rold turned toward his name.

"Hello, Gordon, Thomas," he said nodding to each man. "Good to see some friendly faces."

He looked through an observation window and confirmed his suspicion: an idle transport was on fire, with its top half-blown away.

"What's this?" he asked nodding his head toward the window.

"Just a few minutes ago," Gordon said. "Some explosion. It looks like a cargo transport. No people hurt, I would guess — or no one significant."

"That's a bit cold-hearted, Gordon."

He shrugged. "They use apes mostly."

Rold knew it was not a cargo transport. It was the Old Earth Express.

"Simms," Gordon continued, as if this were a normal social gathering. "What is it you've been working on exactly out there in that desert of yours?"

"Water resources. I do most of the data gathering in the high desert and mountains."

"Caljunna," Thomas said. "Rather dismal planet, isn't it? All these wretched natives."

"I don't deal with the people very often. I'm mostly locked up with the computer. Although I do get out from time to time. I go rock climbing to relax. There are some excellent climbs in the Choshoon mountains."

"You'll get your neck broken one of these days, Simms. And where would that leave your father?"

Rold wondered how much these two knew.

"So, Rold, what brings you here, of all days?" Thomas asked, as he eyed Tyler.

"Gentlemen, my sister. Vivian Tyler Simms. Tyler, this is Thomas, and Gordon."

Rold was distracted by an argument between the attendant and the two policemen left guarding the entrance. Tyler's eyes were glazed and she remained silent.

The suited men now approached Rold and his companions. He watched in fascination as they pushed through the crowd. "Something's afoot now," he mumbled, thinking about the damaged transport.

Gordon and Thomas looked at each other. Rold thought he saw complicity there — of what he was not sure. *I've been at this too long*, he thought. *Now I don't even trust Scientists!*

"Mr. Simms?" one of the policemen said. He waved a probe about Rold's body, pronouncing him "clean" then did the same with Tyler. He produced a hand weapon, an energy-wave propeller.

Rold's skin crawled at the sight. He wondered if Tyler had ever seen such a weapon. He was sure she had seen little violence in her life, having been sheltered by her social position. The Scientist Party was a component of the new aristocracy, and the Simms family association with their class, had allowed Tyler, perhaps forced her, to move about in antiseptic surroundings. She looked up at Rold, beseeching support. He smiled at her, hoping it gave her some comfort.

"Yes," he said calmly.

"Sorry, sir, but you and your sister are under arrest."

"On what charge?" Gordon burst in.

Rold held up his hand to silence him.

"The O. E. transport has been attacked by terrorists. There's evidence that an explosive device was left in the passenger luggage hold, just above your sister's seat."

"Why are you talking like I'm not even here?" Tyler said.

Rold tried to shush her but she continued, "I didn't put a bomb in that transport. It's simply a mistake. It sounds incredible that an explosive small enough to fit into luggage could do that!" She pointed to the vast steaming hole in the five hundred meter long transport.

"We thought Mr. Simms might have an answer to that."

The room had quieted, and all eyes were on Rold.

"I'm not budging until we have council."

"Do you realize who you're dealing with?" Gordon interrupted again.

The policeman stared silently. Discomfiture shown in his eyes as he quickly laid out a compromise.

"Very well, sir. You may wait here until you receive council. But you'll not be allowed to leave this room. I'll have to talk to the Boss. I'm sure the port attendant here will find a solicitor for you."

The men turned and strode to the door. Tyler was visibly frightened.

Rold still maintained his icy glare.

"Look, Simms," Gordon said, placing his hand on Rold's shoulder. "It's all a mistake. A bit of hot air. The Industrialists love to see one of us in trouble, but not you — not with who your father is. Don't look so glum."

Rold tensed as Gordon patted his shoulder. His only thought was for Tyler. He was angry, ready to scream at her, perhaps take her across his knee. That thought softened him. He knew then he would not let his temper frighten her. Reality would do a good job of that quite soon.

"You had no idea," he started, looking down at her. "You couldn't have known."

He took her by the arm and escaped to a deserted corner. "This is what they've been waiting for," he continued in a lower voice.

"*What?*"

"They followed you. They saw an opportunity to use *you* to get at me. You had no way of knowing. And now, somehow I have to keep us alive. This *could* be it. This could start the whole goddamn thing!"

"Start *what*? Rold, what are you talking about…"

Their faces were close together, noses almost touching. Tyler's brow was drawn down into a furrow deep enough to get lost in. Rold stroked her cheek with the back of his hand. They stood like that for a long moment.

"Be strong," he said as he held both her arms firmly. "You have to get your mind on surviving. It's not your fault; I know that. Did anyone suggest you come here?"

"No. No one knows I'm here — not even Father."

She buried her head into his chest. She straightened up, wiped her eyes, and took a deep breath. Rold was lost in thought.

"Somehow we've got to get you to Newert. We've got to convince them you knew nothing about it. They've got me. What else do they want?"

"I don't want to go."

"Excuse me, sir," someone said from behind them. "I think I can offer you some help."

Rold turned and saw a short man with a thick abdomen, square face and gray beard, dressed in desert leathers. He looked more out of place in this lounge than Rold. The man grinned, showing lost teeth. He spoke in Ameranglo with a thick accent and odd phrasing, but somehow differently than the Caljunnese Rold was used to.

"I know, sir," he continued. "I don't belong in this fancy room. No, you're right. I just came to make arrangements for a couple of customers — Industrialists, you know. They're the only kinds who usually hire me. I couldn't help but overhear — of course nobody could help but overhear. You got a little trouble. Now, I'm not saying I can help with the Boss, but I can maybe help get the young lady to her destination. To be honest, I already knew she was stranded — kind of knowing the port the way I do, I hear things.

"I'm sorry, I didn't introduce myself. Blikki, call me Blikki. Me and my daughter run safaris on a wilderness planet. I've got my own ship."

Rold looked at the man quietly. *How does he know so much?* he thought. *Who said Tyler was "stranded?"*

But he looked harmless enough. His smile seemed genuine, his demeanor typically Caljunnese, with an air of deference to aristos that barely hid a dislike of the ruling class.

"No, no. Blikki — you said your name was Blikki? You don't understand. My sister needs to get to Newert. That's all the way to the other end of the Commonwealth. A small charter can't make a trip like that."

"Just wait; I haven't explained it all yet. I know I ramble a lot. We're on our way to Salkinia — the third planet in this system. Take us maybe a month or so to get there, sub-lumina. Ore barges come and go all the time there — empty ones in, full ones out. There's one that goes all the way to the New Earth system using wormy holes, takes on passengers at times. Goes to a neighbor planet to New Earth. Pontano I think it's called."

Rold brightened. "Pontain. You mean Pontain. Yes, then she could get a shuttle to Newert. That sounds good."

Almost too good, he thought. "I'll pay whatever fare you require. No need to quibble over the price. You just name it. But first we need to clear up this mess." He looked toward the entrance. "When do you leave?"

"We'll be ready in a couple of hours, but I'll wait as long as tomorrow morning. Then we have to be on our way. We're at the charter terminal, gate eleven."

"Thanks, Blikki. I'll get her there somehow." He sighed as he shook Blikki's hand. *Why am I trusting this little man?* he asked himself. *Because he had not real choice.*

Blikki backed away, disappearing in the crowd. Rold's smile disappeared quickly as he looked around for Gordon and Thomas, who were nowhere to be seen. He had a sour taste in his mouth and a burning in his stomach as his resolve hardened.

They stood for a half-hour or more, quietly discussing news of home and other happenings in their recent lives, avoiding the present situation. Finally Rold grew impatient and crossed the room to the entrance. A server offered him another drink, and he shoved it aside. The ape fell to the floor, the drink tray spinning through the air. Rold's eyes widened at the scene, his whole body shaking. This was their chance to escape!

The commotion drew one of the policemen. Rold acted quickly, without thought. He shoved the policeman, expertly it seemed, his size adding to the effect. The man was down, pulling his weapon. Rold jumped to the floor and wrestled it away. The second policeman rushed in, trying to tackle Tyler and use her as a human shield. Mindlessly Rold fired a spray of energy at him. Another step and Tyler would have been in the way. The man crumpled into a quivering, paralyzed heap. Neither man had activated personal shields. With a moment of hesitation Rold looked at his work with grim concentration. There were screams from the few people still in the lounge. Tyler was frozen to the floor. Rold swept the room with his eyes, pointing the weapon as a warning, then stuffed it in his belt. He pushed Tyler through the door, and started running.

The chase was on. They raced down the empty corridors, making random turns until completely lost, with sirens blaring overhead.

They stopped at an isolated alcove which housed communication panels and an entrance to restrooms. Tyler coughed and doubled over, panting furiously. Rold straightened as he caught his breath and began evaluating his surroundings. Each corridor at the space port looked alike: blue plastic floors, glossy white walls and ceilings, and metal railings along the various ramps that allowed elevation changes for pedestrians. He both berated and congratulated himself for his impetuousness. Then he slowed himself long enough to think.

"What are you doing!" Tyler said through labored breaths. "We're just getting into more trouble."

"I love you dearly, Tyler, but shut up."

"Where are we?" he asked rotating his head about the protective nook.

"CALJUNNA SPACE PORT," an assistance audio stated.

"Where within Caljunna Space Port?"

"TERMINAL FF, LEVEL 2," the voice said calmly. "AUDIO ACCESS AND HUMAN WASTE DISPOSAL APARTMENT 209."

He checked his watch then swept Tyler along, mapping a theoretical path to the charter terminal where he hoped he would find Blikki.

Seconds flashed with the thudding contact of each foot to the soft floor. Most of the people had been cleared from this sector, but the few stray travelers wandering the gigantic tube-like corridors gave little notice to anyone running. People were constantly late to connections, and the size of the building added to the problem. In fact, they passed another person running to catch a transport. The alarm going off was no different from the warning signals for transport departures. Maybe they could escape?

Rold began thinking about the start of all this: the damaged transport. What kind of explosive had it been? Some dense emulsion, he thought. Probably a frozen hydrogen base. What's the vulgar term used by the *Fashatta*?

Ice cream. Yeah, I've heard that somewhere. He angered at the thought that Tyler could have been one of the victims of the explosion.

The thunder of feet followed them, heard but unseen. Blikki's terminal was a level below them, and Rold knew that an elevator could be secured by the police, while the ramps took too much time. At a railing that overlooked a plaza below them on the lower level, Rold made a quick decision to jump. It was a good four meters down. Tyler stood frozen at the railing as she watched her brother hit a shrub in a planter box and roll to his feet.

"Jump," he called up to her. "I'll catch you."

"I can't!"

"Yes you can. Hurry, they're coming! Do it now!"

She straddled the railing, closed her eyes, and let herself fall, bottom downward. Rold was there and caught her in his arms, the two of them collapsing on the plastic floor.

"You *have* grown," Rold said with a smile.

Tyler frowned at him; he grabbed her hand and pulled her to running feet.

The terminal was in sight. As they approached, Rold saw Blikki strolling toward his departure gate.

"Blikki!"

The little round man stopped and looked over his shoulder. He smiled then was startled by a commotion off some distance beyond Rold and Tyler. Rold stopped also and turned sharply, following Blikki's stare. An army of police were scrambling in their direction, weaponry snapping to the ready. Rold jumped as he gave in to his instincts and pushed Tyler and Blikki along with him, who picked up the pace.

"Do we have passage with you?" Rold asked.

"Only if you can run a little faster, sir."

"Are you coming with us, Rold?" Tyler asked.

His only answer was a blast to the rear with the stolen hand weapon. He did not even look to see what damage he might have caused.

They dashed through the gate and into an open portal. Blikki closed the heavy, pivoted door. It clanked and hissed as it sealed them in.

"Thank you." Rold panted with his heart in his throat. Explosive taps and thuds rang the hull.

"Let's get moving," Blikki said. "Those wave blasts could do some damage after a while. But no worry. Caljunna has no space fleet, no military to speak of. Once we're a few kilometers into space we're out of their jurisdiction."

A woman entered the cramped tube where the two men stood. "Father, they're all tucked away and everything's buttoned down."

"My daughter: Yosana la' Kunda."

Rold nodded to her. She was very young and plain looking, slim, with light brown hair, brown eyes, a dry complexion, dressed in cotton pants and tunic. Rold thought again. *She was not so much plain as masked in plainness, attractive, but unconcerned with her own looks.*

She was not smiling. She stared intently, to the point that Rold finally averted his eyes as he spoke.

"Good to meet you, *zelita*."

Yosana surveyed the situation, checked a monitor that showed the massed forces outside the transport, then looked at another one that showed the clear tarmac.

"We have no time for introductions," she said, somewhat relaxing her stony face. "They'll break the door if we don't get out of here. Hurry." She retreated and the others followed. The four of them moved toward the flight deck.

"Get seated and strapped in," Blikki said. "We're about to leave this little home of mine. The centrifugal sling'll break your neck if you're not stabilized."

Yosana shoved Rold into a swiveling chair and then collapsed into the one at the controls. Tyler slowly found a seat and began fastening the restraints.

"You appear to have anticipated our arrival," Rold said as he connected a wide elastic band of fabric across his abdomen. He watched Yosana and Blikki attaching theirs and mimicked the procedure. The chairs resembled cocoons, protecting their occupants. Yosana touched a button and the brightly-lit paved ground sank below them. Darkness soon swallowed the spaceport, shrinking it to a few sparkling lights.

"Times being what they are, sir," Yosana said keeping her attention to her instrumentation.

"We thank you," Tyler said.

"Yes," Rold joined in. "Though I wonder why you risk so much for strangers."

"A simple answer," Yosana said. "Money. You're paying for the trip. And a little extra for the trouble."

She then spoke in Caljunnese under her breath: "Damn rich aristos! Getting our ship all beaten up. They'll pay, damn it."

Rold understood some of what she said and smiled at her grumbling, glad to know where he stood.

The small transport creaked and moaned. They were instantly hurtled into deep space. Caljunna was reduced to a small pinpoint. Blikki sighed and shook his head. A slow feeling of relief permeated the small globular cell.

Yosana popped out of her bindings. Rold attempted the same motions but could not get his fasteners undone.

"Helpless." Yosana shook her head. She knelt beside him and freed him of his cocoon.

"How do you know to call me 'zelita?'" she asked, making conversation as she returned to her instruments. Blikki excused himself quietly. Rold watched him leave, feeling slightly abandoned.

"Your name: la'Kunda. It's Caljunnese. I've lived in the desert. Learned the language. Perhaps I presumed. Should I call you *odamma?*"

"You may call me Yosana, sir." *I'll have to watch what I say,* she thought. "And your names?"

"Rold. I thought you knew already."

"And I'm Tyler."

"Hello, Tyler. Interesting name for a woman."

"It's actually Vivian Tyler Simms. Tyler's an old family name. I *hate* Vivian. Your name is beautiful."

"Thank you. And you're Scientists?" She seemed preoccupied but willing to talk.

"Politically, yes," Rold said. "Occupation? Not exactly. I'm sort of the black sheep."

"No you're not!" Tyler said taking Rold's hand and looking into her brother's eyes with innocent admiration.

"I studied philosophy rather than science."

"But you work, don't you? What does a philosopher do besides teach? You weren't teaching on Caljunna."

"I'll be teaching on Old Earth soon I hope. But you're right. I was doing science."

As the transport accelerated to its maximum speed, Rold examined the flight deck. The walls were that of a sphere encrusted with button switches, lever switches, photo displays, and metal grills. He hated the design. Pretty old, he thought. Dr. Schiller probably designed it. Gadgets. There must be a couple of thousand moving parts in all of this. Who maintains it all? Then he noticed the jury-rigged thermal keyboard and nodded his head.

"Excuse me," he said, feeling oppressed in the cramped cell. "Is there more to this . . . vessel?"

"We have plenty of room. Only one other party. The Jenkins are in hibernation. They have no idea what's happened. How about you? I'm sure you can afford the drugs."

"No, I don't think so. But I would like to get settled. How about you, Tyler?"

"All right with me. My head's still spinning. I just got off a star jumper, got arrested, flattened some policemen — actually Rold did that — and ran to catch your ship. What a day!

"Are we going to be all right now, Rold? I was really scared back there. What's going on, anyway? I'm no terrorist. And neither are you . . ."

"We'll talk about it later. Let's get some rest."

"Follow me." Yosana checked the pilot controls then stepped to an oval door which led into another tubular hall.

The transport was like a beehive; Rold was immediately oppressed after the open spaces of Caljunna. They followed the short hallway to a commonroom that was much more comfortable. There were blue fabric drapes on the walls and floor pillows which shined with primary hues.

Like night and day, Rold thought as he plopped on a lush sofa made of the glossy pillows; the flight deck was so mechanical. Tyler found a group of pillows and curled up, quickly falling asleep.

"I wish I could do that," Rold whispered. "It's a talent I lack."

He relaxed his throbbing eyes for a moment then blinked them open and saw Yosana waving a bio-scanner around his face and shoulders.

"You're in pain," she said. "You should've said something."

"It's not bad. Bruised my shoulder."

She opened a purse that hung from a loose belt around her hips.

"I have some anti-inflammatories here," she said still searching.

"Please, no. I don't use chemicals. I'm fine. Really."

"Oh, that old priggish Scientist rule doesn't mean anything in deep space. Nobody really pays any attention to that."

"No thank you anyway."

"Very well." She shook her head, having to bite her tongue. "Would you like to go to your cell?"

"I think I'll just stay here with Tyler for now. This is quite comfortable. I still feel like I'm racing."

Yosana only nodded and walked briskly through the room to return to piloting.

Soon fatigue grabbed hold and thrust Rold into a stack of pillows as a drain sucks wash water from a tub. Cerebral juices swirled about the top of his head making him dizzy. Sleep came slowly but completely. No dreams interrupted his rest.

Yosana walked in once and dimmed the sheet-light in the smooth ceiling. She unfolded two blankets woven of natural fibers and covered the sleeping hulk of Rold Simms and his young sister. Rold stirred and thought he heard her whisper something: "It's him all right. Damn it!"

Then she left.

CHAPTER 2

*Mysteries enshroud the name of la'Kunda
Margona as woman shall break the silence
And ease the heart of the Rider.*

From "The Song of Margona"
by Pitallela-Sim

Rold woke to a cozy warmness, though a small shiver rippled down his neck. His shoulder was sore, his back stiff. The room was dark except for one dim red light that appeared as a dying flame upon a stone hearth. The room was much larger than he remembered: at least fifty paces across in either direction. As he rose from his blanket he suddenly realized Tyler was not there. Yosana entered and switched on the sheet-light, which grew in brilliance slowly so that Rold's eyes would accommodate the radiance without pain. He saw that the fireplace was real enough, though the flame was an animated projection. Yosana walked to a corner alcove that was bordered with a counter and stools. She began sifting through cabinets and drawers, clicking and clanking, sliding and slamming, but not angrily — in fact, efficiently it seemed to Rold. The sound was the symphony of an early morning kitchen, which brought a smile and memories to Rold.

When he had been a boy, his family had lived in a small bungalow by the sea. His bedroom had been just off the kitchen. His mother and father had always been up early, puttering around, making breakfast and talking quietly. Rold would lie in his warm bed and listen through the cracked door, knowing that he could laze a while, all cozy, before having to get up. While smelling breakfast cooking and listening to the comfortable sounds, he would dream up some adventure for the day. Frank would come along; he had always followed Rold into any mischief, though reluctantly. Rold smiled at the thought.

As he moved to stretch, he began thinking of the previous day, how crazy it all was. He felt some satisfaction that Tyler was safe, though he feared only temporarily.

"Do you know where my sister is?" he asked as he stood and tried to smooth out his rumpled clothes.

"I showed her to a room early this morning."

Rold walked to the galley, sat on one of the stools and leaned over the counter. As Yosana rose from bent knees they bumped heads then looked at each other, Rold smiling, Yosana frowning and rubbing her crown.

"Butting heads already," Rold said. He expected her to laugh at his little joke, but she kept her impassive expression.

She quietly served him a platter of yellow cheese, a salted meat hash, and malonta bread — a curious, heavy brioche of oat and corn meal, which Rold recognized from Caljunna. He ate in silence as was the custom of the Caljunnese. After eating as much as his stomach could hold, Rold stood and stretched and rubbed his face and beard.

"Want to freshen up?" Yosana asked as she cleared the counter.

"Yes. In a moment."

Yosana stopped her puttering and looked at Rold silently.

"The exploding transport," he said then paused.

"Yes?"

"I want Tyler left out. It was a mistake she got involved. I'm probably telling you too much. I don't want to endanger you as well."

"I can take care of myself, sir."

Rold nodded, not sure if she was playing games or if she simply did not care.

"Your sister," Yosana said.

"Yes?"

"She's a very special person."

"She's always had that effect on people. I'm not surprised she's charmed you so quickly."

"She's quite different than most of your class. Believe me, I've seen plenty of aristos. Forgive me for speaking so bluntly."

"I don't mind. But I'd guess you've dealt with Industrialists mostly."

"There's really not much difference between the two parties. No offense, sir."

"Stop calling me 'sir.' Call me Rold. And it would have to be something personal to offend me — not your dislike of my party."

Yosana displeasure was apparent in her twisted face. Her expression relaxed to a non-committal lifelessness. "Very well, *Rold*."

Rold felt dissatisfied with the conversation but decided to drop it for now. There was an itch inside him that needed scratching, but it was hard to identify it.

Yosana showed him to an unoccupied living cell and left to take over piloting chores for Blikki.

The distilled vapor shower cleansed every pore on Rold's body. He used a microbe scrubber, and as a final act of refreshment had his body vacuumed. He stood in a metallic cylinder a meter in diameter. Wide-mouthed suction tubes attacked him, one in front and one in back. He laughed as they passed below his shoulders, to just below his waist. He dragged a comb through his long, tangled hair and left the hygiene closet. Clothing lay on the bed cushions in neat bundles. Without a thought of how they got there, he dressed and went exploring.

Little time passed before he had seen most of the transport. There were only six individual living quarters which he surmised from their portals. Though he could not inspect them, he assumed they were like his own. In addition to the large common room there were a game room and a library. Transportation and living support controls were all managed up front, where they had entered the day before.

The undercarriage, a full one-quarter of the ship, contained the massive gravity emulator which seemed to be on the fritz. Occasionally after some crackling sounds, a brief pause would occur and objects would float then drop in disorder. Rold hit his head once in a corridor as he rose unexpectedly. His breakfast sloshed up his esophagus and churned in his stomach. His first experience with weightlessness had been when he'd worked on satellites as a vacation job between university terms. Since then he had done some asteroid trekking, enjoying his hobby of rock climbing, and had little trouble with the low gravity on the slow spinners. No one was immune to space sickness — though some are more resistant than others — and he had been lucky in that respect.

There were stories about early space exploration, before gravity emulation, in which people died or went crazy. No deep space travel had ever been successful in those days. Not until gravity emulation was perfected did human space travel become practical. Rold thought of all the suffering of those primitive times, somewhat awed by the advances that had been made since then; though when he recalled the exploding transport, his confidence ebbed quickly.

After leaving Rold in his room, Yosana returned to the flight deck. Blikki was there, messing with a display screen. He looked up, feeling her presence.

She screamed in rage, picking up a notebook and throwing it across the small room, hitting the viewing window. Falling to her knees in the cramped quarters, she lay her head on her father's lap and beat on his legs with her fists.

Blikki grabbed her convulsing body and crooned until she calmed a bit.

"Don't like having them under foot myself," he said. "Did he do anything to you? Just tell me and I'll cut out his liver. To hell with his money or his position."

"No, no. That's not it."

She looked up into his concerned eyes.

"But . . . No. I can't tell you! Gwydmonia! She . . . she has me tied up in knots. This Scientist — he's like the others: arrogant, rich. You know what I mean. I can handle him. He's not the problem. I can't tell you now. Not now."

Blikki smoothed her hair from the top of her head to her shoulders.

"The sister is sweet," he said.

"Yes. She's not ruined yet, I guess. There's something about her, though. Like she can see right through me."

"I'm still not sure about the brother."

Yosana looked into Blikki's eyes. There was a pleading there he did not understand. But he had learned not to question his daughter when she went into these black moods.

"Can you make it till we get to Salkinia?"

"I'm fine, Father. All calmed down now. I'll talk to Gwyd when we get there. I miss her."

"Can you tell me what it's all about when we get there?"

"I'm afraid to tell you. If I speak it out loud, it's like I'll believe it then. I don't want to believe it. Some day."

Blikki restrained his curiosity, worried he had already pushed too much.

Yosana rose and straightened herself, wiping her face and smoothing her clothes. Blikki watched her leave and shook his head. *It's very trying having a daughter with so many mysteries,* he thought. *A lot like her mother, of course. Like her sweet mother.*

Rold found Yosana and Blikki staring at a communication panel they had uncovered on the floor of the library.

"Well, that's it then," Blikki was saying as he replaced the cover and flipped back a square of carpet.

"Let me guess," Rold said. "Power communication problem for the gravity emulator. You probably use biotic communications for systems management."

"Yes," Yosana said, irritation clinging to the word as she pronounced it, "and we don't have an on-board lab to manufacture enzyme. It may be an enzyme problem, or it could be receptors."

"What you need is an endocrinologist."

"We can't afford an endocrinologist," Yosana said.

"They don't charge that much."

"We like to be . . . independent," Blikki said. "We'll be all right until we get to Salkinia. Won't be quite as comfortable, though."

"We have some space sickness drugs," Yosana said. "But I forget, you don't partake."

Rold shook his head but smiled with tolerance. He wondered how Yosana was able to keep customers as rude as she was. But he realized most passengers probably chose hibernation, and she was not used to people wandering around the ship like this.

Yosana and he left Blikki to stroll back to the common room. Yosana obviously had something on her mind. Rold wanted to help her open up, but wisely kept silent, knowing he would set off her temper. Then she spoke.

"I want to apologize if I seem unconcerned about your predicament. I know I seem rude. But friends of mine, innocent people, have been hurt by your feud with the Industrialists." Her eyes sparkled with moisture and the corners of her mouth were pulled back. "A childhood friend died last year on my mother's home world by the hands of the Militia. I know it's none of your doing, Mr. Simms . . . Rold. I guess I'm jealous of the comfortable isolation your status affords you."

"I had no idea. Must have been a good friend."

Yosana found Rold's eyes, her mouth grim. "Yes. But good friend or not, his death was senseless."

Rold was excited by her opening up. But he was sure that she was still hiding something.

They entered the common room. Yosana placed her palm flatly on a red rectangular panel on the wall close to the door. With a rumbling hum the wall rolled up into the ceiling revealing a window. It was the height of a man and twice as wide. She darkened the room and the brilliance of the stars threw long shadows back onto the floor and opposite wall. Some of the stars seemed reddish and elongated but there was very little evidence of movement.

"Beautiful," he said.

"What's that?" Yosana said pointing at a star that was growing in brightness and size. It moved in a distorted spiral. Just then a red light flashed in the cabin, and a projection of Blikki appeared floating in the middle of the room.

"We've got a missile heading our way," Blikki said.

"What?" Rold exclaimed, squinting his eyes.

"Someone at Caljunna threw it at us. But the guidance is pretty unstable at these speeds and so far from home. I wouldn't worry about it. Who did you piss off back there, sir?"

"I wish I knew."

"Well, somebody wants you bad," Blikki said.

"Are you going to maneuver away from it?" Rold asked. Blikki's calm manner had not reassured him.

"Would do no good," Blikki said. "It's on us now."

"But you could try, couldn't you?"

"Yeah, but we'd lose as much as a week on our ETA with a course change. Just settle down, sir; it'll miss us. I promise."

"Where's Tyler?"

"She's fine," Yosana said. "It's better that she stay in her room than be moving about the ship."

Rold felt unsatisfied with her answer but quickly decided to trust her judgement. He peered with his nose pressing the glass. The missile was a misshapen sphere slowly tumbling toward the transport. Yosana stood with arms folded beneath her breasts, sweat forming on her temples. They watched in a trance without speaking.

"Hold on," Blikki said as it reached within a hundred meters.

The room shook, rattling everything into disarray. Then the missile passed by and exploded without harm, sending a shower of pebbles tapping against the hull. Rold thought he noticed an unusual cloud surrounding the debris, but at second glance it had disappeared.

Rold turned toward Blikki's image, eyes wide.

"You have a shield!" he accused.

"Not a force shield. A couple of defensive blasters. Got it with my port gun, I guess; automatic tracking. Though I would have sworn it missed."

"But even that's unlawful."

"Got to protect myself, sir. You've been out here long enough to know what the limits of the law are."

Blikki looked down, his hands obviously adjusting instruments.

"Damn!" He shouted as his head jerked forward.

"Did we move off course?" Rold asked.

"Yes," Blikki said. "But not too much, I guess. We'll probably only lose a couple of days. But that's not the problem. We've been hit. Yosana, get up here quick. I need you. We're going into a roll. And damn it, of all the luck! There's another one coming! And it's a big one!"

"Where's that gun!"

"Sir, you don't . . ."

He turned to Yosana.

"How do I get there?"

"This way."

Yosana led him through a crawl space that was under the floor of the main corridor. In seconds they were in a bubble that had a small viewer and controls to a short-range blaster.

"Go back inside; help Blikki," Rold said.

"What do you know about weapons? You're a . . ."

"I said go inside, *zelita*."

Yosana reluctantly obeyed, knowing this was not the time for an argument. She headed back into the common room, on her way to the flight deck, and found Tyler watching the window.

"What was that?" Tyler asked, her eyes wide.

"An attack. A missile . . ."

"No. I know about that. I saw your father's com picture. I'm talking about that glob of whatever. There was a creature, a white, oozing cloud of fluid as big as this transport. Out there!"

Yosana was startled. She took in a deep breath.

"Where? When?"

"Out there, Yosana. I just said that. It came really close to the window. I put my hand up to the glass, and it started glowing. Lights. Colored lights danced around my hand."

Yosana matched Tyler's intense gaze.

"You see strange things in space," was her only answer. "Quickly. Come with me forward. We're not out of danger yet."

Tyler sat in a cockpit chair and watched the monitor for the coming missile. It was approaching on a more steady path than the smaller one. Blikki and Yosana were having problems with the ship's controls. Rold fired, sending sparks of energy flowing back behind the transport. He made a glancing hit; a chunk of the missile peeled off. But the menace kept coming. He fired again and made a dead-center hit. But the missile broke up into twelve smaller warheads, six warheads exploding without harm.

"He's pretty good," Yosana said, eyebrows raised. Blikki and she were feverishly working to stabilize the ship, but each kept an eye on the rear battle.

Tyler smiled at Yosana's compliment for only a moment.

Rold made several successive blasts, destroying all but two of the warheads.

"Damn good!" Blikki added.

They were breathing hard now. The warheads were getting closer. Tyler was about to hide her eyes when the monitor was blurred with a milky haze. Her eyes widened. It was that . . .thing again! In a wink it had vanished.

"What the hell was that?" Rold said over a com speaker.

The remaining warheads were gone, as was the spinning debris of the blasted missile.

"There," Blikki said. "It'll hold for now. Damn scrap almost put us in a spin." He wiped his brow of sweat. Yosana sighed as she stood.

Everyone met in the common room as they rushed to check on each other. Even Yosana smiled.

"Good job," she said looking at Rold. "For a Scientist."

He paid little attention to her compliment.

"Are you all right?" he asked Tyler as she encircled his waist with her delicate arms. She answered with a squeeze.

"Look at this mess," Yosana said.

Everyone began picking up the tumbled contents. Yosana noted that Rold and Tyler helped, thinking how odd this couple was. She was becoming comfortable with them, though.

"Things look fine now," Yosana said. "I have to get back to the controls."

Blikki approached Rold. He had stood back still not sure of this young man who had brought so much trouble aboard his ship.

"Good job back there, sir."

"I'm not sure what happened at the end, Blikki."

"Doesn't matter. You saved my ship. We would've been blasted to dust. What's this all about? They must want to kill you awfully bad."

"I'm not even sure who 'they' are."

Rold turned to the window. The debris from the missile was like a fog that began to clear. The speckles of distant stars reappeared. And he felt his anger boiling.

CHAPTER 3

Mystery recognizes mystery
When placed amidst the battle,
The calling came to Margona the woman
And hushed was the Rider's worry,
For among the stars, the mighty Rold
Came rushing like a storm.

From "The Song of Margona"
by Pitallela-Sim

The next few weeks were tranquil, and little was said about the escape — the first or the second. Rold and Tyler relaxed by playing games or watching recorded plays and musical concerts. It was good to get to know each other again. But Rold still kept a few things to himself.

Yosana and Blikki took one day at a time, which both bothered and pleased Rold. His whole life had been filled with planning, analyzing, thinking things through. Yet here were two people who had little care for what they might be doing even a month in advance much less a year. They managed to keep to themselves most of the time, leaving the brother and sister to their reunion.

Tyler occasionally sought out Yosana, wanting the company of a woman. Rold warned her not to be a pest, but Tyler claimed Yosana did not mind. Blikki was quiet but not unkind if approached. The voyage became a relaxing intermission amid the chaos of the Scientists' escape.

As the proscribed space days passed, Rold began evaluating Blikki and Yosana.

Blikki was full of old tales and was likeable from the beginning. He had a little larceny in him, being a real salesman, or con man Rold thought, and it made Rold laugh to himself. He never believed a word Blikki said, but he was polite and listened. The old man had softened his distrust of Rold after the missile incident. He felt beholdened to Rold for saving his ship and the lives aboard.

Yosana stirred many passions, good and bad. She was a fighter and a bitter opponent of the aristocracy. He actually liked that. Though he missed Society at times, he had always been at odds with the ancient system, as was his father.

The details were not necessary, so Rold did not pry, but it was apparent Yosana's mother had been dead for several years, which explained some things. And that gave them something in common. She had been raised by Blikki, and they were now partners in their touring business. Rold wondered what kind of adolescence she must have had. Her intelligence was impressive, as was her competence at her job. But she seemed angry much of the time. He admired her energy, though she never seemed quite ready to trust his compliments. He would not have given her a second thought if she had simply treated him as a paying customer. But there was something about her when she spoke to him. She was hiding something, something that involved him or Tyler. He sensed it, and he *had* to know what it was.

"Why don't you sit down and relax a moment?" Rold said, patting a pillow beside him. Yosana and he were in the common room. Tyler was off reading or sleeping. He was sure that she had planned to be scarce; she was such a little schemer since she had grown up. For some reason she wanted Rold and Yosana to talk.

Yosana was scanning a display tablet from behind the galley counter. "I'm busy," she said without even a glance in his direction.

"I can see that."

"Sorry," she said, looking up from her work. "Forgive me for being rude. You command; I obey."

She circled the counter, with her head down, and dropped to her knees in front of him.

"You can be so infuriating!" he said. "All I asked was that you relax a minute. Damn it. It wasn't a command!"

"Oh come now. That's just . . ."

"How do you ever keep customers?"

"We do just fine, Mr. Simms."

"Rold."

"I forgot."

Rold snared Yosana's wrists in both hands and jerked her erect from her kowtow. Surprise bulged her eyes and she bit her lower lip. A brief show of anger crossed her face. Rold kept his stern expression as he released her. Then he sighed and turned his eyes away.

"I don't usually treat people that way," he said. Their eyes locked. "I beg your pardon."

"I could have easily slit your gizzard just then."

"I asked you to forgive me."

"The hell I will! You're just like all the rest. You think because you own the Universe you own the people in it as well. But you don't own me, MR. SIMMS. We'll take you to Salkinia. You'll pay us well. And I don't expect to see you again. So that should explain all you need to know."

"You're not being fair. I may not be like all the rest. There must be something special about me. Certainly you don't treat all your passengers with such abhorrence."

She wavered. It was a visible sheen that washed her eyes of anger.

"I don't really feel abhorrence for . . . *you*."

"My position? What?"

"My future. I want to control it. Never mind. Forget it. You're right. I should apologize."

With that said she jogged from the room. Rold calmed himself, letting the adrenalin subside. He shook his head, not feeling any closer to the mystery. They had several meetings just as volatile. He now hoped for a quick end to the journey.

Tyler made sure that she was at the viewing window as often as possible each day. She wanted to see the *thing* again. She was sure that it was real — and intelligent. It had called to her. She was not sure how or why. Every time she asked Yosana about it she became cross. Yosana must know something about the creature, she must!

About halfway through the voyage, Tyler and Yosana were playing their daily game of chess. Yosana was very good, but Tyler always won. She wondered if Yosana was letting her win — because she was a passenger or because of her position in Society. Regardless, it was always fun. It was the only time Yosana did not seem so gloomy.

"Oh, Yosana, how did you do that? I'll never beat you now."

"You'll find a way."

Tyler moved her remaining knight and was delighted to see that it worked well; the game would continue at least for a while.

"There. Check. Get out of this one." Yosana had moved her bishop while Tyler was not looking.

Tyler shook her head. The check was easily managed. But Yosana's obscure way of talking confused her, as always. She wondered if it was the difference in language. Yosana's Ameranglo was of an archaic form: lovely to listen to but difficult to comprehend at times.

"I've been looking for that thing. That cloud thing."

Yosana did not rankle as usual with the introduction of the subject.

"I know," she said. "I guess I should tell you what you want to know."

Tyler looked up from the board, excitement surging through her entire body. She had been trying to get Yosana to talk about this for days. And now . . . maybe now she would open up.

"Tell me. Tell me!"

"First, you tell *me*."

"What?"

"What you saw and felt — or heard."

The chess game was now totally forgotten. Tyler adjusted her seating, wiggling until her back was relaxed. She tilted her head and talked.

"It's big — as big as this ship. Like a giant jellyfish or amoeba. White and billowing like a cloud but shiny like a plastic bag or balloon. Also, I could see a network of tubular vessels through its rubbery shell membrane. Fluid bubbled through the tubes in surges. It spoke to me in two ways: lights — it had flashing colored lights that responded to my hand, and telepathy, I guess. I sensed things, in my mind."

"What things?"

Tyler laughed.

"It's silly. Feelings of love, acceptance. It made me think of my mother and how I miss her."

"Tell me about your mother."

"I haven't told you? Rold didn't either? Well, she died in an accident. It was a senseless accident on a ground highway on Old Earth. Nothing sinister or political, just your everyday statistical accident. Only, it was my mother, not a faceless statistic quoted on the news. I was eight years old. Rold was fifteen. Father fell apart. We had never seen him that way. Rold had to be the *man* of the house. He made all the arrangements; comforted me and father; took on the whole thing. He never allowed himself to grieve — except the day of the memorial service, and then only briefly.

"Mother was beautiful. Light brown hair that she kept in curls. Blue eyes like mine. I have holograms or I wouldn't remember as well. We're all okay now, I think. Father aged over it drastically. But he's all right. I worry about Rold, though. He takes too many chances, flies into things without thinking at times. Like now. I think it has something to do with losing Mother, but I'm not sure."

Yosana listened patiently. Tyler had not realized that the subject had changed from the space organism she saw to her personal life. Yosana was good at drawing out such information, without giving anything away about herself in return, maintaining her mysterious air.

"And your mother?" Tyler looked at Yosana, their eyes locking. Yosana made a little laugh.

"Very well," she said. "A curious coincidence, it seems. My mother was killed in an accident ten years ago as well. A flood destroyed our village on Salkinia, killing several people.

"But we have moved away from our purpose."

"Oh, right! The cloud thing."

"It was a *minah-machacute*," she said. "A living cloud. That's what they're called by my mother's people. But in the rest of the Commonwealth the vulgar term is slunk."

"Oh, yes. I've heard of slunks. But I thought they were like sea serpents at the edge of the world in old nautical myths. So now I've seen a mythical monster for myself, huh?"

Yosana smiled but kept an even tone as she spoke: "They're not monsters, Tyler. Demons to some, perhaps, but not monsters. And . . . I didn't tell you any of this. Right? Our little secret?"

"Yes! Of course!"

"The one who spoke to you has a name: Gwydmonia. She's my melding mate. I am a cloud rider of Salkinia."

Tyler looked at this wonderfully mysterious woman, whom she wished to call friend. Yosana had frightened her somewhat with this last dramatic sentence. But it was fabulously exhilarating. What could it mean? *Cloud rider?*

She was awe struck and hesitated to ask. Then Rold entered the game room. Yosana's face flushed and she nervously reached for a chess piece, knocking several pieces to the floor.

"Is my sister bothering you again, *zelita*?" Rold did not seem to notice Yosana's accident.

"No," she said without looking up. "We . . . we were finished. And no, she doesn't bother me, Rold."

Yosana quickly stood and jaunted to the exit without looking back.

"What was that all about?" Rold said as he placed his hand on Tyler's shoulder.

"She was telling me a fairy tale," Tyler said after a long pause. She was smiling.

"A little old for that aren't you, Tyler?"

"But it was . . . oh, never mind. Did you notice? She called you 'Rold.'"

"No I didn't notice."

"Men!"

*

Two days before arriving, Yosana removed the hibernation equipment from the other passengers' cell. The couple awoke within an hour and stumbled into their hygiene closet. They appeared in the common room that afternoon, pale and limp on their jelly-like legs. Yosana did not introduce them to Rold and Tyler. And so they performed polite nods. The woman had newly grown fuzz on top of her head where she had normally kept a shaved and painted dome; she continually rubbed and scratched it.

"When do we get to this god-awful place?" the man asked. On Old Earth he'd be classified as oriental, Rold thought, though he probably has no idea what that meant. His hair was shiny black and his face was round with a broad mouth.

"Tomorrow," Yosana said.

Rold noticed contempt in Yosana's voice, which the couple either did not detect or more likely ignored.

"I can't believe you talked me into this, Barb," the man continued. "It's one thing to watch beasts killed in an arena, but how exciting can it be all alone on some wilderness planet? With disease and vermin, and savages."

"I assure you," Yosana said, "you'll be taken care of in maximum comfort. We have a land rover equipped with all the modern luxuries."

"I would hope so," the woman said. "That's what we're paying for. I'm sure we'll have a great time."

She turned to Rold, smiling, and extended her hand.

"Barbara," she said. "Barbara Jenkins. My husband, Daryl. There, now we're introduced. And you are?"

"Rold Simms," Rold said finally taking her hand. It felt cold and spongy. "And this is my sister, Vivian Tyler Simms."

Tyler took her hand as well, nodding her greeting, and noticed the woman's unhealthy pallor. She was glad she had not subjected herself to hibernation.

"Well, Mr. Simms, are you two off to safari with us?"

"No. We're just hitching a ride. My sister is on her way to Newert, and ... couldn't wait for a transport on Caljunna. There are transports at Salkinia I'm told."

"Newert?" Daryl asked. "A government related trip? Or just a tourist?"

"Neither. Visiting my father," Tyler said.

"What kind of work do you do? Oh, yes, of course, I can see you're a Scientist, Mr. Simms. In what area are you involved?"

"Weather control. But I'll be returning to O. E. presently to teach at the Southwestern American University."

Barbara shivered and moved closer to Daryl. He took her hand and began rubbing her shoulder.

"I have such a headache," she said. "Is it time for dinner? I'm starved. I'm always starved after hibing. But I wouldn't travel any other way. Don't you agree, Simms?"

Rold nodded silently. He wanted to give an honest shake of his head but resisted. Having Industrialists on board set his senses reeling, but he was determined to maintain his cool.

"I'll have dinner ready in a moment," Yosana said.

She walked to the galley with Tyler tagging along. The Industrialist couple murmured between themselves with an occasional laugh. Tyler looked closely at the graying around Barbara's eyes and throat and wondered if the hibernation drugs caused the dehydration or whether there had not been enough fluid circulating through her system. She skirted around the counter and began searching for plates and utensils.

"What are you doing?" Yosana said.

"I thought I'd help," Tyler said.

"You're a passenger, Tyler. This is my job. Go sit with the other guests and I'll serve you."

"Certainly not. I want to help. I don't feel comfortable having you wait on me — just because your other passengers are around. So quit fussing and let me help. Besides, I need something to keep me busy."

"Very well."

Rold reluctantly joined the others. Tyler began slicing a melon that Yosana had retrieved from refrigeration.

"You might need to check your hibernation equipment," Tyler said.

"Oh?"

"The bald one seems dehydrated."

Yosana shook her head. "The effect of caine drugs. She's a caine addict. Can't you tell? I had to do an analysis while they were on the machine, but I knew already. She was probably born addicted. It's a problem among the Industrialist families."

"No, I didn't know. You . . . know so much. You can read. You know history. You know about people. Why haven't you joined one of the parties?"

Yosana blushed at her exaggerated attention.

"Scientism, Industrialism, sorry but it's all a bunch of nonsense. There's such a thing as being a plain, ordinary human being, struggling through life — eating up life, tasting every moment. I know about politics, those expensive games your people play, but I don't give a damn about it. So, does that make me small, insignificant?"

"To those perhaps," Tyler said nodding her head toward the others. "But not to me. I'm a human being too. And I could care less about those stupid, dangerous games of intrigue and politics. You probably know more about what's going on than I do."

They were silent for a moment, finishing the preparations, then Tyler said, "Even though my father's on the Committee."

Yosana inhaled through her teeth, putting her hand to her chest and upsetting a bowl of fruit. During the whole trip Tyler had managed not to mention what her father was doing on Newert. And neither had Rold. "You mean . . . the ruling committee? *The* Committee?"

"It doesn't change us. I have no Committee responsibilities myself. I love my father, but that world isn't mine, not really. And Rold — well, I don't know about him. There are things he's not telling me. I suspect Father's got him involved in something."

Yosana stood for a moment staring at the floor. The room grew silent. "Do you know how much that scares me? Your position?" she whispered.

The Jenkins looked toward the galley. "Please, woman, our food," Daryl said.

Yosana looked up and sighed at Tyler, gave a concerned stare at Rold, then lifted the tray of fruit and bread.

"I generally don't tell people," Tyler said as she gathered the eating utensils. "It doesn't really mean anything, you know. People react funny. I thought you'd be different."

"We'll talk later." Yosana approached a round table situated close to the fireplace. Tyler hurriedly set the table and helped serve the food. Everyone gathered around the table and eased themselves onto the plump cushions. The Industrialists each dropped a drug in powdered form into a cup of liquid, in ritual fashion.

"I assume this fruit has been microbe filtered," Barbara said.

"Certified by Commonwealth inspectors," Yosana said. There was that contempt again. "You may look at the cases if you wish."

"Not necessary."

"Would you care for an aperitif?" Daryl asked looking at Rold. He held another envelope of drugs.

"No," Rold said. "But thank you. I'm not allowed chemicals. Certainly you know that."

"Very well," Daryl said raising one eyebrow then shrugging his shoulders. "If you can't be civil . . ."

Yosana approached Daryl. He turned with his glass and Yosana collided with his arm, liquid sloshing onto her and him.

"Stupid wog," he growled and swung the back of his hand toward her already flushed face.

Rold grabbed Daryl's forearm just before contact. As soon as their eyes met, Rold dropped the man's arm. Nothing else was said.

Yosana looked like she would protest, but Rold touched her arm above her wrist and gave her a calm look, eyebrows raised.

"I'm not really hungry," he said, turning back to the couple. "Please enjoy your meal."

He nodded his head, stood and walked toward the exit that led to the flight deck.

"Idiot!" Barbara said between gritted teeth to her self-satisfied husband. Yosana followed Rold.

"No, Yosana," Rold said. "You should serve your passengers. Don't let their rudeness bother you; I won't allow any hostility to occur. He won't try that again. Take care of Tyler." He nodded his head for her to return to her charge.

Rold made his way to the flight deck. He detested the old rivalry, the hatred between the two parties. But that Industrialist's behavior with Yosana was inexcusable! At this moment he regretted his station in life, wanting to live as Yosana and Blikki: simple people, doing simple work. But he had always felt a responsibility to his family and thus to his party, his class. But not in a way the majority of the Scientists would approve. He knew the wounds were too deep to ever bring the two parties together, but he always felt there must be some way to effect some change.

"Hello, sir," Blikki said without turning to face him. The words startled Rold from his thoughts.

"Hello," he said. "Please don't call me 'sir,' Blikki. I prefer Rold. Do you mind if I join you? I thought I might look around your equipment here. Just out of curiosity."

"Fine. But it's not mine, it's the bank's. Never mind that. I see you've met our guests. Lovely couple, eh?"

Rold smiled. "Am I that transparent? Well, you know how it is with us. We're constantly at odds with each other, and yet we're forced to work so closely together."

Blikki smiled and nodded his head. Rold moved up and sat beside him.

"I was curious," Rold said, changing the subject. "Your name doesn't sound Caljunnese."

"Ah-Blikkinata," Blikki said. "It means: 'from the old world'. That's because I'm one of the Salkinian migrators."

"Oh?"

"Many of the Caljunnese were originally from Salkinia. Ah-Blikkinata is a fairly common name there. It's been carried down from the first families to move to Caljunna from Salkinia."

"I don't understand. Caljunna was colonized decades before Salkinia. Wasn't it? You're saying it's the other way around?"

"Yes and no. Actually Salkinia's been peopled for centuries. Ethno-migration, two thousand years ago from Earth."

"Oh, that myth," he said. "It was supposed to be more like twenty-four hundred years ago. Of course the nation wars obscured the records from those times. But it's not really clear what happened, or if it happened at all. It's just a romanticized tale. People are always claiming to be descended from one of those early colonies."

Blikki maneuvered a bright pin-point of light about the room by rolling a ball between his two palms. The motion of the ball corresponded to the positioning of the dot of light. The instrument settings responded to his careful ball juggling. Then he set the ball in a black bowl in front of him and turned his chair toward Rold.

"But our knowledge has no gaps," he said. "We know every detail of our migration, the leader's names, the ethnic identity of our people, the dates: everything. A scientist, *Pitallela* was her name. She went looking for a planet with as many Earth characteristics as possible. She didn't live to see the new world. It took generations to arrive here. But the Great Mother must have smiled on her because the planet had a single moon with phases and relative positioning much like that of Earth's moon, which was important to my ancestors. And as it happened, it was a good choice."

"So, who are your people, Blikki? Which group?" Rold was smiling. There had always been anthropological searches for these colonies, with no success.

"The Commonwealth named the planet Salkinia after Admiral Salk, the man who discovered it two centuries ago. But my people still call it Earth, and themselves hunters of the *pitah*, the buffalo, or Teton from an ancient people on Old Earth."

"American Natives!"

"Yes. Of course they weren't really all American Natives. Not nearly homogeneous. The only thing that brought these people together was their claim in having a scant of American Native blood and a romanticized idea of what life was like for some brief shining moment in Earth's history.

"A great leader was born who became the father of our people upon landing on the planet. He's worshipped today as a spirit. His name was *Chomata-te*, which means 'golden eagle.'"

Blikki glanced back at his console and flicked two switches. Rold sat quietly for a moment, trying to piece this story into his own understanding of human history. His skepticism was only slightly dented.

"Perhaps you should join our safari and see for yourself," Blikki said.

"I have to get Tyler to Newert."

"Yes." Blikki turned back to his panel of switches and lights.

"But I may need some place to . . . regroup."

"Lay low, you mean?" Blikki laughed.

"I think I need some rest," Rold said. "Perhaps tonight you could tell me about Salkinia and why people left to go to Caljunna."

"Certainly, Rold. Tonight."

Rold left the flight deck and walked back to the common room. He tried putting away Blikki's story so that he could turn his mind to his current predicament but found that he could not shake the subject. Questions arose that burned hungrily within him.

After wandering the small ship, deep in thought, he returned to the common room and found it deserted. Everyone must have left after the meal. It was dark, and the viewing window was left uncovered. He was startled by a flash of light outside the ship, close to the window. He went to the window and fell into the trance of the stargazer, watching the slow movement of the tunnel of light through which they now traveled. Briefly he thought he saw another flash of light and an undulating white cloud in the distance. But soon it disappeared or blended in with the mist of stars.

CHAPTER 4

The White witch brought her soldiers
To bury the brother,
Strike down Margona, they did try
But her will was too strong, as was her future.

From "The Song of Margona"
by Pitallela-Sim

The Committee Hall rose one hundred fifty meters above the gray hill. As the yellow sun of Newert broke free of the jagged city skyline, its rays melted through the translucent prism of the phallic Hall and turned the hill into emerald, a breeze washing over the tall standing uniform grasses.

In the lingering shadows of dawn, between two glass pillars that dressed the circling steps of the Hall, stood a woman and a man. Come to govern within the hall, the two Committee members, dressed in Committee robes, spoke privately before entering the monument.

"Young Simms is on his way, Ruth," the man said in a twittering voice. "We need not worry now."

"Without my worrying," the woman said, "we would both be on a penal rock by now." She had an old voice that rasped when whispered.

"Now listen," she continued, "Malcolm Simms will be in the Hall today. I'm not ready for him to know his son has been detoured. Timing is crucial. Certain records must be refined, massaged. And anyone who had any direct connection with the Industrialists: make them disappear. Only you and I must know that there was a connection."

"I see. There is one thing."

"Yes?"

"The daughter."

"What about her?"

"The operatives used her to push Simms to his . . . final destination."

"So they are together?"

"As far as I know."

"Good. Good. We'll have him now, the way he dotes on that girl."

"As I thought as well."

"Yes. He would stop us, you know. He's too liberal. Allowing Industrialists to sit on the Committee! He must be mad.

"Any clue as to where they've taken young Simms?"

"They're being quite secretive. To a factory world, I would expect."

"That would be the logical choice, but I'm not sure. Doesn't matter now. As long as he's in Industrialist hands."

"Hush," the man whispered and circled his head about his neck, peering into corners. "This plan must work or we're all in for a rough ride."

"And it will work as long as Malcolm Simms is out of it until the tide has turned, as they say. Then he'll be as committed as we. We shall see the Industrialists struck down."

"They've stuck their necks in it, all right. Brilliant, Ruth."

The two parted as the sun more certainly shone on the steps. More Committee members approached the entrance as they arrived on subway transporter walking paths from the nearby apartments set aside for visiting members.

Ruth waited patiently, nodding to friends as they passed. She bowed graciously to Malcolm Simms. His white hair and beard separated him from the predominately young crowd. He was the only member from Old Earth — a prestigious position. Though no member was formerly head of the Committee, seniority meant power; and Old Earth meant tradition.

"Good morning, Ruth," Malcolm said. "I see you're here early." His voice crackled with fatigue from a sleepless night.

"Good morning, Malcolm," she said without smiling. "You look tired. Up late?"

"Well, yes. I've been up trying to locate my daughter. It seems she took a detour on her way here. She's coming for a visit until her return to O. E. Did I tell you she's entering the university?"

"Yes, you mentioned it. I'm sure she's in transit by now. Probably out of packet range, don't you think? You do look weary, though, Malcolm. Perhaps you should've used some chemical stimulants this morning as some of our new Committee members do."

Her sarcasm filled the air with a sour twinge. Malcolm shook his head.

"You're right to be critical of such practices, Ruth. I'll not fight you on that."

"Then you agree the Industrialists have brought some bad influences with them into these chambers. Some feel they should be expelled — the rule given back to the Scientists totally."

"There is a difference between orthodoxy and reactionism, Ruth. There is reason behind our tradition of not using drugs — but expulsion? Certainly you're not among the rumored usurpers."

"There is reason behind a Universe ruled by Scientists. But of course, I'm not a violent person. You've known me many years, and certainly you've learned that. But you do see my point?"

Malcolm pursed his lips and blew a sigh through his nose. After pausing a moment longer he motioned Ruth toward the doors that led into the Hall.

"Let's debate this within the Hall where everyone can hear and comment, as is our duty," he said as they walked out of the sunshine.

Deceleration had begun before dinner. It was an unusual phenomenon for Rold who had traveled space at sub-lumina only a handful of times, and this trip was with a defective gravity emulator. At times he felt that his body was expanding in all directions, becoming bloated and elongated. It affected his digestive organs even more than the occasional lapse in gravity. Again he passed on dinner and realized he must seem obsessed with fasting.

He looked at Yosana sitting across from him. The la'Kundas had invited Tyler and him forward to join in the landing. Yosana was watching the growing sphere that was Salkinia, showing only her profile to Rold. With his eyes he traced her jaw from her chin to her hairline, then followed the curve of her ear. Her long hair was pulled back and swept across her shoulders and throat. Her skin was dark in this light and without blemish. He wanted to follow the path of his eyes with his fingers, gently brush her soft, serious face. But he drew back, wondering at his growing feelings for this woman who so hated his class. He then thought of Tyler and her safety, still worried about the details of her return to their father. And he thought of the dream he had that kept him awake in the early morning hours.

It had washed through him in slow, pulsating waves. At the crests it was so clear, so real; at the valleys it was so dim he thought he would lose it. A golden eagle, now extinct on Old Earth, was floating in a purplish blue sky, suspended in an updraft. The sun caught its brilliantly colored breast: white and gold. It suddenly compressed into the shape of a missile and dropped from the sky as if propelled by engines. Its talons grew to grotesque size and slammed onto Rold's naked shoulders as he groped on his knees in desert sand. The impact was that of two hammers striking his upper back, forcing his face deep into the powdery soil.

Then he had wakened, sweating, having thrown himself to the floor beside his bed. He had searched the covers of his cot for Yosana but realized that was from an earlier dream. She had never actually been in his room, not for the whole trip. Now he wondered at his unconscious obsession with her.

I'm like a child, he thought. I'm having dreams after listening to Blikki's tall-tales about Salkinia.

He turned toward the window. They were approaching the blue planet of Salkinia. Fingers of white clouds mottled the blue oceans and taupe continents much like Old Earth. Caljunna had little or no precipitation; mostly underground water running through channeled carbonate rock. It looked red and desolate until the cities could be seen which were large and modern. Also, Caljunna was so much larger than Old Earth in circumference. In contrast, this planet could be mistaken for Old Earth, though the continents were unfamiliar.

"Salkinia," Rold said. Until this point the room had been quiet.

"Shhh!" Yosana gave Rold a stern glance. Then she whispered: "Father is trying to communicate with the port and is having some problems hearing their signal."

"Stop whispering, child," Blikki said. "It's no use. Something's going on down there. But no matter; I'll land near the Smith and Hargess mine. You're sure to catch a ride there. They make weekly runs."

One more problem, Rold thought. So many odd things had happened lately that his hackles rose at any suggestion of trouble.

"Salkinia's not a highly technical world," Yosana said. "It's not unusual to go in blindly like this. Also, it's a rowdy place. But we'll have no problems."

"Somehow that didn't make me feel better," Tyler said and gripped the arms of her chair. Rold gave her a smile for confidence.

The cocoons were fastened, and a warning signal was sent through the transport for the other passengers. Blikki projected his image to the stateroom where the others were awaiting the landing.

"Hold on to whatever feels best," Blikki said, "we're going in."

As quickly as had been the departure from Caljunna, the transport brought the planet of Salkinia to its belly. All was a blur until the final thud. The sound of mechanical rotors winding slowly to a stop deafened Rold's ears, and a tingling began at the base of his spine and rose to his neck. He was slow at unfastening the chair restraints, feeling some dizziness. But quickly his curiosity began driving his thoughts.

Tyler was slight trembling. Yosana stood beside her and rubbed her back, smiling.

"It's just the shock of landing," she said. "You're a bit nervous still. You haven't gotten your land legs yet."

"I do feel a little queasy, but I'll be fine. This is the correct region of Salkinia, the right port?" Tyler asked. "It's a big planet."

"This is the only mining port on Salkinia. Minpana is the only Commonwealth city. Let's get out of the transport and take a look. You'll feel a lot better once you've breathed some fresh air."

"It's all so exciting," she said smiling. "I've never been to a wilderness planet before. I hope we can spend a little time here before I have to go."

"Tyler," Rold said, taking her by the hand.

They stepped into a blazing desert sun. The deep blue sky overhead weakened at the horizon where a dusty haze partially hid violet, round topped mountains. A sea of iron rich red sand dotted with blue-green brush and yellow grasses spread before them. A dust devil swirled to the right, reaching for the noon sun, then flattened into a wide, pulsing rhythm before dissipating into the desert. Rold felt the warmth of the baked sand enter his boots. He noticed this more than the heat of the sun, which was lessened by a cool, dry breeze. The sweet smell of the grasses in bloom mixed with the flinty smell of dust. Further right, around the nose of the transport, Rold could see the mining machines, painted white, and the red brick buildings from which the metal bits and pieces of derricks and cranes grew. A deserted freight shuttle sat on pavement, its skin turning pink from the blowing, red dust. Mining shavings rose in huge mounds which looked like volcanic cones, reaching two hundred meters above the desert floor.

As they walked around the transport, Rold stroked the vessel's hull, in perhaps an absent-minded caress, then was struck by the sight of some taller buildings of the city of Minpana. He continued walking until he was able to face fully the panorama of the skyline. The city was much larger than he expected. He felt a certain relief upon seeing the possibility of civilization so close. At the same time he sympathized with this primitive, innocent world into which the Commonwealth invaded. He noticed behind the city a giant wall of snow capped mountains. The snow tops glinted in the sun and seemed to float like clouds. But Rold nodded his head as he confirmed to himself: it's snow not clouds; real snow.

"It's so much like Old Earth," he said as he saw Yosana approaching.

"Really? I've often wondered."

"Uncrowded, though. Old Earth is teaming with people. But it must have been like this once. The mountains beyond the city there look cool and inviting."

Their heads turned together toward the city.

"You said this is the only city?"

"Yes. I know what you're thinking. You see, Salkinia has conservation status. It was arranged many years ago. This one area was given as a concession to the Industrialists, for the iron and bauxite. Minpana grew to accommodate the operation. But believe me, they'd love to get their hands on the whole planet."

A stream of dust grew along a barely distinguishable road several kilometers away. A dark speck led the orange cloud toward the mine.

"Someone's coming," Blikki said as he hopped to the ground. "Things are certainly odd today. No one seems to be at the mine. But I suspect that's some kind of welcoming committee on its way from Minpana. I hope it's friendly. I have all the correct permits right here in my pocket." He patted his left thigh where a long pants pocket bulged. "We're perfectly legal."

The other passengers slowly emerged from the rear exit of the transport. A large cavity presented itself there. Blikki had been hard at work depositing the land rover from the transport. The couple walked around the land rover and joined the group at the front.

"Why didn't we land in the city?" Daryl asked.

"No clearance there," Blikki said. "Communication was out. But we're fine here. I have permits to use the mine's landing ground. We'll have to pay a fee for leaving the transport here while we travel. The Commonwealth port is cheaper, but that's life."

Presently a group of five land vehicles arrived. Dust blew around the area, getting into everyone's hair and teeth, and stinging their eyes. The vehicles bore the plain green disc emblem of the Industrialist Militia. The machinery was very expensive hover craft technology, which explained the exorbitant dust. The lead machine opened in front and two Industrialist Militia stepped out holding energy weapons across their bodies. Rold's throat dried immediately, and the noon sun finally drew sweat from his body. Beads slid slowly down the bridge of his nose. Tyler grabbed his hand and tightened her grip. Blikki jaunted over to the three men, waving his plastic data cards at them.

"We have permits," he shouted over the noise of the engines. "So just get along with yourselves. We need no provisions or maps or advice, and certainly no bureaucratic delays."

"We don't wish to delay your party," the front man said. He pulled back the visor of his helmet, slung his weapon over his shoulder and pulled off his gloves. "I'm Colonel August. I have orders to arrest a Rold and Vivian Simms who are believed to be with your group."

"Arrest?" Yosana said. She moved to Blikki's side. "You're Militia, not police."

"I'm afraid Minpana is under martial law for the moment. Several acts of insurrection have occurred in the last few days. We're simply trying to aid the local government — maintaining peace."

A fourth person emerged from the Militia vehicle, a woman dressed in tan slacks and tunic.

"Hello, *zelita*," the woman said as she saw Yosana. "I must thank you for your assistance. The Caljunna authorities almost destroyed our plan, but you showed your resourcefulness. We'll take him now."

Rold was confused by the conversation. He noticed the recognition in Yosana's eyes, and a certain shock there. The smiling woman looked familiar to him also. Her hair was cut short and was streaked with gray, though she appeared very young, younger than Rold. Of course being an Industrialist she probably had youth treatments. He could not place her but was sure he knew this person.

Yosana turned to Blikki and whispered: "That's the woman I mentioned to you earlier, the one who told me about two Scientists needing a ride off Caljunna. She followed us here. We've been used. They're kidnapping them, Father. This can't be legal."

Blikki looked squarely at the colonel.

"You have no jurisdiction here," he said. "Rold and his sister can stay with me or go with you as far as I'm concerned. But don't push too hard."

The colonel squeezed his hand, and the other vehicles burst open pouring green uniformed Militia upon them. In a moment each member of the party was being held by two Militia: though with a nod from the colonel, the Industrialist travelers were released. Energy weapons discharged in warning. Yosana shrieked and lunged toward Tyler. The two men holding her arms stood fast, hurting her shoulders as she strained without success.

"You wouldn't want to lose those permits, would you?" August said. "Cooperate and all will be well. The Militia is now in charge of government on this planet. So no trouble, please."

Tyler was able to pull loose, scrambling like a cat to get to Rold. One of her captors caught her by her robe and in one motion flung her to the ground. Rold burst loose, smashed his fist into the throat of one of the Militia, crushing his wind pipe. The man fell to the ground writhing until dead. Rold was quickly at Tyler's side helping her to a sitting position.

Three men jerked him up and dragged him away. He kicked, and screamed Tyler's name.

"Hold!" the woman shouted. She stood before Rold. "This could be quite simple, Scientist, if you would just answer a few questions."

Rold relaxed a bit, breathing heavily.

"Now," she said. "Who knows you're here?"

"What do you mean?" Rold said.

"I need to know if you'll be followed."

"You mean rescued!"

"We don't need any more complications."

"I have nothing to say."

The woman took her hand weapon and clubbed Rold across the side of his head. His ear burst, blood spewing onto the man holding his arm side.

"Talk!"

Rold simply stared. He seemed to feel no pain. The safari group stood and watched the brutality, the Industrialists enjoying the show. Yosana felt a certain resentment and fear of Rold, but she now regretted her part in his capture.

The woman pointed her weapon at Rold's face.

"Rold, no!" Tyler screamed.

"Do you refuse?" the woman said.

"You wouldn't dare kill me," Rold said.

"Still the pompous brat you've always been. Well perhaps if I kill your precious sister."

She turned her weapon toward Tyler.

Rold exploded, pulling from his captors, but they were able to control him until he calmed again.

"All right," he said. "My father knows I was on Caljunna. But he doesn't know I'm here. I didn't have time to get word. Satisfied? No one knows. They'll figure it out, though."

"They won't be quick enough," she said. "But I'm afraid I don't believe you. You are a spy, and you've been planning something for some time. We know you were behind the Swansflight Factory sabotage on Monda. And you were on Caljunna for a reason. What was it?"

"I don't know what you were talking about. You can't harm us. The results would be disastrous for you."

"I can't? Watch me."

So quickly that it took everyone by surprise, the woman fired her blaster straight at Tyler's head. To Rold the scene seemed in slow motion: he watched the energy flow from the weapon, concentrate in a fine beam and strike Tyler's head just above her ear. Chunks of flesh and bone exploded, blood gushing and staining her neck and shoulder. She was thrown backward two meters, her feet leaving the ground.

Rold immediately went mad. He saw his sister lying on the ground, her blood mixing with the red dust. But he could not break free. Eventually he lost all strength, barely able to whimper a last "No!" then the militia dragged him to the vehicle.

"Thank you again, *zelita*," the woman said walking past her to Rold. She stared at Rold as he was placed inside the craft. His breath pounded in and out of his nose. He felt the woman's hatred pouring from her eyes and returned it in full.

"Any one who follows you here will be dealt with the same way," she said.

Colonel August ordered his troops to their machines and stood with his readied weapon as a warning to Blikki's party, Yosana finally freed. Tyler's body was tossed over a man's shoulder and thrown in a separate craft.

The vehicles churned dust in their retreat to Minpana, Yosana collapsed, trembling. The others sighed in relief, Daryl laughing nervously; Blikki shook his head.

"To think, a criminal in our midst," Barbara said.

Blikki bent over his daughter and helped her to rise. She clung to him desperately.

"I know," he said. "We must pray to the Great Mother for the soul of the little one."

"You don't understand," Yosana said pulling back and looking into his eyes. "It has started."

"What? What's started? What are you talking about?"

"The *war*. It has now begun."

"A premonition?"

"No, no. Rold, Tyler. Their father is on the Committee. A Scientist! And Tyler's been murdered!"

Blikki grunted, loudly enough to attract the others' attention.

"This is too large a crime to go unanswered," Yosana continued, now in Caljunnese. "He'll be used as a hostage."

"I'm old, but I'm not stupid. And Rold will probably die like his sister — and a lot of others, too — because of this stupid, ancient political dichotomy. I've told you it was coming. Didn't I? But now. And we're somehow a part of its beginning. There's nothing we can do. They let us go. We should make our money on this safari and then what?"

He patted her shoulder.

Yosana stood back and wiped the dust from her clothes and shook her head, making her long hair fly about. Then she pulled her hair back and pushed a leather head band over her crown to just above her eyes. She despised herself at that moment. No matter how she felt about Rold, he did not deserve this. And Tyler! Poor Tyler. Yosana blamed herself. She was now a part of the stupid war.

Blikki jogged around to the rover and began packing the luggage from the transport. Daryl found shade beside the transport and sat on a smooth rock. Barbara pensively approached Yosana, her lips pressed tightly together.

"Quite a scene," Barbara said. Yosana looked at her, fire in her eyes.

"I somehow doubt that Mr. Simms or his sister could commit a crime worthy of such a display," Barbara continued. "But, you never know. I hope this won't impact our holiday."

"Certainly not," Yosana said curtly without looking at the woman.

Instead she watched the dust shrouded machines until they disappeared.

The trip to Minpana seemed to last for hours. The hover machines approached the city at a leisurely pace. Rold was strapped to an inside chair but had a clear view diagonally through the right front window. The machine rose and fell with each hill showing glimpses of the sandstone boulder strewn landscape. A meter-tall cloud of sandy dust spread from the vehicle, angling behind them as a wake. Rold noticed that most of the yellow and red he saw was not sand or clay, but dry grasses. Occasionally brush would scratch the hull, and once they mowed down a blue-green succulent tree that must have housed twenty birds, which scattered quickly into the hot air above them.

As Rold began thinking they would never arrive, he saw the city wall. Blikki had described the Wall to him. There were four gates; two major, two minor. The Militia were entering through one of the major gates: Desertgate, which opened in the middle of the broad side of the Wall that faced the desert. The other gates were Mountaingate (a major gate on the opposite broad side), Rivergate (a minor gate where a river entered the city), and Farmgate (a minor gate on the opposite end that led to the irrigated fields that blanketed the hills radiating from that end). The Wall itself stood thirty meters above the ground and circled the city in a perfect ellipse so that the sides were a continuous curve. The material was a light bluish metal, three meters thick and without a visible seam. In places apartments grew from the Wall.

Rold watched, wide-eyed, as the three-storey tall gate slid to one side to allow their entrance.

Once inside, the city was less forbidding. Most of the buildings were adobe boxes. The natural materials lent the city a warmth, a quaintness. However, at the core the city grew gigantic buildings made of glass, plastic, and metal. They were each tall, slender cylinders that reflected the desert hills and blue sky. The streets were filled with people; many were Commonwealth settlers, Rold guessed. They shrank from the Militia cavalcade.

Rold's captors abruptly turned down an ally that presented less traffic congestion but forced the vehicles into single file. The alley soon opened onto a thoroughfare that bordered a narrow, green park. A single, small building, much like the other adobe huts, stood in the center of the green. Here the machines stopped. Rold was jerked out of his chair and rushed into the structure. The woman followed them into an elevator car that presently dropped smoothly down its shaft.

"You don't remember me, do you?" the woman said. She had a monotonous smirk that enraged Rold. And, yes, he did remember her now.

"Rachel Meacom," he said. She turned toward him, startled. "I'm sure Ambassador Meacom would be quite proud of his daughter today. Butcher!"

"Hold your tongue, Scientist trash, or you'll lose it. My father is now a member of the Committee. And, yes, I will make him proud."

"I didn't know things had come so far."

"You've been away."

"What have you done with . . . my sister's body. I want to see her."

"Do you really? How maudlin. I don't have time, nor patience, for courtesies, Simms. Perhaps it's best that you remember her as she was: a martyr for your cause."

He lunged but was restrained by his guards. *I have no "cause" any more,* Rold thought, *except revenge, you bitch.*

A blackness consumed him. No longer was he on a "fact finding" mission for his father. Now his only purpose was getting even. And as he thought of all the ways he could kill the people responsible, he grew more and more excited. But soon he would have to do more than plan: he would have to act.

The silence grew, erasing even the hum of the elevator. Rold forced himself to relax. He did not want to show any curiosity or impatience. He hoped that his lack of interest would annoy Rachel. He knew this was her father's plan — some grand scheme to extort what? Power? Rold had met the Meacoms on his one and only trip to Newert with his father five years before. Like his father, he had wanted so much to trust the Industrialists — to mend the schism. But the Meacoms had obviously mistrusted the friendship Rold's father had offered. Rold could sense their apprehension the moment he met them. So here he was, facing torture, death, thrust into a situation which could easily touch off a galactic war. He really did not have to ask questions; the answers would be all too predictable.

The elevator stopped as smoothly as it had begun. Rachel stepped out first, then Rold with his guards. They were in a dim, granite tunnel, crudely hewn, with a ceiling of about three meters above a dusty floor. The guards constantly shoved Rold as they walked. They passed a series of metal doors with small, unglassed windows the size of a man's hand which were placed at about eye level. The smell of stale urine was overwhelming. Rold started coughing. He could hear people shuffling about behind the doors, and occasionally one would call out a muffled plea.

"Lovely hotels, here in Minpana," he said.

He received a slap on the top of his head by one of his guards by way of reply. The group stopped as a jailer approached them with confused and worried eyes. He wore no shirt but had on trousers and a huge metal ring around his neck that circled about his chest. Several old-fashioned metal keys for mechanical locks hung jangling from the hoop.

"There's no more room," he said with his hands up. "Forgive me, but the last cell has been filled."

"Someone will have to share," Rachel said losing her smirk. She rapped on a cell door. "Put him in here."

"With the tribal chief?" the jailer asked.

"Is that wise?" Colonel August's voice rumbled through the tunnel as he approached. The squeak of his boots echoed before him. "This native is a dangerous creature. I lost two of my men in his capture."

Rachel laughed. "Let's go, August. What does it matter? What can he do in this hole?"

"He could kill Simms."

She laughed again and turned.

"Before you're locked away," she said as the group began moving forward again, "perhaps you would be interested in what your sacrifice is buying, Simms."

"Don't bother. I think I can guess."

"No, I don't think you can," Colonel August said.

"Let me, August," Rachel said. "No, poor Rold, this isn't a terrorist abduction — an attack of Industrialists against Scientists — but an attack against the Committee itself. We have Scientist allies in this. Or how else could we have accomplished anything so dangerous?"

"*No*," Rold said. Now he was panicking. His trembling was racked with a powerful shudder, then his guts almost jumped out of his throat. "You're attacking my father, that I know, but what Scientists?"

"Ruth Poundstone."

Rold laughed. It was all he could do. Perhaps laughing would wake him from this nightmare — for it must be that; it had all the characteristics of a dream, a confusion of reality. Then as quickly as he had started laughing he stopped. A brilliant thought occurred to him — an awful, terrifying thought. And slowly he nodded his head.

"Rachel," he said hoarsely, "you've been used, even more treacherously than you've used me. Ruth Poundstone hates Industrialists."

"But she hates the Committee more — and your father. She's jealous of his implied rule."

"No. I know I can't convince you, but no. She'll turn on you. It matters little now. The damage is done. The war is coming."

"No!" Rachel said stamping her foot. "Not a war, a *coup d'etat*!"

"Time will tell," Rold said. "But I suppose I'll not live long enough to find out. Am I right?"

"We had not planned on killing you," Colonel August said. "Though survival in the Minpana Hold is rare."

"Tell me," Rold said, after swallowing bile, "why did you go to so much trouble to hide the fact that you were kidnapping us? Why didn't you just take us back there on Caljunna?"

"We needed time," Rachel said. "We arranged for the la'Kundas to be at the terminal on the day of your departure. Other friends planted the bomb. We also made sure you'd escape. Those Caljunnese police got carried away; especially firing missiles. You killed two of their men and almost ruined the whole show. But, luckily, we got it under control."

"I thought it was too easy. And Yosana? She was in on it?" He was barely able to ask his question. He did not want to believe that he had been so wrong about her.

"She served her purpose. Everyone needs a little cash from time-to-time. Yes? And the la'Kundas are known to be discrete. Quite mercenary, though. They play both sides. A dangerous game. But they're insignificant little pawns in my bigger game."

The jailer inserted a key into a lock illuminated by a handheld electric torch. Rold watched in desperation. The thick door swung open and he was shoved in. The door was shut and the lock clicked automatically; Rold assumed it must have metal tumblers. His heart pounded faster as he heard his captors shuffling back down the hallway. He could hear the motors of the elevator, then he turned to face his fate.

The cell's dimensions were obscured by darkness. The only light was from the tiny window in the door, so it took a moment for him to sense the true depth of the room. There was no furniture, no toilet — no plumbing whatsoever — and not even a pad or blanket. There was straw on the floor, obviously to absorb bodily wastes. It stank and was soggy under his feet. A man was kneeling facing the back of the room. Rold walked around him and received no response. He feared the man had died in that position and had become rigid. But soon the man relaxed his head and arms and stood.

"You have come," the man said in what Rold recognized as Caljunnese though with an unfamiliar accent.

"Yes," Rold said. "They put me in here. There were no empty cells."

"I know."

"My name is Rold Simms."

The man said nothing. Rold tried to find a less noxious-smelling part of the cell, sat against the wall and tried to calm his stomach. He breathed deeply, trying not to weep for his sister. He wanted to scream, but he was determined to remain dry-eyed. There would be time enough for that when her murderers were dead. Exhausted from his efforts, he drifted off into sleep, unable to fight his fatigue.

No dreams came, and when he woke, Rold berated himself for performing such a calm sleep at a time like this. The dim room became clear again, and the silhouette of his cell mate appeared within inches of his face. Rold jerked away and bumped his head against the slime-coated rock wall.

"Don't be afraid of me, Mountain Bear," the man said.

"Why were you so close?" Rold said rubbing his head. He felt something wet but could not tell whether it was blood or slime.

"I was awakening you. You've slept for more than a day."

"That doesn't make any sense. I wasn't that tired."

"I put you to sleep with a mystery my people sometimes use on enemies."

"I'm not your enemy."

"Perhaps. But you needed rest. We'll be leaving today, and I needed to prepare you, Mountain Bear."

Rold frowned and wondered if this native could see his face in such low light. He started to correct the man's use of Mountain Bear, for his name but felt it was not worth the effort. He had the same problem on Caljunna: his name sounded like *wolsooms*, Caljunnese for a type of bear that lives in cold climates or in high elevations.

"How do you know we're leaving?" Rold asked. "Are we to be moved?"

"We'll be freed by my people."

Rold smiled. "I hope so." But he realized how unlikely such a prospect was. Neo-primitives probably had little real knowledge of the Commonwealth and its power. But why destroy the hope of a savage? So he let it go and began pacing. To believe in hope!

"This damned darkness," he grumbled and futilely beat on the door.

"You want light?" the native said. He had spoken in his native language, but Rold quickly noticed that he had himself made his complaint in Ameranglo.

"You speak Ameranglo," Rold said.

"I speak English, yes. Some French and of course the language of the Teton — it's a language we adopted as a common tongue hundreds of years ago."

Rold stood motionless, astounded. The man laughed.

"I can read your thoughts," he said. "Through your face. My people preserved a library brought from Earth. All chiefs are required to study at the Library for several winters when they're young."

Rold nodded. Too many questions floated about his head. "Light. Do you have a torch or something?"

The man laughed again. "Very advanced technology. There are fungi on these walls that feed on urine. Water the wall and be dazzled!"

Rold was disgusted by the suggestion, but his bladder was aching, and he had noticed there was no toilet, so he relieved himself in a corner. A small triangle of light rose from the junction of the two walls and floor, then grew to a meter in height. The color of the light changed from red to yellow then white so bright it hurt Rold's eyes. He turned away and beheld his companion smiling in the middle of the room. He looked just as Rold had imagined the Native Americans from the pre-Columbian era would look. But also different: the artistic detail of his body decorations did not have the same characteristics as the relics Rold had studied on Old Earth.

The man — the chief — wore a leather head band encrusted with small, multi-colored gems and a single feather that jutted downward toward his right shoulder. The only other clothing he wore was a plain leather breechcloth. His body paint was beautiful: feathery strokes of orange, white and yellow covered his chest and arms, circled his neck, and arose in a symmetrical fan to engulf his face. Rold wondered how he had managed not to erase or smudge the paint. Perhaps it was a tattoo. Shining amid the splendor of his decorations was his glowing smile. His body shape seemed perfect to Rold: well developed muscles, but not overly developed as some people attained from training, developed moreover from actual, physical work; smooth golden skin without hair; and his facial structure exhibited the hawk-like features and thick black head hair Rold expected.

The light began to fade, reversing its color pattern, and the man knelt in front of Rold, who was now sitting.

"My name is Pentat," the man said. "Chief of the Eagle village. I was captured while on a spirit quest in the Red Hills. My village was attacked as I was returning. I was prepared for the ceremony, and that's why I appear as I am: in paint. But I dare not soil my paint in this pit of filth, so I've been in a trance off and on to preserve my calm."

"I see."

"You asked me, now I ask you. How do you know the language of the Teton?"

"Caljunnese. I lived on Caljunna. Do you know of that place?"

"Yes, of course. Ancestors of ours who came to work here in the city many winters ago left with the Whites to live on one of their worlds."

"I came here with a Caljunnese family." Rold could not say their names. He was confused and angry. *How could I have been so stupid?* he thought. *They'll pay for Tyler!*

Pentat nodded, though Rold could not see it in the dark of the cell.

"I'm here because I'm a danger to the Whites," Pentat said after some time. "And you as well, I would guess. The war we've been awaiting, dreading, has come. I fear you may have some part in it."

Rold wondered how Pentat knew of the possibility of galactic war, but realized his concern was probably for a local conflict into which, it seemed, Rold had also stumbled. A coincidence? But what was the use speculating when there was no hope.

"My sister was killed by these bastards," Rold said, his eyes pointed toward the dark floor. But the floor was not what he saw; he saw the memory of Tyler's tiny body, twisted in a ball, lying on red sand.

Pentat nodded, his hidden expression as grim as the walls about him.

CHAPTER 5

The pridda flew through White walls . . .

From "The Song of Margona"
by Pitallela-Sim

Moments passed then hours. Rold tried to relax his abhorrence of the filth on which he rested. Pentat had returned to his fanatic calm. Rold could not sleep any more — though he wished, silently begged his body, for unconsciousness. He could have easily been tempted to use sedative drugs if some were available. He had never been very patient at learning the calming exercises taught to him when he was a child on Old Earth. He had never had a problem with tension, and, in general, he was very lucky — considering the risks he took.

But his life had not been so totally free of pain. He began thinking of the few brief brushings with death and injury he had growing up. When he was about nine years old, Frank and he had been paddling around in a wooden boat they had built together. They had been in a lagoon that emptied into a shallow ocean bay checking crab traps that belonged to Frank's father. Frank's family was poor and lived on this lagoon as their ancestors had, fishing and farming for a living. He was the first of his people to enter into the Scientists' schools. He had passed certain tests and showed an interest in the proper topics.

Coming close to shore the two boys had jumped from the boat, wanting to take a swim. Rold jumped from one side and Frank the other. Rold felt something scraping along his leg as he sank swiftly from his dramatic jump. He felt the scratching for only an instant, giving little warning that he was falling on a submerged metal pipe standing upright, hidden by the murky bay water. The pipe, a fist in diameter, tore into him low in his belly, just above the groin. The gray-green water turned brown from the stain of blood, and all Rold remembered was waking in a hospital bed. Surgery had saved him, though the pain almost killed him afterward. He had never practiced his biofeedback techniques enough and suffered for it.

Sitting on the floor of his dark cell, watching Pentat kneeling, his knees spread wide, his buttocks resting on his heels, calmly breathing with his back erect, Rold thought of the pain from that accident and began his exercises, the breathing. He rubbed his scar from childhood, his constant reminder.

To be like him, he thought staring at Pentat. To be calm, confident, self-sufficient in a primitive world.

"Hello," Rold said in a soft voice.

Pentat's shoulders slumped, and he slowly turned. Rold wished he could see his face, his eyes, to see if he was angry for being disturbed.

"Yes," Pentat said.

"Forgive me for disturbing you. I was just thinking that we might be able to help each other."

"Of course. Forgive my self-indulgence. I needed some time to prepare. But since we're to spend this ugly moment in the hands of the Whites, whether we be friends or enemies, we must now act as comrades."

"Thank you. There are things I must know. I've had little diversity in my life, a few cuts and bruises, but all in all a good life, an easy life. Sometimes I think too easy."

"Don't be ashamed of an easy life. There's no honor in living a hard life, only honor in living a hard life well, when it's forced upon you. No one should wish for a hard life. It makes no sense."

"I see that, of course. But I feel ill prepared. I'm not helpless. Believe me. But an unfamiliar world . . ."

"Yes. That's a problem."

Pentat moved to a sitting position with legs crossed. Rold stood and began to pace as he let pour a cascade of emotion.

"The worst thing," Rold said using his hands to punctuate each syllable, "is this hopeless confinement.

"And what about these odd coincidences: What war are you speaking of? You're fighting the Industrialists? Perhaps that's it. This is a testing ground for them. But you wouldn't know the answer to that. To you your war is your war. But that must be it. Or else why would I be brought here? Damn it. I'll be dead soon, and others will die too. Death, death, death. Humans love death, don't they?"

"Sit," Pentat said. There was a firmness, a fatherly firmness to his voice — not anger, but an unwillingness to tolerate nonsense.

Rold sat without a word. A shiver shook his shoulders as his hands touched the soupy, rotting-straw-covered floor. He wiped them on his pants legs and felt his stomach jump and just managed to hold back his vomit.

"Now is not the time for philosophy nor retching, though you Whites seem to do a lot of both," Pentat said. "Are you listening?"

"Yes." Rold's eyes were shut, and he faced the floor. "I've lost my sister, and my world is coming apart at the seams. I'll not apologize for my behavior. But I think I'm past the worst of it now. I'm ready for action."

"There are two things you must learn," Pentat said. "And quickly. The sun has already set."

"How do you know that?"

"Can't you feel it? No matter. First you must learn silence."

"No problem. Next?"

"Escape."

Rold laughed. It was a hoarse, evil sounding laugh.

"Yes, then no talking, no mumbling, no singing, whistling, or humming. Nothing from your mouth. And no stumbling or shuffling. And I'll enforce this silence. Make a noise, and I'll silence you."

Rold wanted to protest such handling but realized Pentat was simply being a good leader; and in this situation he must assume that role. Rold was definitely out of his element.

"All right, I'll be quiet."

"Next. We'll leave through Mountaingate. Do you know of it?"

"I got a description of the Wall from . . ."

"Follow me. Be my shadow. Lose me, and we both die. Stay with me, and we live."

He began wondering about Pentat's plan. What would they do if they actually did get out of the Hold? Would there be any use in it? How far could they get? With the technology available to the Militia, they could track them to any corner of the planet. Was it not useless? Revenge was a better plan. Kill and die trying. But how and with what weapons? Perhaps escape should be the first priority. A few more hours, perhaps days, above ground, out of this septic hole would be worth it. Wouldn't it?

"I see you have doubts," Pentat said. "Though you crave hope. Yes?"

"Yes. Yes, I'll follow you."

"Good. Now, my people won't descend into the Hold. We must get out ourselves. They'll be waiting above, hidden. I pray the Great Mother forgives us the lives we take tonight."

How the hell are we supposed to get out of here? Rold thought, and began readying himself, for what he did not know. Pentat walked to the cell door. He scraped slime from the wall, working with both hands until he had a significant amount, cupped and dripping.

"Get some more," he said, and Rold worked at the wall where he stood. Pentat began yelling curses through the tiny window. For several minutes the jailer paid no attention, then several other prisoners took up the chant. He came grumbling to the cell door.

"It's very simple, monkey," the jailer said. "Shut up or I'll shut you up.

However you like it. You've disturbed everyone."

Pentat did not answer; he flung the dripping slime through the window. A bright flash could be seen that lit the black cell. The jailer screamed and angrily fumbled with the metal keys about his neck trying to unlock the door. Rold surmised that sweat must react with the slime in the same way as urine had earlier, producing not only light but heat.

"At his face," Pentat said, and Rold stood tensed, awaiting the opening of the door.

It took several minutes, and Rold could hear the jailer moaning and weeping. "Don't hesitate," Pentat said.

Rold wondered if he could actually read his mind, for he was beginning to feel sympathy for the poor oaf. But then the door exploded. Rold slapped two handfuls of the messy stuff onto the man's face and throat. Pentat had been ready as well. To Rold's disgust, he was urinating up into the jailer's face. The light from the fungus was brilliant. The jailer stopped his groaning and fell writhing on the floor. He stopped moving completely at the moment the organic light faded to blackness. Pentat knelt and relieved him of his keys then signaled Rold out the door.

Rold started to speak but Pentat covered his mouth roughly and made a sign with his other hand that resembled a knife slicing his throat. Rold understood this meant to be quiet and nodded. Other prisoners were screaming for freedom but were ignored. Rold followed, though not as quickly. He was weak and confused by the row.

"I'll say this once," Pentat said. "Until we are beyond the Whites' reach, we will not speak. My people use signing. It shouldn't be too difficult to understand; a child can understand without being taught. Stay in my shadow."

The car was not down on their level. It had to be activated by an identifier card which the jailer must not have had. So the jailer was a prisoner as well, Rold thought. A slave, at least. He looked at the reader panel and shook his head. Pentat grinned and jumped into the open shaft. Using the cables that hung tightly against a wall, he began climbing. Rold followed. His rock climbing skills came in handy as the two men silently ascended the black hole. Rold thought: what a strange culture! Such varying technologies — mechanical locks and optical locks in the same edifice.

The cell block was deep into the earth, at least forty meters. They had to stop occasionally and rest, finding perches on the rough rock walls. Then they would attack the climb again and inch themselves up, occasionally slipping on the greased cables.

Once they reached the final landing, Pentat signed something to Rold that he did not quite understand. But he assumed that there would be guards about the surrounding park, and that was what Pentat was trying to say.

This brought to mind the Militia scanners. Rold knew that with their technology he would be found. But who knows what this little rabbit-run might cost the Industrialists in time? An incident like this could upset their strategy, if only for a moment. Stranger things had happened. He would be caught and, yes, killed no doubt, but the delay, the energy expended, could be a help. And who knows who might go down in the dust with him? Rold was now determined to play out the whole game.

Pentat approached the door of the building. He smiled at the moonless sky, then dropped to the ground and began crawling across the cool grass. He had moved so quickly that Rold found himself twenty paces behind him and losing him fast. He was unused to such a mode of travel, but the freshness of the air and the clean grass invigorated him and soon he was catching Pentat. He drank in the wonderful air, the clear night, the thick brush-strokes of stars that lit the grass with silver sprinkles. The elation was hard to control. It wiped all memory of the filthy hole from which they had escaped. Suddenly he wanted to live. He wanted to go on drinking in this wonderful air. He promised himself never to take such things for granted again.

He hit something with his head. It was Pentat. He felt silly and wanted to laugh until he saw Pentat's hand signing to be quiet. They were about three-fourths of the way across the grass. Rold hoped Pentat was taking them in the right direction. It would be a long way if they had to circle back. They saw a small light, its beam swinging about the park. The light slowly approached but never shined directly on the two. The black form of a man could be seen holding the light.

"Who is it?" he shouted. "You're surrounded by Militia."

"They're in your area," said another voice to the right, off some distance.

"I know," the man with the light said. "But they're being as still as rabbits."

Rold saw something; he thought it might be a bird flying low to the ground, just above his head. He heard the swish of air then a thud and a sound something like a rock being smashed by a hammer. The light wobbled then turned toward the sky as the man holding it dropped to the ground. Then more of these flying things swished overhead in many directions, with the same resultant thudding and cracking sounds. So many flew overhead that the light of the stars was blocked from sight. Thousands it seemed were crisscrossing the sky. Pentat raised his hand well above his head. Rold wanted to grab it, protect him from the silent missiles, but they stopped; so suddenly that the stars dazzled Rold's eyes for a moment. There was moaning, weeping, and screaming in a circle around them, a wide circle; the human sounds of pain were faint and fell quickly to the ground.

Slowly the scene materialized in front of them: bodies, alive and dead, or at least not moving, of uniformed people, each with a halo of rods or sticks protruding from their flesh. Fletched darts: arrows! A half moon was now above the mud buildings behind Rold and Pentat. It painted the people with blue light, the arrows throwing ugly, angular shadows against the adobe walls and sparkling grass.

Pentat stood and Rold followed. With only a simple nod of Pentat's head, the silent, invisible hoard that were his people burst upon the grass like vermin in a cupboard. They fell on the victims with such speed, Rold assumed they would consume the flesh off their dead bones here and now. But what he saw amazed him. They attacked the automatic weapons rather than the bodies. They beat and crushed and destroyed all the hand-weapons they could find. Then Pentat raised his hand one more time, and they stood quiet, at attention. Rold wondered if there was some subtle differences in the way Pentat lifted his hands that signaled different actions. If he was supposed to distinguish between this hand in the air from another, in this pose or that, he was sure he would fail miserably. But Pentat's people understood, and obeyed.

Barbarous, Rold thought. But he felt a slight touch of satisfaction at the results.

The warriors gathered about them. To Rold's surprise there were only a dozen of them — two of whom he thought were women. They were dressed in leather, as befitting their ancient cultural habits. *And they used bow and arrow,* Rold thought, shaking his head.

He assumed he was to remain silent, though the warriors had made quite a bit of noise slaying the Militia and performing their symbolic emasculation. In fact, lights began appearing in windows and some traffic could be heard close by. Again another quick hand signal and the band raced to a corner of the park — Rold trailing, feeling as if he were being dragged along with a leash. Upon entering a damp, dark alley, the group split up into pairs. Rold stayed with Pentat. Each pair ran to different block corners then headed along parallel streets that rose and fell over low hills. Rold was running and gasping as he had at the spaceport. He felt he was moving in slow motion, fatigue cramping his limbs, as if he were trying to run in water a meter deep. When would he be able to stop running?

At another corner they entered an unpaved road, and there Pentat stopped and crouched along side a rough wooden rail that followed the edge of the road. Rold did not notice the arrival of one of the warriors in the dark because of his weariness after climbing the lift shaft and making this run. Pentat startled him by grabbing his tunic and pulling him up to a standing position. Before them stood a warrior holding leather reins for two mounts.

Rold's eyes widened as he saw they were not horses. Cloven hoofed, antlered mammals of tremendous size stood snorting and rattling their heads.

He remembered seeing pictures of extinct deer from Old Earth called elk that these resembled, but they were not of this size or coloring. These animals were as large as horses and their coats were speckled with camouflage like tropical cats. Heavy fabric girded their middles.

As Pentat mounted one, Rold saw the rest of the warriors trickling into the road, some already riding their mounts, others leading them toward Pentat. Rold jumped up on his mount with more grace than Pentat was expecting. He patted Rold's shoulder, then with another signal all were mounted and off down a single path together.

The animal behaved like a horse: it was used to a human load on its back. Rold had ridden extensively on O. E. when he was growing up. He knew horses well. But this gait was quite original. Each stride of the gallop was an arched leap with all four feet leaving the ground. He felt that he would take off and fly with each leap. The speed was much greater than a horse, but of course no match for hover craft. He had been enjoying the ride, but now began thinking of how useless it all was — well, perhaps not useless, but definitely doomed. Fearing the animal's antlers as it tossed its head with each step, Rold began scooting backward until he was on the animal's rump. But from there the ride was so bumpy he had to brave his way forward again only to get his jaw swiped once from an antler point. He felt blood dribbling down his throat. The bleeding somehow turned him into a wild man: the sound of the gallop, the rushing breeze, and the thought of blood drying on his face made Rold want to whoop and scream.

The single file of hopping deer twisted and turned along the narrow road that was now composed of clay brick, the small cloven hoofs clicking against the hard surface. They ascended a steep gradiant and then zigzagged into a tunnel with a ceiling that produced a greenish chemical light. Gray shadows splashed against the brick. As the exit appeared, the train of warriors suddenly stopped. Rold must have missed Pentat's signal, but he was able to halt his animal noisily. Everyone jumped down, moved their animals to the walls, across from each other, pulled their mounts down onto their knees, and prepared their bows as they crouched behind the elk, sandwiched against the walls. All this occurred in a single, fluid motion as if practiced many times. Rold found his mount cooperative to the point that he did not know who was the master of the maneuver: himself or the elk.

The shuffling quieted, and Rold heard what Pentat must have heard already: a faint rumbling approaching. Rold could see that it was a company of individual roadsters ridden in tandem by the Industrialist Militia. The miracle of the situation was the way the Salkinian warriors went unnoticed until the roadsters were upon them. The animals blended in with the rough brick walls of the tunnel and were as silent as the inanimate baked-red silica.

Rold marveled at the scene that he interpreted as a battle between low and high technology — a very simplistic notion, he soon found out. He assumed he would die on this spot. He wished for one of the weapons the Teton had destroyed in the park, feeling naked without anyway to defend himself or help his rescuers.

Then the arrows flew as they had before. But now he could watch the entire procedure in the green light that turned the ensuing blood gray. Of course the Militia did not suspect a thing. Certainly they had been told of the escape — but this close to Mountaingate, in this particular tunnel? It was impossible, but here they were.

The tunnel clogged immediately with fallen roadsters and dead or dying Militia. Energy blasters streaked the gray tunnel with yellow light and heat, but the tunnel was too confined, too constricting, to allow any direct hits. Dust and crumbled brick fell from the walls and ceiling as the blasts missed their target. The warriors mounted, and the sure footed beasts jumped the piled machines and bodies like boulders on a hillside. The warriors rode reinless. The forward group held up circular convex shields adorned with paint and feathers. The blasters could not penetrate whatever material was used to construct them. The rest followed with volleys of arrows, all except Rold and Pentat. Within just a few strides they were through the mess, the rear guard pulling up shields as they passed, and the forward group turning round on their animals and shooting one more round of arrows. The end of the tunnel appeared and the speeding band spit forth and headed for the massive gate that was now in view.

The road was set at an angle and crossed an open area. A semicircle of about an acre bounded the gate clear of any buildings. The Wall blackened the horizon; hills or mountains loomed above it, blocking out half the sky. Rold was just wondering about the time of night when he saw violet blooming above the serrated peaks and smelled a dawn breeze.

He followed dumbly, keeping his eyes on Pentat, refusing to think any further then the next stride. It was not his place to solve problems, though several presented themselves. But problems arose and were surpassed so quickly on this run that he gave in to confidence in the native leader.

Another problem ahead solved itself as the others seemed to. Mountaingate was opening as the rescuers approached it without missing a step. With dawn, merchants were entering the city with produce and artifacts of the hill folk. As Pentat and his cohorts passed, the merchants swiftly clogged the open gate behind them, cheering the escaping heroes. The gate-keepers were taken by surprise, but managed a single energy blast that spilled a warrior and crippled his mount. Without stopping he ran, almost as fast as the trotting animals, and using a small boulder as a step leaped onto Rold's animal behind him and grabbed Rold around his waist.

Following Pentat, the group left the main road and followed a dry creek bed that led them quickly up into the foothills. The creek was fairly clear of debris, giving the animals little problem with footing. As the sun broke free of the white crystalline peaks they turned again and climbed more earnestly, making numerous switchbacks. The short brush of the lower hills was replaced with gangly conifers that had rooted themselves in the brittle rock.

Rold kept looking over his shoulder. His passenger would smile and shake his head. Such confidence, Rold thought. He imagined the Industrialist Militia's machinery massing outside the Wall, preparing for their ascent. Tracking would be so simple: fourteen people on thirteen mounts moving slowly up the side of a mountain. Scanners could be used to pinpoint the group. Sniffers could be used to follow their trail.

They stopped at the summit of the hill they were climbing and surveyed the canyons below and high mountains beyond. Still using signing instead of speech Pentat ordered the band to split into three groups. He pointed to three canyons that were the forks of a large river that glistened below them. Without hesitating the company broke up, Rold and his passenger staying with Pentat and another rider. The ride down was alarmingly steep, but soon they had entered the southern canyon. Upon turning a sharp corner they entered a very narrow stretch where the river had sliced through the rock in short order. The cliffs darkened the trail and almost touched, it seemed, three hundred meters overhead. Here Pentat spoke.

"Now we're safe," he said. "These walls will protect us."

"Why's that?" Rold asked.

His passenger answered. "The Whites have no eyes or ears beyond here."

Pentat smiled. Rold screwed his face then wiped his eyes with one hand.

"Lampa means the Whites' instruments for searching won't operate here," Pentat explained.

Rold still looked confused or perhaps just tired. Pentat lagged and rode beside him on the narrow path. He pulled a knife from his belt.

"Watch," Pentat said. He then lobbed the knife toward the cliff wall. The wall seemed to lunge for the metal blade. It rang as it hit the wall and adhered. Rold, amazed, stopped and retrieved the knife, having to slide it along the surface to free it.

"Magnetic ore," Rold said. "An incredible deposit. There must be ions jumping all over the place. Is it in the other canyons as well?"

"Yes. Otherwise the Whites would easily assume to follow this one."

"They could follow them all. And probably will. This path wouldn't be that hard to follow, let's face it. Their scanners would be blind, but they can still just search until they find us."

Pentat pointed up the wall ahead of them. At first only appearing as a speck far above them, a wooden platform was being lowered by ropes from the top of the cliff. As it reached the canyon floor Rold could see that it was large enough for all three mounts.

"It's big enough, but can it hold all of us at once?" he asked, worried about the delay if each had to be lifted separately. Seeing the smiles of his companions, he knew the answer. His face ached from the silly grin he was wearing. He could not describe his emotions: relief, joy, and wonder.

He started to hand the knife back to Pentat, but he refused it.

"Keep it, Mountain Bear. You have no knife and you'll need one now that you are with the Teton."

Rold smiled, shoved the knife into his belt, and the two men clasped forearms.

The lift met the canyon floor with a thud, and the three animals and four men boarded the giant bucket, as the Salkinians called it. The ropes creaked as the heavy weight was lifted, and the escaping Teton disappeared up into the slit in the sky above the canyon.

Later the Militia would swear that they had actually vanished, melted into the rock.

CHAPTER 6

Life histories tangle in the minah-machacute web,
The Mountain Bear roared as he sped to his destiny,
With Margona's resurrection unknown.

From "The Song of Margona"
by Pitallela-Sim

Ruth Poundstone was working late as usual in her chambers at the Committee Hall. The majority of the Committee members had returned to their home planets spread through the Commonwealth, scheduled to return in a quarter cycle to battle new debates. But Ruth was a resident of Newert, as were a handful of the Committee — the ones with life terms — all except Malcolm Simms. He should be here, but he did things his own way, and no one seriously challenged him on his residency. He clung to the old world while building a new universe. Newert, though, was not that new, and was still linked to Old Earth by its traditions, values, art, and genes. It had been a cozy world, a haven for scientists so many years ago. They had developed their power base on Newert. Ruth wanted to preserve the cohesive strength of decades of Scientism which her ancestors had built. She could not, would not, regret the human sacrifices for which she had been responsible in the past few weeks. The protection of Holy Science was her number one priority. Though she did not care for murder, it was not something to cry over.

Working at her desk with a single light that brought to life her small workspace and draped the rest of the chamber in deadly dark, she was notified of a communication that was about to appear from her projector. She pressed a button in response to a blinking yellow light, and a snowy blob began resolving in front of her, emitting the crackling noises of static. The image sharpened and became Rachel Meacom. No identifiable artifacts from the source of transmission could be seen, so Ruth had no clue as to where Rachel was at the moment. She could guess that she was no longer in the field since she was dressed for night play. Rachel's hair was done in a current Industrialist style: first braided, then coiled on top of her head and encased in a translucent blue plastic sculpture. The fad was to have molten polymers actually poured on the hair, then have a glass blower perform his art. Jewels and specks of gold were held in suspension in the glass.

The practice disgusted Ruth. *Probably going to some party to destroy her mind with drugs*, she thought. But she held her tongue, not wanting to miss anything important in the transmission. The image was turned so that Rachel spoke to a wall. Ruth maneuvered a lever, rotating the image until Rachel was facing her. Then she lowered it so that their eyes were level with each other.

"The Militia has failed us," Rachel said.

Ruth was appalled and full of questions. It was a one-way transmission, probably sent several hours before, so she had to fume in frustration at not being able to immediately reach out and strangle the woman.

"Rold Simms was apprehended," Rachel was saying as Ruth rubbed her eyes, "but escaped his imprisonment with the help of a small group of native rebels on one of our planets. Colonel August is now searching the surrounding areas, but as yet has not been successful. I have sent a similar message to my father. I urged him to dismiss August for his incompetence. However, in my mind, we are not yet beaten. Who is to say we don't have Rold Simms in our possession? The locals here have a very low technology. They will not be able to send transmissions or transport Simms offworld. And they will not evade us long. Also they may have kidnapped Simms themselves, seeing the importance we placed on him, with hope that we might be willing to pay a ransom. He may already be dead. These people are little better than savages. I am sure for some payment we may at least get his body back. The Simms girl is dead, as was reported; at least she can't cause us trouble.

"It is my suggestion that our plan not be delayed nor perceived as hindered by these events. I hope you share my confidence."

The image of Rachel Meacom then dissolved. An encrypted return address was left on the communicator for Ruth's reply. Ruth did not like sending a message to an unknown address, and realized she dearly wished to know where they had taken him. But the encryption included a self-destruction of the address if tampered with.

She's probably at a brothel, on god knows what planet, Ruth thought; it could be any of a hundred of their factory planets spread out there in the Twin Sisters quadrant. No matter.

She keyed in a command to reply and encrypt the transmission.

"I agree," Ruth said staring at the camera. "We will go on as planned. But it's very important that Rold Simms is recovered, and soon. Dead or alive. Perhaps you should assume command. I'll talk to your father about it.

"I can just imagine your precious Militia getting caught with their pants down.

"And don't worry. You'll be involved in the coup when it occurs. Come home when you have everything under control."

She started the transmission and returned to her desk. *This helps me more than it helps her,* Ruth thought. *Yes, we'll go on as planned. When Malcolm gets the news of the kidnapping and no word from his daughter, he'll assume they're both dead. Probably young Simmis is by now. Then things will begin to move a bit faster.*

Before turning off the machine she dispatched another message. She did not know to whom it would be sent. The conspiracy had attracted some anonymous members who had somehow extorted their way into the organization. She had been given a customized encryption program for reaching this particular member, who managed the dirtier duties for the Committee. The message was simple: "Have the Meacoms disappear — father and daughter."

Sighing deeply with fatigue and age, Ruth stood, joints and tendons aching as they were stretched. She turned off the one light and shuffled through the dark to the door and entered the brightly lit hallway that led to a fire escape. She used that exit because it was close to her office. Each night she would set off an alarm and the one human security guard would see her on his monitor, smile and turn off the alarm. Tonight was no exception. She walked into an overcast night. The shadows were dark, but the sky was bright from the city lights reflecting on the low clouds. With slow, confident steps the weary old woman headed home.

The warm summer nights of Minpana exacerbated the stench of the mounting cadavers in the state-run hospital; an overworked orderly moaned at the sight of more bodies arriving. Attacks by the rebels were becoming more frequent, and the workers spoke quietly about the high number of Militia dead among the bodies. Very few natives were ever brought in. They wondered at the competence of the Industrialist recruits.

Chictampa and his wife, Sompica, had been working at the hospital for over thirty years, long before a Militia had existed. They were Salkinians, Teton, drawn by the opportunities of the urban market, intrigued by the White way of life. They had never been politically-minded. But since the Militia had come, atrocities had mounted. And the rebellion had grown. They were old now with few regrets, but they secretly felt a yearning to return to their village for the remainder of their lives.

"Sompy?" Chictampa said, as he wrestled with another gurney in the dark hallway that led to the morgue. "This White girl, why is she here? She is not Militia. Could she be what they call a Scientist?"

"Why do you care? Quiet now. Don't ask questions. We have twenty more dead to take care of before we can go home."

"But there's something wrong here. Ah!"

"What is it!"

"She . . . breathes!"

The gray couple stood over the child, her head crusted with dried blood, dried mucous almost closing her nostrils. Chictampa stroked her matted hair.

"We must get her help," he said, in the Teton language.

"You risk our jobs; you risk our lives."

"She is an enemy of the Militia. Why else would she be here? Dumped like an animal found dead by a road? We must take her to the Swilla village. It's close. They have medicine, a Library-trained doctor."

Sompica looked at the pitiful lump of a girl, curled up, still as death. She put her ear close to the child's mouth and confirmed that she breathed.

"Then we leave forever," she said looking at her mate with frightened eyes.

He nodded. It was now time to abandon the Whites. This child needed help immediately. He wrapped her in a sheet, covering her head as well, and carried her potato sack fashion into the dark of midnight. Sompica followed, watching behind them, but all was quiet. They picked up a few belongings at their adobe apartment then stole to Rivergate. They knew a gatekeeper there and managed to quietly pass beyond the Wall with a barely breathing girl child, and their lives.

Rold woke shivering. Condensing vapor escaped his nose and mouth as he breathed. Experimenting, he blew lightly through his mouth and watched the smoky cloud form and dissolve in front of his face. He could smell a wood fire, and his stomach ached as he caught a whiff of cooked meat. Just a glimmer of sunlight could be seen through the branches of evergreen trees; the sky was purple. Being disoriented, he could not tell whether the twilight was dawn or dusk. He stood then waded through shoulder high bracken toward the group of sitting warriors that circled a small, smoky campfire. The sky darkened slightly as he crossed the marshy clearing. Pentat rose from the group and held up a charred animal haunch. He no longer wore his paint — in fact he wore no adornments: no feathers, no beads, only a leather headband to secure his long hair.

"You've slept all day," Pentat said and some men laughed. He handed Rold the haunch and sat him down beside him facing the fire. He basked in the heat. Pentat rubbed Rold's arms and shoulders trying to warm him. It embarrassed Rold, though it did feel good. "It's good to be rested," Pentat said. "Eat. Regain your strength. We must travel tonight."

"Where are we going?"

"We must find my family."

Rold thought to ask why but kept silent. He had only one aim now: *revenge.*

"We will head for the grassy plains to the northwest," Pentat said. "We will find who we seek there."

"We would be exposing ourselves that way."

"It would be an unexpected direction. They'll think we're headed for my lands east of this plateau. My warriors will continue on to our village, throwing off the trackers along the way. But you and I, we'll head north, through the mountains then down to the grass sea. We will need their help. You agree?"

"Yes," Rold said grimly. He quelled his impatience with his thoughts of revenge. A well-formed plan would achieve the best results. He had to keep reminding himself though. "I still have hope of stopping the war . . ."

"Your war."

"Yes."

Rold tore into the dripping flesh and found it addicting, until his stomach ached from fullness rather than hunger. He studied the band in silence. They spoke little and used sign language as a part of their natural conversation, speaking a word aloud occasionally to make a point. They laughed freely, and when they looked at Rold he saw a warmth in their eyes that relaxed him and also made him feel a little sad.

These were a new group of men. Upon reaching the top of the mountain ridge, they had left the mechanism that had plucked them from the Militia and crossed onto an alpine meadow where they'd camped. The raiders had assumed the sentinels' job as the sentinels came along with Pentat and Rold. He wondered what Pentat had told the group about him. The thing that was still puzzling was why he was so accepted. He was a "White." He supposed his imprisonment made the difference. He asked Pentat, who just laughed at his question.

They were preparing to leave — all of them. Pentat saddled his and Rold's animals. A warrior approached Pentat and spoke to him in whispers and signing.

"And who is this White?" he asked. "Why do you take him with you?"

"I'll tell you this: his face is not unknown to me," Pentat said. "I saw him in a vision."

"Is he the one, Pentat?" the warrior said. "The one foretold by the minah-machacute?"

Rold noticed the conversation. He heard the word minah-machacute and asked: "The what?"

"Living clouds," Pentat said. "Tellers of the future."

Rold nodded. What does that mean: *Living clouds?* He knew that the warriors were curious about him. They kept looking at him. Why had Pentat helped him?

Pentat wondered what Rold had heard.

"Can you throw an arrow?" Pentat asked.

"Why not shoot it . . . Oh, I see, throw means shoot. No, I've never done it. I'm sure I could learn."

"It's not something that can be learned in a few minutes like firing a blaster. It takes skill and practice. Perhaps you won't have to learn its use. Hopefully we will find my father soon. He can help you with your quest, and then you will know your future. Now up on your pony."

Rold jumped up on his animal and sat with a rigid back, aware of the points of the antlers. His jaw still stung and felt inflamed. *There's probably lots of stuff here I'm not immune to,* he thought. *This dumb scratch on my chin will probably end up killing me unless I can develop some immunity quickly. With a little work I might train my antibodies.*

Pentat attached a pack to some straps behind Rold, then stuffed an unstrung bow vertically into gathered fabric beneath more bindings.

"What are these animals called?" Rold asked. "You have no horses?"

They left the others and began leisurely climbing a rocky ridge that stuck out above the trees. The sun had set and no moon had yet appeared. The stars, though, were bright enough to light their way as long as they stayed in clearings on the plateau.

"I know of horses," Pentat said. "I have seen pictures. Our horses perished a thousand years ago. My ancestors brought many animals with them: cows, horses, chickens, and sheep. All died the first year except the eagles and hawks, which were released to the wild. The *pridda*, these ponies, were trained for riding soon after. There's a story of how Chomata-te spoke to the leader of a herd of pridda, and he consented to release fawns for training in exchange for a promise never to kill the pridda for food or sport. It's a children's story of course." He laughed softly.

"Go on. Tell it."

"Well, as it is told, Chomata-te promised the stag that the Teton would never kill a pridda, and in the spring one hundred fawns appeared at the settlement. At that time the pridda were not spotted as they are now. They were as horses: reds, bays, blacks, whites. And within a couple of years the fawns grew and were trained for riding and carrying packs. But some wilder people who had decided to live away from the village began killing pridda for food. The stag came and spoke with Chomata-te again asking him to stop the slaughter. The killers were tracked down and humiliated and told to leave the plain — which they did. All except one band that hid in the Red Hills. But soon it was evident that more pridda were being killed. The stag returned to warn Chomata-te to keep all those that were dear to him inside the village for the night, for the pridda were going to destroy the killers. That night a thousand pridda stormed into the foothills and killed everyone of the outlaw band. The blood of the people splattered the pridda, who had never killed before, and it's said that the blood stained their souls. From that time forward the pridda have had spotted coats, and not a single pridda has been killed for food or sport by a Teton."

"Chomata-te. That's the leader who was born during the exodus from Old Earth."

"You have heard that story, have you?"

"There's so much more I'd like to know."

"Ask."

"I have so many questions. Like: how is your war related to the war that's brewing in the Commonwealth? Who are you at war with?"

"War is not a pleasant subject. And more to the point, it's not a pleasant business. We are not a warring people. In a thousand years there has not been a single war among our people here. But your Commonwealth began invading us a hundred years ago, and you're destroying us with your technology and your nihilistic ideas. Your concepts of life, love, society are self-destructive. You are what we escaped two thousand years ago, and now you have caught up with us to torture us again."

Rold choked on his rebuttal. He was about to charge in with an elegant defense of his culture when he realized that Pentat had used words, ideas, that should be foreign to a regressed culture like this. Also he was speaking in Ameranglo. But the worst thing was that Rold was being included in the attack. He was a part of the enemy. His society was the problem. And now thinking of how rotten things had become in his society he felt he could not defend it. Something was wrong with it, and he knew it.

"Am I your enemy then?" he asked lamely, not knowing what else to say. He could not see Pentat's face, only a dark mass bouncing with his pony's trot.

"Mountain Bear," Pentat said, "you are not my enemy. I can see that the Whites fear you. They see you as their enemy. And so we can make a bond to be friends, to fight the Whites, to avenge my suffering and yours. And by the great eagle I swear to this bond.

"The eagle is, as you might say, the mascot of my village, or tribe. When I have pain dreams an eagle is always present. Ten days ago I dreamed on an icy rock that looked out on the desert. I saw many things: battles to come, death — much death — but good things too.

"This war is bad for us. It has divided our people. There are those that would adopt your technology, steal your weapons and turn them against you. To me that is a sign of defeat. Also there are those who don't understand the true danger of the Whites. So I went to the high mountains, climbed above the timberline, and sat for five days without food so that I might have a dream that would tell me what to do. I was told in my dream that you were coming was a sign. In fact, it was a strange sending. The message was really just 'stay alive,' and your coming meant we would not have to wait much longer. Who knows about these things? I was skeptical about the pain dreams when I was younger, and I had been educated at the Library. But having a dream and seeing the reality of it — well, seeing is believing, as the old books say."

Rold shook his head; he knew Pentat could not see it in the dark. Undeveloped or regressed cultures always exhibited some formalized beliefs based on superstition, or more accurately mistaken coincidences of thought and deed. Because of pressures of fictionalized media and the remnants of ancient cults such as Buddhists and Christians, anyone might at times imagine that a dream, a daydream, *deja vu,* or a simple scene or phrase has some psychic importance. Rold recounted these teachings he took for granted. Even he had moments that seemed to point to something unexplained — like his own dream of an eagle. And now the thought of that dream fed a hidden hunger of escapism. He had to calm himself and walk through his own skepticism, pragmatism.

But he did not wish to offend Pentat with challenges to his simple beliefs in sendings and dreams — and gods no doubt. So he battled it out with himself, as he often did, playing games of rhetoric which tended toward solipsism.

"I have no romantic ideas about saviors," Pentat said. "You may be a great ally, a terrible warrior, but I see you as a source of knowledge that we may use to find a weakness in the White armies. In this way you may contribute.

"I see hatred in your eyes when you speak of those who killed your sister. This I can understand. Too many of my people have died at the hands of the Whites. But let me ask you: Instead of pouring your hatred into a single blow of revenge, as I'm sure you have dreamed of doing, why not join me, as my dream has indicated, and do something more lasting, more noble perhaps? You have to follow your own mind, I know. But I would welcome your help."

Rold wondered why Pentat kept arguing this point. He supposed Pentat was trying to make sense of Rold's importance to the war if he believed such dreams; Rold would be puzzled by that point himself. But why worry about it? If he was not killed in his attempt at revenge, he would soon be leaving Salkinia to report to his father.

"Whatever the outcome," Rold said, "I must thank you for helping me escape. I never thought we would make it this far. Perhaps your eagle god is really looking over us. But I prefer to believe that you made it happen, and I thank you. And your soldiers — or warriors. What is the word you use?"

"Sampita. It's hard to translate. Really it means 'hunters,' but you might say 'warriors of the buffalo.' As I said, we are not warriors — we are hunters. We consider ourselves enemy to no one. But if someone or something makes itself our enemy, then we must use our skills at hunting to defend ourselves. The pitah, buffalo, is a fierce and cunning animal — unlike the ancient bison of Earth. We have had to learn to defend our villages, for he is vengeful and attacks us, his enemy. We mourn the cruelty of our war with the pitah, but also we rejoice in the fact that we survive."

Rold kept silent, letting the conversation sleep. He was fascinated by this new culture but did not want to be too drawn in by it. To romanticize life in a regressed culture could be dangerous, especially for an outsider from a highly-developed society who had been educated and honed to a fine sophistication. He could not put his finger on it, but there always seemed to be something amiss with a regressed culture like this — it lacked something important. But listening to Pentat, Salkinia sounded utopian — brutal in some respects, one had to expect that, but well organized in an informal way. The advantages of a small population which acquiesced to ecological pressure seemed undeniable. But he knew he was not seeing the whole picture, and it did not matter anyway — he would leave eventually, or die trying.

The trail narrowed, and little light filtered down leaving them blinded. But the pridda lumbered easily along the path, with hidden creatures singing and buzzing as the air warmed along the descent. Rold dozed on and off after the two men gave up talking all together. Occasionally he was woken by the crack of a twig or a rustling of birds or night animals, then would sink into a bobbing state of unconsciousness. Finally he slumped forward and snored loudly. Pentat stopped and threw a thong around Rold's back and secured him to his pony and settled him in a balanced position. The two pridda started again, needing no rein to direct them down the little trail.

The moon rose late in the night as the canyon grew into a wide valley of small rolling hills carpeted with tall, dry grass. Pentat woke Rold so that he could tell him of their new direction. They left the river and followed a trail to the south that meandered between two blue, moon-lit furry hills. Dawn warmed their backs, and soon the sun lit the grassy hills with gold. There was not a tree in sight, not even in the weathered nooks and arroyos — only dry grass that whipped in the wind.

The hills became smaller and smaller until the two men were on a plain with an infinite horizon to the west and south. Over his shoulder Rold looked at the towering mountains that stood as a wall. He was lost, of course. He had no idea which direction Minpana lay — not that he wished to return there at this moment, but it was where he had entered Salkinia, where his sweet sister Tyler had been lost, and he wanted to use it as a reference point. For now he must trust Pentat.

Certainly Pentat was exhausted, Rold thought. Has he been able to sleep at all these last couple of days? He has let me sleep. Why does he pamper me?

A large cloud shadow drifted across their path much faster than the wind was blowing. Rold looked up, shading his eyes with his hand, and was startled to see that it was not a cloud but a huge bag of protoplasm, an organism of some sort, hovering in the atmosphere. He did not understand the propulsion mechanics of the creature and how it manipulated gravity — unless with light gasses. Seemingly from nowhere, two more smaller organisms appeared. Some after-vision images showed Rold from which directions the two new ones had come. Such speed!

"Look," he said, pointing up in awe like a child.

Pentat looked up and smiled. He had grown up with such scenes. The minah-machacute lived in large numbers around Salkinia and had no fear of human beings.

"Living clouds," Pentat said.

"That's what you were talking about! Living clouds! They're amazing. And . . . ugly. Are they dangerous?"

Pentat laughed. Then looked serious. "No one told you about the minah-machacute? I'm surprised. Well, no, they aren't a danger, in the way you would think. They would not harm anyone physically. But don't make the mistake of trusting a minah-machacute. They are very unreliable. My sister has reasons for believing in them; she is a rider. But listen to me, don't trust your life to one. They're like children who play games all the time and have no sense of what is important. Everything is a game."

Rold sensed bitterness in Pentat's words and wondered if he had had some practical experience with these creatures that had turned out badly.

They looked so ugly in the daylight with cerulean sky behind them. Occasionally a real cloud would float by, and the minah-machacute would be lost in them. After an hour or so they disappeared all together.

The terrain began changing in the afternoon. Low shrubs appeared, and the grass thinned. The soil was white with a caustic compound that looked lifeless. To the north a large, dry lake came into view, and some bluffs rose ahead of them, taking them back onto high grasses. The plain was alive with noises — so unlike Old Earth which had lost most of its wildlife. Here there were birds, insects, snakes, rodents, and wild cats. Rold saw a fat little roosting bird in the brush, some small red birds with scissor tails playing games from twig to twig, and two hawks. Pentat pointed to a rodent he called a rabbit, but it looked more like a monkey with long ears to Rold, who had studied zoo animals on Old Earth.

As they entered a saddle along one of the bluffs, Pentat motioned to stop and rest in the shade. He produced some food from a purse he wore strapped to his waist. It was a wad of cooked meat wrapped in a large leaf. Rold watched Pentat bite into the rolled packet and then nibbled his own. The leaf was tender and had a faint minty taste. The meat was a bit dry and salty, but together with the leaf it tasted good. Pentat had also brought water bladders, and passed one to Rold.

"Pitallela did an admirable job in finding this planet," Rold said after wiping his mouth of water. "It's more like Old Earth than Old Earth is anymore — or any other planet in the Commonwealth for that matter. The animal life, the plant life, geological structures, it's amazing. No wonder it was given conservation status."

"Yes. But there are other differences with the Old Earth you speak of, some obvious and some not. It's said that the phases of our moon drove many people mad early in our history. You see, Pitallela looked very hard to find a planet with a single moon that revolved within twenty-eight rotations of the planet. Our moon here revolves at twice that rate. It was something that seemed unimportant, but some chiefs from the early days blamed the moon for anything that went wrong: storms, babies dying, small summer kills of pitah, and mostly people losing their reason. Who knows?"

"Perhaps you know this already, but there are other dangers on a new planet, such as microbes — bacteria, viruses."

"Yes, I know of them. Such knowledge is not lost to us. In the beginning the weak died, and the strong produced children who were not affected by diseases. Your people take drugs made from our blood to make them strong."

"Not my people, Pentat. People of my 'tribe' don't introduce chemicals into their bodies. The Industrialists who live here are the ones you are talking about."

"Then you are in danger here."

"Perhaps. But I'm trying to communicate with my body to fight any foreign microbes. So far I feel fine."

"Then you meditate?"

"Sort of."

Pentat smiled. "I could tell you were different. I didn't know how you could be different, but now I see."

The cool rest was short, for the horizon beckoned the sun, and Pentat wanted to get on the road, still hoping to find the safari before dark.

Once past the bluff the trail found its way onto flat grassy land again. The tall, yellow grain threw long shadows back toward the travelers as the sun shown red in their eyes. A warm breeze kicked up, whipping the grass for leagues in all directions. The sweet smell of the air forced a smile upon Rold, who inhaled it as if it were his last breath. In fact he drank it like an addictive drug. Pentat turned and nodded his head.

"You like our air," he said waving an arm through it. "Be careful. It has a very high oxygen content."

Of course, Rold thought. That's been it all along. He just thought it was clean, which it was, but he had not guessed at the gas mixture. But he was troubled again by Pentat's knowledge — this time of chemistry. And that comment about microbes. He knows so much, Rold thought, like Yosana.

Pentat stopped, and Rold halted close behind him. As before in the battle Pentat jumped down from the pridda, pulled the pony down; Rold managed to get his animal down as well. Pentat motioned for silence and notched an arrow. Rold could not see or hear anything, but Pentat obviously could, and was concentrating on the bluff they had just left. Just as Rold began growing impatient and lost interest he was violently startled by the sound of a roaring and galloping animal that was very close and had appeared seemingly from nowhere. Pentat aimed calmly and shot. A scream of pain came from the animal and started the pridda howling. Pentat leaped to his mount's back and was off chasing the wounded prey. Rold watched for a moment then climbed on his pridda and followed at a gallop. They were both falling behind the beast. It was twice as tall as the pridda and twice as broad with a reddish-brown shaggy coat. It had two curved horns and a huge head. Rold was amazed that it could run so fast.

After a long, hard chase they began to slow and give up, but then the animal stumbled. As it went down its head exploded, and a second later the delayed sound of the crackling of a blaster echoed against the hills. Pentat, without hesitating, sped up to investigate. Rold thought he was being too reckless and followed at a slower pace.

From hunting blinds covered in dry grass emerged three hunters. Rold could not tell much about them. They were in shadows and some distance away, but as he came nearer he recognized one, then guessed at all of them. It was Blikki and his party. His stomach felt hollow, and a tingling shot down his back.

Catching up to Pentat, he tried to grab his reins and halt his animal. Pentat angrily pulled away, looking at Rold as if he had lost his mind. But Rold persisted until the pridda crashed into each other, spilling their riders.

"What is it, Mountain Bear?" Pentat said as he stood and rubbed his aching shoulder. "What danger do you see?"

"These people. They're dangerous. They were responsible for my capture."

Pentat looked at Rold as if he were speaking an unknown language.

"No, Mountain Bear, that's not possible."

Rold grabbed Pentat by the shoulders and looked into his eyes, wanting desperately to make his point.

"I tell you, damn it, they can't be trusted!"

Pentat forced Rold's hands from his body.

"And I tell you, Mountain Bear, that is my father, Ah-blikkinata la' Kunda. And he would never deliver you to the Whites unless he were tricked himself."

Rold's confusion about Yosana and Blikki suddenly thickened. Pentat had taken him right to them. A coincidence? Or is Pentat betraying him as well? But his feelings told him Pentat was not capable of deceit. He was determined to solve this mystery once and for all.

"I'll follow you," Rold said. "But on my guard."

They mounted and stepped up their pace until they were moving at a flying speed.

"The people that are with him know I was arrested," Rold shouted. "They belong to the same party as my captors."

"Whites. Thank you, Mountain Bear."

"I just thought you should know."

The two were practically brushing their legs together. There was a thrill to the ride that put a smile on each of their faces. The feeling was quite different from what was felt on the anxious ride out of Minpana. Rold got caught up in the moment, forgetting his anxiety about the la' Kundas.

Pentat looked at Rold, his eyes shining wildly. "Freedom is like water to a thirsty man — or riding a fast mount," Pentat yelled. "Do you feel it?"

Rold whooped and threw both arms up, showing off his riding skills.

"Drink long," Pentat said. Feeling compelled to compete, he performed tricks composed of leaps from one side of the animal to the other and finishing with screams and brandishing of his bow which was decorated with dangling feathers. He was claiming the kill to be his by his show and easily commanded the attention of the entire party.

Rold could see Blikki waving and dancing as they approached, a grin spreading across his face. He looked but could not find Yosana. They arrived and spilled to the ground from their excited pridda, laughing and teasing each other with slaps and embraces. Blikki approached, obviously amazed to see Rold and Pentat together.

"Where's Yosana?" Pentat asked after catching his breath.

Rold stood aloof, determined to find what kind of people these really were before committing himself again.

"She's at camp," Blikki said. "But how the . . . To see you, Rold, this is a wonder. And with my kinsman. How did this happen?"

The smell of blood reached them as a dusty gust of wind swirled through the gathering. Barbara was recording pictures of the dead animal. Everyone gathered around the kill, examining it for their own purposes.

"We met in prison," Rold said, his eyes glued to the corpse. He gingerly brushed the fur with the tips of his fingers.

"Pitah," Pentat said.

"It's huge," Rold said.

"It's a bison, you fool," Daryl said. He seemed slightly intoxicated. He mumbled a couple of words then laughed again.

"I take it you were released by the Militia, Mr. Simms," Barbara said. "Certainly your arrest must have been a mistake. We all were quite shocked."

"Well," she continued after clearing her throat, "please, introduce us to your companion. Our guide here seems to already know you, sir."

"Pentat, chief of the Eagles," Rold said.

"A chief. How impressive. Well worth the trip. Will you join us at camp for the evening? Quite a surprise, Mr. Simms; quite a surprise."

With that said Barbara and Daryl started for the camp. Blikki called to them, "But what of the animal? We must dress it."

"Let it rot," Daryl said. "I destroyed its head. The trophy's ruined. Just forget it." He turned and continued walking.

Blikki, Pentat, and Rold stayed behind, keeping silent until the Industrialists were out of sight. The sun touched the gray rim of the plain, and Blikki produced electric lanterns to light his work, then pulled his knife that was strapped to his belt and dug into the tough hide of the animal.

"There's no place to pack the meat," he said as he struggled with one of the giant legs. "Forgive me, son, but we can at least take the coat." Pentat put his knife to work without complaint. Rold sat and watched.

"Sorry about your sister, Rold," Blikki said, breathing hard. "That woman who killed her should be dragged through cactus and left to be eaten by the vultures."

"Thank you . . ."

Rold was still on his guard, not sure if he could trust Blikki. He had allowed himself to ease his guard with Pentat, but that could have been a mistake as well. But he owed Pentat for his escape.

"Should've know those bastards were up to no good," Blikki continued. "We got you into this because we took you on. Yosana got the tip that you needed a ride. You probably figured that out. But we meant no harm. Certainly didn't want your sister. . ."

"That's behind us," Rold said quickly.

"Yosana . . . well, Yosana can tell you herself. I just think you should know she took it hard."

"Thank you for telling me."

Rold was beginning to be convinced that the la'Kundas were innocent of deliberately delivering him to the Militia. He knew he should not accept these people so easily. But he seemed to have a hidden desire to believe them. He decided that their mercenary habits made them blameless, though perhaps not completely innocent. Trust was a different matter. But he must reserve his revenge for more worthy targets.

"So you were released?"

"Not exactly," Rold said.

Blikki stopped for a moment, wiping his brow. "I see. So, Pentat, you were involved, I guess."

"Yes, Father. We were imprisoned together."

Blikki stopped and touched Pentat on the shoulder. They both stopped working. "It has gone that far?" Blikki said.

Rold thought he saw tears in the old man's eyes, but it could have been sweat.

"I won't go back, then," Blikki said. "As I said many times, the Whites are not all bad. But I can't live among them if they treat the Teton this way. Yosana and I will stay here. We had already decided. With the big war coming . . ."

"But you have to go back," Pentat said. "At least one more time. To take Mountain Bear. He has to get word to his people, to his home world."

Blikki sighed. "It won't stop the war, you understand," he said to Rold. "Things are too far along for that. Even if I could get you to Minpana and a packet transmitter. But if you wish to go, it'll be no hardship for us. Though we must do something about these Commonwealthers. They'll insist on finishing the safari. And perhaps that would be the safest thing."

"But why?" Pentat said. "We would lose too much time."

"You know so little about these people. They're important. They could be terrible enemies. They would get suspicious if we turned back now, make trouble for us all. Your showing up has probably already got them talking.

"Let's say we declared war here and now and abandoned or killed these people: the Industrialist Militia would be on us in minutes. And no, I'm not killing an innocent man and woman. You see, Pentat, war requires deceit as well as killing. And I would just as soon play this game with my hunting party for a few days then risk getting us all killed. I know you would like to just forget the pretending and die an honest hero. But I've seen how the Whites make war, and we must adapt or be beaten."

"Their philosophy is worse then their technology," Pentat said.

Rold was quiet through all this, feeling too exhausted to argue on either side. Blikki was right, though he hated to admit it. They should finish the safari as planned. Then he could somehow get to Minpana and do what he must do — if things were not already happening . . .

In much less time then Rold thought possible the pitah was stripped of its auburn hide. Blikki and Pentat laid the rug on the trampled ground and dried the blood and scoured chunks of flesh from it with sand, until it was more pink than red. They expertly rolled and folded it, packing it in a bag that Pentat flung over his back. Leading the pridda while remaining on foot, Rold carried one of the lamps while Blikki carried the other to lead the way to camp.

CHAPTER 7

The rider revealed herself in the moonlight,
At the bite of night, Mountain Bear saw her secret
Already succumbing to the magic of clouds.

From "The Song of Margona"
by Pitallela-Sim

Yosana knelt beside the small camp fire poking it in an effort to look busy, her mind far away from her chores. When Barbara had announced the arrival of Rold and her cousin Pentat, her self-control had almost snapped. Barbara noticed Yosana's anxious manner, but said nothing, only acknowledging it with her eyes as the two women greeted each other outside the land rover.

A jiggling light approached, and Yosana stood, her stomach churning and gurgling. Above the sounds of the insects and wind she could hear laughter coming from behind the light. She broke free of her self-imposed bindings and ran to greet the guests. Pentat saw her coming first and shouted her name. He opened his arms and smiled. Rold felt something odd. He had thought only of Tyler, and the coming war, since his abduction, never thinking he would see Yosana again. His feelings for her had never been resolved. Part of him was not looking forward to her biting comments and resentment of his station; but then he found himself pleased to see her, perhaps as a reminder of his last few happy moments with Tyler aboard the ship.

Without hesitating, without slowing, Yosana crashed into Pentat, their arms wrapping around each other. They had all stopped just a few paces from the camp, allowing the reunion to take its course. Rold found himself smiling at their loving hug.

They parted and Yosana looked at Rold. She was still smiling from her greeting to Pentat, but a sadness seemed to melt her smile as she extended her hand to Rold. He was taken aback by this welcome; he found that he had hoped such a greeting, though never expected it. He took her hand silently.

Rold did not think of himself as a sentimentalist. Since his mother died he had hardened himself to the world of emotions. But losing Tyler had opened old wounds. He felt a surge of energy bursting from his heart. His only good friend in this universe was Frank — and he would have loved to see him now in this time of trouble. But Yosana's sympathetic eyes seemed to fill him with that same warmth that Frank was always able to produce. He shook his head, wondering at himself, not so sure he liked this vulnerability that Tyler's death had created.

"I . . . I am glad to see that you still live," Yosana said in a low, sweet voice. "I'm sorry about Tyler." Her eyes sparkled in the lantern light. Anger and sadness mixed themselves in her voice and shining face. "If I had known! If I had only known!"

"Thank you."

She could not find more words.

"Rold and Pentat were in the Minpana Hold together," Blikki said.

Yosana looked shocked, as Blikki had upon hearing that a Teton chief had been imprisoned. She gave Pentat a look of pain, but her eyes kept returning to Rold, his eyes never leaving hers.

"I didn't think I'd see you again," Rold said. He appeared so calm, not cold or distant, but in control. He felt tired, though — drained. The danger of repressed emotion had been vented by physical exercise; that was the only explanation he could think of. He should be jumping, screaming, crying, doing something, but he just stood with faltered speech and a confusion that no one could see in the dark. Yosana was looking at him, trying to read him, trying to decide whether to be hurt or relieved by his cool expression. She was madly searching there, in his face, for something to tell her what he felt. Did he hate her? Did he blame her for Tyler's death?

During the land journey, after leaving Rold to the henchmen, watching Tyler struck down by the dragon's blaster, she had spent a tortuous time, wondering if she had contributed to his capture, wondering if he had guessed the same and hated her for it. She struggled desperately against the shackles of fate, fighting each inevitability. She needed to talk to Gwydmonia, to understand why this man had come into her life. And had Tyler had to die?

The three men put away the folded pelt and washed using the facilities of the land rover while Yosana stayed by the fire. A cold dampness descended from the night sky, freezing her fingers and nose. Realizing the time was late and the night was becoming uncomfortable, she entered the vehicle. There was a small galley with a booth that seated four in the main compartment. The land rover was designed to transport four easily — but she and her father slept in a tent outdoors, which had to be pitched each evening, leaving the air conditioned rover to their guests.

Barbara was taking a stroll while Daryl recuperated on one of the beds. After washing, Blikki gave Rold some clean clothes and Pentat a blanket.

Pentat grabbed a hunk of malonta and went outside to sit on the grass with Blikki following. Rold changed his shirt in the galley.

Yosana watched silently out of the corner of her eye, finding here words still caught in her throat.

Rold took one deep breath, which made him dizzy for a moment. He felt tension in the air. Yosana was conspicuously quiet. He took a long look at this woman whom he barely knew, this person who judged him for his position in society, who never seemed to relax her anger — who had befriended his sister.

"There was something between you and Tyler," he said matter-of-factly.

She jumped at his words, surprised by the interruption of the quiet about them.

"She sought a woman companion for a long voyage in cramped quarters, that is all," she said. "I was flattered, to be honest — considering how I behaved with you."

"And how you feel about aristos."

She smiled. She could not help herself, knowing he could take advantage of such a weakness.

"Yes," she said. Her smile disappeared as she looked off into some distant place, her eyes squinting in anger. "She was an innocent. Those bastards trampled on her like she was a meaningless flower growing in the road. So now do you see? Do you see why I'm angry — angry with your whole world of useless games that end in the death of innocents?"

"I'm not ready to quit the game, if that's what you're getting at. I'm going to make them pay. But I'm going to make it count, be smart about how I do it. I want to destroy their whole world . . ."

"You could destroy your own world, and ours, in the process!"

"I know. But I'll be damned if I'm willing to let another Tyler be killed by pretentious, political hoodlums. I will stop them, Yosana. I swear it! And beware anyone who gets in my way!"

Yosana was moved by such courageous talk — and, yes, even inspired — no matter how futile such determination might be in reality. *Have I misjudged this man?* she asked herself. But then the thought of who he was, what he meant to her future interrupted her growing admiration with fear and resentment. Her heart and her head were in a terrible battle.

She led Rold out of the land rover and into the tent, in an attempt to stay out of the Industrialists' way. The tent was cold, but warmed quickly from the heat of the two people as they moved about as they got settled, and by the burning lantern.

"Where are Blikki and Pentat?" Rold asked before they began eating.

"Talking. They haven't seen each other for several months. Father wanted to know all the news about the village raids. We heard rumors that Teton were being used for forced labor."

"Slaves?"

"Quite fashionable among the aristos to own slaves."

"But it's illegal!"

"On a frontier planet? And do you think your Scientist friends don't own slaves as well? It's not unusual. But what we hear now is that large numbers of Teton are being captured and used for some big project — not as personal slaves."

"I'd like to hear Blikki for myself . . ."

"Stop, Rold."

Yosana put her arm in front of the tent flap to block his exit.

"They need to be alone with each other. You must respect that. Relax here. If I know Pentat, he pushed you pretty hard."

"I was up to it." Rold sat again and smiled.

They could hear the Industrialists talking loudly, but the closed land rover muffled their words.

"You're not performing your duties," Rold said.

"They can manage by themselves one night."

"I'm surprised they didn't demand your service. I guess I'm being rude again as well by avoiding them. But they don't seem too concerned now."

"Barbara . . ."

"The one with the shaved head."

"Barbara probably took care of things. She's one for taking control. She tried to be friendly, but I still don't trust her."

"Imagine that."

Yosana smiled in spite of herself at Rold's teasing. Then she returned to her serious tone.

"She asked a lot of questions about you and Tyler."

"You didn't tell her . . ."

"No. Only Father knows about who your father is and what this all means."

"And I suppose you know what it all means?"

"Typical Scientist. You think all us lowly common people are mentally deficient."

"Very confident, aren't you?"

"Why not? Scientists aren't the only ones who have brains; they just prostitute theirs. The Industrialists pay for it, and the Scientists perform."

Rold laughed while Yosana sat with fists on her hips. She had a look that would set a tree aflame.

"Perfect description," he said. "I'll have to tell my father that one."

"Giggling like children," Pentat said loudly as he entered the tent.

Yosana made a sound that was anything but a giggle.

"Must I sleep here with that kind of greeting?" he teased.

"This . . . White has a talent for causing me to lose my temper," Yosana said, her eyes never leaving Rold.

"And that temper of yours so seldom causes you problems." Pentat's smile was barely discernable, but it was clear he was enjoying this.

Blikki walked into the large tent, stooping at the entrance.

"Stop teasing her, Pentat. She's enough trouble as it is without being all riled up."

Yosana started nodding her head.

"Ganging up on me, are you?"

"Forgive me, little sister," Pentat said in a deep, gracious tone. "I've missed you . . . and your temper."

"Then I won't disappoint you."

Silence again, as they settled. A pulsing hum of insects drowned out any other sounds. Yosana told Rold they were crickets, a name he did not recognize.

Late in the night, after Rold and Pentat had told the story of their escape, Yosana stole inside the land rover and absconded with more blankets. As she entered the tent a loud thunder-clap shook the ground.

"Rain," she whispered and handed out the bedding.

"Sounds like a storm," Blikki said just as the sky began to pour large, icy drops of rain.

As everyone settled for sleep, Pentat noticed Rold's discomfiture at being placed beside Yosana. Yosana's behavior seemed strange as well. Finally he spoke.

"The Teton family sleeps together in their lodge, Mountain Bear. Yosana will not bite you. I don't think. . ."

Yosana batted at Pentat with her fists.

"Put away your embarrassment for tonight, child," Blikki said as he held his daughter's hands. "This rain is going to cause us a lot of work tomorrow, so please let us get some sleep. Strange to have such a cold storm when it's still full summer. Just one more worry. Good night."

Rold realized how trivial it was to be worried about propriety at a time like this. He quickly turned his thoughts to his pain, his loss of Tyler, and the coming horror of war. His eyes, though, would not stay open.

The blanket was comfortable, fending off the cold. The rhythm of the rain riveting the plastic fabric produced a calm, secure feeling, soothing him finally to sleep.

Yosana dreamed once of Militia weapons ripping through Rold's body, and she woke with a cry. Blikki spoke to her with a grunt, and she went back to sleep.

Light from a red morning leaked into the tent, waking Rold. Several birds were barking at each other, their shadows crisscrossing the tent roof. Rold needed to relieve himself, but lay still for a while not wanting to wake the others. Pentat touched his shoulder and signed to be quiet and follow him outside. Rubbing his eyes and stretching, Rold emerged from the opening in the tent and immediately hissed: "What!"

Pentat stood, arms folded. The land rover was gone, and the tracks led south to Minpana.

"I didn't hear a thing!" Rold said. He looked at the tracks, scratching his head.

"What is it?" Blikki said as he joined them. "Great Mother! My rover! Damn those people. What do they think they're doing. How the . . ."

"They rolled it, Father," Pentat said. "See the foot tracks on this side? Then they started it, I'd say, below the hill. Though it's hard to say with the rain last night. Everything's mud."

"They've stolen it!" Blikki was hopping and stamping and swearing. He ripped his tunic off and threw it toward the tracks. Then after much snorting and grumbling he picked it up and shook it out, calming down.

"Can you still ride a pridda?" Pentat said.

"The day I can't ride a pridda I'll personally slit my own throat," Blikki said. "'Can I ride a pridda.' Huh! You just don't understand, Pentat. You weren't brought up with the Whites. You don't understand the value of a machine like that. You don't just let people walk away with things like that."

"I think we have more to worry about than the cost of a damned land rover," Yosana said. She had dressed and joined the men outside.

Rold swallowed down his initial panic. He wanted to strike out, smash someone's face. But his enemy was not here. He was here: stranded!

Then from the clean sky, a purple-blue, the call of an eagle sent shocks through the air. Everyone looked up, seeing the bird circle, all but Rold who was too lost in himself to hear the sound. It made a downward arc that usually brought a smile to Pentat. He had always rejoiced in watching an eagle's grace, but he lost interest and began thinking of a plan. As everyone withdrew their attention, the eagle fell in attack. They heard the swishing air too late. The bird knocked Rold to the ground, his face in the muddy grass; then it disappeared over the bluffs to the east.

Yosana was immediately beside him. The eagle's talons had slashed his shoulders. She stroked his brow and frantically called his name. He regained consciousness, shaking his head, and at first thought he was back on Blikki's ship but quickly remembered where he was.

"Are you all right?" Blikki was now beside him as well.

Rold sat cross-legged and looked at the concerned faces of his companions then started laughing. They did not laugh with him.

"It seems I've been visited by your eagle, Pentat," he said and winced at the pain on his back. "Shit, that hurts."

Pentat smiled. Yosana stared at him as if he had lost his mind. He looked into her hazel eyes and wiped his face, spitting sand and pieces of grass.

"I'm all right," he said. "But my shoulders will never be the same."

"Damned strange," Blikki said and helped Rold to his feet. "I've never seen a bird act like that. Have you, Pentat?"

"I never question eagles," Pentat said.

Yosana gasped, placing both hands over her mouth and turning aside.

Rold shook his head. He refused to succumb to superstition. The parallel of this incident with his on the ship dream was pure coincidence. He would not allow himself to be influenced by this exotic place, these people and their culture.

"It's something like my pain dream," Pentat said. "You see, Mountain Bear, I have seen your face before. I knew you when you came into the Hold. And now . . ."

He turned Rold so that he faced his back then ripped off Rold's shirt, revealing the bleeding scars left by the eagle. "And now you have the marks of an Eagle tribesman, Mountain Bear." Pentat turned his own bare back to Rold's eyes. Faint, white marks striped Pentat's shoulder blades, contrasted by his tan skin.

Blikki turned his broad back toward the two men and Rold saw the wide scars there.

"And you, Yosana?" Pentat took Yosana by her shoulders and forced her to look at Rold. "What do you know about this? You have seen this before as well, I think."

"No," she said, her face ashen as she looked about her at the three men. "Gwyd showed me something else."

Pentat spat a word that Rold assumed was an expletive.

"I can't . . . talk about it," she said.

Everyone was silent as Rold stood. He winced with pain. His head was reeling with what had happened. He had never believed in such things: portents of the future. Worldly things never frightened him. He never ran from a good fight or wavered at the sign of trouble. But this was unnerving. Too many coincidences, he thought. Which generally means correlation is possible, causality. Someone or something is controlling this, causing this. What does it mean? He found himself trembling but overcame it with great effort.

Yosana regained possession of herself. "Let me clean those wounds before they get infected. May I use an external antiseptic, or is that forbidden like internal chemicals?"

Rold's back pulsed, aching miserably.

"If it denatures bacteria, it'll denature skin cells. So, no. Just use water."

As Yosana began rummaging through supplies, Rold looked about him at the vast plain. Not a single sign of a human's touch could be seen.

"It looks like you're stuck with me for a while," he said. "You'll be in danger as long as I'm with you."

"I must say things have been rather exciting since we met you," Blikki said. "Have any ideas, Pentat? You're always one for plans."

"You'll be in danger as long as I'm with you, as well," Pentat said.

"How bad is it, son?" Blikki said.

"We killed Whites when I was taken. And when we escaped. Father, I've never seen so many White warriors. The time for waiting is gone. They raided our village when they took me. They'll either enslave us or exterminate us. And so we must fight back."

He turned to Rold.

"Are you a leader among your people, Mountain Bear?" Pentat asked.

"No, not really. But my father is."

"The son of a chief."

"Yes, you could say that."

"I was the son of a chief. And when he died I became chief. I am beginning to understand some of your words. Your war — my war. You and me. Somehow they are related. The Eagle has brought us and our wars together. But for now I must act as a chief. Your plans for revenge will have to wait. There will be a time when you must do what you have to do. But for now you must stay with us; let us help you in your quest. Certainly, you couldn't make it on your own.

"For now we must hurry and find my village. I've been gone too long, and we must not be found here. We'll go to the Red Hills. With only two pridda we'll have to walk. The pridda can carry packs. I fear the Whites that stole your machine won't be friendly towards us and our cause once they've been questioned by soldiers in Minpana."

Rold was silent. Though Tyler had not been a part of the plan, much of his mission had worked out perfectly. If he could get to Minpana, he might get a message to his people and possibly save lives. If not, his father would still find him, and the rebel Industrialists would be put down. If he died trying to get that message out, he still accomplished his mission — though he would be no further help dead.

He at least had a chance of survival with Pentat. And with that he could return and seek his revenge. His decision was clear.

Pentat and Blikki began sorting through what was left on the ground as Yosana found water and gently cleaned Rold's wounds. When done she packed the open slashes with gauze from a first aid kit and gave him one of Blikki's tunics.

"I thought Blikki was Pentat's father," Rold said after Blikki and Pentat left to round up the pridda. "He calls him father. Who was this chief he spoke of?"

"Pentat's mother and father and my mother were killed in a storm fifteen years ago. Father and I were his only living relatives. So Father adopted Pentat, and he in turn honors him by addressing him that way. But he wasn't a child when it happened — he was twenty and had to become a chief."

"How did it happen? You and Blikki weren't with them."

"Father had taken me to Minpana with him on business. Mother was Teton and didn't approve of his doing business with the Whites. But he couldn't help himself. And I loved going with him on his trips."

"So after your mother's death he took you back to Caljunna."

"Yes. But we come here two, three times a year. And we visit Pentat. I love him like a brother. But he's always seemed distant to me. I suppose because I was saved — I wasn't there to help with the disaster. I was safe."

"But he survived. What happened?"

"You'll have to ask him. He won't talk to me about it. All I know is his hatred for the living clouds began with the disaster."

"Yes, the living clouds."

"So you know of them? Pentat explained?"

"He said you could tell me more."

"Not now."

Rold helped Yosana tear down and fold the tent. The coolness of the morning was gone; the sun shown hot in the cloudless sky.

"What was a lone pitah doing out here anyway?" Blikki shouted as he tied the pelt to one of the pridda.

Pentat walked up leading the other animal.

"Scouting I would guess. He'll be missed by today. We'll need to be alert for the herd. They could be dangerous in this heat. Especially after a rain.

"Now are we all ready?"

"No," Blikki said. "I want to dig a cache for things we're not taking."

"You have too much pride in possessions, Father. We can't afford the time."

"I suppose not. But it took a year to earn enough to pay for all this. The damn rover's gone, and the transport. I guess that's a blessing; it's just that much less money I'd be paying the Industrialists."

"My wealth will mean very little now also," Rold said.

"Yes, your Goldbase account won't buy you much in the Red Hills," Yosana said.

"Sort of makes us even."

"You'll miss your privileged life on this trek — if you survive."

They began walking with Pentat in the lead. The two pridda were tied in a train so that Rold only had to lead one, and the other followed.

"Are you going back to the plateau?" Blikki asked curious about the route.

"No," Pentat said. "They'll be searching there. We'll circle north and enter through the Spotted Valley. It'll take longer but will be safer. Also I want to visit the Library. They must be told what's happening."

"What's the Spotted Valley?" Rold whispered to Yosana who walked beside him.

"It's hard to describe. But it's a safe entrance to the Hills because the only way to get through is on foot."

"Is it narrow then, like the canyons in the mountains?" Yosana smiled. "No, in fact it's several kilometers wide and very flat. But there are . . . obstacles. It's a holy place for the Teton. You'll just have to see it. It humbles even the Librarians."

Ruth Poundstone leaned casually against a pillar at the gateway where Malcolm Simms was just exiting the transport from Old Earth. She meant to look impatient, but appeared too much like the cat that ate the canary. She straightened herself as Malcolm walked toward her. He had a different-looking entourage than usual. He had brought two men she did not know. He looked tired — vulnerable she hoped.

"How nice of you to meet us here, Ruth," Malcolm said. The words were gracious, but the tone was not.

"Well? Is this enough for you?" she said, too anxiously. She joined the men as they headed for ground transport at a brisk pace.

"Ruth, I just got here."

"Forgive my impatience. It's just that I'm distraught over this. And I'm . . ."

"Seething for revenge? I can see it in your eyes, old friend."

"And you're not?"

"I want my children back."

"And if they are dead?"

Malcolm stopped and wiped his face.

"Comrade Poundstone," said the younger man in Malcolm's party, "can't you see he's in pain? Have you no heart?"

"Who the hell are you?" she said.

"Sorry, Ruth. This is Francisco Diego, a close friend of Rold's, and Captain Shama of Committee security."

"How do you do," she said.

"Tyler's not dead," Malcolm said. Ruth's face went white. "I just know it — I feel it. And Rold . . . well, he can take care of himself."

She relaxed.

"Not very scientific," she said. "But of course we all hope so. In any event, the kidnapping has been taken as an act of war."

"I will not have it!" Malcolm said. "As far as we know, this is an isolated act of terrorism."

"You must not have heard. The Industrialists have left Newert. Comrade Meacom was involved in the kidnapping. We have evidence."

"What have you done with him?"

"He has disappeared."

"This is what I wanted to avoid. I don't want any aggression, at least until I perform my own investigation."

"Very well. But I tell you, these Industrialists have proven to be the treacherous filth I knew them to be. Intelligence says they are massing offensive weapons and their Militia at some isolated system — which we have not located as yet. There's evidence that they have been preparing for this for years. They have an army of Zenians training with their Militia."

"I've heard that name before," Frank said. "Who are they?"

"Humanoids from Zenia," Malcolm said.

"You see," Ruth said, "Zenia's a slow rotating world. The Zenian humanoid specie lives on the daylight side. They have developed a metabolism that allows them to remain in a waking state indefinitely. They're desert people."

"The point, Frank, is they're formidable mercenaries," Malcolm said. "They're perpetually angry, and they never sleep. They're considered criminals, pirates. It's is forbidden for Commonwealth officials to hire them; that's why you probably know so little about them."

"The Industrialists don't follow such laws, Comrade," Ruth said. "As I have said before, they have no honor. Their militia is not a militia but an army — against Centauri Conference articles."

Malcolm did not protest the slander. Ruth knew he was weakening. Soon she would be able to lead the war in his name, and the Industrialists would come tumbling down.

"First we must find Tyler and Rold," Malcolm said. He held Frank's arm with affection and looked into his eyes. "Frank has volunteered to lead the investigation."

"Where will you start?" Ruth asked. "The terrorists have not even asked for a ransom. It's totally political."

"I plan on tracking him from Caljunna," Frank said. "The criminals have done a good job of covering their tracks, but if there's something, some kind of clue, it will be on Caljunna."

Ruth made a mental note to have Rold's tracks not only covered but obliterated. She was not overconfident, and believed in doing a thorough job — no loose ends. There should be no ties between her and his kidnapping. However, it would be good to know where Rachel Meacom had taken him. She filed that thought away.

"There's a proposal for a declaration of war on the Committee floor already," she said.

"It will die if I protest it," Malcolm said.

But you won't, Ruth thought. *Not after I'm through with you.*

Ground transportation arrived, and she joined the three men on their way to the apartments. A mauve twilight reflected gray in Malcolm's sunken eyes. He closed them as dusk ushered in night.

A small, smoky fire fueled with dried roots of marsh reeds became the center of attention for Rold as his mind drifted to thoughts of his revenge against Rachel Meacom and the Militia. He missed Tyler. He had not seen her for some time, not thinking of her often, but fondly when he did. Now he would never see her again, and anger surged when he thought about it. But now there was Yosana his new-found friends. Could he accomplish what he set out to do? Should he put these people in danger?

"What are you analyzing now?" Yosana asked as she handed him a cup of tea. She sat beside him and took a sip from her own cup.

"You think you know me, don't you?" Rold said.

Yosana's cup hid her mouth. He could not read her reaction.

"You're eyes were lost in the fire," she said.

"I was thinking about . . . everything."

"Like a good Scientist."

"Just stop it, Yosana. I don't want to fight with you or even play with you now. The only thing that matters is to deal with these criminals."

"I know. And I believe that you mean that. Survival will take all of us working as a team. I'll control my temper, and you drop your airs."

"Agreed. But I need to be in Minpana eventually. I have something I have to do."

"You must understand: we can't go back. At least for now. We have to get Pentat to his village. And at the Library, we'll find some answers."

"Of course."

Rold looked at the mysterious woman and wondered at her changing moods. He then downed his drink and stood, stretching his aching legs. Two days of walking had certainly tested his stamina. But he managed easily enough. Backpacking and rock climbing had always been his main recreation. He enjoyed the challenge of self-propelled travel, of "roughing it." His feet were seasoned, and his lungs. Though this was no park full of trails posted with electronic nature guides and campsites at the end of the day with rest rooms and showers. And this was not for relaxation.

"How much farther?" he said loudly to Pentat who was tending the pridda across camp. Pentat finished what he was doing and walked to the fire.

"Three more days to the Spotted Valley," he said.

"And then?"

"It'll take a day or more to pass through the valley then perhaps the Eagle village will be in the hills. If not we'll continue on to the Library. You'll be safe there. The Librarians may be able to help you. They maintain certain technology forbidden to the average Teton."

"Yes. Yes, of course!" Yosana said. "Rold, the Library has a museum of ancient artifacts — things brought here with the Migration. It's an ancient technology, but they do have some communication devices."

"Centuries old?" Rold said. "Probably radio."

"Yes."

"It takes radio waves years to travel in space."

"Like a note in a bottle; I know. But it's something. With your knowledge maybe you could do something with it."

"My knowledge is not much use without a certain level of industry available. I'll have to see this museum and this Library."

Once in the night a large shadow floated over the camp. The late moon had shone consistently through the night, but it was blackened by the shadow, which woke Rold. At first he thought it might be another storm, but he heard no thunder, and rain never fell. As he sat up the shadow vanished. The moonlight returned as if a light had been switched on. He lay back down, but could not go back to sleep. He looked around the tent and was startled to see that Yosana was missing. As quietly as he could he left the tent and walked in the moonlight, not really knowing where to look.

He blinked several times, trying to get his eyes adjusted to the soft light, when he saw Yosana standing on a knoll. She was unclothed, her back to him, her long hair dancing about her shoulders in the breeze. He smiled at the vision of this naked young woman, bathed in moonlight, and decided to remain where he was, quietly so that she would not notice him. But then a shadow covered her, making her almost invisible.

He stumbled from the shock as he saw a living cloud descend to the knoll and rest beside her. It was huge and undulated in slow surges. In only a moment it rose, and he was astonished to see that Yosana was no longer there. He started to panic; the thing had somehow taken her. But he was able to calm himself, and instead of waking Blikki and Pentat, he decided to stay there at the foot of the knoll. He dropped to his knees, hugged himself for warmth, and waited.

CHAPTER 8

The teller of this story came into being
On this ride of rides
As Rold and the mother rider were joined
With the brave Gwydmonia as servant of the future.

From "The Song of Margona"
by Pitallela-Sim

The yeasty smell of bread filled the adobe hut. A yard bird squawked as it swooped upon the head of small boy who was threatening a nest of eggs in a fruit tree nearby. Rays of sunshine intruded harshly with forceful angularity through a large window. Wide polished beams of wood striped the ceiling of the hut, and were the first sight of the young injured woman as she awoke. Blood pulsed in her temples, her head spinning from pain. She fought hard to hold back her nausea and moaned in the effort.

She pulled herself up on her elbows, then hands, but collapsed from weakness.

"Ah-ee, girl," a woman said with a deep, aged voice. "Don't move now." But the words were foreign, and the young woman did not understand them. Though she could do nothing but obey as her head felt as if it would explode.

"Where . . ." she said in a whisper.

"You're safe," came the answer, now in Ameranglo. "Relax. I'm Sompica, wife of Chictampa. We brought you from the Militia hospital. You've been hurt."

"Where is my brother?" Tyler said with her eyes closed.

"You were with another?"

"Rold . . ."

"We found no other." This was a different voice, a man's voice. Tyler opened her eyes, wanting to see who was speaking to her, but the harsh light made her head hurt.

"Must . . . tell . . . Father . . ."

With these last three words, Tyler fell unconscious again.

Chictampa motioned his wife to his side in a corner of their new home.

"This brother must be the one they look for, the one that escaped from the Hold," he said.

"Old man, you don't know that. You always think the worst of people. This is an innocent girl, barely a woman. What would she have to do with the Hold?"

"I don't know, Sompy. But they may look for this brother here. They may be looking for her too." He nodded to Tyler, whose breathing was labored and raspy.

"They think she's dead. They won't come looking for her."

"In another moon she must be well enough to travel. I have decided we are to travel to the Library. Several here are going now."

Sompica looked at the sleeping young woman in her care. She knew, as did Chictampa, that she was unusual and probably meant trouble for them both. But she could not abandon her.

Suddenly the crackling sound of energy blasters shot through the warm summer air. People screamed, and the noise of rushing feet came to the hut. The door burst open. Three Militia poured in, weapons drawn.

They silently looked about, moving like cats, poking into cupboards and cabinets.

"Who is this?" one said pointing at Tyler.

"My . . . grand daughter, sir. She had an accident."

He threw back the blanket that covered her and appreciated her naked form. Pushing her head to one side by holding her chin, he examined her wound, then roughly tossed her head back. Sompica attacked the man's arm. He shoved her across the room where she fell against the clay stove, falling in a quivering heap.

"Let's go," he said, and the three left abruptly.

Chictampa rushed to his wife. She had already calmed, stretching her back and rubbing her shoulder.

"They are gone," he said. "How are you?"

"I'll be all right, old man. Don't worry about me."

He went to the window and watched as a company of Militia moved about the common circle of the village.

"We're safe now," he said. "They won't be back. Grand daughter, eh? Good thing she didn't speak, with that funny accent. We'd all be dead."

Sompica stood weakly then crossed to Tyler's bed. She covered her up and confirmed to herself that she was not harmed.

"But you're right," she said. "We must leave as soon as she is able. Talk will follow us. We have some trouble here in this child." But she found herself smiling as she looked at Tyler, the young woman's injury healing. Tyler's slumber was less troubled, and her porcelain skin glowed with returning health.

The night chill forced Rold to get a blanket from the tent. Pentat opened his eyes and made an approving sign. Rold assumed he was acknowledging Rold's concern about Yosana. But Pentat quickly closed his eyes and snored as Rold returned to his vigil.

The cold, the dark, and Yosana's disappearance caused a trembling in Rold that he could not stop. The moon was low in the sky, and the hills cast large black shadows across the plain. He stood with the blanket around his shoulders and stomped his feet, then sat again and began thinking about Yosana and where she might be, what might be happening to her. After a time his eyes drooped and his head nodded. From black sleep he awoke with Yosana's hand on his shoulder. He stood suddenly.

"Where were you?" he asked in a harsh whisper.

"You were worried?" It was too dark to see her expression, but he knew she was astonished.

"I thought . . . well, now it seems like a dream. I saw you and one of those living clouds. Then you disappeared. I guess I fell asleep. You're all right?"

"I'm fine, Rold. But you should be in the tent, asleep. You're going to be tired tomorrow, and we've got a lot of walking to do."

"What about you? Don't you need sleep?"

"This was more important."

"You might as well tell me. I'll make a nuisance of myself if you don't."

There was silence. The two walked to the fire circle of the camp and sat beside each other on the ground. The coals were dead but the smell of smoke lingered.

"I'm a cloud rider," Yosana began. "The living cloud you saw was my melding mate, Gwydmonia. We had a . . . conversation. I needed to talk to her about what has happened here . . . about you, and Tyler."

"So you actually make physical contact with it? These creatures are safe? And intelligent?"

Yosana smiled at his surprise. "Yes. But that's all I'm going to tell you. It's a private thing, Rold. You mustn't badger me about this. I know we've had our differences, but I'm asking you to let this alone. Can you do that?"

"I don't know. I'll admit, I was worried. I thought the thing had taken you to its lair and consumed you or something. Actually I don't know what I thought."

It was still dark when the two settled in their bedding. Yosana inexplicably took Rold's hand and squeezed it then released it and turned over to go to sleep. Rold felt a surge of pleasure at her touch.

The blisters on Rold's feet, after tearing and bleeding, were finally hardening into calluses with the aid of nightly bathing and rubbing with sand. He used the short rests during the day to relax the spasms in his digestive track and enhance his immune system. The weather was cooling as they climbed the northern plateau, and he fought a cold.

The climb entailed walking up and down rolling, grassy hills and following switch backs down gullies and back up again. They were close to the Spotted Valley which Rold imagined must be a wide canyon among these hills — this being the ninth day of walking. Food stores were getting low; there had been only a single pack left outside the land rover. All the other food had traveled back to Minpana. Water at least was replenishable from the few creeks swollen from the recent rain. Pentat had decided to stop for the day far from sundown, not wanting to enter the valley at night. The routine of making camp was finally comfortable for all involved, each tending to his own chosen duty — and it was managed quickly.

All was quiet until the faint sound disturbed the camp. Each person turned at the same time to hear it better.

"Jetcraft," Rold said. "Coming fast."

"Quickly," Pentat commanded, "spread out and pull grass. Cover everything, including yourselves. Then find a ditch to lie in and blanket yourselves with grass. I'll hide the pridda. Now hurry."

Rold jumped into a ravine filled with the yellow grain and began pulling handfuls. He tossed the straw into a pile close to camp. The sharp corns and stems cut his hands and bare arms. Before long he was itching from little bleeding nicks. Everyone worked hard piling the stuff then swiftly spread it over camp. Blikki struck the tent and spread grass over it. Rold and Yosana found a ditch that was about two meters wide and deep and lay in it, covering themselves with the yellow grass. Rold stung and itched all over from it.

Everyone lay quietly somewhere waiting for the flying craft to speed overhead. Time went by slowly, but the sound of jet engines did not go away. Then a shadow drifted over them. Rold looked up and saw a huge living cloud hovering twenty meters above them. It stopped. A jet fighter flew above it, cracking the air. Another jet nosed about the hulking thing, then moved on. Rold kept Yosana down in the ditch until the sound of the jet engines was totally gone — or at least until they could not be heard over the noisy birds and insects that seemed to infest every inch of Salkinia.

Everyone returned to the camp site. The sun was still above the horizon as they cleaned up the grounds and raised the tent.

"No fire tonight," Pentat said.

"Gwydmonia might protect us if we kept a small fire," Yosana said.

"I won't trust my life to a minah-machacute."

"She just saved your life."

"She saved yours, Yosana. You're the cloud rider. We just happened to be with you."

Pentat left the camp.

"You know how he feels," Blikki said. "He can't help it. Thank that demon friend of yours for us. We do appreciate it — even Pentat."

Blikki looked up at the blue sky. Rold looked too and realized the creature was no longer above them. He caught sight of it beyond a close hill top. It seemed to be resting on the ground.

"What is 'cloud riding?'" Rold asked.

"Yosana was chosen," Blikki said, "to learn the language of the living clouds and meld her flesh with theirs. Her mother was a cloud rider."

Yosana went to Blikki and hugged him. He put his arms around her and rocked her slightly.

"I love you, Father," she said.

"Love you too," he said.

"Come," she said to Rold, "Gwydmonia says its time to show you what it means. You want to know, don't you?"

"Be careful, son," Blikki said. "Don't let her boss you around too much. She can be wicked at times." He winked.

"Hush, Father," Yosana said. "I've got to keep him in the right frame of mind."

"Now wait a minute," Rold said. "What have I gotten myself into here?"

"Don't pay any attention to Father," she said. "He's just jealous. Let me show you something you've never seen before — even in your dreams."

They climbed the hill that ascended to where the creature sat, pulsating, oozing, and still hovering centimeters from the ground. Brilliant spots of colored light burst in a diamond pattern about the middle, or at least what Rold thought was the middle, of the creature. Yosana smiled and used a signing, it seemed, to communicate with the thing. She moved flat palms about in a diamond pattern, much like the colored lights of the creature.

"This is Gwydmonia?" Rold asked.

"Yes."

"Does she belong to you?"

"No! Of course not. You might call her my fairy godmother."

Rold laughed, and the lights grew brighter and had more brilliant hues. He smiled in fascination. Caught unaware, because of concentration on the lights and the overwhelming size of the glob of living flesh, he was startled by an appendage growing toward him. It was as tall as Rold and as wide and stuck out from the main body three or four meters; it never seemed to stop moving.

"What a fantastic creature!" Rold said. "I've never seen anything like it."

"You may have heard the Commonwealth term of *slunk*."

"Of course! I should have realized. So this is a slunk. The shy giants of the frontier. There have been so few sightings that if it weren't for the merchant marine documentation these things would be thought of as pure myth."

"Gwyd is real enough. You can touch her if you wish."

Rold reached out slowly and placed his hand flatly on the pulsating flesh. It was rubbery but warm and slightly moist. Sparks of light rippled around the outline of his hand. He jerked it away, then felt slightly embarrassed by his childish response.

"It's all right," Yosana said. "She was just saying hello. She's asking us to go for a ride."

"You mean she can actually take us somewhere?"

"You'll see."

"Then why have we been *walking* for days?"

"She's not a pony. Minah-machacute give rides to riders only, or their guests, and only when they feel like it. They choose the time and place — not us. It's a rare privilege to be allowed to ride."

Lights flashed and another appendage jutted out beside Yosana. With its movements a new sound of gurgling appeared.

"What do we do?" Rold said. He was getting excited about this ride, seeing it as another adventure: an experience to add to his collection. Since he was child he had had a driving need for experiences. Whether intellectually stimulating ones or physically dangerous ones, he craved more and thought little about the risks.

Yosana hesitated. He could see it in her face, which had lost its smile. His own anticipation waned on seeing her indecision. She almost looked frightened.

"What is it?" he asked.

"Oh Rold! This is the one most terrifying things I have ever done. Gwyd tells me I must, so I will, but . . ."

"Is this dangerous? We don't have to do it. I admit I'm intrigued, but we can do this another time. We do have other priorities — other things that matter right now."

"There's no way to make you understand. I didn't know you'd be so compliant. I didn't have to coax or trick you into this. No, no. It's not like that: it won't harm you. Please trust me. It's just important; that's all. We have to do this, and I'm frightened."

Frightened of what? Rold thought.

"I placed barriers between us," she said. "I wanted to hate you, but I couldn't. I knew we would go cloud riding someday. Gwyd told me. And I fear it because . . . it means things will change in my life that I'm not ready to give up."

Rold looked confused. His eyes begged for more information, something to tell him why she was in so much pain.

"What do we do?" he said finally. He did not know why he was still willing to go through with the ride, but its importance, the mystery of the thing, made him anxious to begin.

Yosana seemed to recover. She gave Rold a smile.

"You must trust me."

"I'm not sure why, but I do."

"First, take off your clothes. They would be absorbed anyway, so we should save them to put on when we return."

He raised his eyebrows, thought about it for a moment then said with a smile: "Ladies first."

"So you're a voyeur, eh?"

Rold shrugged.

Yosana was already stripping off her tunic. Rold stood for a moment and admired her breasts and small waist until she noticed and blushed. He then gave in and undressed. The cool breeze of early evening gave him a chill; he rubbed his arms and moved his legs, walking in place.

"Now stand here," she said and backed a few steps away. "You should probably use those calming exercises you Scientists do. This is going to be a little frightening at first."

"Why am I doing this?" Rold said, shivering. "Oh, what the hell, if you can do it, I can do it."

Yosana rolled her eyes. "A couple more things. Keep your eyes and mouth closed. And don't panic. You'll not suffocate. That's what most people think is going to happen, but it won't."

"All this time I thought we were going up to the top of this thing, that it was going to lift us up there somehow."

"Our bodies will meld with Gwydmonia. It's hard to explain. She'll explain it. She'll speak to you. When you hear her you can open your eyes and begin to breathe. Now stand still."

Rold was going to make one last protest when the slunk began oozing about his body. He calmed himself by repeating the hypnotic phrases that he had learned as a child. He remembered to close his eyes and mouth and found he could not move his arms or legs. Every inch, every pore, of his skin was being encased in the jelly-like, milky substance that was the bulk of the slunk. Even the bottom of his feet were covered as the slunk lifted his body from the ground. The slunk gel was warm and sticky, but soon he felt numbness all around him. He could not tell where his limbs were, what position they were in. The contact between his skin and the slunk had no feeling to it at all except for the warmth.

In rapid succession he felt things hitting him in odd places. "See," a voice said, so he opened his eyes. His head was capped with a clear sphere filled with air. Attached to the bubble were a mass of tubes or fluid vessels. He breathed the air, and it seemed good. His chest was able to expand and contract within the rubbery enclosure. Beyond the sphere he could see nothing but the milky gel and occasional flashes of colored light.

"Close your eyes and see." He heard the voice again. Closing his eyes he relaxed his mind, and an image appeared as clearly as if he were looking at it. It did not flee as most dream images do; it was stable and allowed him to inspect it. The image was himself frozen within the middle of the slunk, but he was viewing himself as if he were another person. He was startled to see what the slunk was doing to him. A catheter was inserted in his anus, another in his penis, and still more tubes were connected to his abdomen, back, neck, and head. He could sense that ganglia were piercing his skin, searching for nerve connections.

"They are what you would call life support," the voice said. "The ducts provide saline fluid and oxygen and also remove waste fluids, solids and gas. Also, I must touch your nervous system. But relax. There is no permanent damage."

"Am I hallucinating?" Rold asked aloud.

"No. I am Gwydmonia."

The image changed to Yosana. She was hooked up in the same manner as Rold. Her words came to his thoughts in sync with the movement of her lips.

"Hello, Rold," she said. "She's showing you to me now and me to you. If you speak aloud she can transfer the image and words to me."

"This is incredible!" he said. "I'm trying to stay calm. You sure this thing isn't going to digest us? The enclosure scared the hell out of me. My bodily functions are out of control."

Yosana laughed. Gwydmonia laughed too. Rold then broke into a nervous cackle but stopped as he felt his equilibrium sloshed about in his head. He immediately tensed, as if ready for battle, and the image of Yosana disappeared. He calmed himself again and there she was again.

"We must be moving," he said.

"Yes," Gwydmonia said. "Relax, and I'll show you where we're going."

Now in his mind Rold could see the grassland and hills shrinking below him. He seemed to be getting higher and higher. Off in the distance he could see a valley that had a grid of black dots strewn across in a regular rectangular pattern. The Spotted Valley, he thought. The land diminished at greater speed now; the shadows from the setting sun were deep and dramatic. In very little time they were far enough away from Salkinia to assume they must be in space. Could this creature help his cause? Get him offworld? But Pentat had said not to trust the living clouds. And Yosana had said they would do only as they wished. But where was it taking them?

"Here," she said.

"What?"

"I have taken you here. To see this beautiful planet from close space. I love watching it from here.

"Did you not think I could read your thoughts?" She laughed. The quality of her voice was that of a matron: deep but feminine. In fact, she sounded a great deal like his mother.

"Yes," she said. "I'm using your mother's voice from your memory. Her phrasing as well, if you don't mind. I want you to feel comfortable."

"Then can you answer some of my questions?"

"Perhaps."

"Can you help us? Help me prevent this war?"

"No."

"Can not or will not?"

"Will not."

"But why!"

"It's not my purpose."

"Then what is your purpose?"

"Entropy."

"What does that mean?"

"You ask a lot of questions. Are you sure about this fellow, Yosana?"

"You picked him, Gwyd," Yosana said.

"So I did; so I did," Gwydmonia said. "I should indulge him a bit. I'm what you might call an agent of entropy. Of course this is only a small job in a much larger purpose. But entropy is my purpose, my central program."

A lot of good it does to ask questions, Rold thought.

"Forget your questions," Gwydmonia said. "Let me give you some answers you have not been looking for. What you see now is your reality. Now I'll expand your small concept by showing you my reality."

Rold could see Yosana in his mind, preserved in the slunk gel; then the gel, the tubes, Gwydmonia herself, vanished leaving Yosana naked, floating in space. Behind her was the black void smeared with the speckled light of stars. He stifled a scream, thinking she would be destroyed by the vacuum.

"What's wrong?" Yosana said. He calmed down, seeing that she appeared unharmed.

"Don't worry," Gwydmonia said. "She's not really out in space unsupported. I'm toying with your image of her. In fact I can do more."

Yosana moved her arms and looked at her hand. *But she can't move!* he thought.

"You try it," Gwydmonia suggested. "But remember, concentrate on the image, not on your reality."

As Gwydmonia said this, her flesh disappeared from around Rold, and there was no longer a milky screen between him and Yosana. He opened his eyes, and the air bubble and fleshy tubes appeared again.

"Use your thoughts," Gwydmonia said. "Keep your eyes closed. Or better yet, I'll stop that . . ." And suddenly Rold was blinded. The image of Yosana was persistent and came back. Now with eyes open or closed he saw only the image of himself and Yosana floating leagues above Salkinia. He moved his arms. He not only saw, or imagined, his arms moving, he felt them move! He kicked his legs, and the motion sent him into a spin; he had to fight hard not to panic. Slowly he came to a stop and was close to Yosana.

"Are you all right?" she asked. "You have to take it easy at first."

"I'm losing my mind," he said.

"In a sense you have lost it to me," Gwydmonia said. "But I'll give it back, if you really want it."

"Well," he said, "not yet."

"I thought so."

Experimenting, he kicked his way over to Yosana and grabbed her hands. As he watched himself do it, he was amazed that he could actually touch her. He rubbed her hand from knuckle to knuckle, the bones were hard and the flesh firm but pliant.

"Impressive," he said. "Do you feel it? Are you experiencing the same thing I am? At the same time?"

"I feel my hands in yours if that's what you mean," she said.

"Don't look now," Gwydmonia said, "but your imagination is developing a hunger."

Rold looked down and saw that he had an erection. He could not seem to control his passion. A spark of anger jumped through his body as he watched himself take Yosana into his arms. She was not smiling, and he resented being manipulated in this way. But Gwydmonia suppressed his anger before he could stop himself from attacking her body with a ferocity he had never experienced. Yosana received him with the same intensity. So, floating among the stars and planets they made love. Everywhere Rold touched her, kissed her, the sensation stayed true to what he imagined it would be like to have her. The smell of her hair, the taste of her skin, everything was perfect, beautiful.

The gymnastics in what seemed open space were effortless, and it made them both giggle once as they spun in their coupled position. He devoured her body, his mouth finding every spot that made her quake. And she returned his efforts twofold. Rold's thrusts were savage at first, but soon the rhythm became paced and artful. They climaxed simultaneously and the orgasm was convulsive; they felt engorged with ecstasy.

Exhausted, they cradled each other as they watched the sun disappear behind the planet leaving them in only starlight.

A slow realization crept into Rold's consciousness. A spark of anger returned as he thought of how he had been used. Suddenly he found himself snapped back into the gelatin prison of Gwydmonia's body — feeling abandoned, wanting desperately to hold Yosana again and apologize or thank her, he was not sure.

Then, with that thought, Gwydmonia brought him back to the image of floating in space. Yosana was there again, looking deep within his soul through his eyes.

"Rold?" Gwydmonia said.

"Yes?" He had a hard time speaking. He had hoped to hear Yosana's voice, resenting the slunk's intrusion.

"Sorry to disturb you, but I had a question myself. When you were a child didn't you ever imagine, or try to imagine, what was outside the Universe? Beyond the stars?"

His breathing had calmed, and his regrets — if that was what they were — had subsided somewhat.

"Everyone does, I'm sure. Why?"

"Would you like to go there?"

"We'd love to," Yosana said. "I'd like to see Rold's idea of Heaven."

He watched her speak and thought that her words were like precious jewels to be cherish. Then he shook his head, wondering where in the world such sentimental thoughts had come from.

"What do we do?" he said, though he assumed the slunk would orchestrate whatever was necessary.

"Do what you've always dreamed of doing," Gwydmonia said.

"What do you mean?"

"You know. The *door*."

Rold laughed. "When I was very young," he explained to Yosana, "I thought there was a door out there in the night sky that had stars painted on it, and you could go up to it, open it, and leave the Universe and enter who-knows-what. I don't think I ever got any further with the idea; I was so fascinated with the door itself. It's not too original, but at six years old it impressed me."

He looked into the depths of space and saw a rectangle drawn in white light. They moved toward it.

"Go," Gwydmonia said. "You must reach for it."

"I . . . can't," he said. For a moment the image failed. A true memory of the door intruded upon Gwydmonia's simulated scene causing Rold to slip back to his own reality — but only at a certain level: that of tactile sensations.

"I'm frozen again," he said. "I can't move."

A warm relaxing feeling washed through him. The image sharpened; he was holding Yosana's hand.

"I almost lost you," Gwydmonia said. "Your memory has power. But never mind. What I want to show you is how we tie knots in space, manipulate gravity, and so on. You imagine there's a door — so there is. That's not quite the reality, but probably as close as you'll get.

"From what I've seen of your culture you have migrated to just a small corner of this small galaxy. That's because you don't understand space. You've learned to move fast, and to pierce space with your propped open worm holes; that's all. Though we do worry you're close to mutating into beings that can sense the additional dimensions. Then all you have to do is understand the energy considerations."

"Sensitivity to dimensional junctures?" Rold said. "Is that your trick? Is she always this talkative?" He looked at Yosana.

"The concept is actually quite simple," Gwydmonia said. "Bring the mountain to Mohammed. Oh, you wouldn't know that one. What I mean is: move the point in normal space where you want to be to you rather than you to there. Understand? I can see you're getting bored. Just go through the damn door."

Rold and Yosana drifted to the door holding hands. It opened wide, and they floated through. They found themselves standing, naked, on a city street — a city of cubed glass, metal, and plastic buildings and millions of people. Rold immediately covered himself in embarrassment; Yosana did not. She was watching wide-eyed, almost terrified, the mass of human beings walking, riding, all constantly moving, seething.

"Can they see us?" Rold asked.

"I don't think so."

"I wish we had clothes on; this is like a bad dream."

He heard Gwydmonia laugh and immediately they were wearing the clothes they had discarded on Salkinia.

Yosana moved into Rold's arms. They had been placed on a corner, out of the way of traffic. "Why do so many people live this way?" she asked. "It's horrible. So close they can't move without bumping someone. It's like . . . it's like a pantry full of insects."

Rold smiled. "This is Old Earth. What I want to know is if we're really here."

It was daytime, and a gray-brown haze hung over the buildings smelling of ozone. The noise was one big clashing roar at first. A group of young people walked by, pushing and shoving, laughing. They were eating something from a bag that was being passed around. Sirens blasted from two different directions; their wailing danced in the city canyons, bouncing off tall, glass walls. The young group scrambled across the street, stopping traffic. They laughed and made rude hand signals at the angry drivers. As they pushed past, Rold thought he would be tumbled over, but they walked through him as if he were a ghost."

"I'm not perfect," Gwydmonia said.

"So we're not really here," Rold said.

"You tell me."

Yosana still clung to Rold. He could not understand her reaction. Certainly she had been in big cities before, right? And she was so quiet. Of course it may be because of Gwydmonia's limitations at simulating such images. There was so much he did not know or understand. He was convinced though that there were rules to this new reality; it was not like a dream or hallucination. He just had to learn the rules then he could move around with a little more confidence.

"This is where you're going to live?" Yosana asked.

"No, not this city. This is a very old city, very large; in a province much to the east of where my family lives. The university is more than a thousand kilometers from here."

"Is all of Old Earth like this?"

"What's wrong? It's just a city. Can't you feel how alive it is? There's so much to do here, so many people to talk to, to teach, to learn from. There are concerts and plays performed by *real* people.

"I know it's different from Caljunna — and certainly Salkinia — but there are beautiful places on Old Earth too. Much of it's inhabited. There's one city after the other on this continent, from one ocean to the other. But each city has its own charm. There's so much art and a fascination for knowledge that it energizes everything. The variety of food never ends, from one culture to the next."

Yosana was smiling at his enthusiasm. He smiled back then looked beyond her up the sidewalk. Brightly lit signs decorated the first story building facades. Armies of people marched beside those facades. He breathed in the air. Even though it made him choke, it also made him nostalgic.

In an instant, as quickly as a blink, the streets were empty of people. Rold did not startle. He was growing accustomed to the quickly-changing sights in this world of images. The sky was blue, and the only noise was the wind gusting around the corners of buildings.

"Oh, you weren't supposed to see this," Gwydmonia said, and just as quickly Rold was back in black space floating a small distance from Yosana.

"Wait a minute," he said angrily. "That meant something, didn't it? Was it something symbolic — representing the effect of the war? Please tell me."

"You have a very powerful imagination," Gwydmonia said. "You manipulated space all by yourself. I had to stop you before you got hurt, or hurt my sweet Yosana."

"But what did it mean?"

Yosana's image vanished; then Rold was again embalmed in the body of Gwydmonia, breathing in the air bubble, fluid gurgling about him through ducts. He knew they were moving because at one point he must have been on his left side — gravity pulled on his internal organs. Then he was upright again. The bloated, milky tissues began receding, and he stumbled, naked on cold sandy ground. It was dark, but he could see Yosana lying a few steps away. Gwydmonia hovered above them now, dark and massive. She presently floated straight up until she was out of sight.

Rold tried to stand but fell back from weakness. Yosana stirred and called to him. Rock shards and pebbles cut his knees as he crawled to her side. They were both shivering.

Rold looked around trying to orient himself. They were nowhere near where they had began the ride. They could have been halfway around the planet for all he knew. A camp fire sparked below them in walking distance, and he recognized the tent which made him sigh with relief.

"Put these on before you freeze to death," Pentat said.

Rold jumped and landed in a battle-ready stance. Pentat stood before them, dark against a starry sky, holding a bundle of clothes. Rold relaxed and straightened, all sense of modesty suppressed, taking the clothes from Pentat's hands.

"I didn't hear you coming," Rold said.

They clasped forearms then Pentat strode down the hill.

Rold wanted to look at Yosana but kept his eyes averted as they both dressed. His chest swelled with an unknown vigor. He felt ready to conquer the world, as though a battle glamour surrounded him. He was ready to defeat any enemy, with his bare hands if necessary. The ride had given him a physical satisfaction unlike any training or contest in his life.

"What actually happened?" he said. "Did we? Did you? Did I?"

"Yes and no, Rold. We didn't really make love."

He was beyond anger now. His body was surging with wild desires.

What did it mean?

"Gwyd provided a virtual experience. We didn't actually touch each other. But the image was the same for us both. She brought out a hidden hunger in us, wiping away all inhibitions. And, the most important thing: you did ejaculate, and I did receive it. Gwyd transmitted the sperm. She wanted me to get pregnant."

Rold stumbled. Yosana was beside him and attempted to help him rise. He pushed her away as he righted himself.

"You know there are clinical ways of getting pregnant, if that was all you wanted," he said, resentment ringing in every word. "Or I'm sure you could have a young buck from here."

Yosana swung as hard as she could and slapped Rold flatly on his cheek. He grabbed her wrist and started to slap her back but resisted. She pulled away, wanting to run, but the bond that Gwydmonia had tied between these two was not easily broken.

"Do you want me to explain, or do you hate me now?" she asked.

"I don't know how I feel, yet. I'm not angry with you, really — though I wonder why you went along with this. It's that *thing* that I'm angry with. But you . . . How can I trust my feelings now? I have an uncontrollable desire to tell you that I love you. Do I really love you, or has your Gwydmonia made me feel this way?"

"I know, Rold. I feel the same. I've never taken a man for a cloud ride before, though I knew the danger. There's so much more to this than you know."

She took his hand and they both sat on the ground. Rold was too exhausted to fight anymore. He crossed his legs and waited. "I'm now the last cloud rider," Yosana began. "There were a half dozen when I started riding. But with the Industrialist raids on villages, accidents, and plain old age, all have perished. I'm the last. Twylompa was the only other, and she died two months ago. She was very old, lasted beyond what should be expected; but finally her poor body gave up. I found out on our trip here. Gwyd came to me soon after we left Caljunna.

"I have known the time would come when I must produce a child — a child who would be another rider."

"Why could you not choose someone to train? I don't understand."

"Riding is lethal to a normal human being. The melding is toxic. For generations riders have been produced through this method:　sex within a minah-machacute. The living cloud alters some genes of the zygote at conception, giving the child the difference, the protection, it needs to ride a minah-machacute and live."

"But I rode. I didn't die. Or will I? Have I been sacrificed for your religion?"

"No. You're fine, Rold. Through me and my blood you were protected. If you rode alone, you would certainly die. Besides, you're a man, and riders are always female. Don't ask me why. The minah-machacute always produce female riders. Perhaps its caused by the change to the genes; I don't know."

After a long pause Rold spoke. "It has changed me."

"Yes."

"I don't know how or in what way, but I'm different now. I do love you, Yosana. It's like I fell in love with you at first sight, back there on your ship, but it took this . . . experience to realize it. I was so angry: angry with you, angry with your minah-machacute. And so — I'm to be a father?"

"It doesn't always work. Just like through the normal way of doing things, it may abort or not fertilize. I'm afraid to know."

"Why? Now that it's done, it seems like a good thing — no matter how it came about."

"Another little detail. We're among the Teton now. Having a child here is a grave thing. Much responsibility. The Teton are rather egalitarian as far as primitives go: women can be hunters, warriors, even chiefs. But the one restricting factor is raising a child. Once a woman has borne a child she can't join the hunt, she can't sit in council, nor certainly go to war. The child is all important, and the woman assumes that responsibility. This is not an cosmopolitan world. Winters are harsh — as you'll witness. Survival is an everyday struggle.

"I've lived a very free life until now, moving about this stellar system. Working for a living: I can take care of myself. And I've never run from a fight. But now . . . now, if I'm pregnant, I'll be required to sit on my haunches and watch you men exercise your natural freedoms. I had sworn to myself I would never be in this situation, I would never be tied to a man or a child."

"So why did you do it? Does Gwydmonia have that much control over your life? If so, then you were never really free."

"Who is? Freedom is relative. I can't explain the bond we have. I'm a part of Gwyd, and she's a part of me. I can't give that up; it would kill me."

Rold knew he would have to think about all that had happened. It was too much to digest in such a short time.

At first gingerly, then with more fervor, the two came into each other's arms.

"Can you forgive me?" Yosana said holding Rold closely.

"For this?" He stood back and rubbed her abdomen, then they began walking again.

"No. I mean, how I treated you — at first. You're . . . so much more than you appear. I feel foolish thinking of how I acted. You should have seen yourself then. But there's no excuse. I was prejudiced in our first meeting: by your wealth and status and also by what you meant to my future."

"Now I understand."

"Tyler knew, somehow. I had a silly hope in her that was destroyed by her death. I thought that Gwyd might be able to take Tyler, change her, so that she could become a rider. Something happened on the ship between Tyler and Gwyd. Gwyd won't tell me what exactly. Tyler told me she talked with Gwyd, though she didn't know who or what she was then."

"She never mentioned it."

"She didn't have time . . . Oh Rold! Why did she have to die! And you loved her so. It showed in every thing you said and did when you were with her. That's when I knew you were different; anyone who could love someone and show it so unashamedly, that person is worth something. But I fought it. I didn't want to like you."

They stopped and looked at each other.

"I don't know what you're talking about. I'm no saint," Rold said. "I think I'm changing. This place has changed me. But don't give up the fight. I need to be prodded. I want you to love me not worship me."

"This is always a danger of riding. I saw much of you –maybe too much of you. You are . . . more important than you know."

"So you got into my head. Is that it? She didn't let me inside yours. But, Yosana, I would think looking deep down into any person's mind would be overwhelming. I'm not special; people are just special — period. Do you understand what I'm trying to say?"

She made no answer.

They turned and continued down to the camp. Blikki was sitting by the fire. The camouflage was cleaned away, and all was in order.

"I'm starving," Yosana said, looking at Rold. "I think it's your turn to do supper."

"Now wait, my lady, I'm no cook."

"Then it's a good time to learn."

Blikki slapped his knee and bellowed a big, long laugh. "I told you," he said. "I told you to watch out. Now she knows you inside out, and you'll never have a minute's peace. Her mother did the same thing to me. But it's heaven. Heaven."

Pentat held up a freshly flayed carcass of some small animal. "Here, cook."

Rold felt challenged now, so he grabbed the meat and skewered it with a sturdy reed then sat calmly and began roasting it over the small fire. He wanted time to think about what had happened to him this evening. It had all been so strange. He thought he had a good, general grasp of all the various phenomena know to science — all the weird, interesting, quirky things that had been studied over the years. But he was sure this odd inter-species melding was undocumented, unstudied. He shook his head. *Don't analyze it*, he thought. Feel it. Hate it, love it, deny it, worship it, but by hell don't analyze it!

"Don't burn it," Yosana said. Rold grimaced as he fumbled with the stick, trying to turn it. Yosana sat beside him and laid her head on his shoulder.

"Will we make the valley tomorrow?" she asked looking at Blikki.

"Pentat wants to rest a day," he said. "We'll stay here one more night, then enter the valley."

"But why?" she said.

"Because of your ride," Pentat said, his back turned to the group. "You've been through enough for a day."

"I don't see the problem," she said.

"Yes, I know," he said turning to her. "It was very foolish, though, Sister, to perform your tricks on a journey such as this. You've put us at risk. The Whites are everywhere. And now we'll be exposed to them another day."

"We can make it through the valley," she said. Rold watched her fists dig into her hips.

"You've seen the valley," Pentat said, "but you've never walked through it. Now don't argue. You need rest. We'll stay one more day."

"Personally, I agree," Rold said. "I could use a rest."

Blikki shook his head, and Rold was just able to read his lips silently mouthing: "Wrong." Yosana glared at Rold, stood and tore into the tent. Pentat sat down beside him, sighing.

Blikki came around the fire, put his arm around both men and said with a little laugh: "There may be three of us men and one of her, but I think we're outgunned." He patted their backs firmly and followed Yosana into the tent.

When the meat was done, Rold and Pentat shared it. Rold ate like he had not eaten in days. The cloud ride had left him hungry and wide awake, so he and Pentat sat up talking for several hours. The clear night filled him with energy, and the late, slivered moon struck him as extraordinarily beautiful. Pentat told him stories of the early days on Salkinia and about local animal lore and about his village: two new babies were born that he had not yet seen.

Rold finally went to bed though still wide awake thinking about the cloud ride. At first all he got from Yosana was a "humph" and a cold backside, but not too long after he was settled she turned and cuddled for warmth. He accepted it as if they had been lovers for years and drank in the elation it produced.

CHAPTER 9

The demons of the desert bent Margona to their will
Not knowing of her power and their tangled future.

From "The Song of Margona"
by Pitallela-Sim

The next day Yosana had totally forgotten her indignant reaction to the delay and busied herself with sorting through and organizing their gear and supplies. Rold practiced shooting arrows at a straw dummy Pentat had fashioned, while Blikki went hunting. Pentat stayed behind to instruct his new pupil.

"What am I supposed to be shooting at?" Rold asked.

"Your enemy."

"I never believed in enemies when I was younger. But now, revenge sharpens such images."

"The Teton always know who are their enemies. An enemy is one whose death gives you life or your death gives him life."

"As a rule the Teton aren't warriors, as I've said. We don't kill unless it's the last and only way to survive. To live this way takes great discipline."

"What do you mean?"

"You must respect all things of this world, not harm what needs no harm. But living like this may make you soft, so that when you're tested with a true enemy you'll be too weak in body or mind to do what you must. It's very hard. The undisciplined person will be one way or the other: mild and easy prey or vicious even to those who aren't enemies."

"So, what are you trying to tell me?"

"You should be fierce with your enemies and gentle with all else. Don't let pride in your ability to kill, or your desire to be compassionate, lead you one way when you should go another. Don't hesitate to strike down your enemy but be able to cease the killing when it's not needed."

"I suppose on a wilderness planet life can be that simple: someone is your enemy, or they're not. But in my world things are not so black and white. Though my sister's murder was certainly clear enough. I'm not confused about that. I see your point about discipline. Maybe people in my world complicate things that are actually simple. Teach me. I need to have such discipline, I think, for what's coming. Please."

"First learn the skill of the bow. Then you must learn how to recognize your enemy. That's the biggest step."

Rold practiced more with his bow. Pentat watched him and criticized his movements until all he could do to improve was practice. Afterward his wrist and forearm ached from the slapping of the bow string.

"You know, an energy blaster takes less skill and does a whole lot more damage," Rold said as he began building a fire.

"Such technology is not *gisha-ga*," Pentat said. "The English term is self-industrial, I think."

"That's an idiom I don't recognize," Rold said.

"It means," Yosana said as she knelt beside him, "that a single human being can't produce a blaster — at least easily or efficiently — by himself. The Teton use this as an ethical measure. They believe in self-sufficiency. A blaster would require mining the metal, purifying it, forging it, shaping it, and assembling it. Also it requires energy charging, crystals, optic fibers, and computer cells. The Teton culture depends on maintaining basic survival knowledge within a small group of people. The villages are small; they can't specialize enough to have heavy industry nor do they want to become dependent on outside industry that may be taken away from them. So, they manufacture traditional artifacts: bows, arrows, natural fiber weavings, leather, wooden utensils, pottery."

"Stone age," Rold said.

"Not quite, but yes to some degree. That doesn't lessen the complexity of the culture. I can see you've already made that mistake."

"I'm just trying to understand. So, they're anti-technocratic, but . . ."

"No, no," Pentat said. "Listen. You're not listening."

"I thought you were a philosopher," Yosana said. "Open your mind."

"Now you're ganging up on me," Rold said. "Just forget it. I'll learn to use the bow."

Pentat shook his head. "Technology is not bad if it has roots in your civilization and you can support it. But your technology is like poison to us. He'll never understand, Yosana. They never do."

"Think of your silly rules about drugs," Yosana said. "Commonwealth technology is to the Teton as drugs are to your body. They can relieve obvious symptoms and even cure some ailments, but if you become dependent on them they can destroy you. Or think of pollutants in a fragile ecological environment."

"Yes," Rold said. "I understand. But, as in the argument of drugs, there are those who would promote an influx of technology to solve the problems of hunger, disease, education."

"As it happened to us before," Pentat said, "on Earth. When you force your technology on people you force your culture on them, and their culture dies or the people die."

"And if the only way a dying child could recover is through some higher technology, would you deny it to her?"

"Quality of Life is all important in my culture, Mountain Bear. If someone dies in my village because we don't have your technology available, well, that is a small price to pay for maintaining our continued peace and happiness."

"And if the technology is available? Easily at hand? Would you deny it to save the child?"

Pentat thought for a moment. "No. I would save the child. But only because I'm disciplined; I have confidence I would not be tempted to welcome such technology into my village permanently — where we would become dependent on it. But in an instance where a child could be saved, anyone could be saved, yes, I would risk that one moment. But I don't know if I could trust another to handle such a decision."

Rold began to get an inkling of how harsh life in this primitive world was — and had to be.

The conversation was interrupted by Blikki's return. Instead of bringing back slain animals for supper he held up two giant crayfish with enormous pincers.

"Boil some water, child, and we'll make a feast," he said, laughing. The crayfish were still alive and jerked his arms as they tried to leap to the ground. "No you don't, my little monsters. You're my dinner tonight."

Pentat laughed with him. "No doubt Bana's people will be angry when they see you've been poaching in their streams. How far did you go?"

"No one saw me. And I worked hard for these beauties. I'll not give them up."

Pentat froze. The only sound Rold could hear was the crackling of his newly lit fire and Yosana's rummaging in the packs. But then Pentat drew his knife and Blikki dropped his catch and retrieved his knife as quickly. Rold pulled out the knife Pentat had given him and stood ready — for what he did not know.

A ring of native warriors popped up from the ground like seedlings of the yellow grass, totally surrounding the camp. Rold wondered how they had been able to sneak up on them in the daylight; the day had grown old and shadows were long, but there was a good hour before the sun would finally set. They had straw attached to their hair and shoulders and legs. Yellow paint streaked their bodies. A leader emerged who began signing to Pentat. Rold tried to follow the silent conversation, but it was too complex, too elegant, for his limited experience. All Rold could think of was what Pentat had said about the Teton not being at war among themselves. But Pentat never eased his protective stance the whole time he was signing to the other leader.

The ring of warriors dug their lances into the sandy soil, everyone relaxed. Several of them left the camp; others began sniffing around the packs or evaluating the pridda. At one moment they were organized, disciplined, the next free and unruly.

"Rold, this is Bana, chief of the Rabbit village," Pentat said. "He saw that you're a White, and I had to convince him you're not an enemy. Even the Teton make mistakes sometimes."

Blikki snorted as he clumsily tried to hide his poached meal. Bana was quickly at his side with arms folded and a tapping foot.

"I would ask you to join us in this meal, but I didn't catch enough," Blikki said and raised an eyebrow. Bana roared with laughter and took the old man in his arms.

"It's good to see you, old thief," Bana said. "It's good to see you alive. And you, Yosana. All of you. You should feel fortunate. The green moon warriors have burned our village. Only two dead, but one was a child. My brother's child. They're looking for you, Pentat, and this White, I think." He turned to Rold. "There's an offer in the city: a house and one year of food to any Teton who brings your head in to the green moon warriors."

Yosana's arms reached around Rold in frantic squeezes until settling down around his waist. Bana watched carefully and nodded his head then sat beside Pentat.

"The two of you have stirred them up like a flying ant nest," he said. "The Eagle village is in Cold Canyon. Your scout, Kikina, came to warn us. The Whites searched for you and almost found the village in the mountains, but they were gone by then. But now the Whites know you came to the grass sea, our land. They looked for you in my village."

"Forgive me, old friend," Pentat said. "I regret your loss."

"You're not my enemy. The Whites, they're our enemy. Also, I have word from the sea villages and the corn eaters that they'll follow you in this war. I'll follow you, of course. The old master has called for a meeting at the Library."

"Good. It's time. Mountain Bear is my sign. He was in my pain dream and signals the beginning."

Bana looked at Rold with new interest.

"You've ridden a cloud," he said.

"How did you know that?" Rold said.

"She sticks to you like a suckling child. But soon it'll wear off, and she'll be like any other woman: giving orders, thinking for you . . ."

Yosana gave Bana a look that destroyed his smirk.

As quickly as they had appeared, the Rabbit village warriors were assembled for departure. Bana led them from the camp at a run while signing his farewell to Pentat. Rold noticed that at least five of the warriors were women and wondered at the confused sense of rights and privileges that a neo-primitive culture must bear.

"Blikki, quit playing with those two river bugs and cook them," Pentat said. The strain was becoming obvious in his face; the news had bled the laughter from his eyes. "We need to sleep early tonight. Tomorrow will be a challenge for us all."

The pridda were noisy with complaints as Blikki and Rold strapped on the packs. The morning sun shot streaks of purple and yellow up into the sky as it burned its way above the distant icy mountains. Its radiance warmed the back of Rold's neck which felt good after a cold, achy dawn. The march began with everyone full of energy and urgency. Five kilometers slipped by before the sun fully warmed the rising hills. Rold was falling in love with Salkinia. He breathed in the sweet air and plodded joyously along the sandy path. Even the smell of the dust elated him. His body was trimming and tightening from the constant labor of hiking.

Sometimes he felt guilty about his new-found joy. He should be trembling with anger, but right now he wanted to enjoy the beauty of the land and his companions, and Yosana. He no longer questioned his feelings for her, nor hers for him. They had known each other for such a short time — days, weeks — but it was right. It felt right. Everything fit together like a puzzle. He felt whole, symmetric as the physicists would say. How much of this was manufactured by Gwydmonia? He shrugged at the question.

There was no rest at midday. Yosana passed around bread, and each person had been given a water canteen. There had been short rests, but Pentat wanted to make it to the valley before stopping.

In the early afternoon they climbed a rounded ridge of bare sandstone. As they neared the top Rold was startled by a metallic object that rose slowly beyond the ridge. He felt his heart racing in his chest, and he feared breathing. The object stopped, and he could see it was a bronze dome of about two meters across; its finish was matted but uniform. It dropped from sight just as slowly as it had risen.

"What was that?" he said in a loud, harsh whisper.

"We're at the edge of the valley," Yosana said. "Come and see."

They jogged to the very top of the hill. Below them stretched a small valley of about fifteen kilometers square. And spread about the valley in a regular, grid-like pattern were metallic spheres — floating at various heights, from ground level to the top level of the surrounding hills. The dome they had seen was the top of one of these balls. Each one moved up then back down again over an individual spot on the valley floor. They were in a random display of various elevations almost like three dimensional game pieces for giants. Each was uniform in size and color — two meters in diameter and dark bronze.

"It's incredible," Rold said. The questions came popping into his mind faster than he could sort through them and decide what to ask first. Obviously these were not an artifact of the Teton. But who put them here? How do they work?

"Let's rest here before climbing down," Pentat said. Rold went back down and secured the pridda. Yosana followed and broke out some rations of meat and cold herb tea.

"We can't stay long," Pentat called to them. "It will take three hours to cross the valley, and we must do it before dark."

"Why's that?" Rold said as he returned and sat on the very crest of the hill.

"The balls are very close together," Pentat said. "They move up slowly but down much faster. You could be crushed between two of them or under one — especially if you can't see them. Even in the day it's difficult. There's a method to crossing the valley that few people know. It's like a game. But I know the secret and can get us through. I've been here many times."

"Especially as a boy," Blikki said with a smile. "I seem to remember you and your friend Bana were caught and scolded once."

Pentat smiled. He had been so serious all day –concentrating, worrying. It made Rold feel good to see him smile. Pentat was almost embarrassed, and of course only Blikki would be able to accomplish that.

"What did you do?" Yosana asked wide-eyed.

"When we were young and in training at the Library," Pentat said, "we hiked here often. We did it many times without anyone knowing."

"Coming here's not allowed?" Rold asked.

Blikki laughed with a stringy piece of meat still hanging from his mouth.

"Nothing is exactly forbidden," Pentat said, trying to ignore Blikki's laughter. "But we did a very foolish thing for boys of ten and twelve winters. We each climbed on top of a ball that was resting on the ground then managed to stay up there while it rose up and then went back down again."

"Pentat!" Yosana said. "You could have been killed. Foolish boys, indeed. What if you had fallen from that height?"

"But we didn't fall. And the view was wonderful. Actually the ride up was slow and boring. So to liven things up a bit we did tricks like standing on our heads, dancing, seeing how far to the side you could hold on without falling, or jumping from one ball to another."

"I'm surprised you didn't fall," she said.

"Well, I did once. It was not that far from the ground, but I broke my arm. That's how we got into trouble with the master Librarian."

"I should hope so," she said.

"I'm ready. Let's do it!" Rold said, his eyes twinkling and his head nodding toward the valley. Pentat returned his smile and grasped his shoulder in approval.

"Oh no you don't," Yosana said. "You're not foolish boys. And stop laughing, Father. You're as bad as they are."

"No, little sister, you're right," Pentat said. "We must get through the valley before dark. And there are greater things we need to do. Maybe someday our children will come and balance on the balls."

They finished eating, and Rold retrieved the pridda. They were moody and slow going up the hill and more so as they stumbled down a makeshift grade. Rold could barely contain his curiosity and felt a trembling in his knees. He slipped once, stirring up dust and scraping skin from his hands. But quickly, silently they made it to the bottom where they were at the very edge of the grid. A sphere sat in front of them, dust clinging to its bottom that had been splashed upon its landing. Rold felt a ringing in his ears that soon became a powerful, low pitched hum. As balls across the valley landed with thumps, the ground shook slightly. The landings sounded like bass drums. The wind whistled through the passages between the spheres, which caused little eddies of dust.

"What's the sound?" Rold asked wanting to hold his hands to his ears.

"The wind, vibration in the balls, who knows?" Pentat said. "Now follow me closely. Blikki, help Mountain Bear with the ponies. They're going to be jumpy in here. Is everyone ready?"

They nodded and walked in unison into the wall of bronze bubbles. "Can we talk?" Rold said.

Pentat laughed. "I would not deny you that."

Rold smiled at Pentat's jab at his talkativeness. "Anybody would be curious. I just want to know who made these things. And what are they?"

"The Great Mother placed them here," Yosana said. "That's what the Teton believe. The Spotted Valley was like this when they landed their spacecraft over two thousand years ago. No one really knows."

"Turn here quickly," Pentat said as a ball dropped loudly in front of him. They turned to the left then back to the right. Another ball fell behind Rold and his animal jumped and knocked Yosana over. He grabbed the pridda and scolded it.

"I'm all right," she said and dusted herself off while she joined them walking again, not wanting to hold up the train.

Rold looked up above him as he firmly took hold of the pridda's halter.

"There are thousands of them," he said. "They look like metal."

"They feel like a mineral of some sort," Blikki said. "Don't be afraid to touch one that's on the ground."

Rold did; at the first opportunity. *Manufactured in space,* he thought. *They're so perfect. But what mechanism? And why? For what purpose?*

"How long is each cycle?" he asked. "From ground then up and then down again?"

"Oh, probably fifteen times from sunrise to sunset they reach the top," Pentat said.

Rold decided not to bother everyone with questions for a while. They could not tell him what he really wanted to know. It would probably take generations of anthropologists to even develop a theory, and then it would go unsolved for eternity. He settled into his hiking mode — that of plodding one foot in front of the other, letting his body manage the walk by itself, while his mind wandered through topic after topic. He forced himself back to his project on Caljunna and went over several of the formulations he had packaged and sold to the Industrialist firm that had hired him. It helped ease the tension by forcing a certain concentration required to solve mathematical formulas. But even with such concentration he was able to keep pace with the others.

Pentat led them through several more turns. It was as he had said: like a game. He alone knew the precise rhythm of the floating spheres and used that knowledge to ease them through. Shadows from the surrounding hills soon grew large enough to cover the valley. The sun was no longer visible though they had a good half hour before escaping the arduous path. It was then that Blikki faltered. He stumbled in front of Rold, letting loose the pridda he was leading.

"I'm not sure I can go on," Blikki said. He was panting and wiping sweat from his forehead.

Pentat was at his side in a moment, as was Yosana. Rold stood back, taking hold of both animals.

"Of course you can, Father," Pentat said. "You must. It'll be dark soon. Let me help you."

He lifted Blikki from the ground and stood him on his weakened legs.

"I apologize," Blikki said, still breathing hard. "This pace is a bit much for me, I guess. I should be able to manage it better. I thought I'd be the last to tire."

"It's all that soft living," Pentat said. "And your round belly."

Blikki laughed and slapped his stomach.

"I have to admit," Rold said. "I'm feeling a bit weak myself. Sort of sick to my stomach."

"Me, too," Yosana said, looking at Pentat.

"It's the power of the valley," Pentat said. "The hum, the vibration. But we must overcome it and go on or things will get much worse."

Yosana and Pentat supported Blikki on either side and began walking out of the valley. Rold pulled along both pridda which were now swaying and calling loudly like cows. Occasionally the scene ahead would blur and a tingling would start on top of Rold's head. He let his feet carry him; and finally they climbed up into a narrow ravine that was beyond the spheres. Pentat and Yosana looked grave but unharmed. Blikki was barely conscious where they laid him. Rold examined his own arms and hands in the last pink glimmer of light and saw a paleness that looked like death. He dropped to his knees with his face in his hands. He was not sure how long he had been in that position, but he was roused from it by the smell of soup and wood smoke. Pentat was busy stoking a camp fire and stirring a pot above it; Yosana was beside her father wiping his face with a wet cloth.

"Forgive me," Rold said. He felt like retching for a moment, but it passed. "I see you made camp already."

"How are you feeling?" Yosana asked.

"Queasy. What happened back there? One minute I was fine then — boom!"

"It hit us all," Pentat said. "But Blikki the most. His age and physical condition. I don't know how to explain it to you, Mountain Bear. It's something that happens sometimes in the Spotted Valley. It's like a sudden gust of wind that carries a poison."

"How is he?" Rold asked as he crawled over to Blikki and Yosana.

"Sleeping now," Yosana said. "He's running a very high fever. You look feverish as well."

"You're lucky to feel as well as you do," Pentat said. "After going on your foolish ride the night before — exposing yourself to that demon."

Rold had never heard Pentat speak so sharply. There was anger biting on the tail of each word.

"Gwyd is no demon, you pompous buffalo eater," Yosana said, squaring off.

"Now wait, you two," Rold said. He tried to stand between them but staggered and dropped to his knees. Yosana was beside him, her face moist and sparkling yellow from the camp fire light.

"This is why!" Pentat said throwing his words mercilessly at them. "You foolish child. This is why you must be prepared to enter the valley. Now you're sick — all of you. And we still have so far to go."

He kicked dirt into the fire and upset the pot of boiling meat, then disappeared like a cat into the dark.

Rold fell back, exhausted, aching from fever. He wiped his sweating brow and nose and noticed a rash was beginning on his arm. Yosana's comforting face floated above him occasionally descending to kiss his hairy cheek. Then he dozed.

When he woke the night was late with everyone quiet, asleep. A couple of embers stared at him from the melted camp fire. He found himself beside a sleeping Yosana, the two of them under the large buffalo robe that was now beginning to stink. Rold wondered for a moment if it was the animal skin or himself that smelled so terribly. He was sure the skin rash he had developed was from being so filthy. His fever must have broken because he was now as cold as ice and shivering. Without closing his eyes he imagined hundreds of bronze spheres dancing in the valley and the wearying hike that he and his companions had managed as if through a maze. Worried about Blikki he looked about the camp site and saw that the tent was standing not far away. Pentat and Blikki must be inside, he thought. Yosana stayed outside under the stars to avoid a fight.

He startled at hearing a sound, a twig snapping perhaps. A curious animal, he thought; the breeze maybe? He listened for a moment and heard nothing else then tried warming himself against Yosana. After concentrating on a monotonous thought for a time he fell asleep, and did not wake until dawn.

The late summer Beldine sun reflected miserably off the sand and metal hull of the la'Kunda space transport. The ringing of metal tools wafted on the dusty breeze to Rachel Meacom's burning ears. The scene was filled with busy soldiers, busy machines, a busy sky of jet fighters and transports. She looked on as she crouched over a flat display panel that had been plopped on the sandy ground. A dynamic graphic of three maps were pieced together on the display in a montage; two of the maps were zoomed windows of small sectors of the one large map beside them. But she was ignoring the picture; her eyes were drawn to the la'Kunda transport which was being picked apart, stripped, and salvaged. Militia drones were climbing about the outside and inside of the large machine which was beginning to look like a slaughtered whale being gutted on an ocean shore. A young man, dressed in a beige jump suit with a large green disc emblem on his chest leapt from the open cockpit and ran to Rachel where he stopped and stood at attention. She choked dramatically from the dust he stirred.

"Well?" she said, shading her eyes with her hand as she looked up at his face.

"Commander, there were no interstellar transmissions."

"Are you sure?"

"Every second of the trip from Caljunna to this planet was recorded and accounted for. No one made any hyper transmissions of any sort."

"Good. Now over at the mine there. That group of men. One of them is my father, Comrade Meacom. Ask him to join me here as soon as possible. That is all."

The Militiaman turned and jogged away stirring up more dust. Rachel looked down at the map and pressed a red circle that was displayed along the bottom border. A five-centimeter slot opened in the plastic frame where she inserted a data card. An array of green dots now splattered the map showing the positions of the many search groups. Such a large area had been covered and still no sign of the la'Kunda party and Rold Simms. The large map covered four thousand square kilometers, but that was a small portion of the giant northern continent of Salkinia. The northern continent wrapped three-fourths of the way around the globe and from the pole to the equator with only a few ocean gulfs eating into the coast line. The southern continent was really no more than an island that had broken away from the main continent a few million years earlier. Such a large land mass was difficult to patrol, especially with a single metropolitan center for a base. But the la'Kundas could not have traveled far without their land rover, though certainly they had been aided by the local natives.

Rachel leisurely moved from her squatting position to be seated on the warm soil and pulled her knees up to her chest. She sensed her father arriving from behind her, where he stopped.

"Tell me your news," he said. "Is it as bad as mine?"

"How important is it that we find Simms?" she asked turning her head to look up at her aging father. The skin about his jaw hung in withered folds, and age spots freckled his balding head. He had lost weight, and she wondered if he had been ill. Ill with this mess of failed intrigue, she thought.

"So you haven't found him, I gather," he said.

"At first we thought he might be dead. As I told you in the transmission, he escaped with some natives — bows and arrows were their only weapons. How ridiculous! But there were rumors he was killed. I think some of the Militia circulated that story to save themselves some embarrassment. At any rate we lost him."

"So you told me."

He circled around the map and sat on the ground with his daughter. His body shook with weakness as he let himself down. Rachel helped him sit by holding one of his arms.

"But I understand he's been spotted," he said.

"Yes. This transport is the one in which he arrived. He somehow caught up with the safari group that were with him on the transport. It consisted of a guide and his daughter and two Industrialists — one of which was my agent."

"Oh, I see. Yes. The original plan. One of these passengers was a part of the abduction."

"Yes. Barbara Jenkins. She's an old classmate of mine."

"So why didn't she bring him back? Or at least kill him? You really have a mess here."

"*We* have a mess, Father. It was stupid. Her husband wasn't in on it. In the night he panicked and drove the land rover back to Minpana. Barbara tried to get him to turn around, but he ignored her. That's her excuse any-way."

"Badly handled."

"She volunteered for the search. I have her in charge. We hired some local guides who have no love for the native uprising, and who seem to love our money much more."

"Tell me about this local problem."

"It's really very small. Nothing to worry about. We've estimated the native population to be less than five hundred thousand for the whole planet. And this little uprising involves just a handful."

"But they could align with the Scientists and give away our position."

"They have no technology. Their religion forbids it. The most trouble they've given us is that they seem to be hiding Simms."

"Very smart. Well, perhaps you're right. He's not really that important anymore — as long as he's not allowed off the planet. I could care less whether he's dead or alive. We can't afford to expend so much energy in his recapture any longer. A token force would be fine. We can't just forget him. Perhaps offer a reprieve for the Jenkins woman if she finds him. Or else she'll have to be reprimanded. She's married, you said?"

"Yes."

"Don't let her husband leave the planet. Lose him in some bureaucratic office or something like that. Leaving Simms to the natives is a nuisance. On second thought, maybe you should get rid of the husband. You don't see any use for him do you?"

"No . . . I guess not."

"Don't get soft on me!"

"I'm not. It's just, Barbara has had contact with these people. I need her expertise, her cooperation. I don't want to jeopardize that with knocking off her husband. Even if is seems an accident of war, or something. She'll be distracted. I'll just lose him in red tape, as you said."

"We're lucky, Rachel, to be in the position we are in. Things could be worse."

Rachel turned off the display and folded it into a carrying case.

"No messages were sent from the transport," she said. "Our security is preserved."

"Are you sure Ruth Poundstone has no clue to your whereabouts?"

She spat. The sun evaporated the saliva before it could sink into the sand.

"The bitch has no idea," she said, then she laughed, obviously thinking of something else. She saw the questioning look on her father's face.

"I was just thinking," she said. "Rold Simms knew. I don't mean he was in on it — he just figured it out. He told me I'd been conned by Poundstone, that she would betray us. All she wanted was to lead us into this war, not really hand us the Committee. We should have known. It was too neat, too clean. But I'm glad it has finally started. I'm glad that I'm living in these times so that I can be a part of the downfall of the Scientists."

"There aren't too many people in the Commonwealth that are pleased with being in this war. The computer simulations are showing at least a hundred billion deaths. That's about twenty-five percent of the population."

"A natural consequence. But with such sacrifices we must assure our victory or the Commonwealth will suffer. My only fear is Ruth Poundstone. She plays rough and smart."

"We must be as smart. And, dear, there are a few other things we need to be worrying about as well. Security is number one. I'm not so convinced these local trouble-makers are harmless."

"Please, Father! They're a stone age regressed culture. Knives and spears for god's sake!"

"You underestimated them once."

"I was not in charge of Simms' incarceration."

"You had him put in with the native chief."

He stood, with much more vigor than he showed being seated, and dusted off his clothes. Rachel sat staring at him then got up slowly.

"You've read Colonel August's report," she said.

"You sound surprised. I'm in charge of the Industrialist offensive forces. I have to review such details from time to time."

"August can't blame me for that. His men were defeated by bows and arrows."

"As I said, let's not underestimate these natives. They're not a real threat, of course, but we can't let them gum up the works here."

"What are you trying to tell me?"

"My news. Salkinia has been chosen for staging. It's seclusion and security, the fact that we have a substantial force here already, has convinced the operations people to move everything here. The Scientists hardly know this stellar system exists. And Salkinia is a good planet for the Zenian mercenaries — it has deserts."

"Zenians! I didn't know."

"What did you expect? We plan on winning this war."

"But they're not . . . human."

"We have apes piloting star system destroyers. Is it that different?"

They were walking toward a small jet that was to take them to the city.

"But can we control them?" she said.

"The Zenians will be the leading edge of our offensive on Newert. They can't be defeated. And their loyalty is to wealth. We control the wealth of the Universe now. The Scientists have nothing — no industry. But we can't be weak. We must strike hard and wipe them out if possible."

"But Zenians? God!" She shuttered. "They're so disgusting. Have you ever seen their women?"

"They're the best fighters I'm told."

"I'm sure that's true. But what I mean is their . . . physical appearance. What are they called? Marsupials? They have this hairy pouch on their stomach. It's disgusting. They keep it uncovered by clothing. Barbarous!"

Her father laughed and stopped walking.

"I hope you can get this disgust out of your system," he said. "Because the first column will be here today. They don't take insults well."

"They'll have to from me if I am to command them. How many will there be in all?"

"Ten million."

For the first time the seriousness of this war became a reality for Rachel. Ten million Zenian ground troops could easily secure every civilized star-system in the Commonwealth. They had inhuman strength and endurance and could learn to hate any enemy. They thrived on hate. Killing was their religion.

They reached the jet and boarded with a silent Militia captain. He settled into the cockpit after seeing that the Meacoms had been seated and secured. The loud engines roared and pushed the aeronautical vehicle into the air. They made a sweeping turn and headed for Minpana.

"Ground troops of that number will require hand weapons," Rachel said. "We don't have that kind of arsenal here."

"A manufacturing complex is to be built here in the city. That will be my job. We won't have easy access to our traditional production planets like

Fordstar and Stallia."

"You sound like we're in hiding. Certainly security is important — surprise is a good ally — but Stallia could never be breached by Scientist fighters. My god they have no real army anyway. Not an offensive one."

"We have already abandoned Stallia and left it to the Scientist police. Fordstar is under marshal law locally; we weren't able to get everyone out. Ruth Poundstone was ready, had been ready I would guess for a long time. But you're right, they have no real offensive forces. They don't know how to fight a war of this type."

"Does anyone?" She felt fear for the first time. Her father had scared her. She was glad to know the truth of their position, how desperate it was.

"If you can't handle it," he said, "I'm sure August would appreciate his command back."

She frowned at his cruelty. It was evident that this was no longer her father: this was a man who must murder a quarter of the population in order to rule the survivors.

"The day August can control ten million Zenians I'll gladly resign," she said. "And I have no fear of that."

"I certainly am trusting a lot to you, my daughter. But I can trust no one else."

"Thanks for the confidence."

"At least you understand why we're doing this. Some of our cohorts are a bit crazed with vengeance for our centuries of subservience to the Scientists. But the Scientists are not evil vermin to be exterminated. It's the System we are trying to change. Certainly you understand that."

"Now who sounds weak?"

"It's not weakness. I find that my passions are stirred much more by a true understanding of reality. We need scientists; we can't do without them. But they must work for us, not the other way around. We can't afford to throw ourselves into a dark age."

"All I know is I hate the Scientists. Nothing would please me more than to see their complete extermination. I want to change the System too, as we had hoped with our first plan that failed. But that failure brought out an anger in me I didn't know was possible. Ruth Poundstone and the Simms family. I would love to send Rold Simms' head to his father as a present." She laughed and looked away.

"That's why you'll command the Zenians," Comrade Meacom said. "It suits you."

"Now what are you going to do about these locals?"

"We've already impressed most of the city dwellers. They seem, well, if not loyal, at least obedient.

"But let me worry about it, Father. You have more important things to do than try to solve such a trivial annoyance."

"You're right."

The jet stopped its propulsion engine and fired its vertical engine for a hover landing on a small concrete pad that was nestled among the modern buildings in the Industrialists section of Minpana. The cluster of glass buildings were to the south and west of Rivergate, what was once a vast park for the city.

"What's the schedule for the arms factory?" Rachel asked.

"Probably a year before peak production will commence. Eighteen months before we'll be able to launch an offensive. I mean to shorten that."

"A long time to keep this place secure and quiet. News media may find us. Or Scientist intelligence."

"Get your people out there, damn it. Don't let the news hacks in. And handle the spies. My god, do I have to think of everything?"

"No, certainly not. Of course I'll begin building our network immediately."

"Go over to Intelligence and view their status reports in detail. There are at least three groups searching for Simms that I've heard about."

"I'll take care of it."

"Another class mate of yours is one of the people searching for Simms. Frank Diego. I thought you should know."

The machine finally landed with a couple of bounces. The engine loudly wound down.

"But that's enough talk of war," he said. "Please have lunch with me. I have imported a cellar full of *puff beny* wine from Benson Monda."

"Will I ever see Monda again, Father? It's the only home I've ever had."

"Monda will be our home again some day. We'll center our empire there — create a throne."

They crossed from the jet to a glass elevator and laughed arm in arm while the low hum of a troop transport landing at the city space port bounced off the slick-walled buildings. The first column of Zenians had arrived.

"Why do you ask so many questions, little one?" Sompica said as she packed for the trip.

"Things are happening here that need to be known," Tyler said.

She was up and dressed in farmer trousers and cotton tunic. Her hair covered the wide gash on the side of her head, which now was scarring. Her determination at finding Rold had strengthened her demeanor — and added years to her life. She fumbled with a walking stick, feeling the smoothness of its finish, absently looking for splinters.

For several days a native doctor had visited the hut and applied salves to her wound. The smell was atrocious, and her hair was so filthy from lack of washing that it hung in stiff fingers about her face. But daily her wound healed more; her headaches disappeared, and her blurred vision sharpened, until now she was strong enough for the journey. Washed and well fed, she was unexpectedly full of energy.

"Need to be know by whom?" Sompica said. "We know as much as we want. We're leaving to protect you. And also because we're getting old and want to join our people in the mountains. The Whites are here by ever increasing numbers. What else is there to know? Knowledge can be dangerous."

Tyler sighed, but did not reply.

Chictampa returned to the hut with water bags and a pack for Tyler to carry.

"We must leave. The search is stepped up. The Teton will protect us if we can find them. A scout from this village will take us as far as the Red Hills."

The old couple, Tyler, and Sinwok, their guide, left the farming village and began their trip onto the plateau. Sinwok was a sturdy, middle-aged man with a wife and three children he was leaving behind to escort Tyler to Teton lands. He did not view himself as Teton, though that was his heritage. He was a farmer and lived close to the White city. The trouble that had entered his village frightened and confused him. His wife praised this brave act of escorting the young girl, but secretly cried on her bed as her husband walked out of sight.

Three days into the wilderness, the foursome was stopped by Industrialist Militia. They were a force of only a half-dozen or so, with one land rover and individual speedsters. The questioning was brutal and pointless. It was obvious that these travelers knew nothing of escaped prisoners.

"May we go now," Tyler said with a commanding tone; she spoke Ameranglo but with a faked accent. "My companions are on in years and get fatigued easily."

"We'll make that decision," a woman Militia said.

As she spoke the underwood of the forest seemed to writhe as a larger force tramped through. The Militia stood relaxed, obviously expecting the visitors. Tyler watched in fascination as a group of twenty suited giants approached.

"Monsters!" Sompica screamed.

The faces of the new contingent were barely seen through their helmet visors, but it was plain that these were not human. Their faces were covered in a fine fur with melanotic noses and lips. Some had exposed hands, which were also furry and claw-like. They stood almost three meters in height, walking with such powerful strides that the knee high brush was crushed flat in their path.

A leader stood forward and approached the questioning Militia, speaking in a language Tyler could not recognize. The Militia woman spoke in the same language, but not quite as gruffly.

"This . . . company has tracked the fugitives to this point," she said, turning to Tyler. "They wish to question you as well."

"What are they?" she asked, her voice trembling. She regretted revealing such a weakness.

"Zenians. Horrible creatures, aren't they? I told this one that I was finished with you. I'll be just as glad to clear out of here. I can't stand their stench."

With these last words the Zenian leader emitted a loud grunt. The Militia's eyes widened as she realized he understood Ameranglo. She moved backward one step and the Zenian instantly sprayed her with a wide energy blast that melted her on the spot. The other Militia responded slowly, but in their movement, were destroyed in their tracks.

Sinwok turned to run but fell face down as his legs were melted into liquid carbon beneath him. His chest exploded from the heat of the blast, his body aflame. Tyler was frozen as the scene unfolded. This last atrocity focused her consciousness and she turned to the Zenian leader ready to propel herself at him without any concern except to kill him.

Chictampa and Sompica stood holding each other; each in horror of their situation. The Zenian leader laughed, or that was what Tyler assumed he was doing as he grabbed her by both arms and practically snapped them in two.

"You," he growled. His voice was like a power hammer at full speed, crackling in a deep resonating blur. "You are a Scientist bitch."

Tyler struggled. Her strength was not quite what it should be, she knew. But she knew her fighting would be futile even at full strength, so she calmed.

The Zenian shouted a command in his own language and the group started moving. He pulled Tyler along for a few steps then pushed her ahead, pointing his weapon at her. She took the hint and began walking. Sompica called to her, but Chictampa held his wife back. The Zenians ignored them, seeing them as no threat. It was the last time the old couple would see Tyler.

CHAPTER 10

*Most accounts of the Spotted Valley have been
vague and contradictory. Although I never saw
the valley myself, Rold Simms made sketches and
calculated the extent of the outlay of spheres to be
in excess of ten thousand.*

From "The Chronicles of Rold Simms"
by Francisco Diego

With Blikki on a litter, the trip to the Library took longer than Pentat had hoped. The climb out of the valley was the most difficult and time-consuming segment. Rold and Pentat had to help the pridda pull the litter up a winding, treacherous grade on brittle red sandstone. Rold's health had bounced back quickly, giving Yosana ammunition for her lectures on the benefits of cloud-riding. She could not let it drop. Each time Pentat grunted at her about the living clouds she would retaliate with a newly formulated argument; she had to have the last word, but with the sincere hope that she would finally make her point clear and change his mind. Rold was continually troubled with the bickering and uncomfortable to the point of having second thoughts about his feelings for these people. But all he had to do was look at Blikki's tepid expression as he bounced along on his mobile bed or feel Yosana's hand in his or see the weary frown on the once smiling, haughty Pentat, and he knew how he felt.

On the last day before they reached the Library Blikki began complaining about his treatment, about being lashed to a pile of sticks that were shaking his guts into mush, about the sun, the dust, the food; in short, he complained about everything in his waking world. Finally Pentat stopped and sat down beside him laughing. He laughed harder each time Blikki spoke another complaint. Soon they were both laughing, everyone was laughing. Rold could see the love that Pentat felt for this man. Through this whole trip Blikki had been in the background: it was hard to outshine a personality like Yosana or Pentat. Not that they were in competition, but Rold realized that until this fever he had been taking Blikki for granted. And all this time Blikki had been the rock on which they had all found footing.

Yosana interrupted the laughter to check Blikki's fever and give him some broth and medicine. They could see in her eyes the smile of success, meaning the fever had broken, and she hugged her father for a long moment.

Blikki insisted on walking, which accelerated the pace slightly. But mid-afternoon came, and they were still a good distance from the Library — in wilderness still, Rold thought. He said the word wilderness in Ameranglo, and Pentat laughed and explained that there was no Teton word that corresponded to it.

"You cannot tame the land," he said.

They were now climbing a foothill to a small range of arid mountains. Blikki was breathing hard and leaning on one of the priddas. But his color was better, and a sparkle was growing in his eyes.

"Some people stick to a piece of land like a tick on a pitah," Pentat continued. "The Whites have always done so. But sitting on land and sucking it clean of life does not make it yours.

"There is a story about a White who sat on his land during a drought. The animals left. The vegetation died. The top soil got blown away. But still he sat: because it was his land! And no one was going to take it from him! So he sat there until he starved to death. Even the smallest of creatures were smarter than that White."

"That's the silliest thing I've ever heard," Yosana said. "Propaganda. You make people who believe in owning property sound like fools."

"I don't have to do that," Pentat said. "But yes, it's a children's story, and it's not like life. A real White farmer would steal more land after ruining the land he was on. To own property means having the right to destroy it. Is that not the way the Whites think?"

"How did we get into this anyway?" she said.

"Wilderness," Rold said. "But, Pentat, whether people own the land or not, they do sit on it, as you say, and, thus, it's no longer wild."

Pentat was quiet while he thought. A cool gust of wind twirled some dust as it shot around the bend of the hill. Rold caught sight of a white peak that jutted above the grassy crown of the group of mounds they were crossing. As they walked farther he could see that it was a snow-capped cone, much taller than the mountains to the south, from which he and Pentat had escaped. And beyond, through hazy clouds, there were more mountains, a beautifully wooded and snow streaked range that seemed to appear from nowhere. He could smell a subtle hint of evergreen, and the crispness of the air tickled his nose.

"I see, Mountain Bear," Pentat said. "Then perhaps we can agree then that wilderness — to use your word — is my world, and what makes it not wilderness is the disease of the White culture. In our understanding of things the idea of owning property is not unlike the evil of parasitic growth. We try to live in symbiosis with our environment; since we are dependent on flesh for sustenance. That is one point that can't be talked away. So we're not apologetic."

Rold shook his head as he huffed oxygen rich air, struggling up rocky steps to the hill's summit. He was amazed again at Pentat's scholarly discourse.

"Why are you two jabbering philosophy when you should be saving your breath for climbing these rocks?" Blikki said. Pentat had him by the arm as a few rocks crumbled and bounced down the gentle slope. "You Library-educated brats are always so talkative."

"Stop your grumbling, Father," Pentat said. "We'll be there soon enough."

"We must be close," Rold said.

"The scouts already know we're here," Pentat said. "We'll be expected. Did you notice them, Father? Something odd is happening. Two scouts spotted us this morning but didn't approach. And they were village scouts, not Library scouts. Does that make sense?"

His question was answered before he finished uttering it. As they reached the top of the ridge a fantastic scene lay before them. It was especially fantastic to Rold, for he had never seen the Library. Though his attention strayed to the Library's structure often, the more pertinent surprise was in front of the Library on the fan-shaped meadow. In circular groups spread about the terrain according to the random selection of sites were hundreds of Teton villages — thousands of people. Rold guessed that there were perhaps half a million or more. Obviously Pentat was shocked. He stood with his mouth open, his trembling hand wiping his face. First just a few, then more, like a wave moving across a pond, people's faces turned up to them. Arms jutted out pointing to them. A second wave, that of a chant, moved across the gathering: "Pen-tat! Pen-tat! Pen-tat! . . ."

Louder and louder the two syllables were roared; children's voices mixed with warriors, old men's voices with women's. A chill shot down Rold's back, and he froze for a moment in awe. Then he forced himself to turn and look at Pentat, the fatigued, frustrated warrior chief whom he had first seen with his body painted golden in light produced from a fungus. Pentat stood proud and grim; he did not shirk the exaltation but accepted the awful responsibility he knew it to be.

Yosana hugged Rold's arm and kept her eyes on Pentat. She soon became giddy from the blasting chant. But Blikki wore an angry scowl and turned his eyes from the assemblage.

"A nasty business, son," he said. "You know that. Your people are ready to be led to Heaven, but it'll take crossing through Hell to get there."

"You sound like an old woman," Pentat said.

The words were a slap in Blikki's face, and Rold was angry at Pentat for the first time. Blikki took it like a rock. He stared at this new leader whom he cared for as a son. But it was Pentat who almost crumbled. He spoke without turning.

"Forgive me, Father. As you say, I know that war is the true monster, not the Whites. But they'll destroy us surely. War will destroy some but save others. So, it's war we must choose. And I'm sure you know that to win this war we must be united; we must believe in a positive result. I'm asking that from you now."

The prickling roar grew louder by the minute, accompanied now by hundreds of musicians. Rold felt himself being hypnotized by the scene and Pentat's words. He knew he would follow him anywhere now, into the field of battle if asked. But he had an itching thought that shook him from his bewitchment.

"But you can't win this war!" Rold said now animated, losing his hesitation. "Not against the Industrialists."

"There are things you don't know," Pentat said. "Whatever weapons are used, to win a war is possible if you have heart and discipline. We were defeated before on Earth, almost exterminated . . ."

"Yes, by technology and numbers!"

"The Whites are a disease, a parasite. We must simply find a poison that will destroy the parasite but preserve the host."

The group began moving down the gentle slope. The pridda were stubborn and took much pulling, almost dragging, by Rold and Blikki to get them down the hill. As they neared the first tier of chanting people, Rold was able to see better the musical instruments that had been dragged out for the reception. There were large drums of stretched hide and hollow logs and rattles and flutes, large and small. A long twisted rope of leather thongs was stretched twenty feet from one man to another. The ends were wrapped around limber wooden dowels, and the whole thing was as tight as a spring. A handful of people stroked the strings of their hunting bows across the taut rope producing a low pitched hum that threatened to burst everyone's ear drums. The men holding the ends were able to change the pitch by increasing or lessening the stress on the rope. The hum managed to enhance the rhythm of the other instruments but mostly added to the deafening cheers and chants.

The smiling people were in organized groups, though the organization collapsed behind the travelers as they advanced toward the monstrous Library. Each group was a village, Rold surmised — a village being a self-maintaining unit that was primarily nomadic. At first glance the members of the race of Tetons looked much alike, but Rold noticed quickly that each village had its own cultural differences. Some were dressed in furs with little adornment. Others had woven fabrics and metal and gem jewelry as well as paint and various contrivances of head hair. But a good many dressed as Pentat and the other Eagle village warriors whom Rold had already seen: in tanned leather, with body paint and feather jewelry.

The march was like a Roman triumph. Toward the end of the crowd, at the steps of the Library, something of a regal reception awaited. A handful of people dressed in brown hooded robes stood with arms crossed. In the center of these was an old man with long silver hair and an open, smiling mouth with missing teeth. He wore the same type robe, but his hood rested on his shoulders. He extended his arms in welcome then raised them trying to quiet the massive gathering. From the crowd, on the left, a woman sprang, running toward the travelers. Her hair was dark and braided over either ear, the braids flying two feet behind her. Dust stained her cheeks where it stuck to tears and was smeared from the constant wiping of her leather sleeve. What Rold thought at first was a back pack was actually an infant strapped back-to-back to the woman. He remembered reading of this custom on Old Earth but had never observed it in any other culture. Even the Caljunnese did not practice this. She was beautiful Rold thought, as beautiful as a queen. He had already guessed the truth. Pentat ran to her, the two people crashing into each other. They embraced and kissed each other until Rold thought they must have cleaned each other's face of grime. Pentat looked at the child nervously then took it from its pouch, held it aloft, above his head, and now the crowd really sent up a cheer.

The procession began again, now Pentat leading with one arm around the woman and the other holding the child. Yosana clung to Rold's arm.

"His wife?" he said.

"Yes," she said.

"He never said anything about a family. Why?"

"Until now he wasn't sure they were still alive. Several people of his village died when he was captured."

"He told you this?"

"No, he told Father. I had no idea Tachina had given birth. And he asked that the subject not be spoken of until we found the village. Sort of a superstitious wish not to bring bad luck. Pentat's biggest problem is his pride. The fear of losing his family has been burning inside him. He has already lost his parents. But look at him now: his heart is about to burst, and his face will ache from smiling. I'm so happy for him. Tachina is a wonderful person. And now a son, whom he's seeing for the first time."

"How do you know it's a boy?"

"The baby wears a red bracelet. Red is a male color."

Seeing the homecoming, Rold's thoughts rolled back to Tyler. He blew a sigh through his nose and felt the anger and pain well up. But he forced his feelings back down, though his determination was never more pronounced. He watched his new friend walking with his family, his pride and happiness shining like a glamour mist.

The sun was setting; light washed the sky to a bright new pink. Shadows from the mountains fell on the crowd like a blanket, and cooking fires and torches flared into brilliance, keeping the scene alive. A rumbling of thunder preceded the arrival of a large bank of clouds that circled but did not cover the congregation. Rold soon realized that the formations above them were living clouds. He could distinguish twelve as they silently paid homage to the returning hero. The Teton marveled at the appearance, many kneeling and gasping and chanting prayers. But Rold could not get it out of his mind that the slunks were snobbishly observing the festivities as curious anthropologists or were simply viewing it as an entertainment. But it was an impressive sight — all these huge, ugly globs floating above them, the fire light and setting sun reflecting off their rippling, elastic shells. Pentat looked up astonished as well. He seemed ready to curse them, but nothing could anger him now.

The heat of the day lingered even in twilight; a warm and muggy atmosphere was also produced by the mass of celebrating flesh that surrounded Pentat and his followers. As they reached the Library Rold realized that the pridda had vanished. Someone must have taken them to be fed and unburdened. Rold, Yosana, and Blikki were motioned to the left where Rold recognized a couple of the warriors that had been a part of the prison rescue. He saw Lampa, the warrior that had ridden behind him after losing his own mount. They found they could not speak over the noisy crowd and tried greeting each other with signing. Lampa was glad to see that Rold and Pentat had made it safely to the Library. Rold did not understand all that he tried to say but gathered that the Librarians called for this gathering and that the villages would be wintering here. Rold tried to show his wonder at how to feed such a large number of people, especially if winter was cold in these hills. Lampa indicated that there would be much snow in a double moon, and, yes, food would be a problem. But he smiled confidently.

A hush rushed through the crowd, sentences being stopped in the middle, coughing and cries of children gaining recognition as the chanting stilled. Rold turned toward the Library and saw that Pentat had ascended the steps to a point ten meters above the heads of the villagers. Beside him stood the silver-haired man with arms raised to quiet the celebration. A small, robed assistant pointed a long pole toward the man's face. The man spoke, his voice amplified by an electronic public address system.

"Teton," he began, "we have called you here to spend your winter in peace and safety. All villages are welcome: the hunters of pitah, the farmers, the fishers, yes, even those who live in the White city. But when this winter passes and the sun warms our land and brings life to us all, we must face our enemy or accept our extinction."

A roar went up, too quickly and too loudly. Rold could see a frown on the old man's lips. The man held up his hands again and calmed the people.

"Today you have cheered the return of a great warrior — perhaps the greatest warrior of our time. We must place our trust in him and give him our love, for in his hands he holds our future, and the future of the Earth."

The burst of human cheering shot into the sky. The energy expelled from the lungs of those people could have powered a space transport. Rold was exhilarated and also frightened. He thought the man's statement about "the future of the Earth" was a bit much, but all in all it was a powerful introduction. No one actually heard the man when he pointed and said, "Pentat," for the chanting began again.

"Pen-tat! Pen-tat! Pen-tat! . . ."

Pentat stood before the microphone, which was attached to a jury-rigged boom, obviously put together in a hurry for this special situation. The crowd quieted themselves, wanting to hear what this new, powerful leader had to say. Pentat kept his arms folded and scanned the faces he could see. From the back of the crowd he looked like a glowing insect.

"I do not want to fight a war," he said. A moan reverberated about the villages. A man's voice rose up from the front and challenged him, "There must be war!"

Pentat spoke a little louder, "I do not want to fight a war, and neither do you! Fathers, mothers, children will be killed. We might all be killed. But . . . we will all surely die if this White plague is allowed to grow and destroy our home.

"Listen! Hear me. I do not want to fight a war. What I want is to defeat my enemy! This we must do; we have no choice."

The chant went up again. Pentat now had little chance to speak, but Rold imagined that he had little else to say. The microphone was taken away, and Pentat stood alone staring at his people. A cool wind picked up and swirled around the steps lifting debris and dust. Rold welcomed the relief from the muggy sweat he was feeling.

Pentat spoke to one of the Librarian's aides, pointing toward Rold. The young man quickly descended the steps and as he gained Rold's attention motioned him to follow him back up.

As Rold pushed his way through the standing and sitting people to get to the steps, the true wonder of the evening occurred. The breeze they had been feeling grew stronger. Looking up people could see that it was being generated by the living clouds: they were circling the gathering like a wreath, turning in the circle faster and faster as if in a race. Sparks of light flashed in each slunk, as Rold had seen before, but the intensity of the light was growing until bolts flashed from one slunk to another making spokes to the wheel they had formed. Now all eyes were turned up; people were gasping or screaming or simply standing with mouths open. The minah-machacute now spun so quickly that they were only a blur. From the center of the circle, where the bolts intersected, a blast of light shot at an angle down to the Library steps and struck Pentat. Thousands of eyes followed the light to him. He stood stunned and bathed in a continuous stream of yellow-white light that formed a halo about his entire body. Faintly from some corner, then growing louder the chant began: "Pen-tat. Pen-tat. Pen-tat . . ."

Rold tripped over himself trying to get to him. He knew these regressed natives would see this as a religious sign or something, but he feared the physical harm the radiation might cause. He had no thoughts about why the minah-machacute were doing this nor was he sure of what he could do about it; he just knew he must get to him. And he felt alone in his effort. He looked for Yosana and Blikki, who had been beside him just moments before, but all the faces were a blur. Climbing the steps seemed to take forever, and once he made it to the top he was still a good forty or fifty paces from Pentat. He walked like a drunken man; the light blinded him to the point that he lacked balance or a sense of direction. And then a second column of light emerged from the spinning living clouds. It caught Rold and froze him to the terra-cotta steps. The crowd now saw two images illuminated side-by-side. The halos that circled the two men merged between them as Rold tried to reach Pentat, and a picture took shape. It was an eagle; a golden eagle was superimposed upon the two men. Silence took hold of the people. They stared dumbly at the projected picture, frightened and awed. The robed librarians fell flat upon the steps and top landing. A single voice, a woman singing softly an old hymn from Old Earth, could be heard from one end of the meadow to the other.

> *Shadows of the eagle's wings*
> *Stretch across the land*
> *Green corn reaching for the sky*
> *Turning golden as it stands,*
> *The eagle comes to share its song*
> *And protect the children of the sun*
> *With mighty wings of gold*

For him we have waited so long.

All the thousands of people could hear the pure, sweet notes and slowly joined in until the ground trembled with the vibrato. The eagle image faded slowly then the cascade of light blackened; the minah-machacute had disappeared. The singing dissolved into murmurs; both men staggered then fell to the hard steps. Librarians were quickly at their sides; Yosana and Blikki were there as well, after much struggling through the congested crowd, though the area around the steps did clear slowly.

The majority could not see the steps well enough to know that the two men were stretched out, unconscious. Each person withdrew to his own village for merry and inspired conversation with friends and family about the wonderful sign from the Great Mother who sent the Eagle to honor the chief of the Eagle village. But who was that other person with him?

The librarians wondered as well. Rold and Pentat were taken to a large room that was filled with green, growing plants, heated with warm, humid air. Felt pallets were laid out for them to rest on. Both were somewhat conscious though disoriented. Blikki sent the librarians away after some arguments. Yosana sat holding Rold's hand for several minutes before he was able to speak. Tachina stood beside Blikki holding her son, perhaps afraid to be too near her husband after such a display, not really understanding it.

"I'm all right," Rold said in a croaking voice, his eyes closed. Yosana fell upon him with kisses and hugs. He returned them weakly but with a warm smile.

"I love you," he said.

"I know."

"My head!" Pentat said. "What happened?" He tried standing, but Tachina got over her shyness and pulled him down to the pallet.

"No," Pentat said, "I know what happened. Minah-machacute. Mountain Bear. The light."

"They've cemented your cause," Yosana said. "The Teton will follow you to their dying breath now — both of you."

Pentat looked at Rold and nodded. His brow was in folds and the corners of his mouth were pulled tightly, but he was not angry as much as he was in pain. "The living clouds shined their light on both of us then?" he asked.

"Yes," Blikki said. "But of course, son, you couldn't see all that happened. The two of you together — you were each the wing of an eagle. The villagers saw it; we all saw it."

"You now have no reason to criticize the living clouds, Pentat," Yosana said. "They've just given you power beyond anything any Teton leader has ever known. Can't you see that they do care about us? Finally?"

"Perhaps," Pentat said, rubbing his face and trying out his eyes for the first time since regaining consciousness. "But I don't need their help. I don't want their help. They should just stay out of it — as they usually do."

"Well, I don't know about the rest of you," Blikki said, "but I'm thirsty after all this excitement."

As if summoned by his words, two robed men appeared with platters of fruit and pitchers of liquid. The old man with silver hair walked with them. Rold hesitated at reaching for a cup when he saw him. Blikki did not. He grabbed a cup, sloshed some drink into it, threw back a big gulp, then shook the old man's hand heartily. The greeting was returned in kind.

"Welcome, Little Mouse," the man said turning to Pentat.

Yosana laughed aloud until she saw Pentat's icy face.

"Mouse?" she said. "I've never heard you called that before."

"It's a name he had as a boy here," the man said. "I haven't used it in a long time, Yosana. But seeing him lying there in Tachina's arms like an exhausted young boy brought me back many years.

"Tell me, Yosana, did you arrange this . . . spectacle?"

"What?" she said. "Do you mean the living clouds? Of course not. How could I? Why would they follow my wishes?"

"You're Gwydmonia's rider, and the others follow her lead in most things. You are the last, you know. It's just so unlike the minah-machacute to . . . involve themselves in our affairs."

The man laughed. "Please, introduce me to this man you have brought with you. Young man, you seem to be an important part of this whole drama."

"Master Chaka," Yosana said, "this is Rold Simms. He helped Pentat escape the Whites."

"No, no," Rold said. "Pentat helped me escape."

"The minah-machacute seem to think you're important," Chaka said. He looked at Yosana then back at Rold. "Oh, I see. She has taken you riding. You poor man. I'd say you have been through a lot for one who is not a Teton."

"He carries the sign of the Eagle," Pentat said. "He's the one, Master. I'm sure of it."

"Such good friends you have, Rold Simms," Chaka said and turned to Pentat. "I think you and your family should return to your lodge tonight, Pentat, if you think you can walk. Tachina will help."

"We're on our way," Pentat said with a smile. Tachina helped him to his feet as he held their baby under one arm.

"We can accommodate the la'Kundas here if you wish, and Rold Simms."

"All I want is a bath and a bed," Rold said.

"I'll join you," Yosana said.

"I'll have another drink," Blikki said.

"And I'll join you, old friend," Chaka said then took a cup, delicately poured the golden liquid into it, and sipped as he sat with Blikki.

Yosana took Rold by the hand and pulled him from his mat. "Come," she said. "I know my way." He followed, with renewed energy.

"Can we slow down a bit?" Rold said. He was not tired or faint or dizzy. He simply wanted to take in the sights of this great structure and also absorb the past few hours that had moved by so quickly. His itching skin begged for a scrubbing in clean water, but his eyes were too full of the sights and sounds of the Library, and his mind was too full of the sights and sounds of Pentat's triumph, and of course questions.

"Things have been moving a bit fast for me today," he said. "Well, really for the past few weeks, I guess."

"You've already said that," Yosana said. She walked along a worn path etched in the wooden floor. She strolled with confidence, the confidence of royalty, and Rold realized she was probably considered royalty here. And yet she chose to live in the Commonwealth where she really was no more than a servant.

Her face was chapped and grimy as was his own, but he still thought she was beautiful, not the plain girl he had seen at the Caljunna space port. He reached for her hair and gently brushed it with the back of his fingers. She took his hand and kept walking.

"I haven't been here since I was a little girl," she said. "You're still a little girl."

She glared. "I'm not that much younger than you, Rold Simms."

"How old do you think I am?"

"I know your age, my love, and much more. We rode together. Remember?"

At first he felt vulnerable, naked; no one should be so wide open to another human being. But then he relaxed and sense the bond that had been formed between them, or among them, for certainly Gwydmonia took part in that bond.

"How far do we have to go?" he asked.

"It's a kilometer from one side of the Library to the other, and that's where we are going."

"Tell me about this place. Who is Chaka?"

"The Master Librarian, of course. He's the spiritual father to all the Teton. He keeps the knowledge of their race."

"Was that a slip? Are you Teton or not?"

"My mother, as you know, was Teton. And the Caljunnese were once Teton. But genes are not what make someone Teton. I don't claim to be

Teton because I don't live as one."

Rold had no idea what knowledge was maintained in these halls, but the edifice was impressive. They were now walking through a large domed chamber the size of a stadium large enough to accommodate fifty thousand people. It was open and free of walls and full of the yellow light produced by electricity jumping through a vacuum in glass bottles. Varied groups of people were strolling through aisles lined with stacks of bound tabloid books, an ancient technology for storage of language-based knowledge. Shelves and cabinets stood in clusters from one end of the hall to the other smelling of dust and decaying celluloid.

As Rold and Yosana reached the far end of the hall they could see another group of people straightening up piles of yarn, as a last chore before going home for the night. Unfinished products were laying about: knitted squares with glossy, wooden needles still attached and looms half-filled with fabric standing up or on the floor. This area smelled of dye and wool, and the clicking of wooden utensils from the labors of the remaining people echoed in the unseen recesses of the dome.

"Such a strange building," Rold said. "I can't imagine the Teton constructing it. Was it built by someone else? It doesn't exactly fit the level of technology they seem to maintain currently."

"You don't recognize it? I thought you were something of an historian. The Library was once a space transport — the one that brought my people here from Old Earth. This large dome was once filled with buildings, homes. It encased a whole city. There are four other domes connected to this one. They were used for farming. But it was all cleared out hundreds of years ago. The only things kept were the books and Earth gadgets for the museum. It's in one of the other domes. One dome was destroyed in the landing. The smallest one is used for living quarters."

"Fascinating. But where were we with the others? Where the pallets were?"

"That's new construction. It's a sanctuary."

"It's all fantastic. But this is too large a transport to land on a planet. Isn't it?"

"It crashed here against these mountains. By the time the transport had made it to Salkinia there was no one who really knew how to manage the orbit. It was amazing that anyone survived the landing, but most did. There are stories about it. It's hard to tell what's true and what's myth. Ask my father. He's the story teller of the family."

"I will. But I like listening to you better."

"Let's just get to the baths," she said.

"All right. I'll stop needling you."

"No you won't."

Rold took her in his arms. She resisted only a fraction of a moment then nuzzled his chest.

"You have such a temper," he said, smiling.

"I know. And you're the perfect trigger for it. What we need is some rest. Crossing the grassy sea and red hills on foot is no easy job. And especially for us who aren't Teton. So lets get cleaned up and get some sleep. You do stink, you know."

Tyler was exhausted by the forced march. The Zenians had given her water but no food for three days. The nights were cold and she had no blanket; her captors had their environment suits that provided the warmth they needed. She was worried that she was becoming ill and knew she was growing weak.

"You will either have to carry me or bury me if you don't give me some food and a blanket," she said in a horse voice.

The leader, apparently the only one who knew Ameranglo, squatted beside her where she sat cross-legged.

"You complain, you will die," he grunted. "And we will not bury you, as you say; we will let the vermin of this rotting world consume your smelly flesh."

"I'm not frightened anymore, pig-face. I'm beyond that. So save your threats. Can I at least have a fire? The higher we get in these hills the colder I get. From what I can tell, you people would die even at these temperatures if you didn't have your suits."

The Zenian winced at the thought of cold. Tyler saw fear in his full-pupiled eyes.

"A fire. If you can make it yourself. Gather fuel. We have no food that you could consume safely. If you find raw food in these hills, you are welcome to gather that as well."

Tyler took a deep breath, determined not to show her pleasure in this small victory. She was pleased to know that the idea of *cold* was a powerful image that she could possibly use in the future.

The leader assigned a soldier to accompany Tyler in the night as she gathered downed limbs from the scrub trees that were sprinkled about the dark hills.

CHAPTER 11

No turning back now; the path had narrowed
When the city of dreams sprang up from dust,
The Teton accepted their fate.

- From "The Song of Margona"
  by Pitallela-Sim

The planet of Caljunna crept into view on the monitor until it erased half the black void with its yellow surface. Frank Diego fiercely studied the scene. This was his second visit to the dull world of the Beldine stellar system in a span of six weeks. The last time he had been here he had left with new hope, being directed by yet another clue only to be bashed against a dead end and rebounded to the starting point. This was the last place anyone had seen Rold Simms. He had lived and worked here, and yet no one seemed to know anything about him or about his departure. The space port was crawling with Industrialist Militia. Computer records were a shambles. But certainly someone, somewhere on this huge, clumsy rock, knew something.

Frank was forced to assume a cover: that of a Industrialist salesman dealing in farm equipment, something he knew about from his more humble origin. Caljunna was now in the hands of the Industrialists. They had seized much of this frontier; since it was so far from Old Earth, Newert and the Three Sister Worlds of Knowledge, which were Scientist strongholds. Rold had let himself be captured. That was all Frank knew. He was supposed to lead the Scientists to the new Industrialist stronghold. But the clues had been erased. Tyler was the random factor that had corrupted the neat trail Rold was supposed to leave. Frank had learned of her *incognito* arrival. What was she doing here? And now they were both lost.

Frank calmly responded to flight control monitors as the transport gently sank into the atmosphere. He was good at playing an Industrialist and seldom worried about being discovered, though he wearied of the game and wondered how important his task was any more. His personal reasons were clear: he loved Rold as a friend, a brother, and ached at the thought of losing him. But though the abduction had started the war, it was no longer an issue in the minds of those who were fighting. Three million people had been killed in these first few weeks of the conflict — one whole planet disintegrated. The Industrialists were exterminating human beings and sweeping up the debris as if they were an infestation of vermin in a barn: kill the rats and pile them on the fire. This "housecleaning" effort had so far been aimed at planets of little consequence. The prizes of the Commonwealth would be taken carefully, the citizens indoctrinated. The Scientists were entangled in their own politics, but they were slowly becoming organized. A buffer around the seven stellar systems that were the basis of their aristocratic hold had been formed and maintained successfully.

Frank was constantly being apprised by encrypted hyper transmissions from Malcolm Simms. And he in turn had sent back notices of his constant failures. Producing Rold at this time would not stop the war. If he had only turned up before things had really gotten started! But Ruth Poundstone could not wait. Of course she was now considered a hero. And probably she was; her haste made possible the buffer, but it also allowed millions of casualties. Frank would not give up, though. He cursed the war and determined to find Rold at any cost to himself.

His transport landed with a bump and little notice. He was amazed at how unaffected by the war the planet and its people appeared. *They should enjoy it while it lasts,* he thought.

He exited into a gate area much like those constructed for passenger transports but much smaller. An idea blossomed and struck him as so elementary that he felt ashamed he had overlooked it. Sub-lumina! Rold is still here — somewhere in the Beldine system! With a little hope that sparked a modest amount of enthusiasm, Frank walked into the Industrialist world again.

A cool, morning breeze leaked into the bedroom that Rold and Yosana had chosen. Hides covered the windows and the door allowing a draft where there were not proper seals. The crisp air was a sign of autumn, and it felt good now, as a relief from the dry summer air, but Yosana warned that it was only a hint of the bitter cold that was coming. With the draft yellow beams of sunshine also leaked into the little room beckoning the lazy lovers from their bed. For two days they had rested there, made love there, taken their food in bed like honeymooners. They talked and talked, telling stories of their childhoods, their hopes and dreams — no matter how ludicrous that seemed under the circumstances — and explored each other physically until they were exhausted and slept the remainder of their time in bed.

Only once did they venture out, and that was to allow Rold the chance to view the museum and try his hand at the radio set. He sent a coded message over fifty different frequencies. But without a computer to automate the process, he tired quickly. A computer would allow him to maintain a continuous message over hundreds of frequencies, like a beacon. But all the computers from the original star ship were gone, and he had little hope that these few messages would alert Frank — who he hoped was listening. But perhaps it was just as well he could not automate the beacon: he was sure the Industrialists would pay little attention to a radio signal; however, it could be used as a homing signal.

The room was a single cell among a row of cells that half circled the main dome. From the window they could view a beautiful scene of snow-painted sierras rising above a green meadow partially planted with corn and beans. The camped villages were not in sight from this side of the Library, but the noise of activity made its way to the living quarters. The sound of the mass of people sparked a desire in Rold which burned slowly until the second day. He missed the crowded streets of Old Earth cities, and the Teton villages sounded and smelled so inviting that he finally could wait no longer. He dressed in clothes provided to him by the librarians: leather trousers, a linen tunic, a leather vest, and soft soled, leather boots which they called "feet." The outfit felt cozy and warmed his body down to his toes; he wondered if it would be too warm when the sun rose a little higher. Yosana dressed in the travelling clothes she had been wearing, though they had now been cleaned. Rold liked the glow on her face which she had acquired in the two days of rest. He started thinking about the other women he had had in his life. The list was short. When he was quite young, and his mother was still alive, he found girls to be good companions, good to talk to. But he had never fallen in love. As a man he had thought he loved a woman once. He found himself craving her presence: she was his opium. But she had tired of him and left to fulfill a career. His work had replaced her as his drug, and all his passion had been poured into it. It seemed healthier to him to vent his energy into hypothesis construction rather than something as fragile as a relationship.

"Tell me about your other women," Yosana said interrupting his thoughts. He was struck by the uncanniness of her statement, and it showed on his face.

"Is this a side affect of cloud riding?" he said. "You were reading my mind."

"So you were thinking of someone else then. I don't think I've ever been so insulted." He could see the starting of a grin at the corners of her mouth, though she was trying to hide it.

"You're so wicked," he said. "No, I wasn't thinking of anyone in particular. I was just thinking of how I've changed over the years. You've made me feel like a kid again."

"When your libido was alive and kicking?"

"There you go again reading my mind. How do you do that?"

"No magic. I just know you, from our ride and our travelling. I like you, Rold Simms."

"So long as we're not butting heads."

"Even then."

"Me too."

It felt good not to have to pretend to be sophisticated or mature and just relax and act as he really felt. Rold grabbed Yosana, picking her up, twirling her around; then they both fell onto their bed. As they did the skin-covered portal opened, and the Master Librarian and Blikki entered.

"At least you're dressed," Blikki said. "That's a step forward. Now how about joining the world again, you lazy bums."

"That's exactly what we were going to do," Yosana said. "Rold wants to see the villages. I thought I'd take him to Pentat's lodge to meet the family."

"That's what it looked like you were doing," Blikki said.

"Father!"

"May we accompany you?" Chaka said diplomatically.

"Yes, sir," Rold said. "I need to talk to you. I need to get a message off planet. We were hoping . . ."

"In time," Chaka said, "in time."

Rold stooped to exit through the portal with Chaka behind him.

"You'll have to work hard for a month to pay for your two days of food and rest," Blikki said. He slapped Yosana's backside as she climbed through the door.

"And I suppose you've been hard at work and fasting the whole time, eh, Father?" she said in return.

"Hard at work telling stories," Chaka said.

"Story telling *is* hard work," Blikki said.

"Rold has been out. But, yes, I've been lazy. I admit it."

Yosana hugged her father and planted a kiss on his cheek. For the first time Rold noticed that she was slightly taller than Blikki, and had to lean down a little to kiss him.

The foursome traveled through hallways lined with portals until Rold was quite lost. He had paid little attention to the route the day they arrived; Yosana had led him by the hand. But soon they were back in the large dome, an echo enhanced babble spreading through the room.

"Sir," Rold said as they wove their way through the islands of book-shelves, "I must warn you that there is another war, a potentially more dangerous war beginning in the Commonwealth."

"Yes," Chaka said. "Blikki has mentioned it."

"The civil war of the Commonwealth could be affected with the information I have."

"But is it not too late, Rold?" Blikki said. "Both sides have been itching for it for years. Things are moving, and it's going to take a lot of energy and probably a miracle to stop it."

"I know. But it could be shortened, lives saved. If my father knew what was going on here . . ."

"I don't know what you could do, Rold," Blikki said. "Your people are going to destroy each other surely as the sun will shine tomorrow."

"The outcome of the Teton revolt here will mean little if the civil war touches the frontier. Beldine could be turned into ashes. And the Industrialists are here for a reason. So many Militia running around. Don't you see? I have to make contact. With someone. I don't know how or with whom. You have radio transmitters here. But the chances that anyone would be listening to radio signals is slim."

"Antiques, yes," Chaka said.

"And then there's the problem of the Industrialists sensing the transmissions and locating the Library. I doubt they monitor radio frequencies. Of course neither will my friends. But it was worth an attempt."

Blikki clasped Rold's shoulder, his small, strong fingers massaging it. "Let us see Pentat. He may have a thought about it."

"I haven't given up, Blikki. But I have a lot to do, and there's little time."

"There's time," Chaka said. "Winter is coming. We must bring in our harvest, but after that the snows will come and our season of rest begins."

"The Industrialists will not rest," Rold said. He panicked for a moment at the thought of being hold up an entire winter before going into action. He began to regret following Pentat here.

"And neither will we," Pentat said as he climbed the Library steps to meet them.

Rold greeted him as if they had not seen each other for months. Pentat looked ten years younger, refreshed, and his smile was back. The cooler temperature had him wearing a vest over his tanned skin and leggings. His hair was loose with no headband or feather.

"Our lives continue to parallel, Mountain Bear," he said. "I think we've been spending the last two days in a similar form of relaxation."

"You seem well informed," Rold said.

"It's my job," Pentat said. "Come. Let me take you to my lodge. We have a gift for you — for you both."

He hung his arms around Rold's and Yosana's necks, sandwiching himself in between. They walked down a makeshift thoroughfare that formed down the middle of the collected villages. Each village had maintained its autonomy by setting up its own corral of pridda and circling its lodges. Chaka explained that a gathering of this size was unprecedented. It was not unusual for two or three villages to winter together, and in that case they would form a single circle. But it was decided not to combine villages here in order to avoid factions forming.

"The Teton must be united but maintain their individuality," he said.

This made no sense to Rold so he simply nodded.

The walk was taking some time so Rold could not wait any longer to begin his questions.

"What about the Industrialists troops?" he asked. "You seem to know something."

Pentat formed a serious expression and thought a moment before speaking.

"What I hear is very disturbing," he said. "The Whites have brought a race of monsters onto our world."

"Monsters?" Yosana said.

Rold stopped walking. "Zenians," he said.

"Yes," Pentat said. "Human-like creatures but very dangerous and very ugly, the messenger said. They don't sleep, ever. But they're only used to dry, hot weather, and so my scouts think they will suffer during our winter or at least have to be housed the entire time. I'm anxious to view one because my scouts' descriptions make little sense. There are female warriors among them they say who carry their young into battle in a pocket that is a part of their body. And if the warrior is in combat and is threatened, she aborts her live young to die on the ground. They're training in the western desert. The Whites don't seem to like them much, but they've brought them here anyway."

"But not to battle the Teton," Rold said. "They're here to train to kill Scientists. Do your scouts have an estimate of their numbers?"

"In the millions," Pentat said.

Yosana gasped. "How are we to fight millions?," she said. "And you look so cheerful, you . . ."

"She has a point. We can't fight so many — monsters or men."

"Let's go to Pentat's lodge," Chaka said. His vibrating voice had a calming effect on everyone. "We'll discuss this there." Yosana nodded her head and followed the men without talking.

A noon sun warmed them as they approached the Eagle village. It looked deserted. Pentat explained that a hunting party had gone out that morning, men and women, and the only ones still there were those who could not ride or were busy tending to their prescribed crafts. They came to the lodge which was a five-meter tall tent made of painted leather, ribbed with strong, slender wooden poles. The floor of the tent was a patchwork of fur rugs with some woven rugs where beds were made. The floor was round and almost ten meters across. At one side was a stove that had a chimney disappearing out a hole in the wall. The stove was carved from a giant gourd that was the height of a man. A modest fire smoldered in the belly of the stove where a crockery pot was filled with boiling soup. Pentat's wife sat tending the pot and only smiled as a greeting to the people entering her home. The baby was lying in a mess of blankets, his eyes wide open, his mouth gurgling.

"Mountain Bear," Pentat said. "Forgive me for not introducing you the night of our arrival. This is my wife, Tachina, and our son, Chomata-te."

"Hello," Rold said.

"I must thank you," Tachina said, "for bringing Pentat here. All of you — Yosana, Blikki — thank you. The Whites kept several of us captive in the hills. But they didn't know I was the wife of Pentat, or they wouldn't have let us go. But now we're here together. I am pleased to meet the dream-man."

"She means you," Pentat said to Rold. He had his hand on Rold's shoulder.

"Everyone," Tachina said, "please sit."

Yosana rushed to the baby with eyes sparkling. She picked him up and kissed him. "Oh, 'China, he's wonderful," she said. Tears were beginning to redden her eyes. "He looks just like you, so beautiful. Thank goodness, he looks nothing like that husband of yours."

"Humph," Pentat said.

He nudged Rold as the men sat in a circle on the floor. The gesture finally dawned on Rold. He looked at Yosana's glowing face and felt a trembling in his knees.

"Your face is pale, Rold," Blikki said. "Are you all right?"

Rold took a breath. Having a serious relationship with a woman was a new thing for him. But the thought of a child was something as scary as anything that had so far happened to him. He refused to think about it and shook his head.

Yosana sat beside Rold holding Chomata-te. Pentat pulled Tachina beside him by the hand, and she sat while taking the baby from Yosana for feeding.

"Yosana," Pentat said. "We wish to give you a lodge — to you and Mountain Bear."

Rold looked at the smiling faces around the circle. Yosana, though, looked serious.

"Rold doesn't know what that means," she said.

"Yes, of course," Pentat said. "If you don't accept it, I'll not be insulted. But for the time being I would like you to stay with the Eagles."

"I don't think you understand what Yosana is saying," Tachina said in her warm, soft voice.

"Oh," Pentat said,nodding his head. "Did I jump to conclusions? You did take him riding."

"Yes, but . . ." Yosana looked at Rold with worried eyes.

What are they talking about? Rold thought. *I certainly wouldn't mind staying here rather than at the Library. But what is the fuss?*

Then he knew.

"I understand. You're talking about marriage," he said.

He took Yosana into his arms.

"Pentat," he said still holding Yosana tightly. "I'm not sure what the custom is here, but I wish to have Yosana with me in our own lodge — for as long as I stay with the Teton. I thank you for your gift."

Yosana pulled back and stared at Rold, embling. Her expression was one of anxiety and stress rather than exuberance, but Rold could see she wanted the lodge. She turned to watch Pentat and then her father.

"Why ask?" Blikki said. "She always does what ever she damn well pleases anyway."

"Are you not pleased?" Yosana said, still troubled.

"I'm very pleased," Blikki said. "Damned pleased. You took him riding. What a question!"

She finally smiled and kissed Rold hard on the lips. "Are you sure you understand?" she said.

"Do I have a choice?" he said.

"But, Pentat," Rold said. "What can I give you in return? I have nothing any ore."

"You don't understand our ways," Pentat said. "Giving a gift is an honored gesture among my people."

"Yes, I know, and I don't want to insult you, but it is hard for me to accept. You've given me so much already."

"We'll talk of it later," Pentat said. "For now we must talk of war before the day gets too late. Chaka has been patient with us long enough this morning. There's much to do."

Rold looked at the Master Librarian sitting with hunched back and constant grin, or grimace — it was hard to distinguish. His wool robe draped about his shoulders, arms and chest as a father's clothes would swallow a young son who was playing dress-up. His silver hair fell to his shoulders, not limply but stiffly, coarse and uneven. Folds of skin circled his brow and jaw much like his baggy robe. Silence had come to the lodge. And before Chaka spoke he retrieved a small, leather pouch that was hidden inside his robe. The movements of his hand were calculated and graceful; his black eyes fixed on

Rold, unblinking.

"This is a mystery bag," Chaka said. "It's my gift to the right-wing-of-the-eagle, the dream-man."

Rold began to protest, but felt pretentious in doing so. He accepted the gift without speech and attempted to keep his eyes fixed on the old man's eyes. Chaka then produced a second bag and handed it to Pentat.

"And for the left-wing-of-the-eagle, the Eagle chief," he said. "Rold Simms carries a part of you, Pentat, in his bag, and you a part of him, that you may be a part of each other always."

"Thank you, Grandfather," Pentat said.

"Yes, thank you," Rold said.

"Now," Chaka said. "We must speak of a plan. Our world has been invaded by Whites and an abomination. How will we be rid of them?"

"May I speak?" Rold said. Chaka nodded.

"I don't know the solution," Rold began, "but you need to understand the power of the Whites. Several million troops is frightening, I agree. And Zenians are inhumanly strong. But these troops are for controlling a population, not destroying it. If they want to destroy us, they can do it in a single stroke: nuclear explosives. They can split apart an entire planet or wipe out a single city. What I fear most, though, is the selective bombing of a small area."

"What are you saying?" Blikki asked.

"Having the villages winter together here at the Library was tactically all wrong. They could wipe out your entire population in a moment if they found this place, and if that was what they wanted to do."

"Nuclear bombs?" Tachina said, her face stricken. "Like on Earth? They would destroy the whole world with poison?"

"Well, no," Rold said. "Things have come a long way since the Nation Wars that you've heard about. They have radiation sponges these days. The real power of a nuclear explosion is heat radiation; that's what does all the damage. The particle radiation can now be cleaned up so an ecosystem isn't totally destroyed. So, they could bomb the Library, drop a radiation sponge over a fifty kilometer radius and be rid of us, and not really harm the rest of Salkinia at all."

"Describe this 'sponge,'" Chaka said.

"That's just what it's called. It's actually little pebble-sized chips of a material that absorbs radiation and becomes inert. They dump tons of it over the area from jetcraft. It's light and floats for hours in the air.

"I fear this tent city will be discovered."

"Yes," Chaka said calmly, evenly. "Any ideas, Pentat? Blikki?"

"I'm getting old," Blikki said. "I'll not jeopardize your leadership position, son. I promised you that standing on that damned hill. But Rold is right; the Whites will simply snuff out the Teton like so many trees that need to be cleared for farming. Can we fight against so many?"

Pentat grew red, but did not throw angry words back at Blikki.

"I know what we must do."

"You do?" Rold said.

"The Whites are going to destroy all of the Teton. And we will make sure that it will happen."

"Make yourself clear," Chaka said.

"Of course! You have a place in mind?" Rold said to Pentat.

"First Colony. Hundreds of winters ago it was a thriving settlement — back when the first of our people tried to stay in one place. But year after year the game — pitah, boars, and birds — began to thin and learned not to come too close to First Colony. The hunters had to travel farther and farther. Finally the settlers took up an ancient practice of following the pitah. They built lodges that could be packed and moved. They would be at one place in summer and another in winter. And they began breaking up into smaller groups: the moves were cumbersome with a large village. And so we have done for winter after winter, though some have settled into farming or fishing. First Colony was abandoned but is still considered a holy place, much like the Library.

"We must trick the Whites into thinking the Teton have all gathered for winter at First Colony, not at the Library. It's not uncommon for several villages to meet there; it's a good place to winter. It should be believable. Then we must get the Whites to make a nuclear strike on the site, either through provocation or intrigue. They must think they have destroyed us, destroyed us all."

"You understand, there would be nothing left of your First Colony," Rold said. "No artifacts or ruins. Nothing."

"It's a sad thing," Chaka said setting his emptied plate aside. "But it must be believable. In fact, it makes more sense than this preposterous gathering at my Library. And if we can manage this we'll have gained the initiative, much power."

"Is it possible?" Yosana asked. "So many details! How are we going to make it look like thousands of Teton are camped at First Colony? And what would make them bomb it?"

"Yes, that's a point," Rold said. "We must force them into it. And they must believe they have succeeded."

"Yes," Blikki joined in. "We'll need spies. It's the only way."

"As I was thinking," Pentat said. "A diplomatic delegation should go to Minpana to throw down the gauntlet, anger them. The Whites have been trying of late to seduce us into joining them in their space war. We must flatly refuse and make our position clear. Then spies can plant the information about the gathering."

"We need to also consider what happens after the bombing," Yosana said. "Let's say it works — this deception actually works. How can we use that to our advantage? They'll have expended a bomb or two, but no one will be hurt, hopefully, on their side or ours."

"The main thing we'll accomplish is protecting our people here at the Library," Pentat said. "The random raids on scattered villages will stop, because we'll all be together here, and the Whites will think we're all dead. We'll be free to plan our offense with some time on our side. This won't be a quick war, my family, unless the gods intervene. And on top of it all we must still live through the winter, feed ourselves."

"Winter is almost here," Chaka said. "When will this illusion be posed?"

"No more than a quarter moon," Pentat said. "Less if possible; before snow falls on the plateau. I want Blikki and Bana to begin setting up scrap lodges in circles around the city. Someone should bring pridda there and set up camp fires. As many details as we can think of must be added to insure a believable gathering of Teton. The Whites don't know of our numbers. We don't have to pretend to have as many people as there truly are. I'll lead the expedition."

"And will we get them there, with bombs no less?" Yosana said.

"We could use Rold as bait," Pentat said. "And myself. Perhaps Chaka is wrong, and they're still concerned with Rold and me. We can have our spies give information about our whereabouts, and they can say I'm planning an attack."

"This could be dangerous," Chaka said. "What you plan on telling the Whites is too close to the truth. First Colony is not far from here for their flying machines."

"They'll not find the Library," Pentat said. "They won't even be looking for it."

"Well then, let's get started," Blikki said. "At least we've got something concrete to do, and it doesn't even sound too dangerous. So 'China girl, how about something to drink to wash down this talk."

"Certainly, Father," Tachina said. She dipped a golden liquid into gourd cups and passed them around.

"I guess I was getting a bit restless," Blikki said. "It'll be good to get back to the trail and have some work to do." He held up his cup. "Here's to Yosana and Rold: May you be as happy as your mother and I were when we lived with the Teton."

Everyone drank. Rold choked and coughed. "This has alcohol in it," he said. Laughter circled the lodge.

"It's beer," Yosana said. "You'll have to drop some of your prejudices if we are to stay here for any length of time. You've insulted Tachina."

"Forgive me," he said. "I wasn't expecting it." He swallowed his pride and a small sip of the warm beer. It was not as unpleasant as he had first thought.

"So much to do," Tachina said.

"Yes, I will gather the chiefs . . . ," Pentat started to say.

"No," she interrupted. "I mean for Yosana's lodge. We'll give a feast for our village in celebration."

"Of course," Pentat said. "Father, we'll have to do some miraculous hunting in the next few days if your daughter is going to have a proper celebration.

"You'll have to accept it, Mountain Bear. We have all managed to live through such a feast. But there's something I must ask of you that will require more courage then taking a lodge with my sister."

"Yes?" Rold said. "Anything, Pentat. I am in your debt."

"I want you to accompany me on a spirit quest. I was interrupted on my last trip to the buttes, and I feel I need to prepare myself for the coming labors. When Teton are young their first spirit quest is performed with friend, and they share their pain dream. The experience is a cleansing one and produces a lucidity of thought that's necessary for planning a war — or considering a wife. I ask that we share this."

"I have no idea what it entails, but I'll go with you," Rold said.

"Good," Chaka said. "If Pentat had not mentioned it, I would have. Yosana, you'll have to wait on your lodge for a while. I suggest that Pentat and Rold Simms begin their journey in the morning. While they're gone we'll begin preparing for the trip to First Colony. I would also ask that the lodge feast be delayed until after the work is done. Time is running out."

Yosana accepted postponing the move to the village with little thought. She was now thinking more of Rold's spirit quest, and looked at him with proud eyes. She realized he had no idea to what he had agreed. He was so naive, and so foolish for rushing into the unknown for the love of a friend. But that was what made her proud.

A cold, howling wind whipped through the closely sprouted young white barked trees. The straight trunks striped the dark horizon like a fence, bordering the swampy meadow. The Zenians were moody in this cold, crisp air. Their e-suits protected them, but this high elevation was unnerving. They were used to flat desert, as on their home world, or the urban battle fields of the crowded human worlds. Chilly mountain forests were hated and feared.

They were drawn to Tyler's fire.

"How many are you?" Tyler asked the leader, as she chewed on raisins she had found in the forest that day.

"Like the stars," he grunted. "We train . . . to kill Scientists like you!"

"Why don't you kill me?" She looked at him with courage though her heart raced within her chest.

"You are prize. For Meacom. Also, you are . . . unusual. Not supposed to be here. No Scientists on this rotting planet. Why are you here?"

She did not answer.

Growls went up around the camp. The sky was full of clouds; a storm was coming in. Tyler looked up to see at what the giants were pointing. Living clouds! Her breathing increased. At first they seemed to blend in with the real clouds but they moved faster and closer to the ground. The Zenians sensed they were organic. Several fired blasts into the sky, the energy streams piercing a living cloud, seemingly without harm. For it passed slowly across the sky undisturbed. A large one stopped directly overhead. It was awash with flashes of light as it descended. The Zenians went crazy blasting the thing.

While all attention was on the living cloud, Tyler grabbed a blazing stick from the camp fire. She attacked the leader from behind, searing a hole into his suit at the neck as she beat him fiercely with the brand. He turned as if to simply swat her aside but then felt the heat on his neck. He started dancing about as he grabbed his neck, trying to arrest the flames. His helmet came off the top part of his suit ripped down to his waist. Tyler jumped at him and pulled a blaster from his belt then stepped back and blew a hole through his chest. He toppled, it seemed in slow motion.

The remaining troops turned and watched their leader crumble into a heap and cried out in rage. Tyler turned to run to the woods, still holding the blaster. She stumbled over a rotting log then decided to make a stand behind it, blasting wildly toward the group. In seconds the fallen log was aflame from the Zenians return fire. She thought she was dead. A few disconnected thoughts about her restive attempt to escape and its failure blinded her to what was to come.

The living cloud that had been descending came to the ground between Tyler and her assailants. A quiet returned to the meadow. It was the quiet that finally awakened Tyler from her thoughts of death and failure. She looked at the ugly mass of the living cloud. A diamond pattern of lights rotated in front of her. As before, on the la'Kunda transport, Tyler placed her palm in the middle of the diamond. But this time she was actually touching the flesh of the creature. Cilia crept into the pores of her hand, swiftly shooting into her arm. She felt her arm going numb, to her elbow then to her shoulder.

"You are safe," a voice said within her.

Tyler wanted to jerk her arm away but the desire was quelled by the intrusive cilia. She felt she would swoon at any moment.

"Mother?"

"No, Tyler. I'm Gwydmonia. You know me."

"Yes . . ."

"The abominations that held you are no more. You are free. Go now. Find Rold."

"But where? Where am I?"

A rush of images riveted Tyler's mind. She saw the mountains, plains and desert from above. The sensation of flying enveloped her as the images changed rapidly. She saw the meadow where she had camped then followed a trail to an alpine plateau covered in trees and house-sized granite boulders. Moving eastward the trail led down into arid, rocky foot hills then onto a scorched desert.

"Here, Tyler," the voice said. And Tyler could see the ruins of a city. Crumbled buildings with no roofs sat along streets that were the spokes of a wheel: the outer boundaries of the city made a perfect circle.

Then the living cloud released its clutches on Tyler. Her hand fell loosely at her side; her arm tingled. The living cloud rose and the cold wind rushed in. Left on the dark ground were several bodies, the corpses of Zenians, barely recognizable.

Tyler slowly crossed the meadow, averting her eyes when passing the mangled bodies. She found her campfire still blazing but soon low on fuel. Dropping a couple of large pine knots on the fire, she lay beside it, cradling her head as she watched the flickering yellow tongues of flame and quietly fell asleep.

CHAPTER 12

The dreamers dreamed in snow and ice
And the Eagle did appear.

- From "The Song of Margona"
 by Pitallela-Sim

Ruth Poundstone paced the war room floor dressed in infantry armor that was designed especially for her; it was molded to make accommodating bulges where bulges were needed. She caught her reflection in a wall-sized display screen and laughed at how silly she looked. It was the first time she had realized it.

A man entered dressed in Committee robes. She turned on him quickly.

"You're late," she said. "The war council will be here at any moment."

"I only just arrived to Collinsville," he said.

"What do you have to tell me of Frank Diego?"

"We lost him once. He left Caljunna secretly about a month ago, and our people couldn't find him. But we were lucky, and he returned to Caljunna. An agent spotted him at the space port."

"Very lucky. Now go on."

"He then entered the city on a lead he somehow got at the port. But then he rented a flat in the city and is maintaining a semblance of living and working there."

"Do you think he's on to something?"

"He seems to be waiting on someone to return, a gate attendant who's away."

"So you've been monitoring him."

"Yes. And this time we put a homing device on his cargo transport."

"Good. I know that man is reporting to Simms, but Simms isn't sharing any of the details. We have to handle this delicately. Any information that would link us with the abduction must never get out, and Diego has become a potential threat. But also I'm convinced that wherever Rachel Meacom took Rold Simms is their strong hold. In that blasted frontier somewhere they're preparing. These little attacks on unguarded planets are just tests.

They must be getting ready for an offensive.

"You must leave. Keep me informed on Diego. He'll lead us there, I know it."

The man left as quickly as he had come, leaving a coded report with Ruth. Within a few moments the council began assembling. Ruth paced until all were present. Malcolm Simms sat at the table, alone, while the others milled about fishing for information on opinions. He looked haggard as usual, but more than that he looked as though he was fading like a shadow as the sun sets. Ruth was confused by his appearance, his apathy. Such devotion was beyond her comprehension, thus was suspect of having any rational grounds. He did have enough energy to call the meeting to order, but from there Ruth took over. She was actually grateful for Malcolm's loss of command, for she could now have full control of the war effort. It was not so only a few weeks before. Then he was still making decisions, questioning expenditures, strategy. But soon he had begun losing hope, and pieces of vitality dropped from him as rotting flesh; now the worms were having their turn.

"Any announcements?" he asked. The procedures were so routinized now that a recorded voice or an ape could have been substituted.

"Two more weeks and all evacuations and placements will be completed," one man said.

"Manufacturing management training classes start in two days," another said. "All intermediate supervisors on Newert are to attend. Twelve hundred classes have been organized."

Silently everyone looked around for anyone to speak.

"Who has the program today?" Malcolm said.

"I do," Ruth said. "We're to begin our offensive planning."

"Are we ready for that?" one asked. "How stable is the defense? Aren't the renegades still gobbling up planets?"

"It seems that effort has slowed," she said. "I have information that points to a regrouping by the Industrialists. They seem to be preparing for their own large scale offensive. I'd say Newert, Tridia, the Holofax systems, and straight on to Old Earth."

"That sounds very ambitious, Ruth," Malcolm said. "Do you think the push will come soon?"

"They're building a new base, new weapons factories, and training grounds; this we learned from at least three sources. It'll only be a matter of months before they're ready."

"And where is all this taking place?"

"That we don't know as yet. But we're very close to finding out. In my opinion we're better prepared at the moment, further along in arms and training. In fleeing, the Industrialists have left several of the heavy industry planets in our hands. That's why I am proposing an offensive of our own. As soon as we know the location of their base we should attack."

"Slow down now, Ruth," another man said. "Yes, we have the factories, but we don't know anything about producing weapons — even though we've been stumbling along okay. And as far as training goes, yes, we're making a good effort. But Industrialists don't need training. They can put together a full-fledged factory in days and have it running at capacity. And they have troops already: Zenians."

"The Zenians are ground troops to be used for invasions. They can be wiped out quickly from close space bombing. If I could present my graphics, I think you'll understand my position more clearly."

"Very well, Ruth," Malcolm said. "Show us all the gruesome details. Anything that will prevent a protracted conflict would be welcomed."

Everyone nodded. And as Malcolm Simms' eyes began to glaze, Ruth threw up her presentation with animated gestures and the smile and enthusiasm of a salesman.

Rold found the lodge that Yosana and he had been given very comfortable. It was smaller than Pentat's but was accommodated in much the same way. He looked around at the tent walls, the fur carpet, stove and beds and wondered at the vast time spent of human labor. Just knowing that human beings - specifically Tachina, and perhaps some relatives — had made all that surrounded him produced a solemn awe that surpassed any impression he had ever had of rich palaces made from the work of machines.

The day had been long, and the soft bed pulled at every muscle with a song of sleep. Yosana had lagged behind at Pentat's home, and Rold fought sleep waiting for her to come into their new home. She took so long that he became irritated, but all anger was forgotten the moment she entered.

"I'm awake," he said. He had started a small fire from twigs in the stove before undressing, and a red ember still glowed, the soft light dancing against the walls and Yosana's face.

She seemed distant, a two dimensional painting against the domed tent cover.

"I was waiting for you," he said. "What is it? There's something wrong. Come, sit here with me."

Yosana dropped to her knees and crawled to Rold's arms. He asked no questions, which made her smile at how understanding this man could be at times, for she knew how hard it was for him to stay silent.

"We're living in sin," she said.

"That's an archaic phrase. In all my life I don't think I've heard anyone say such a thing. Is that how you feel?"

"Yes . . . no. I don't know. On the trail, in the Library we were still citizens of the Commonwealth. Here in the village though, my sleeping with you isn't approved."

"Your own brother, the chief of chiefs, gave us this lodge. Certainly he doesn't object. What am I missing?"

"I know how these people think, and I've been getting looks all day."

"But it's more than that, isn't it?"

She took his face in her hands, feeling his rough beard against her palms. "You don't know me," she said. "I don't know you, not really. The cloud ride opened you up to me, but I don't really know you. I love you; I know that. But I worry about whether . . . whether I'm worthy of you."

"Having cold feet?" he said and laughed, then stopped as he saw her trembling lips.

"Who really knows one another?" he said. "Yes, there are things we need to learn about each other if we're to be together. But I'm ready to learn."

Yosana laid her head on his chest and relaxed her body beside him.

"I've loved two other men in my life," she said. "The first time I was very young, and the man was twice my age. I had run away from my father to live in the White city. I hated the desert on Caljunna. The people there had no sense of who they were. The Whites have destroyed whatever Teton was left in them. They no longer know how to live without the White's products, and so their poverty is true poverty. Children are sick and hungry. After living here with the Eagle village as a child, Caljunna was hell. I loved my father, as I do now of course, but I chose the Whites' world. Caljunna was too much in between. I felt that living among the Whites, passing as a White, would be better.

"So I ran away with a wholesale grocery salesman. And don't laugh; at least I ate well. I realize it doesn't sound very romantic, but at first it was. He was an Industrialist but a fairly educated one, and he was infatuated with my young body. But once we were in the city he changed. There are no visible scars now, but he was a violent man when on drugs. A very lonely, sad person. I tried living by myself in the city, but it was too lonely and too confining for me. So I went back to Father. The desert looked better to me then. My memory of Salkinia had faded a bit.

"Father decided I was old enough to accompany him on his trips. He was lonely too. We missed Mother; he especially did. My memory of her isn't very good now. I remember Father grieving the most."

"I guess I was lucky," Rold said, "having a family, a privileged one at that. I know I'm spoiled. But Pentat said something to me about not glorifying a hard life or being ashamed of having it easy."

"Sounds like him."

"Well, what of the other man? You said two."

"The other was a short romance also. He was younger than I. Alfie Gridna was his name. A scared little boy, but so precious. We had a summer together in Caljunna. We did everything together: hiking, camping, working on equipment for Father, shopping, everything. I loved him, I think, more as a brother, but he worshipped me. So much so that I felt guilty all the time and worried about taking advantage of him, which I'm sure I did. I was his first love. And then at the end of the summer he was drafted by the Militia, and I never saw him again. Never another word."

"Such sad stories."

"Not really. Any love that doesn't last seems sad, but each one makes you grow. The pain can be as rewarding as the ecstasy."

"You amaze me," Rold said and kissed her forehead. "Are all Tetons philosophers?"

"I'm no philosopher; that's your expertise. By the way, what do you really do for a living? I've never understood."

"It's boring, really. I can get excited about it when I accomplish something that requires some hard work. But all-in-all, it's rather ordinary. My whole life has been ordinary until recently."

"There you go avoiding talking about your work. Do you dislike it that much, or do you think I'm too stupid to understand it?"

"No, Yosana, I'm sure you would have no problem with the concepts, but really, I just thought you were being polite. But if you insist . . ."

"I insist. But first let me get under the covers with you. I'm freezing."

The fire had burned down to orange speckled ashes, and a bright moon lit the lodge with blue light through seams and folds in the coverings. Yosana slipped under the pitah skin that covered Rold and placed her icy, bare feet against his thighs. He moaned in complaint.

"I guess I have to expect this," he said.

"What else are men for?" she said and settled back into his arms. "All right, tell me about what a professional philosopher does."

"What it amounts to is constructing hypothesis. You see, a scientist may have a project in mind that he wants to study. Or an Industrialist firm has some project with no known engineering solution. A philosopher is hired to develop a system of theories based on his knowledge of physics and then the scientist performs the experimentation to prove the theories. The engineers then take the results and build whatever it is the Industrialist wants. It's the natural cycle of technology. An example is, say, the gravity simulator. A philosopher named Harlan Cole originally hypothesized that energy could be converted into matter and concentrated into a grid that would produce a two-dimensional field having gravitational characteristics. It really sounded silly a thousand years ago. But once there were mechanisms for creating that heavy grid of matter, it worked."

"Yes, I see. It's a matter of specialization."

"Exactly. I guess the distinction for a philosopher is that he has to be creative."

"What have you worked on? What kind of projects?"

"That's the boring part. Waste recycling systems. Transportation through fluid atmospheres. Nothing very important."

"What were you doing on Caljunna?"

"Atmosphere stimulation. Caljunna is in a transition phase. In another ten thousand years it could be a dead planet: little or no atmosphere. Each year there's fewer and fewer photo organisms; and less rain fall. I had an idea that the planet could be stimulated into releasing water to its surface, and then algae could be introduced to start a new biological cycle for producing oxygen."

"Did you do it?" she asked with a yawn.

"I didn't do anything. I came up with some theoretical possibilities. It all really depends on inducing fragmentation of the planet's crust by injecting a large amount of energy into the magma. This would release water to the surface, reforming oceans. It's all possible . . ."

Rold stopped for a moment. Yosana was sound asleep. He had sensed it from her breathing.

"You see," he whispered, "I warned you it was boring." He kissed her lightly on her sweet smelling hair then let the cool, quiet night steal away his consciousness, leaving him in a heavy sleep with only a few roaming, harmless dreams.

The next morning he was awakened by a scratching at the entrance to the lodge. Trying not to wake Yosana he pulled on a wool robe and crawled to the round flap that was the door. Pulling it aside he saw Pentat crouched, dressed in leggings and a vest. Dawn was moments away. The sky was still dark overhead, and a slim, pink line rimmed the horizon of evergreen trees and jagged mountains. Dew was on everything and began forming on Rold's nose as he stuck it out of the tent. Pentat signed that Rold should dress and follow him, quietly. Rold went back in, kissed Yosana and carefully stepped into his new leather clothes. Although he tried to be quiet, he tripped over the threshold and shook the lodge, falling to his hands and knees on the entry mat. Pentat ignored him, tolerantly, and led them to the perimeter of the camping villages. Rold could smell breakfast cooking in the air, but the villages were still mostly quiet. They entered a lone, wooden lodge, of moderate size which must have needed several trees, cut and split, to build. Inside was a fire with little flame but hot glowing coals and a sink of smooth river rocks. The room was thick with steam.

"We must cleanse ourselves before we travel on our dream quest," Pentat said. "This is a sweat lodge. It's an ancient practice brought to this world on the great journey. Have you heard of it?"

"Of course, as a health treatment. But you use this in some ritual fashion?"

"It makes the body pure and calms the mind."

The two men stripped to nakedness. Pentat ladled water onto heated stones producing the hissing steam that filled the room. The dampness mixed with the resins of the wood siding, infusing the air with a pungent odor. They sat there, adding fuel to the fire and water to the stones, keeping silent, dripping in sweat until salt muddied their skin, for several hours.

"It's time," Pentat said finally.

The afternoon had now slipped away, twilight washing over the gathering.

"We'll travel in the dark?" Rold asked as they dressed.

"While the moon is up. Then we will camp. Tomorrow we'll walk with the sun."

"And when do we . . . dream?"

Pentat smiled and shook his head. "You don't even know what a pain dream is," he said and ruffled Rold's hair as if he were a young boy and hugged him with such force he almost pushed all the air out of his lungs.

"No, I don't," Rold said. "I just know it's something I have to do because you asked it. And I don't even know why."

Pentat motioned Rold to take off his vest and tunic. From a small bag he retrieved a small wooden bowl filled with gold paint. He began applying the paint to Rold and then himself, recreating the feathered drawings that he wore while in the Minpana Hold. He seemed disturbed by Rold's beard. He stopped and began shaving it off with his knife. Rold stiffened at the attack. He had no special attachment to his beard; he had one simply because he had not had the opportunity to shave. But this hacking by Pentat was embarrassing if not painful. He did not want to lose his nose or ears in the process. He motioned to his face but could not find the words he needed. Pentat laughed and began rubbing grease into his beard. This at least made the shaving a bit more comfortable. Once done he finished the paint job.

"Now we go," Pentat said. Rold followed him out of the lodge and onto a northern path. He felt self-conscious in the body paint, and his beardless face pleaded for rubbing, but the paint was a part of whatever they were doing, and he was determined not to spoil the experience.

"Where now?" Rold asked. The moon hung low before them and shone on their faces as they trudged along the gravel trail.

"We'll go to those bluffs over there," Pentat said. "It'll take until midnight."

Rold looked to the northeast and saw some rocky hills about twenty kilometers away. They had to cross a gently rising meadow with few trees, so the hike would not be hard.

"What's the purpose of having a pain dream?" Rold asked.

Pentat laughed. "Must you start your questions so early in the journey?"

"I'm following you to god knows what end. I'd like to know what I'm getting into."

Pentat thought for a moment. Rold listened to the rhythm of their feet crunching the fine gravel of the path and the riot of birds and insects that were so noisy at twilight. A stillness had fallen on the meadow, and the smell of grass and leaves was strong.

"A pain dream is a planning tool," Pentat said finally. "In preparing for an event such as a battle, a hunt, or a joining, there's a need for awakening the soul from its lazy complacency. A good slap in the face to jar loose some protected thoughts. Dreaming does this, and also it can give insights not only concerning what you are or have been but what you will be — what is possible."

"These last couple of months have been a pain dream of sorts for me," Rold said. "If I understand what you are saying. Tyler, the war, have definitely slapped me awake."

"Yes, that's the idea. But that energy of awakening has to be concentrated, precisely, in order to provide enlightenment rather than confusion. Though I'd say nothing in this world will ever satisfy all the infinite questions that lie inside your head, Mountain Bear."

"Every question that is answered generates more questions. I can't help it."

As the evening wore on Rold's body started giving signals of fatigue and routine hunger — having left with no meal for the entire day. He paid little attention to it at first; the meadow offered many distractions. A monkey rabbit jumped between the two men once; birds were everywhere. Rold was engrossed in observation in the moonlight. His heart fluttered at hearing the whoosh of a dozen birds flying close to the ground, heading east. By midevening they had to ford a wide, shallow stream which felt icy through his soaked boots.

"Are we going to stop and eat?" Rold said.

"A part of the ritual is fasting. We have no food with us."

"Oh."

"It's necessary to produce the right effect. If you want to turn back, you may. There's no pressure from anyone back there for you to continue. I won't lose respect for you."

"You would be disappointed." Rold was smiling. His affection for Pentat would not allow him to be angry. He felt honored that Pentat wanted him along on this adventure.

"Don't worry," Rold said. "Fasting is something I do well. I can adjust my metabolism fairly rapidly. But what other surprises do you have in store for me?"

"None really. But it'll perhaps take days of fasting and probably some cold nights before we can return."

Midnight came and Pentat found a rock to block the wind. Here they sat for a while and spoke of their lives and the war to come. But soon they were asleep. Rold dreamed. But when he awoke, he knew that it was just a normal dreaming: confused scenes of the past few days and thought of his father — and Tyler.

Pentat had them moving again, before the sun had fully broken free of the horizon. The cool morning wore on with little talk. Their feet simply plodded, one after the other. The mountain meadows on this plateau were full of beauty. Late summer flowers spread out before them. Creatures large and small swarmed in the sunshine. Rold was hypnotized by the idyllic sur-roundings when suddenly the monotonous buzzing around them was silenced.

Pentat stopped still and quickly motioned Rold to the ground. They both dropped to their knees.

"The wind is against us," Pentat said. "It's too late."

"What?"

"Our scent has been blown to the enemy. Pitah."

Rold finally heard the rumbling. Three brown specks approached from the hills leaving a cloud of red dust. Soon they were visible, about three hundred meters away. They stopped abruptly, their heavy bodies shaking the ground. The dust billowed about them then settled slowly; the animals snorted from breathing the cloud. Then they trumpeted their arrival. Pentat said it was a challenge or battle cry. The pitah knew there were men in the grass; they could smell them but not yet see them. Pentat and Rold had no weapons except their knives. Pentat began searching the ground for stones. Rold crawled to a low, woody shrub and broke off two limbs. He stripped them of twigs and returned to Pentat. Pentat then began sharpening the ends of the sticks.

"This will have to do," he said. "Throw stones first. If we throw fast and hard, many stones, they may scare off. If not we must defend ourselves with these sticks.

"I seem to draw trouble every time I plan a dream. I'm sorry I have endangered you, Mountain Bear."

Rold did not speak. Sweat was now streaking through the golden paint on his face and chest. Wild animals were not foreign to him; he knew that most of them were afraid of human beings, even the large dangerous ones. But he had heard of bloody species that were vindictive and killed for no good reason, much as humans had in their history.

The pitah charged. Pentat and Rold began tossing pebbles and stones, shouting as loudly and as angrily as they could. The animals did not slow nor even swerve. The men began to run. Pentat motioned Rold to one side, and they both jumped to a boulder just as the pitah made their pass. Rold impatiently threw his stick, inexpertly, at them as they rushed by. It was broken under their hooves. The pitah overran the men by a considerable distance before being able to stop and turn.

"Pray," Pentat said.

Rold closed his eyes. Then he heard a peculiar sound: a crackling or clapping, like several whips cracking. He opened his eyes and saw a flash of light in the sky, flicking on and off and coming close to them. The pitah stopped and fled in terror. As the light came closer Rold could see that it was an electrical arc flashing, like lightning, between two points in the sky. And as it was upon the pitah he could tell that the two points were the heads of two huge birds. They looked like vultures with wing spans of three meters. They flew close together and occasionally would look at each other at which time the bolt of electricity would jump from one to the other. The pitah were running scared, but the birds corralled them; then they forced one between them and sent the arc through the poor beast. The smell of burning hair and flesh made Rold's stomach heave. The pitah dropped with a thud that sounded like an avalanche. The other two pitah came down in the same manner. The birds let out a screech that echoed against the bluffs, which were now close by. Each attacked its own buffalo, ripping away the soft underbellies of the carcasses with their powerful beaks.

Rold collapsed onto his back, breathing rapidly.

"I thought we were dead," he whispered. "Even though they rescued us, I'm more afraid of those birds, I think." He panted and wiped sweat from his face, smearing his paint. "They're just like Orian condors. They have an electrical charge defense system. I've seen them in zoos. It's amazing that a similar species would evolve here . . ."

Pentat grabbed Rold's mouth and signaled silence. He nodded his head and forced his heart to slow and his limbs to relax, and he eased his breathing. He could see that Pentat was angry and frightened. He kept looking at the sky. Rold signed a question about seeing more birds, and Pentat gave a negative reply. Rold then asked with his hands if they were still in danger. Pentat explained, with many gestures, until Rold understood, that the birds would think that the men were trying to steal their food and would attack if they showed themselves while the birds were eating. He also explained that the birds would gorge themselves so that they could bring food back to their family. It was not normal for either the pitah or these condors to be in this meadow this time of year. That was the reason for his sudden moody behavior.

The birds became irritated and squawked and fought with each other for a few minutes. Then with loud, slow battings of their wings they left the buffalo and flew low to the ground in a wide circle that crossed over the men. Pentat was rigid, kneeling and sitting on his heels; Rold remained on his back, holding his breath. But the birds maintained their circling pattern until they were high above the meadow. As they finally disappeared Rold felt a chill; then a few rain drops splashed him like icy needles. He sat up and saw that the rain was actually snow flakes a meter or two above the ground which were melting on impact.

"Is this why they left?" Rold asked out loud.

"Yes. The snow is early this year; a double moon early. But it's too warm to stick."

"Will we go back?"

"No. We must go on."

Pentat looked at Rold as if a bolt of lightning would connect between the two men at any moment as with the strange birds.

"We are cold. And we have almost been killed and eaten. This will be a most powerful dream we'll have. But not a pleasant one I think." Snow flakes caught in his hair, and his wet shoulders looked like they were coated with ice.

"Is a dream worth death?" Rold said as they both stood, helping each other. "Hypothermia is a real threat, as real as those birds or the pitah. And pneumonia. These are sicknesses caused by exposure to cold weather."

"Yes, I know, Mountain Bear. I'm not a child. I'll not let us die. We're not meant to die or we would be dead now and food for hatchlings."

They began walking again. Pentat brought them back to the trail. Rold followed with questions hanging silently in his open mouth.

"The birds you called condors," Pentat said as they hiked and the sun touched the southwestern ridge of the mountains, "are named here after an Earth legend, *bombosorn*, thunderbird."

Rold laughed. "Of course."

"When the early settlers first saw them they thought that they had found the home of the gods, that the ancient legends must all live here: the thunderbird, pitah, feathered serpent."

"Oh really? There's a feathered reptile native to Salkinia?"

"Yes, but they live mostly on the southern shores of our land, where the air stays warm all winter."

Rold was too tired to continue talking. He managed to stay up with Pentat by sheer disposition alone — by placing one foot in front of the other.

In two more days they reached the bluffs and climbed the red sandstone until Pentat found a flat area where they could sit and gaze at the meadow below. The precipitation had stopped, but enough snow had clung to the ledge to make it cold and wet. As they both sat twilight darkened to night, but off in the distance, toward the eastern plateau a strange red light reflected against the low clouds, turning the sky red.

"A fire?" Rold said.

"Yes. It must be. And look, the lights of a jet flying into the clouds."

Rold saw the point of light that was slowly rising and disappearing.

"What are they doing?" he said.

"Damned Whites! I don't know, but it must be why the pitah were up in this meadow. They seldom come this high when it's cold. Damned Whites. They must be burning the grasses, killing the pitah, as an attack against us. They know it's our life that they threaten."

Rold could hear a very faint buzzing of engines from the jets.

"So close to the Library," he said. "I hope that our plan to decoy them isn't too late."

"They won't find the Library, not by air. It's very hard to fly in these mountains. But yes, it's uncomfortable how close they are. But worse, if they destroy the pitah . . ."

Pentat could not go on. Rold could see the sadness in his face. The red sky reflected against his golden skin and shining eyes. He wanted to express his sympathy but held back, not wanting to insult him. He could not feel the same pain, though. Intellectually he understood the importance of those raging beasts to Pentat's culture, but he still could not feel a part of his culture, could not truly understand the pain, and he assumed he never would. He tried to imagine losing something that meant as much to him as Pentat's way of life did to him. If he lost his people, his culture . . . *That's what has happened to me,* he thought. *Tyler. And Father.*

They were quiet for a while. The red sky faded as the night wore on. Rold was shivering and coughing. His eyelids burned and made him think that he had developed a fever, so he began his meditation to control the inflammation. A living cloud floated overhead toward the dying fire; its shadow fell upon the two men then drifted into the meadow. Rold was amazed with its silence. The only noise was that of the wind it created as it pushed through the air. It stopped at the far end of the valley; the sun that was hidden now still had enough rays to glance the top of the minah-machacute.

"The pitah," Pentat said.

Rold gave up his trance and looked at him.

"They're dead," Pentat said. "The Whites have destroyed them. And look at that cursed pile of floating shit! It just floats there staring down at the agony of those beasts and does nothing, as usual."

"How do you know they're dead?"

"Can you not feel it?"

The power of suggestion, Rold thought. If he let himself, he would be convinced that he too could visualize the slaughter in his mind. But no, he would not succumb to primitive superstition, no matter how accurate Pentat might be in his assessment. Rold preferred to give credit for good predictions to human analytical abilities rather than visions. He looked out toward the amber horizon.

"Why do you hate them so much?" he asked.

"The Whites?"

"No, the living clouds. You hate them so much that it has hurt your relationship with Yosana."

Rold's voice stammered from cold shivers, but he did not give up the appearance that everything was normal.

"They watched my family die," Pentat said. "And Yosana's mother, in the flood. Several people were trapped in a canyon when the flash flood came. I tried riding a pony into the canyon. The pridda had to swim most of the time, and finally I let it loose because my weight would have drowned it. I held onto a floating log and saved myself, but my mother, father, and Yosana's mother were thrown into the torrent and perished. I watched, and the minah-machacute watched."

"But what could they have done?"

"Anything! I prayed to them, screamed to them. They could have plucked my family from the canyon. They could have diverted the water, dammed it into another canyon. Anything! They had the power to save them, and they didn't."

"Do you think they wanted them to die?"

"Yes. Yes! I'm certain of it. They weren't enemies, but they wanted them to die; I could feel it. Not with hatred did they want this, but with cold blood, if they have blood. I can't explain it. And Yosana! She still rides. To this day."

"Does she know how you feel? Or what happened?"

"She must. But I can't talk to her about it. Please, I love her. You must know that. But I feel pain every time she talks of those demons with a smile in her eyes."

"But her mother was a rider. Certainly the minah-machacute would not purposefully have allowed her death."

"They act as they wish. No one can predict what they'll do."

Rold let it drop. He was still quite curious about these strange floating masses of flesh. His feelings for Yosana and Pentat produced an ambivalence that was typical for him. He had so few strong opinions — questioning everything but challenging none. He continued staring at the living cloud that hung so motionless and silent above the horizon until his eyes closed.

He had situated himself against a boulder that was robbing his body of heat, and his shivers woke him several times. But he finally drifted into sleep, exhausted. He dreamed as anyone dreams, with confused characters and settings and unlikely situations. But in an instant, as if someone had turned on a light, he found himself looking at a very real scene, with smells and sounds and people that he knew, including himself. They were in a battle for Minpana; Pentat was leading them against the Zenians. People were dying, blood on their faces.

Then above, in the sky, Rold could see the real battle. The horrifying scale of it stopped his heart, and silenced those around him. Dotting the sky from horizon to horizon, were rocket fighters and space destroyers, hundreds of thousands of them. They were doing battle, firing shots at each other until the sky was a solid sheet of light. They must have been several kilometers above Salkinia, for there was no sound. But in just a few minutes they began destroying each other. Debris came falling as meteors. Rold screamed at the horror of it: the millions of deaths. Several living clouds gathered above Minpana, seemingly watching the holocaust with their typical detachment. Rold cursed them, and Pentat walked toward him unaffected by the scene overhead.

"Why won't they stop it?" Rold said in his dream.

"What could they do?" Pentat said and reached out for Rold's hand.

Rold tried to take his hand, but it was only an illusion. Pentat stood before him like a translucent ghost. Then he transformed into an eagle and flew up to the battle. Rold looked up but was blinded by the light. Standing beside him, in Pentat's place was Tyler. She was smiling, but her smile made him sad not happy. He reached out to touch her.

"Are you awake?" Pentat said.

Rold opened his eyes again and realized he was staring at a very bright sun that had just risen above the far hills.

"Am I?" he asked.

Pentat laughed. "Yes. You no longer dream. It's morning, and the sun has melted the snow."

"Is that it? Was that the dream I came here to have?" Pentat appeared anxious. Rold assumed it was simply the cold and fasting that was causing such a mood. He was not so chipper himself.

"I don't know," Pentat said. "I had a dream, but . . . it was missing something."

Rold stretched and slowly stood up. Every muscle, every bone in his body ached, especially his stomach.

"Can we go home?" he asked.

Pentat smiled again. "Tell me your dream first. Did you see the Eagle?"

"Yes. At the end. It was you, I think. There were two battles: one at Minpana and one in space above the planet. The Teton fought on the planet then the battle in the sky began."

"And which of the two White armies won?"

"None. I think they were all destroyed. And you, you turned into an eagle. And I saw Tyler."

"As I thought. Well, let's climb down this rock. We'll be home early."

"So that's it, huh? I thought you said it would take days." "Perhaps the cold weather hastened it. The Eagle visited your dream, and that's all that matters. Now the air is warmer, so let's get back, Mountain Bear. We must plan our diversion before the snow really comes. I would like to have a peaceful winter to prepare for our first real battle in the spring."

Rold was confused. This was so much less than he expected.

"But I haven't learned anything," he said. "Am I not supposed to learn something from it? I want to understand."

"Your dream is very black. It could be a look at the future, showing much destruction, or it could be a warning, and there's something in it that will save us."

"If it is the future, it's my world that will be destroyed. This world is safe; in fact, you would be rid of the Whites."

"But at what cost? Millions of lives? No, that's not what I want."

"My friend," Rold said, looking into Pentat's eyes with both love and fear, "it might be the only hope for the Teton."

"You would kill millions of your own people?"

"No, no. That's not what I meant. I guess what I'm saying is you're fighting an enormous enemy which grows by the minute. It's not people you fight, but a force, a power. You will not win."

"Your dream tells us we will win. We'll see."

CHAPTER 13

Once there had been a gift from the earth,
Yaddamet, the dark vapor, transmuted our arrows
But all is lost . . .

- From "The Song of Margona"
  by Pitallela-Sim

The smell of rain had wakened Tyler; her body shivered in the early morning cold. After warming herself with exercise, she gathered supplies from the packs of the dead Zenians. Her fear and abhorrence had been supplanted by her determination to find Rold. Gwydmonia had instilled a courage in her that filled her with pride and awe, of herself and the living cloud. She chose a single pack and stuffed it mostly with water containers. And also she found a medium blaster with a strap that she slung over her shoulder. As she walked she examined the workings of the weapon, testing each setting, feeling the kick as it fired.

Navigating the hike was harder than she thought it would be. The image of the trail Gwydmonia had given her was like a map burned into her brain, but here on the ground, the trees, boulders and hills obscured the route. She felt like an insect on a highway. But with her natural sense of direction, along with whatever unconscious knowledge Gwydmonia had given her, she began to recognize the trail and grew more confident with each step.

She walked all day, eating only berries and drinking water. By late afternoon she was exhausted and starved. As she began setting up a small camp on a grassy hillside, she saw a large bird roosting beyond a boulder in the tall grass. She used a fine beam setting on the blaster and killed the cackling fat bird.

The blaster worked great for starting a fire, and before the sun disappeared she had roasted the bird and eaten the best meal she had had for two weeks.

Licking her lips, she lay back, drowsy and full, and looked at the stars as they came out of their hiding in the darkening sky. With the blaster beside her, a fire slowly crackling, and the night crickets chirping, she drifted off to sleep.

Rain drenched the Library and meadow for ten days. With each storm the mountains became whiter with snow until they looked like mounds of sugar, crystals sparkling in the light of day. A group of three hundred Tetons mounted their ponies at the first sign of sunshine breaking through the blue clouds. Wagons and litters were piled with artifacts gathered for dressing up the deception. Rold wondered at the terrible odds for this enterprise. Success would require more luck than anyone deserved — or could count on — even the noble Teton. But it was a morale builder, a single project to which everyone would contribute. It felt good. The weather had broken, and Rold was with his companions: Yosana, Blikki, and Pentat.

Pentat ordered the group to split up into a dozen smaller groups, each having to take a slightly different route to First Colony. This was not unusual for the Teton; they liked to keep the Whites guessing as to their numbers. This took a lot of effort and organization, but the results, though intangible, were an obvious benefit, especially now with the impending war. Rold's companions stayed together with fifteen warriors who were Pentat's body guard. Their course ran through the southern mountains, the range where Rold and Pentat had eluded their pursuers. Pentat explained that First Colony was on a large plain far to the east that once was covered in grass, but now it was more desert than grassland because of a change in climate. It only rained twelve centimeters a year there now, and only one big river flowed through the land which was fed by snow melt in the mountains.

The trip onto the plateau was much easier from the high meadow of the Library than it had been in the canyons east of Minpana. The air was cool and moist, and some snow was present among the evergreen trees that grew in thick groves beside the worn trail. The route took them into deep snow for only one day and then descended onto a dry, grassy plain that occasionally showed patches of alkaline soil and short, thorny bushes. They camped with no fire, eating preserved meat and fruit coated with either salt or sugar. The days were warm and dry and the nights cold and damp. Rold had to fight constantly with illness from the weather or the food, from Salkinia in general. Each new day brought new organisms which his body had to combat.

Pentat rode silently. The pridda were not so quiet; their bounding gallops made a thunder which stirred the insects and rodents from the trail a kilometer away. But Pentat remained grim.

Rold just hoped now that he would survive to see First Colony; a sweating fever had taken hold and was beginning to dehydrate him.

A bright, cool morning greeted the small company only a day from First Colony. But the refreshing weather did nothing to stir Rold. His legs were too weak to hold him erect; his head swam with the burning fever. Pentat stood at the entrance to his tent staring down at Rold and Yosana, a clump of warriors at his back.

"Childish behavior," Pentat said. "If you were going to shit yourself to death, why did you not stay at the Library!"

"Pentat!" Yosana said. Her eyes glowed green in the dark tent like a cat's.

He turned and stamped away. Rold was not sure he had heard him correctly or whether he was dreaming. But he tried to rise. Yosana pushed him down and called for Blikki. In a few moments he was there with a litter and began binding Rold to it.

"This was me only a few weeks ago," he said. "Now I'm fit and your poor boy here is sicker than a pile of garbage."

"Why is Pentat being such a bastard?" Yosana said as she forced a drug laced cup of broth down Rold's throat.

"He's under much pressure."

"Don't make excuses for him, Father. It's not Rold's fault that he's sick, and I'm sure Pentat has had warriors who have become ill on the trail. He should be here caring for him himself, damn it, if he's such a great leader. His problem is he needs to grow up."

"Get your people together, Father," Pentat said bursting into the tent. "We must leave now if we're to stop at the point pool." He then left just as abruptly.

"What's a point pool?" Rold said as he tried to sit, struggling against his bindings.

"You're awake," Yosana said.

"I'm not dead yet. What was that vile liquid you choked me with?"

"What do you mean?" she said.

"So innocent, aren't you. Well, you have me at your mercy and can perform your black magic on me at your whim."

"Don't complain," she said. "You're already responding. I think your fever has broken and . . ."

"And I've stopped babbling. I know. I been fighting it all night. Don't get so angry at Pentat. He's got a tough job and I'm making it tougher."

Yosana shook her head.

"Men. You always stick together."

"Let's get him out of here," Blikki said. "We do need to be moving on."

"You didn't answer," Rold said. "What's a point pool?"

"I've never seen one myself," Blikki said. "It's a thermal pool where the warriors get minerals for their weapons. I really don't know that much about it; it's not something they use except for war, and there hasn't been a war in a long time. I guess we'll see it soon, though."

The warriors erased the evidence of their presence at the campsite and began moving again. Blikki attached Rold's litter to his pridda while Yosana led Rold's mount. They both made sure that the company was not slowed by Rold's encumbering condition.

A light frost had pinched the tips of the short grasses early that morning but was now melting and evaporating. Limestone hills emerged eastward forcing the travelers to climb. Rold kept straining his neck, his body shaking from the effort, to see their path. The Teton seemed to know where they were going though he could not tell where a trail might exist. The hills were a rough and wild area, brambles and boulders slowing their progress. Midday brought a halt; everyone was quiet with no effort at preparing a meal or resting the ponies.

Rold was startled and overturned his litter. He saw eyes staring at him from between two boulders, eyes that seemed to be a part of the rock, alive and peering. Blikki was at his side helping him up. He refused to return to the litter and insisted on standing. He then saw a multitude of eyes materializing from the hillside; about thirty warriors stood among the group. Their bodies were naked except for breech cloths and painted white with chalk. They were silent and spoke in signs, the leader speaking only to Pentat. He was saying that the Whites had murdered ten thousand pitah, destroying them with fire. They had watched, as Pentat and Rold had, the red plain thick with smoke. Also, pridda were killed. Pentat's eyes widened; he screamed a curse that echoed against the hills. The chalk warriors were visibly shocked and dismayed by the breaking of silence, but Pentat dispensed with protocol and strode toward what Rold could now see was the huge mouth of a limestone cave. Rold felt Yosana at one arm and Blikki at the other as they all followed Pentat down into the yawning abyss. Most of the chalk warriors disappeared into the hills, taking some of Pentat's bodyguard with them; the rest followed, pulling the wagons that had been trucked all this way from the Library.

Rold's curiosity pulled him toward the hole until he stood beside Pentat. Pentat smiled at him, and they clasped each other's shoulders. Rold stumbled, still weak from illness; Pentat put his arm around him to hold him up. The noon sun struck them in such a way that their form was reminiscent of the eagle image of the night of Pentat's return to the Library. Upon seeing this the chalk warriors fell to their knees, silent and trembling. Neither Rold nor Pentat noticed since they were to the front of the group. But Yosana saw it and began feeling the inspiration that the others felt, though she remained sober enough not to yield. The magic was broken as the two men parted. Rold waved Pentat aside and began walking again on his own.

"Show me what this is," he said.

As the group moved into the cave, Yosana relaxed and shook away her brief feeling of awe. It was only love that she felt, was it not? Or was it still the effects of the cloud ride?

The warriors also went back to business and trucked several loads of arrows, fletched and pointed, past Rold and Pentat into the torch lit tunnel. The huge room was cold and humid and magnificent with its spires. In the middle was a perfectly round crater, black as night and only a dozen strides across. A natural dike that was made of matted glass fibers circled the hole. A couple of the white painted tribesmen were sitting beside it and were patiently weaving shallow baskets from the pliant glass threads.

"A point pool," Pentat said.

"All these years and I've never seen one," Blikki said. "I've heard the stories about the cloud killer war. How many years has it been?"

"Over six hundred winters," Pentat said. "But the art, the knowledge, of these pools has been kept, thank the Great Mother, so that we're not totally naked in our defense."

"I don't remember ever hearing about this," Yosana said. She stood beside Rold, rubbing his back.

Pentat took an arrow from the first wagon to arrive. The Teton arrows were made of green reeds more than a meter in length. The points were obsidian and small. He walked to the pool and propped one foot on the rim. "We call the vapor in the pool *yaddamet*, invisible paint. These threads that form the mouth of the pool are crystallized yaddamet — at least that's what we think; like ice forming around a pond in early winter. The threads are the only defense against the yaddamet, and so we weave quivers and shields to protect ourselves."

"So, what does it do?" Rold said. "Is it a poison?"

"It's more of a blade sharpener," Pentat said. "I'll show you, then the work must begin."

He dipped the point of the arrow into the black pool. The surface, if there was one, did not ripple, nor did it show the slightest disturbance. Rold opened his eyes wide in the dimly-lit cavern as he examined the point being pulled from the hole. The obsidian point had already been black in color, of course, with the reflective gloss of glass, but now it was dull and black, its form fuzzy and barely recognizable as an arrowhead.

"Watch," Pentat said and tapped the point against the matted threads under his feet then lifted the arrow and walked toward the cave wall. Rold reached to touch it as it passed, but Pentat grabbed his hand roughly. "Your curiosity almost lost you your fingers, Mountain Bear," he said. He then handed the shaft to Rold. "Stab the rock," he said.

"Will it not break the point?" Rold said. "Oh, I see, it hardened it, changed its molecular structure so that it's like a hard alloyed metal or something. Is that it?"

Pentat did not answer.

Rold poked it at the wall and almost fell against it. There was no resistance; the arrow simply entered the rock as if the wall was made of butter. He moved it in and out then twirled it about in a circle. He pulled it out and handed it back to Pentat then examined the wall. The sliced rock fell out into his hands. He touched the smoothly cut limestone and felt the slightest heat.

"I'm speechless," Rold said.

"That's more amazing than the arrow itself," Blikki said with a little laugh.

"This would go through any kind of armor," Rold said. "Even a jet."

"It'll pass through an entire building," Pentat said. "And needing only the power of a bow and a good warrior's arm. I said there were things you didn't know about us, Mountain Bear."

But is this enough? Rold thought.

The painted warriors began unloading the weapons that were to be treated. There were more than a hundred of the chalk people in the cave, some working on shields and quivers, others dipping the arrows. Signs of industry, Rold thought. He noticed that many of them were missing fingers or had large burn scars.

"We'll have enough for our trip to First Colony," Pentat said. "Then on the return trip we'll have hundreds to take back to the Library. Be ready to leave in an hour. We must be at First Colony before sunset."

Rold stopped him by placing his hand on his shoulder. "You've given me hope . . . again," Rold said.

Pentat smiled. "I'm glad you're better. Forgive me for my temper."

"You know I do. But these weapons . . . If the Whites were to find these caves, they could use this substance against you."

"If our plan works and the Whites explode nuclears on First Colony, then they'll have destroyed all the point pools. Each of our groups has gone to a different pool to prepare weapons. All of the sites are within half a day's walk from First Colony. At least all that the Teton have knowledge of."

"Then you'll no longer have the use of them yourselves."

"Of course, but that's why we're preparing now. We've been building up our storage of treated points for months. And making shields, packing away the glass threads."

"Are the arrows recoverable?"

"What do you think? Once they pierce the earth they sink into it until they reach Hell. Once thrown the arrow is no more."

"So many chances," Rold mumbled.

"Will it be enough, you're thinking?" Pentat said. "I don't know. It's the best we can do. We can't count on the blasted living clouds to aid us. This is our only magic!"

Pentat grabbed and shook an arrow that had been freshly dipped. He then pointed it at the ground and threw it down like a spear. The earth swallowed it leaving no trace in the shadowy cave. A few moments later the cave rumbled. A quake rolled the dusty floor. Small rocks tumbled to the ground and dust hung in the air. Then all settled; all was quiet.

"I think the Whites are in for a surprise," Yosana said. "This desert will probably crack into a million pieces when they drop their bombs."

"If they dropped their bombs," Rold said.

"And if they don't," Pentat said with his hand on Rold's shoulder, "then we'll still have a peaceful winter; for if they're not bent on destroying us then perhaps they'll leave us alone for a time."

"Yes," Rold said. "I suppose that's possible. But what of the buffalo — the pitah? It seems they're trying to starve us. Perhaps drive us into dependence on them. The hardship of hunger could divide your people."

"I have no answer for that," Pentat said. "We'll just have to wait and see. I'll have some news at camp tonight, hopefully. A messenger from Minpana should be meeting us there. So let's get going. We have enough weapons for the next few days. Here, Mountain Bear, take these first arrows. I have saved you your bow and brought it along."

"Thank you. I hope if I have to use these things I won't kill any of us in the process."

"That goes without saying," Blikki said.

They left the cave and breathed deeply the warm, clean breeze of the desert. Rold was still weak and resentfully rode on the litter the rest of the way.

Pentat's group was the last to arrive at First Colony. Camp fires were smoldering with small flames, and people were milling about laughing, talking, singing. Pentat had suggested that their presence at First Colony should not be kept a secret: the more noise the more plausible the rumor of a large encampment.

Rold was deposited against a crumbled brick wall that was a part of a maze of ruins. The remains of the colonial buildings were now no more than brittle red clay walls less than a meter in height. Rold wondered if the buildings had worn down and disintegrated or whether the soil had built up and buried the city. But few signs of culture remained in this sandy patch regardless.

As Pentat left to meet with the other chiefs who had led the earlier groups,

Blikki and the warriors began assembling their camp. Yosana sat lazily beside Rold, staring at the endeavors of the Teton.

"Do I smell food?" Rold asked.

"Does that mean you're hungry?"

"Yes. I guess a little."

She smiled. "My 'magic' must have done you some good."

"Yes, yes. I'll admit it. Thank you, again."

Rold closed his eyes and sighed.

"And where are you tonight?" Yosana asked.

He sighed again. "I was thinking of my father . . . and Tyler. Will I see Father again?"

"You will, Rold. You will."

Yosana quietly returned her gaze toward the activity.

"And what's on your mind tonight?" Rold said.

"Me?"

"Are you afraid?"

"No, not really. I guess I haven't quite accepted that a war is really coming. It doesn't seem real yet. Even with the violence that has already occurred. Violence is nothing new to me. When we're in an actual battle, then I'll know it's real."

"Yes, I feel the same way. But, there's something else, something you're not saying."

She looked into his eyes and smiled then abruptly changed her expression to one of fear.

"What is it?" Rold said. He sat up and held her shoulders in his hands.

"I'm pregnant."

"You're sure?"

"Yes."

"I've never thought about being a father. I don't know how much of what I feel comes from your blasted Gwydmonia and how much are my own honest feelings, but I am happy. It's a strange and wonderful thing."

"But when Pentat finds out I'll be confined to the village. I'm not ready for that."

"So, will you resent this child?"

"No! I want to be happy — happy with being a mother, a cloud rider and mother of a rider."

"Instead of feeling like you have been bound in chains by this thing, you could view it as simply a new and wonderful experience. It could actually set you free rather than tie you down."

"A typical male statement."

Rold smiled and Yosana smiled in spite of herself. They held each other.

Yosana enjoyed the embrace; Rold's fever was gone and he finally felt like himself instead of burning hot.

"What's all this kissy, hugging stuff when there's work to be done," Blikki said as he knelt beside them.

Yosana put her arms around her father's neck and held tight. He patted her back.

"Hey, hey. What's all this?" he said.

"We're going to have a baby," Rold said, beaming.

"Well, thank the Great Mother," Blikki said. "I never thought I'd be a grandfather. I guess that means I'm an old man after all. Rold boy, you've made this old man pretty damned happy."

"I had a little bit to do with it," Yosana said.

"I'm sure you had a lot to do with it," Blikki said, laughing.

Yosana pulled away and straightened up, wiping her eyes. "Now both of you," she said, "we must not talk of this until Rold and I are joined in Teton fashion. You know how prudish the Teton are, Father."

"Well, it's not a big surprise, you know," Blikki said. "You took him riding, after all."

As Pentat walked up Yosana whispered to Rold, "Not a word to Pentat. Not until after the ceremony. We've got enough problems."

Pentat sat cross-legged in front of Rold. Everyone quieted their chatter, letting the crackling fire perk their ears.

"Patrols of the monster warriors have been sighted on the desert," Pentat said.

"What are the numbers?" Rold asked.

"Not many. Less than a thousand troops."

"There are only three hundred of us," Blikki said.

"We must seem like thousands if they stumble onto us here," Pentat said.

"There's no problem if they never leave the desert to report on us," Bana said, joining them. The young chief from the grassy hills wore a smile, but Rold took his suggestion seriously.

"Bana and I disagree about this," Pentat said.

"You've grown soft," Bana said. "This White has turned you into a pregnant woman."

"And just what does that mean?" Yosana said, standing.

Bana laughed. "Little Yosana. You have to understand. It's my life's sworn duty to harass this old bull brother of yours. Have you forgotten?"

"I'm not in a mood for teasing," she said.

"I can see that. But we must face the reality that the war is upon us. My hunters are ready to strike down these monsters. And if this grand diversion is to be successful, no ground troops should be allowed to see our make-believe city."

"If it comes to that," Pentat said, "yes, I agree. But the first priority is to build our illusion. So I suggest we begin tonight. I want fifty workers to begin erecting lodges starting now. At midnight relieve them with fifty more. And tomorrow we all work. Fires will be built and pridda corralled."

"You'll sacrifice pridda?" Blikki was astonished. "And who'll keep the fires going? What warriors will you sacrifice?"

"The pridda will be the old and the sick," Pentat said. "And the warriors . . . a dozen will be required to keep the fires going. We will rotate each three days, randomly — the dozen will leave as the others arrive. Perhaps we'll be lucky and have some warning of the approach of the bombers. My name will be placed in the lottery with the others."

"As it must be," Bana said sighing. "And my name as well, old friend."

"So much risk," Blikki said. "I remember you two as boys. You were always tempting chance. Now the whole planet is at stake. I hope you know what you're doing, son."

Yosana shivered as she listened to the discussion. She sat down beside Rold. Pentat left with Bana, and they could be heard arguing until they disappeared into the dark.

The roar of a jet turbine made it impossible for Rachel Meacom to hear her father's greeting. They stood on the plastic pavement of an air base runway that vibrated with the slow cyclic pounding of the deafening engine. A reconnaissance mission was about to begin, and Rachel was on an inspection tour. Coupled with the offensive preparations, local security was still one of her duties, and so the planet was constantly being watched from the air. She jumped when her father's hand touched her shoulder.

"I didn't see you coming," she shouted. "Wait just a minute. The jet will be off, and we can talk." She motioned at the jet craft that was now moving into position for take-off. As it left the runway in an abrupt hop, characteristic of the small, vertical pulse jet craft commonly used for non-combative tasks, the noise lessened, and Rachel's attention swung to her father, who stood as patiently as he could in the gritty wind.

"You've found something?" he asked, getting straight to the point.

"Why do you think I'm here?" she said.

"What I want to know is why I'm here. Please finish this so that I can get back to the Bridge."

They walked toward a hanger that loomed an incredible thirty storeys above them.

"There's a rumor that the natives are having a huge gathering at one of their ruins — a big jamboree," she said.

"I've already heard this information."

"Oh? Of course it's common gossip in the streets. But I have good reason to believe that Rold Simms is at that gathering."

His eyebrows perked. "A prisoner?"

"That's not how it's being told. It seems he has earned a place in their leadership and is planning a revolt against us."

Comrade Meacom laughed and nodded his head. "Not bloody likely."

"Well, maybe terrorist attacks. Who knows?"

"So, what do you suggest?"

"We could use the Zenians. It would be a valuable exercise. Capture him; rub his nose in it. We could have him back."

"Yes. A bit expensive. But as you say, it would be a good exercise for the Zenians. We lost a small group on a patrol, to these natives is all we can assume. They must be good fighters."

"All the Zenians dead?"

She nodded. "I'm sure they took many natives down with them but they removed the bodies. We have no count."

The two stopped and faced each other under a high sun. A shadow drifted from the east bringing a cool breeze. Rachel glanced up, her face darkened by the shade, and saw a living cloud moving silently overhead. Her father looked up, squinting.

"I hate those damned things," he said. "The sight of them turns my stomach. They're so damned big that you can't ignore them."

"You learn to. They begin to blend into the surroundings. They're quite harmless."

"To whom? Have it blasted."

"What?"

"Get rid of it. Blast it out of the sky. You see, it's floating up there and making me sick."

"It won't do any good . . ."

"Do it! That's an order, Daughter."

"Very well."

Rachel touched her jacket collar to activate an intercom and gave a cryptic order. She gave it if only to show her father her power and the sharp conditioning her army had undergone.

Blasts of blue energy sprang from a cannon perched on the roof of a bunker close by. The low pitched rumble of the explosions rivaled the previous roar of the jet engine. But the living cloud simply remained stationary while the bolts passed through it as if it were truly a cloud.

"I hate those things," Meacom said. "Why will it not leave? Is there no getting rid of it?"

"I tried to tell you."

"Yes, well, I'm very disappointed. You can't even rid me of a single, floating glob of pss." Rachel stood frozen. Was he serious? "How are you going to rid me of these natives!" he growled.

Rachel looked up to see the slunk but was startled to see it had disappeared.

"Like that," she said, pointing up.

He looked. "Thank god."

"Like that," she repeated. "Why not? It's cheaper and more certain."

"What are you mumbling about?"

"A nuclear sweep . . . of the native gathering."

"Just wipe them out?"

"All the filthy monkeys, including Simms. Why hadn't I thought of this sooner?"

Comrade Meacom pursed his lips and stared at the ground. They both turned and began walking again toward the hanger. The entrance looked like a huge, hungry mouth. The floor was not the typical plastic pavement, nor even sand, but a white ceramic tile that squeaked as their shoes scuffed across it.

"I would suggest you plan the combat raid first," he said. "If conditions arise that would prevent such an attack, such as bad weather, timing, other commitments, or whatever, then go ahead and bomb. As you said before it would be a good exercise. And good timing too, since we'll have to move the Zenians to the south before winter gets really rough. But of course, it's up to you. Base security is your affair. If you feel more comfortable with bombing . . ."

"I understand, Father. Use the Zenians. That's the first priority."

"But use your own judgment. As I said before, Simms really isn't that important any more. It's becoming some kind of personal thing with you now. If you want to be done with him to ease your mind, go ahead. But Zenian training is more important."

A small hovercraft arrived in the hanger; a porter emerged with a push-cart set with lunch for the Meacoms. Rachel motioned her father to sit on a lounge that accompanied the cart; she sat beside him. The Zenians can be damned, she thought. I'm going to exterminate those nasty little bugs and Simms along with them. I'm tired of worrying about him and these primitives. We need Salkinia as a base. We don't need these irritants distracting our true work.

She stared at the porter for a moment. He stood at formal attention, his eyes focused on the horizon. He looked familiar, yet he was not on her regular staff. He was dark, with black eyes and weathered skin. He looked as though he had aged too quickly. Probably a Salkinian, she thought but wondered why he was so familiar. She put it out of her mind as quickly as it had entered and returned to the issue at hand.

"Leave it to me, Father," she said. "We won't have to concern ourselves with Simms anymore. Or these natives."

"Well, I can't spend anymore time with this topic. So do it your way. Genocide. I'm tired of fooling with them anymore. Maybe those damned slunks will go to some other planet if we get rid of the natives."

They were quiet for a moment while they ate. Rachel smiled at her father's about-face. She hated the Zenians and was glad to avoid such a campaign. Nuclear sweeping was tried and true.

"You have the location of this gathering?" Comrade Meacom asked, his voice muffled by a napkin as he wiped his mouth.

"We're flying intelligence jets over the desert where the ruins are supposed to be. We'll pinpoint it hopefully today."

"A desert, eh? Well, be sure to sponge it anyway. I'd like to keep this planet clean for a while. We have to live here too, you know."

"Yes, sir."

Another reconnaissance flight began filling the hanger with an echoing roar. The sound essentially ended the conversation, and Rachel's eyes followed the jet as it shot into the blue sky until it disappeared over some red sandstone hills.

CHAPTER 14

The desert demons took him away
And left a cloud of nothing.

\- From "The Song of Margona"
  by Pitallela-Sim

In nine days, with grueling labor, over two thousand lodges were constructed around First Colony. From a distance it looked like an army encampment, but walking around the spiral of camp sites Rold shook his head at the fragile armatures they had erected made of twigs and leather rags which smelled of mold and mildew or rot — even in the crisp air of the desert. But all that mattered was what it looked like in a reconnaissance picture taken from a jet or a satellite. Rold helped with certain details that he thought would enhance the possible image that they were hoping to portray, such as worn pathways or roads, latrines and garbage dumps. Pridda were led or ridden over designed paths hundreds of times to make them more real. And now it was time to move on, with hope that it would work.

It was too late in the day to begin the trip home, so Pentat made plans for the warriors to leave the next morning. An outpost would be left some distance from the ruin for rotating fire-watchers. Volunteers were being organized for that now by secret lot. Pentat had already been chosen for an outpost position to be moved to fire watcher in two days after which he could return to the Library. He sat quietly as names were being called. Rold walked behind the crowd of warriors to sit beside him.

"Blikki says he's staying with you," Rold said. "Even if he's not called."

"He'll go back to the Library if he's not called," Pentat said. "Whether he likes it or not."

"He'll have something to say about that."

"He always does," Pentat said smiling. "But . . . we're at war. He'll go where I say that he's needed. It's not fair to the others who would stay here for love of their people or glory or whatever reason. If they're not called they too will return. And besides, I'll need him alive if I am to perish under the Whites' bombing."

They turned their attention to a woman warrior who was reading the names as they were retrieved from a bowl.

"... Mountain Bear, second watch," she said.

Rold nodded his head. "Then I'm with you for a while longer."

"Yes, and your mission is put off again."

The woman finished reading her list as Yosana and Blikki approached.

"We weren't chosen," Yosana said. Her eyes were tired and full of concern as she pressed Rold for a response, but he said nothing. He simply took her hand and helped her sit beside him.

"I'll be damned if I'll go back to safety while my family sits here in danger," Blikki said. "You rigged it didn't you? You rigged it so you'd be picked and I wouldn't. Right?"

"No, Father," Pentat said, sighing. "And I'll not argue with you about it. You don't need to worry about my safety."

"Who said I was worried about your safety. Maybe I was talking about Rold. He's almost my son-in-law — as close kin as you."

Pentat stood and looked at Blikki sternly. Then he took him in his arms and gave him a heavy squeeze with lots of back slaps. Blikki was stiff at first but finally softened.

"Well, don't get yourself killed, damn it," he said as he stepped back. "You either, Rold. There would be no hope left if we lost you, if your people lost you."

"Look!" Rold said, standing. His head was tilted back, his hand shading his eyes. The others turned their eyes toward the sky. Movement stopped about the camp as more people heard the sound. A large jet was flying high overhead; so high it seemed motionless, as the hands of an analog clock.

"Reconnaissance," Rold said. "I just hope they don't find the Library."

"The Library is well-hidden," Pentat said. "The shadow of the mountains protects it."

"Well," Rold said. "At any rate, they have seen us. If they take the bait, they'll be here within days. Hours if they've already made the decision and are just waiting for the location."

"Hours?" Yosana said. "Then we should leave. All of us."

"It's not likely to be that soon," Rold said. "I doubt we're that important to them. But who knows?"

The sight of jets was no longer such a curious thing to the Teton; their vapor trails could be seen across any sky. So the warriors dropped their eyes and continued their labors of tidying and packing. A brilliant afternoon sun warmed the breeze, making Rold feel lazy.

"Where is this winter of yours?" he asked.

"It'll come," Blikki said. "You'll barely be able to see the sun before long."

"The seasons change quickly here," Pentat said. "Winter will drop on us like night in the desert."

Bana strode toward them, leading his pony.

"Anyone for a ride?" he said. "Camp work is not suited to me. I'm restless in such fine weather — there's little enough of it left."

"A ride," Rold said. "How about a race?"

"A race?" Yosana said.

"Is that not a proper thing to do on Salkinia?" Rold said. "On Old Earth we race horses."

"Yes, Mountain Bear," Bana said. "A race would certainly clean off the cobwebs. But what rider should I race?"

"Me of course," Rold said.

Pentat stood silent with a slight grin betraying his straight face.

"Are you well enough, son?" Blikki said.

"I'm fine."

Yosana pulled Rold aside and whispered to him: "Racing is very serious business to the Teton. They have great pride in their pony stock. If a person from one village challenges someone from another, it becomes a trial of honor between those two villages. This isn't something done just for fun. And Bana is probably one of the best riders on the plain. It'll be no disgrace to back out. We can explain that you don't understand the custom . . ."

"I want to race," Rold said. "I know how to ride. What's the problem?"

"If you lose, your pridda will be forfeited to Bana. Thus, the Eagle village will lose a pony."

"Then I won't lose."

"You can be so stubborn."

"Insulting me won't change my mind."

"All right, then think about this: You're a head taller than Bana. He probably weighs fifteen, twenty kilograms less than you. You have very little experience on these animals. You can't win a race against him."

"You shouldn't have said 'can't.'"

"Don't try to prove anything, Rold."

Rold turned back to the group of warriors that had gathered. "What will be the course?" he asked.

"We start at that broken tree over there," Bana said, pointing. "And ride to the stream that bends around that hill toward the plateau. Then back to the broken tree."

"A long race," Rold said. "Anyone else to join us?"

Everyone shook his head. A large crowd began to form around them. The Teton seemed eager for some entertainment. Blikki had retrieved Rold's mount and handed him the reins. Pentat gave Rold a firm pat on his shoulder as they walked to the starting point.

"I have watched you ride," Pentat said. "You're not used to the antlers of the pridda. In another moon these will be shed, but for now they're here. Now listen. Sit more forward — no matter how dangerous it may seem. If you ride between the rack and move with the pridda's head through your turns, you'll be safe.

"I don't expect you to win. But I expect you to honor me, to honor the Eagle village with a good race. Good luck, Mountain Bear."

The two riders hopped onto their animals; the pridda were nervous, their hind legs kicking. Yosana helped calm Rold's pony.

"You crazy Scientist!" she said and kissed Rold as he leaned over to her.

The two men maneuvered their animals side by side. The pridda were sparkling; their spotted coats were sleek with tensed muscles. A low-pitched drum was being hammered at an increasing rate until the vibration from one stroke collided with the vibration of the next. Pentat explained to Rold in a raised voice that the race would begin with the cessation of the drum. The two riders crouched over the antlered heads of the pridda awaiting the silence. The drum stopped, but a pounding continued in Rold's head. Bana and his pony leaped four meters into the desert before Rold sensed the silent signal. He managed to get his pridda to stumble off after Bana, the soft sound of laughter at his back. Caustic dust hung in the air choking him until he moved to the right. The pridda accepted the challenge, perhaps more thoroughly than Rold, and brought himself up to an accelerating pace. Rold was now used to the arcing leaps of the pridda so that he moved with the animal with fluid grace. He felt that they were flying across the desert. He could hear the scraping of hooves against the stubby sage and felt the breeze blowing his hair.

When it seemed they would never catch Bana, the young warrior-chief turned to look at Rold and allowed his pridda to stumble across an arroyo. Neither the rider nor the pony fell, but Rold took advantage and caught them just as they regained their footing and stride.

Green rushes were in sight, defining the edge of the river that was the marker for their turn. Rold was somehow pulling ahead. Perhaps his pridda smelled the water. But just as Rold's confidence was building, his pony slowed and skated on the powdery soil. Bana laughed as he flew past, but his mount began bucking nervously and halted as well. The two men looked at each other, Bana patting the sweaty coat of his pridda. Arising from the stream bank, with a leisurely precision, were a thousand Militia, spread in a broad line four soldiers deep. The soldiers wore the green disc of the Militia on their chests, but Rold could see that these were Zenian warriors. Their heads, arms, and legs were covered in gray fur — not animal skins but their own fur.

The most noticeable clue was their bow-legged stance and long feet. Their height was that of fabled giants.

The monsters," Bana whispered. He looked up and down the crusty ridge that followed the river. "We were foolish to leave without weapons. There's a gully to the north. When they advance head for it and down your pridda."

The Zenians had no vehicles with them. They were known for their speed on foot. In their hands — or fore paws — rested energy blasters. The line began to move toward the two men with greater speed.

Bana and Rold broke to their left at a gallop and dived into a miniature canyon. The pounding of the Zenians' huge feet shook the ground. The men peered over the lip of the gully and saw the advance. But a high-pitched whoop shot up behind them, and they turned to see the entire Teton camp charging on running pridda. The Zenians now began firing wave beams at the gully. Rocks and dirt exploded into the air. The pridda escaped the two men and the blasts. Rold and Bana protected each other from the flying rock. Then in an instant Pentat was beside them pulling them from the suffocating dust.

"Shield and bow," he said and handed each man their weapons and reins of their pridda. All three mounted quickly, Pentat protecting them all with his shield, deflecting energy blasts as easily as creating shade with a parasol.

The sky began raining arrows — much like the night of Rold's escape, but this time he knew what they were. Howls and squeals could be heard over the booming blasts of weapons from the Zenians. They were being cut down like stalks of grain. The earth rumbled from the disappearing arrows, but the Zenians kept advancing. Pentat split his warriors in two, leading half toward one end of the Zenian line and Bana leading the other half to the opposite end. The middle had collapsed. Rold followed Pentat; Blikki winked at him after throwing off a blast with his shield and rode after Bana's group.

Rold could see as they closed on the line that there were some humans among the Zenians — actual Militia. Their faces were screwed with horror as the yaddamet-treated arrow points cut through their personal shields as if they did not exist. The Zenians, though, showed no such horror. Their expressions could not be read. Rold wondered if they even possessed human emotion.

He protected himself with his shield and waded into the battle. He began throwing the destructive arrows at the enemy. Pentat led a brave charge that achieved control of his end of the line. It was not an easy battle; the Teton, outnumbered three to one, fought hard and well. But Rold wondered at the completeness of the quick victory knowing the reputation of the Zenians: They were not known for losing battles. To the south Bana was having a harder time. The Teton were now in hand-to-hand combat with the Zenians, whose energy weapons were being abandoned as useless. They took up knives and began painting the white soil red with blood. Pentat's group had killed or captured all the northern flank so now turned to aid Bana. Rold followed them, a battle frenzy possessing him.

The shadow of an eagle crossed the ground before them. Rold looked up and saw the giant bird gliding in a circle like a vulture. As his eyes dropped back to the battle he was shocked out of his reticence. A lone Zenian, unhindered, was closing on Blikki from behind. Blikki was fiercely engaged and oblivious to this advancing creature. No one else seemed to see him. Rold pulled an arrow from the quiver on his back. Please turn, he thought. Blikki, damn it, turn!

"Blikki!" he shouted. But he could not be heard.

Rold's pridda was galloping now. Rold let loose the reins and held his bow, pulling back the carefully placed arrow. He shot the arrow; it missed. But Blikki heard it or felt the whizzing air and turned. The Zenian was upon him, towering over him like a grotesque tree. Rold screamed as he saw the knife, clutched by the fur covered hand of the soldier, skate across Blikki's throat. His whole chest and shoulders became red, and his head flopped backward as he fell to his knees then in a lifeless pile on the ground.

Rold pulled another arrow from his back and this time jumped from the pony and charged the soldier. He threw down his bow as he reached the Zenian, who was waiting for him. Rold screamed again and slashed the arrow at the soldier, using as if it were a sword. The soldier raised his knife and Rold's arrow caught his arm and severed it from his body. The Zenian had a sick look of shock in his reptilian eyes, then Rold struck again and sliced off his head.

Yosana rushed to her father and knelt beside him. Rold was surprised by her presence — he had not noticed her before. She was dressed as a warrior, carrying a quiver, bow, and knife. He thought briefly of her pregnancy and worried for the baby, but Blikki's bloody body made him forget everything else.

The battle was over. The astounding feat of a handful of Teton warriors defeating a large contingent of Zenians had occurred, but Rold cared little for the fact. He just stared at his sweet Yosana mixing her tears with her dead father's blood. She turned her eyes to Rold. A pleading grief sat on her face; Rold knelt beside her, holding her and rocking back and forth.

"Father!" Pentat cried as he threw himself on the body. He repeated an incoherent chant mixed with sobbing. A silence spread over the desert. He jerked his head up and stared at the sky.

"Look!" he said. "The sign of death; the death of Teton." Rold looked up and saw three living clouds in a stationary circle.

"I have lost everyone," Pentat said. "All of my ancestors are gone. There is now only the future."

He staggered to his feet and walked with crooked steps to his pridda. No one spoke. Prisoners were being rounded up and the dead counted, but only sign language was used. Rold stripped off his leather tunic and wrapped it around the head and chest of Blikki's body then lifted and carried the body to his pony. He managed to place it across the riding blanket and steadied it as Yosana led his pridda, and her own, back to First Colony. He approached Pentat whose glazed eyes were surveying his damaged company of warriors.

"Blikki is dead," Rold said, his voice quivering. "I couldn't save him."

"So now you understand," Pentat said.

Bana was close by listening.

"I have lost my brother today," Bana said. "You have lost your father. The Enemy will do as he must. Don't punish Mountain Bear with your grief. Your grief is his."

Pentat looked at Rold as if he had not heard a word that Bana said.

"Let us pray that we'll prevent more good people from dying at the hands of this plague of senseless, hateful beings," he said. "I don't hate the enemy though as much as I hate those damned living clouds," he said in a soft voice. "Here again, Mountain Bear, you should feel what I feel. They stood by while Blikki was struck down as they did when my mother and father were washed away."

Rold shook his head at Pentat's obsession. He only felt sorrow, and a rage was building inside him. Life would be so much simpler if he would give into his rage, if he would accept the chauvinism of a soldier.

The company regrouped at First Colony as the sun was setting. Twenty-two Teton were dead and three had been wounded. Of the wounded one had been blinded and had lost an ear, one had a minor burn on his leg, and the other had lost both his legs. The dead were placed upon a pyre of dried grass. Yosana was given the honor of starting the flame. Rold stood with her as she broke down into an eerie wailing; after a half hour she sniffled and wiped her eyes, a resolve returning to her eyes. Pentat said a short prayer to the Great Mother. His grief was not visible, and so was all the more pitiable.

Take the dust of these brave souls
As payment for your care,
Great Mother, we ask you,
Bless the spirit that lives on.

He left the burning pile of flesh to question the prisoners. Less than a hundred Militia had been left alive, and were being held at First Colony. Rold watched Pentat leave and was still amazed at how complete this small victory had been — though the price had been too high.

"Oh, Rold!" Yosana said and buried her face in his chest. "He'll never see our baby."

"My poor, sweet Yosana. I love you. I know it is unfair. I feel . . . responsible. If I had only seen that Zenian in time; if I had been quicker."

"No. You can't do that. I need you. Pentat needs you. Don't feel guilt. Just shut up and hold me. My father is gone.   He's gone."

They stood together, rocking each other, Yosana still weeping lightly.

"I need to talk to Pentat," Rold said.

"I'll go with you. I don't want to be alone."

They walked hand-in-hand to a small fire where several of the Militia were seated in a circle, their hands tied behind their backs. The Zenians howled and snorted. They had been brought unconscious and bound with the glass thread from the point pools. Their language was made of a series of grunts and whistles which they spewed in eerie pitches. Two of the captured, however, were humans — Industrialists. Both were officers.

"They're not talking," Pentat said as Rold and Yosana arrived. "The men aren't. These monsters, though, won't shut up."

"You have dishonored them beyond belief," Rold said. "You see, they never lose — especially when the odds are so unbalanced."

"Any suggestions?" Bana said.

Rold motioned Pentat closer.

"The Industrialists look nervous," he whispered.

"As they should."

"Of course, but there's something else. I suspect there may be another attack — one in which their lives would be considered expendable."

"Do you think they know of a bombing?"

"Let's find out. I'll not allow Blikki's death to be in vain. Our diversion must work."

Rold approached the two men. There was recognition in both their eyes.

"Do you know who I am?" Rold said. "I'm Rold Simms. Does that mean anything to you?"

They remained silent though Rold could tell they knew him. "I don't think they're going to talk," Rold said in a loud voice. "I suggest we keep them here over night and deal with them in the morning."

A horror could be seen in the two men's eyes. Rold knelt beside them, anger shaking his entire body.

"Is something happening before morning?" he screamed. "Another attack?"

One of the men started to speak. The other looked at him, his eyes pleading.

"If . . . if you'll take us with you — away from this place — I'll tell you," the man said finally.

"Yes?"

"A nuclear sweep . . ."

Rold smiled. He grabbed Pentat and slapped his back, then sighed.

"Tonight?" Rold asked.

"Yes. Please take us from here. It's your duty under the traditional codes of war to provide officers who are prisoners with reasonable safety and life support."

"And the Zenians?"

"You may leave the disgusting creatures as far as we're concerned."

"You're traitors to your people," Pentat said.

The men stared into the fire.

"There's more," Rold said. "Out with it."

The men cringed as Rold pulled his knife. Pentat's eyes met Yosana's. They had not seen such a display from Rold before.

"Are there more troops close by?" Rold said.

"No troops, but land rovers with drivers, supplies," the talkative one said. "Certainly information has reached Minpana by now of our defeat."

"Will the land machines stay?"

"Perhaps."

Pentat sent some of the warriors off with chores then turned to Bana and Rold.

"We must leave within the hour," he said. "And these machines must be located. I don't want any word of our size to reach the Whites."

"I'm sure if they know of the Zenian defeat they'll think we have thousands of warriors," Rold said. "Perhaps we can send a message to the Whites telling of our false numbers through the land rovers. Also, I think it would be good for them to know that you and I are here. That would give them some additional motivation and satisfaction for their bombing."

"And what of the prisoners?" Bana said.

"Leave the traitors here," Pentat said. "To die by the hand of their own people."

The prisoners screamed obscenities, and though he approved of the news, Rold's heart felt like lead. He looked at the bawling, squirming Zenians and felt sorry for them; they were the most guilty and yet the most innocent players in this disgusting game.

"Well, let's go," Bana said.

"I'm going with you," Yosana said.

"No," Pentat said. "I want you to help organize the return to the Library."

"Damn it, Pentat. I'm going with you. I've lost my father; I don't want to lose Rold. I need to be with him. And I'm not helpless."

Pentat just sighed and left to retrieve his pridda.

As Pentat, Rold, Bana, and Yosana road into the darkness toward an horizon defined by the distant glow of Minpana, the moon began rising from the southeast. Rold looked over his shoulder and smiled at the train of Teton leaving First Colony, their forms shining dusty blue in the moonlight. He lost his smile as he caught sight of the dying flame that was the pyre of Blikki. *So you ended up tending the fires after all, you old pirate,* he thought.

The night was cold and became dark with clouds. As a light sprinkle began Rold wondered how they were going to find anyone. But the lights of a camp sparkled though the rain in a broad valley below them. They had forded the river and were atop a barren ridge looking down at the three vehicles that were shining from lit windows and the reflection of a campfire. The fire bothered Rold. It was not an ordinary habit of Industrialists to use such primitive means for light or heat. But this was a primitive planet — not Old Earth or even Caljunna.

"There's little cover here," Pentat said. "But the dark will hide us and the rain will quiet our approach. How many do you think there are, Mountain Bear?"

"At least two per vehicle. Probably some apes as well," Rold said.

"More hairy monsters?" Bana said.

"Machines that look like people," Yosana said. "An old word is 'robot.'"

"If we can get close enough to throw arrows," Rold said, "we could disable the land rovers, then deal with the Militia."

"Yes," Pentat said. "We'll cut them down as they come out of their machines."

Rold shivered. He was developing a taste for blood, but verbalizing it uncovered a natural distaste that he could not afford right now.

They started down the rocky slope, the pridda slipping and tripping all the way. The hill met the valley at a fault line; they had to cross it in switchbacks in order not to tumble down. Once at the base they found a huge boulder to hide behind and drew their bows. Pentat, Bana, and Yosana each hit a target, the arrows blasting through armor and engines. Rold waited for emerging life to hit. Five Militia jumped out of the land rovers. One darted behind his machine; the others stood dumbly as Rold drilled holes though their chests. They fell where they stood.

"The other was foolish enough to run," Bana said. "Where does he think he can go in this rain?"

They walked to the camp leading the pridda, who snorted their complaints about the weather. Bana checked the machines for other occupants and found none. The rain broke and a slim ray of milky moonlight escaped the black clouds.

"We must find the other one," Pentat said.

"Please hear me," a voice said from the dark perimeter using Ameranglo. "May I come out in peace? I don't want to be killed. I might be of some help."

"Where is he?" Yosana said as she twirled about with a cocked arrow. "Here," the man said as he walked into the light.

With cat-like swiftness Bana was upon him, his knife at his throat. The man struggled and the two were on the ground.

"Wait!" he said between grunts, barely able to hold off Bana's attack. "I'm . . . not an enemy! Please!"

Pentat had been quiet as he watched the wrestling men, then he spoke. "Bana. Hold. He has no weapon."

Bana looked at Pentat, a frenzy lighting his eyes. But he calmed and released his grip. As a signal of his displeasure with having to retreat, he laid one last blow to the man's head, then stood.

The party approached the downed man, eyes circling, wary of others who might be hiding in the dark.

Rold looked at the man, really saw him for the first time. He thought he was dreaming or was just tired. The face was somewhat different: tired, older, bearded. But he knew this face.

"*Frank?*" he said in a whisper. "Frank!" he said louder and took a couple of steps. He dropped his bow in the mud.

"Rold?" Frank said. "Is it . . . is it really you? Oh my god!"

Frank was on his feet, shaking his head after Bana's blow. The Rold helped him rise, took his head into his hands and looked at his face as he rubbed his hair. They embraced silently.

The two friends stood apart to look at each other in the mixture of firelight and moonlight from the clearing sky.

"I can't believe I've been so lucky as to have found you," Frank said.

"You know this man, Mountain Bear?" Pentat said. He spoke in English for Frank's benefit.

"Yes, Pentat," Rold said. "From Old Earth. I vouch for him; he's not your enemy."

"I'm no one's enemy," Frank said. "I detest this war. I've pretended to be an Industrialist only to further my search for Rold. I knew he must still be alive; I felt it in my bones."

"Is that the report?" Rold asked. "That I'm dead?"

"Yes, but your father and I alone have never given up hope." They looked at each other as they held each other's forearms, then they laughed. Rold turned to Yosana and took her hand.

"Let me introduce you to my companions," Rold said. "This is my . . . friend, Yosana la'Kunda."

"So this is why we haven't heard from you," Frank said as he took Yosana's hand and kissed it. "This is a beautiful planet, and you're a beautiful lady for my old and lonely friend. I can understand retreating to an Eden like this."

"You won't consider it Eden in a few more days," Pentat said.

"This is Pentat," Rold said. "Chief of the Eagle village and commander of the Teton forces."

"I've heard of you," Frank said. "You speak Ameranglo well. And you know Old Earth myths such as Eden?"

"It's from the Christian teachings," Pentat said. "They were the first to repress our people; they were our first and most effective enemy. We try to know as much as we can about our enemies."

"I see."

"And this is Bana," Rold said. "Also a Teton chief."

Bana would not drop his suspicion, standing aloof.

"All we need is another White," he said.

Frank said nothing.

"And this, my friends," Rold said, presenting Frank in a formal yet comical manner, "is my friend from childhood, Frank Diego."

Frank nodded with a smile. As he straightened he and Rold could see a look of awe on the faces of the two Teton chiefs. Yosana noticed it too.

"What is it?" Rold said.

"Pitallela," Bana said. "The mother of us all — her name on Old Earth was Diego: Maria Diego. It was her Christian name."

"There are many Diegos on Old Earth," Frank said. "It's a common name where Rold and I grew up. In fact, I know three women with the name of Maria Diego. One is my cousin."

"Then are you Teton?" Bana asked, puzzled.

"I don't know what 'Teton' is," Frank said. "But, if I'm catching on here, I supposedly have some Indian blood — American Native."

"I never knew that," Rold said. "I should have guessed, but how could you keep track of such a thing?"

"My grandmother told me. I don't know if it's true or not. I think she just liked the idea; there's so few ethnic groups left on O. E. that have any definition."

"So, Frank, did you get my message?" Rold asked.

"What message?"

"A coded radio message, a few weeks ago."

"Radio? Sorry, Rold. I was just lucky. I stuck with your original plan and nosed around Caljunna. When the war broke out, the Industrialists were too obvious about movements here. I joined the Militia, and here I am!"

"This is all very interesting," Yosana interrupted, "but shouldn't we be moving out of range of the bombing?"

"You know about the nuclear sweep?" Frank said. "Here we're gabbing away and I forgot how I was going to help you. You must evacuate your city over there before dawn. But, you know about it already."

"Are we out of range here?" Rold asked.

"Yes. And the sweep should occur in, oh, about seven hours. We were to wait here for the Zenians to return. They were to take care of any escaping natives."

"They'll not be coming back," Bana said.

"Oh, I know," Frank said. "We got word of the battle and the tremendous number of natives that attacked."

Bana laughed. "You were right, Mountain Bear. They've over estimated our strength."

"But still you have to get as many out as you can," Frank said. "It's probably impossible to evacuate everyone . . ."

"There's no one at First Colony, Frank," Rold said. "Everyone is safe."

"How could you have known in time?" Frank said. "The decision was only made hours ago! How many people were in your city?"

"About three hundred," Rold said. He could not help but smirk. Frank looked astonished.

The sky was clouding up again; now instead of rain, flakes of snow, the size of large grains of sand, began swirling about the group and settling into feathery piles on the dark earth. The fire sizzled and popped from the contact of the floating ice crystals then was finally extinguished.

"Well, it seems we'll be staying here the night," Pentat said, holding out both hands and looking up. "Winter has found us. Let us hope we're out of range of this bombing that comes at dawn."

"They can be very precise," Frank said. "The city is the target." He began to laugh. "You have actually fooled them. I would love to see Rachel Meacom's face when she finds out that she has bombed an empty city."

"But she'll not find out," Rold said. "There are no witnesses. All the evidence points to a massive gathering of Salkinian natives. Am I right?"

"Yes. Damn it, you are. But, I take it, there'll be a time when you'll confront her and her army. Then she'll know — then she must know of her failure."

"You sound bitter," Rold said.

"And you aren't? You should see what this has done to your father!"

"And Tyler."

"Tyler? Yes, where is she?"

"Frank, she's dead."

"No!"

"Rachel Meacom. Killed her right in front of me. You want to talk about bitterness? I'll not rest until that bitch feels my hand across her face and I can watch her life slowly snuffed out."

Yosana looked at Rold with sympathy and also fear. Pentat shook his head slightly, with no one noticing. Frank was visibly shaken.

"Your father needs to know."

"Yes. Tell him that I live . . . and Tyler is gone."

Everyone was silent for a moment. Frank took that time to shake away the horror and anger at hearing about Tyler. He loved her as if she were his own sister. Then he came to himself, seeing the need to change the subject and get some planning done.

"Would you all like to rest inside the van? I have only a small store of food, I'm afraid. You see, my companions were machines and required none."

The five people entered one of the huge land rovers. As they rested at a settee by a window, Rold stared at the bodies of the driver apes; their forms were being coated by the snow until they were mere bumps in the landscape. He thought of Blikki, wishing he was here to see the success of their plan. The window became foggy from the exterior cold and the interior warmth of the small group of Teton warriors.

CHAPTER 15

"Which is the one?" the minah-machacute asked,
Brother or sister?

\- From "The Song of Margona"
  by Pitallela-Sim

A simple meal was eaten; all was quiet in the land rover cabin while hunger took precedence over speech. Yosana sat next to Rold. They clung to each other as young lovers do — or as a mourning family does. Frank watched them closely, trying to quickly understand their relationship, Rold's feelings, and guess at their plans.

Candles burned on a few of the available surfaces around the cabin. Rold was too tired to question it.

"I must applaud your performance," Frank said, breaking the silence. "You totally destroyed the power packs on all the land rovers. We were listening to broadcast reports from the bomber base when everything went black. I won't ask how you did it, but it was impressive. So, we're stuck. I would offer to take you out of here in style Rold, but I can't repair it. That doesn't mean we can't get back. I have clearances in Minpana you wouldn't believe."

Rold perked up.

"What are you saying?" he asked.

"Let's go home, old friend. I can get us off the planet. We can go to O. E. and see your family. I don't really want to go to Collinsville, do you?"

Rold looked at Yosana and saw a loving smile there. But Pentat was staring at the floor.

"It may be the right answer for you, Mountain Bear," Pentat said. "Perhaps now you have the chance to do something about your war."

Yosana looked into Rold's eyes. Her eyes said she would consider any plan upon which he decided.

Frank looked satisfied. He had read her face correctly. A shutter raced through Rold. He mashed a sob in the back of his throat and looked at his old friend, then at Pentat. They each looked back at him. He stood and paced a moment. Everyone was patient. Bana sat on a couch and propped his feet up, closing his eyes as if he were trying to sleep.

"I'm only one man," Rold said. "I can't stop the Industrialists by myself. I can't stop the war — even though I was a part of starting it. But I can't hide from my duty — to my father, to the memory of Tyler and Blikki. I feel their deaths wrapping around me like chains. I can't simply run home, thinking I'll join the big fight and that should satisfy my need for revenge."

Frank frowned at this. He could feel Rold's pain. He stood and approached him, laying a hand on his shoulder.

"I'm beginning to see how it is," he said. "Then . . . I'll stay here also. I'll not lose you again."

"We could use some intelligence," Bana mumbled, his eyes still closed. "Someone who can move among the Whites as a White."

Rold turned and faced Frank. Pentat approached them, smiling with this idea.

"Welcome, Diego," he said. "We could use your help. Now, are there others here on the desert?"

"No," Frank said. "Just us. This small contingent was to gather up surviving Salkinians after the nuclear sweep. I'm just a driver and a cook. There were some other small groups that were supposed to join us, but they never showed. And I'm told they ran into trouble of some sort."

"Can you tell us when the bombing is to occur?" Bana asked. Frank looked at a clock on a wall that had stopped when the rover had been assaulted. "Probably a couple of hours. They were aware of the battle and immediately sent the bombers. But the base is a couple of thousand kilometers from here."

"Will they send more ground troops?" Rold asked.

"Maybe. But again, it's a long way from Minpana or the base. They could have some here by tomorrow."

"Then at first light we'll go home," Pentat said. "We would leave now, but the snow and darkness would slow us. Let's rest then for awhile — and watch the fireworks begin."

With this last statement Pentat found a bunk and stretched out as Bana had. Rold, Frank, and Yosana returned to the settee and talked in whispers. "How is my father?" Rold asked.

"Bewildered, confused, but still hopeful. I haven't let him despair though he plays the part of a grieving father to the Committee. Ruth Poundstone has essentially taken over. If she knew . . ."

"That I'm alive?" Rold said. "She would shutter. She and Rachel are two of a kind. I blame Poundstone as much for Tyler's death . . . and Blikki's."

"Who's Blikki?"

"My father," Yosana said. She sighed with trembling breath. Tears began again when she had thought none were left.

"I'm sorry," Frank said.

The three talked the evening away. Rold and Yosana told Frank the story of Rold's escape and the trip to the Library. Frank told them of his detective work in trailing Rold to Salkinia. Yosana listened to stories of Rold's childhood on Old Earth — Frank adding a more objective, humbling side to each tale, enjoying his teasing of his old friend. He could see the love between Rold and Yosana; Yosana could see the love and respect between Rold and Frank. Rold felt like a schoolboy again.

Sometime after midnight Rold left Frank and Yosana, as they were getting to know each other, to speak to Pentat. He noticed Pentat was not sleeping. Actually, neither was Bana; both had lost people close to them that day.

"I still don't believe it," Rold said as he knelt beside the bunk. "Or accept it. I expect to turn and see him laughing at me about something, or complaining, telling a story, or helping someone with a burden . . ."

"He was a great man, in my eyes. The best, Mountain Bear. The best. He was more a father to me than my own. My father and I were never close. I could never do anything right as far as he was concerned. And then when he died . . . I felt so guilty. I lost my family and Blikki lost his wife, and we leaned on each other. We had been close for a long time — from my childhood.

"But one gets used to death as an adult. Death is a part of life. And that's not just a statement of philosophy, it's ordinary truth. When something is so familiar it's easier to accept."

"Well, it's not familiar to me. Not until recently."

"You and Yosana will be fine. You have each other. And you can count on me."

"I know." Rold started to say something else on the subject but held his thought. "Listen."

The crackling whoosh of jet engines broke the stillness of the desert night. The bombers were still a good distance from the land rovers, but the sound was beginning to rattle the windows. As they passed overhead the roof was pelted with a shower of tiny pebbles the size of peas. Wind shook the rover, and the whole experience was like a hale storm.

"They're pre-coating the area with a nuclear sponge," Frank said. "They'll do it again after the explosion."

Yosana rushed to the cockpit so that she could look toward First Colony. Frank followed her forward.

"Although we're somewhat protected from nuclear radiation," Frank said, "and the heat won't make it this far, the light from the blast could blind you. Like looking into the sun."

By now everyone had moved forward.

"Face the rear," Frank said. "When the initial flash is over you can watch the fireball."

"Have you seen such explosions before?" Pentat asked.

"Frank worked on nuclear sponge development," Rold said. "They experimented on uninhabited planets, trying to improve the reliability of the sponge."

"An odd vocation for someone who doesn't believe in war," Pentat said.

Frank only nodded his head.

"May we hold you responsible if we're poisoned?" Bana said.

Frank frowned.

The spreading of the sponge took at least an hour. The sound of jets permeated the hills for most of the night. Yosana was beginning to doze when the flash struck her closed eyelids. She opened her eyes a mere crack in time to see what looked like a huge bubble, filled with white light, expanding to mountainous heights until it burst and red flames and black smoke were born from it. A fierce wind hit the land rover head-on, carrying a black wall of dust and debris. The ground rolled and groaned but soon settled. Then the sky was raining ash. It was hard to tell what was ash and what might be sponge being dropped on top of them. But strange rocks began falling. They could be seen from the light of the rising explosion and the still hidden but rising sun. The rocks would fall to the ground and sink into the sand, disappearing. Yosana was the first to see them and point them out and also the first to realize what they were.

"Yaddamet!" she screamed. "From the point pools! The rocks are covered in the invisible paint."

As she said this a couple of rocks fell through the roof of the land rover, falling without loss of speed, as if through perfectly fitted holes, straight down and through the floor.

"What is that stuff?" Frank said.

"Quickly," Pentat said. "Under your shields. Diego, get under here with me."

"Is there fuel in this thing?" Rold asked. "Where?"

"The rear," Frank said as he sat huddled next to Pentat. They had all moved back into the main cabin by now.

"All of us should sit over the fuel cylinder," Rold said. "Here in the back. Make a turtle."

Everyone now sat together on the floor, their shields overhead, overlapping.

More rocks shot through the land rover, some bouncing off the shields and rolling to the floor to sink out of sight. One rolled off Pentat's shield and skidded across Frank's exposed shoulder before disappearing. He did not feel it at first. He touched his shoulder where it itched and brought back a hand covered in blood. He moaned as the pain hit him. Rold dropped his shield, grabbed a towel from the galley and began sopping up blood from the shoulder. He had to wring out the towel several times before the bleeding slowed. He looked at the wound then wrapped it tightly.

"It's mostly skin," he said. "And one deep nick. We'll have to clean it as soon as this shower stops."

By now Frank was in shock. His face was gray and he felt chilled. He had lost a lot of blood. Pentat held him up and moved the shield over him more, the others adjusted theirs.

As the shower of debris stopped, the tremors began. At first there was simply a bump then the land rover was shoved ten meters up and it tumbled over rolling about three times until coming to rest where it lay on its side. Everyone was tossed about; Frank's arm stung from the constant banging. There was actually little damage to the others except for bruises. Bana pushed open the side door, which was now above them, and climbed out.

A light snow was falling again but morning had finally come and light filtered through the winter clouds. The others joined Bana one by one; Frank was lifted handily by Pentat and Bana. Rold and Yosana jumped to the ground and stumbled on the snow-coated scree. The scene was eerie: steaming faults and jumbled boulders were scattered about them where once had been a salt desert. And covering this newly formed landscape was new snow. Smoke rose from the distant ruins and mingled with the low misty clouds. Everyone stood still and stared toward the smoky horizon, Frank holding his bloody arm, Yosana and Rold holding hands.

"Good-bye, Father," Yosana said.

"We've bought some time," Pentat said. "Let's not spoil it by lagging too far behind our warriors. We need a few provisions, more clothing, food. The pridda will get us home. We must make a litter for Diego. We'll use my pony; I'll walk. I think I'm best prepared for walking in this weather."

"I'll let that boast pass," Bana said, "only because you were chosen to lead us."

He looked at Frank.

"We get one White back on his feet, and now we've got another to baby on the road back," he said, with a hard grin.

With no more talk everyone began their preparations, and within an hour they were ready to leave. The pridda had miraculously survived the blast and quake, and were now gathered and packed. Pentat commented that the light snow would cover their tracks nicely. They headed southeast with Bana as scout. The litter glided smoothly over the building snow; Frank enjoyed a peaceful ride — so peaceful that he fell asleep. They skirted the area most affected by the explosion but could see it from the top of a bare ridge. All that was left was a huge crater, perfectly round. But they did not stop long to see it; they wanted to make it to a certain meadow by dusk so they could camp in a protected, flat area — out of the wind and beyond the threat of avalanche. Also, the advanced warriors would be waiting there.

The pace was achingly slow. And as they climbed the plateau the weather grew colder. Rold hugged his pridda from time to time for warmth.

Bana had disappeared at a trot and was gone most of the day. He returned to report that the others had camped in the meadow the night before but were already far ahead of them. He led them down a stream bed into the meadow and showed them a cave at the base of a cliff that ran along the length of the meadow. It had such a low ceiling that they could not stand inside but had to crawl and sit. But it was deep enough for them all to find a spot. The pridda were hobbled and left to forage; a fire was started at the mouth of the cave. The snow had stopped and the clouds cleared quickly. The meadow glowed from moonlight reflecting on the snow, though the fire obscured the sight. Yosana sat beside Rold and sank into self-pity as she drew up a miserable pall around her, along with her blanket. Sadness mingled with the thought of the success of their mission. It was not very satisfying.

The descent was slow but steady. Tyler hugged the boulders that littered the path in order not to slide down the steep slope of the alluvial fan. By the third day her body was hardening; her headaches had lessened. The determination of reaching Rold had steadied her sense of purpose, giving her energy beyond anything she had ever experienced. Occasionally she would see a living cloud and wonder if it was Gwydmonia.

When finally on the desert floor, she saw an army of Zenians. They were not wearing e-suits now that they were on the melting desert; their sleek, insulating fur was totally exposed on their upper bodies. Tyler tried not to panic. She found a rise of boulders and scrub pine in which to hide, holding her weapon in readiness for much of the day.

When night came the army moved on, following a river along its southern bank. Finding courage within her small self, Tyler eased out of her hiding place and began walking again.

The next day was hot and dry. She found herself following the Zenians toward the city ruins. In the distance a cloud of dust rose like a storm. The rumblings of weapons firing and shouting combat reached her as a faint noise on the dry wind. She worried about Rold, her head beginning to ache again, fluid oozing from her wound and dampening the filthy dressing that was still wrapped there.

She stopped again, not wanting to get too close, fearful and tired. She slept until a great, thunderous noise shook the entire world around her. A flash of light as bright as day rocketed toward her. Wind hit her like a wall, knocking her to the ground. She was blinded for several seconds, perhaps minutes. A living cloud appeared as if by magic and buffeted the onslaught of heat and light and deafening sound. The earth quaked as unknown missiles sizzled through the air and into the ground.

When all was calm, Tyler stood again and the living cloud rose. Lights danced within the thing that hovered before her. And as if it were the most natural thing she understood what the lights were saying. They were a code, a message, a way of talking. They said: "DO YOU UNDERSTAND?"

And also as if she were well practiced at it, Tyler moved her hands to signal back a sentence: "YES. BUT HOW?"

"I GAVE YOU THE KNOWLEDGE THROUGH YOUR TOUCHING THE LAST TIME WE MET. I'M GWYDMONIA. DO YOU REMEMBER?"

"YES!"

"YOU ARE SAFE NOW. THE BOMB WILL NOT HARM YOU."

"WAS ROLD DOWN THERE? WAS HE IN THE CITY?"

"YES, BUT NO LONGER. HE IS SAFE NOW."

The slunk moved away from Tyler and swiftly ascended until the darkness of the pre-dawn sky swallowed her.

Tyler looked toward the city. A mammoth crater lay before her glowing red. It's outer rim was at her feet.

She cried aloud a word that echoed across the giant dimple in the earth: "Rold!"

Frank had lain in a corner and was now moaning and shivering. Yosana tore herself from her self-indulgence to see if she could help him. She took some water and her purse to his side.

"Let me see your arm," she said.

Frank tried to sit but Yosana pushed him back down.

"Just stay down," she said.

"I feel like an idiot," Frank said.

"It's all right," she said. "I'm used to you pampered aristos." And she threw a smile toward Rold.

"I know this sounds like I'm complaining," Frank said, "but I'm not a proponent of the war — or any war — and I don't know how much help I'm going to be. Right now I just wish I were home in bed. Rold's the adventurous one. He's been getting me into trouble for years. Ouch! What are you doing!"

"I'm cleaning your wound. Something that we forgot to do this morning. Now drink this. It'll help rid you of the pain."

"Thank you, I . . ."

"Just drink it," Yosana said and she wrapped Frank's arm in clean cloth.

"We're not happy to be in this war either," Pentat said. "My people are not a warring people."

"That's not how the Industrialists view you," Frank said. "They see you as warring savages, hungry for killing. Much like the Zenians. They would have liked to use you, as they have the Zenians, for ground troops. But it seems you couldn't be bought, and you insisted on being trouble makers. For people who dislike war you certainly do it well."

"We train from childhood to fight the Enemy," Bana said. "But you said you didn't make war!" Frank said.

"The 'Enemy' is the pitah — the buffalo," Rold said. "The Teton hunt the buffalo for food and skins. They call them the 'Enemy.'"

"Oh," Frank said. "I see. So you're hunters rather than warriors."

"Yes," Pentat said. "Of course, in our history there have been wars. But those times were brought to an end when starvation became a terrible symptom of that life, and everyone simply stopped. It's said that the women stopped it by refusing to have any more babies because there was no food to feed them. There was an ancient European play that portrayed a people's struggle with war that was somewhat similar. In the play the wives of the warriors cut off their husbands' genitals one by one until they stopped warring."

Everyone smiled at the humor of the black suggestion, though the seriousness of it was felt as well.

"How do you know about ancient Earth literature?" Frank asked.

"The Library," Pentat said.

"You'll see it soon, Frank," Rold said. He moved closer to him and Yosana and knelt with his hands on his thighs. "It's the most incredible thing. Real books! Bound paper folios. Preserved from before the Nation wars."

"From before the last war, at least," Bana said.

"You know of the Nation wars of Old Earth?" Frank said. "How many were there? Scholars have debated that question for centuries."

"When our ancestors left the Great Mother, Earth, there had been two such wars," Pentat said. "What came after we don't know. But it was predicted that if a third war were to come, it would be the end of all life. And from what little we know from our limited outside contact, it seems there must have been at least one more war."

"Well," Frank said, "it didn't end 'all life,' as is obvious, but the world certainly changed. No more nations, and the Scientists became the rulers of the Universe."

A shrieking laugh, the laugh of a woman, came loudly from the mouth of the cave. In the dancing, sparking flames of the small fire a human face glowed. She was a pale woman, her laugh now silenced, but a smile remained. Before anyone vocalized their fear of seeing a ghost or a devil, the woman hopped past the fire, behind which she had been crouching, and crawled in her own shadow into the shallow room. Even though the light was poor it showed the blackened and bleeding burns on her face and arms. She trembled in front of them even as she smiled.

"The Scientists rule no longer," she said and pointed at Rold. "I have finally found you, Rold Simms, though my comrades lay in ash, burned by our own bombs, and the flesh on my fingers has melted away from the flames." She turned her stare to Yosana. "And, *zelita*, you're here with him, of course. And the great chief, Pentat. All alive while your brothers and sisters perished in the holocaust. What cowardice is this?"

She fell to her side and closed her eyes, panting and writhing from the pain.

"It's Barbara," Yosana said rushing to her. "Remember? On our safari."

"Yes," Rold said. "She shaved her head then. I didn't recognize her with those red locks. Is she all right?"

"Burned pretty bad," Yosana said. "Go out and bring me as much snow as you can. Use this skin to carry it. We'll have to get her to the Library."

"The litter will carry them both," Pentat said. "It shouldn't be too much of a burden on the snow."

"But why keep her alive?" Bana said in the Teton language. "Diego is a friend, and I'll stand by him. But she's an enemy. Leave her to die or cut her throat."

Pentat took him by the shoulders firmly.

"Do you see what war has done to you?" he said. "Where's your discipline?"

"But she's a risk — to our whole plan!"

"She's a prisoner, a sick prisoner. At the Library she'll be no risk."

The two men parted. Rold returned with the snow, and Yosana applied it to the most serious burns. Barbara remained unconscious. The others soon went to sleep, but Rold and Yosana tended Barbara until dawn.

The morning brought a cheerless silence to the group. No one escaped the ache-inducing cold. Groaning and curt orders were the extent of the human communication until they were well underway. Cold, dry meat was their breakfast; they chewed it as the pridda splashed through shallow, wet snow. Barbara stared quietly, with some fear, at them all — except Frank, whom she avoided though they were strapped together on the damp, vibrating litter. The sky was clear, without a single cloud — though a couple of living clouds did crowd into the patches of blue that could be seen through the forest ceiling. Green conifers surrounded them until the trail began following a ridge that was the topmost biting edge of a granite cliff. The concave cliff face soon gave way to a more convex dome and then to tumbles of boulders. Here the group took a midday rest.

Bana returned with news of seeing the advanced group several kilometers ahead, down in a green valley below the snow. They seemed too far even to hear his shouts, but he said they appeared in tact and travelling the agreed trail. He stayed long enough to eat something then left again, enjoying the role of the scout.

Yosana tended Barbara's burns and Frank's shoulder while Rold wandered onto some snow free boulders that had been warmed by the sun.

"Where are you taking me?" Barbara asked.

"Don't be afraid," Yosana said. "You're safe. You have Pentat's protection."

"Protection from what? Are we to wander around this wilderness forever? You have no where to go."

"We're going to the Library."

"I've heard of that myth. So it exists. Hah! Rachel Meacom didn't get them all then."

"You have no idea."

"Where's you father?"

"He was killed . . ."

Barbara closed her eyes at the words. Then looking up she saw a living cloud drift overhead then drop below the cliff.

"I hate those things," she said. "They're everywhere, it seems."

"Oh, they're not so bad," Frank said. "I saw Comrade Meacom try to kill one the other day. If he hates them then they must be all right."

"He did what!" Yosana said as she attempted to grab his shoulders. Frank jerked his wounded one away from her grasp.

"He didn't hurt it," he said. "Rachel ordered it shot down, but the energy wave just went right through as if it weren't really there."

"Did you hear that, Pentat?" Yosana said.

"Yes, I heard," Pentat said joining them. "I can't say that I blame them. But such an act can only bring bad luck. The minah-machacute are blessed by the Great Mother. No matter how infuriating they may be, they're not to be harmed. I must say, though, it's laughable these Whites use their guns in such a way. It gives me hope they're too stupid to win this war."

"How else would you kill a slunk?" Barbara asked.

Yosana gave Pentat a threatening stare. He could not help but laugh.

"I'll give no secrets away, sister," he said.

As they were talking, the living cloud drew close to Rold as he sat with his back in the sun. Yosana had taught him some rudimentary signs to use so he thought he would try to say something to this one — at least greet it. He performed a stately "hello" awkwardly, and the living cloud immediately responded. It then flashed the symbol for its name, repeating it several times so that Rold would understand. It was Gwydmonia. Rold had met none of the other living clouds, and was somewhat disappointed by the fact. But at the same time he felt comfortable with Gwydmonia and was glad to see her again. He asked her to slow down her symbols because he was not very good at reading her language as yet. She talked to him as she would a child, but he felt no insult.

"COME . . . CLOSE," she signed.

"I DON'T WANT TO FALL," he answered, looking down the side of the cliff.

"I . . . PROTECT . . . YOU."

"Very well," Rold said aloud as he signed his affirmation. He scooted down a smooth granite pillar that lay on its side wedged between sharply broken ones tumbled around it.

Frank was watching curiously. Rold was too far from the group to hear them chatting. Frank shouted Rold's name and waved. Rold gingerly waved back, smiling. Yosana was paying little attention.

"He's awfully close to that slunk," Frank said.

"Don't worry," Yosana said. "They know each other. That's Gwydmonia — a special friend of mine."

"Yosana!" Pentat said. "What is she up to? She's drawing Mountain Bear to the edge. Is she trying to kill him?"

"She wouldn't do that."

But now Yosana was concerned. She stared with squinted eyes and shaded her brow with both palms.

"He can't ride alone," Pentat said. "It'll kill him."

"I know; I know," she said.

"Ride?" Frank said.

Pentat and Yosana stood and began trotting along the cliff to where Rold sat. Frank followed them. And then, before they could reach him, Gwydmonia shot an appendage toward Rold and in a blur he disappeared.

"It ate him!" Frank said.

Everyone stood at the edge of the slide of boulders and watched the living cloud easing away and drifting out over the valley.

"I don't understand," Yosana said. "Why?"

"Now do you see?" Pentat said in quiet anger. "You lost your mother, your father and now your lover!"

"No!" she said.

"He can't survive without your help."

Yosana could not speak. As she realized the depth of the situation, she started crying. Tears, which were so uncommon in her life, blurred her vision, stinging her eyes.

"We'll wait," Pentat said. "The weather's good. We have food. We'll wait. He's my other half. There's no Eagle without both of us."

After a time Gwydmonia was well out over the valley. No one's eyes left her. But as quickly as she had snatched Rold she now vanished, eliciting gasps from Frank and Barbara.

"I . . . can't give up," Yosana said, trying to arrest her sobs. "She must bring him back. Even if he's . . ."

She turned and walked back to the string of ponies, her body shaking.

"What in the world are you doing?" Rold said. He found himself inside the living cloud as he had been once before. His arms and legs were frozen, suspended in the soft flesh like marshmallows in a gelatin dessert. He opened his eyes to see the bubble of air surrounding his face. Words began tumbling from his mouth until he remembered to "think" his conversation rather than speak it.

"Is Yosana with us?" he asked.

"No," Gwydmonia said.

The voice was the same as before: the husky, reassuring voice of his mother.

"Wait," Rold said in panic. "I forgot to take off my clothes — or rather, I didn't have time . . ."

She laughed. "You only took them off the first time so that you would have them to put on again. I have absorbed the ones you were wearing. A small casualty, don't you think? I'll keep you warm, Rold."

"You'll take me back to Yosana, won't you?"

She hesitated. "I'll try."

Rold decided not to ask further about returning. Obviously there might be some trick to keep him alive, to negate the toxins that were now entering his blood stream, but they would cross that bridge later.

"Why have you taken me?" he asked.

"To talk. The discussion I wish to have is far too complex for the clumsy signing. We need to know more about you. There's an event about to occur in which you'll take part. We want to understand better the part you'll play. And in return I'll answer some of your questions. Perhaps grant a wish. How's that?"

"I have little choice. Of course, you're the larger beneficiary. You'll tell me things to satisfy my curiosity but only so that I'll be better equipped to answer your questions. Am I right?"

"Very quick. Very clever. I see I have to explain very little to you. So I'll begin."

Rold began seeing the landscape in his mind, as he had before, as clear or clearer as he could with his eyes. They were rising. He assumed the rounded mountain below them was where the others were resting.

"Can they see us?" he asked. "Does Yosana know what has happened?"

"She knows. But, no, they can't see us. We're not actually where you think. What you see is where Yosana is camped, but we're looking at it from space. Let me draw back my field of vision a bit."

In only a moment Salkinia shrunk until the curvature was apparent. There they stopped and watched the world creeping about its axis.

"Look," Rold said. "Spotted Valley. You can see it from way up here. You probably know what it is."

"Yes," she said.

"From here . . . well, let's see . . . the rising balls are forming a pattern — a pattern that changes every few minutes."

"Very good."

"Then, it's symbols, communication. If I had a computer I could decrypt it. The matrix is fairly simple. It forms a raster image. Will you not tell me?"

"Eat . . . At . . . Joe's."

"What?"

Gwydmonia was chuckling. Rold angered. He knew he was slowly dying, and this creature joked. She was playing with him, and he found he wanted to join in, despising himself for it.

"You're wasting my time," he said. "I can't fight your induced reactions. It must be the chemicals you're rushing through my body. Now tell me what you mean. Be serious."

"I am serious," she said. "It struck me funny because I've never thought of it that way before. But, because you're from Earth . . . but the wrong century. It really does say something like that. It's an advertisement, a billboard, placed here about a million of your years ago by another species of meddlers. It might be translated: 'Try here. This is a good place to stop over.'"

"True to its word."

"Yes. The Native Americans from Earth saw it. They probably don't realize that it was the Spotted Valley that brought them here. And we're glad they came. They've been a joy for us to watch. They're not meddlers, Rold. They have no interest in controlling the Universe. They have no desire to control Time."

"Are you saying that the Commonwealth meddles?"

"Yes. Of course."

"But so do you."

"No. It's our purpose to extend the life of the Universe. For that we have evolved. The Earth-source life material threatens the Universe."

Rold tried to nod his head but could not.

"Yes," he said.

"You're a philosopher. I think you may understand what I'm about to tell you.

"First of all, your destructive powers are minute. You could annihilate yourselves, perhaps, but little else, much less the whole Universe. The main problem is your talent for collecting things."

"How is that a problem?"

"Quiet your mind, Rold. Practice your meditation. This will take some time to explain and some patience on your part. Do you know the concept of entropy?"

Rold felt himself falling into a drowsy state. He let his body relax. He had been tensing his muscles, though he was completely supported. He tried hard to answer the question.

"In terms of thermodynamics or cosmology?" he said. "Never mind; I know what you mean. The tendency of matter to disperse, spread out, into inert uniformity. Right? On a large scale that's what the Universe has been doing since it started."

"Yes, *this* Universe. There have been so far, thirteen trillion cycles of expansion and condensation within our small sphere which you call the Universe. There's a constant battle between entropy and gravity. Each is the other side of a coin. It's not a battle between Good and Evil as is in your mythology but a striving for equilibrium. We're at an equinox, so to speak, where gravity and entropy are exerting an equal power. Human culture is threatening that equilibrium. You're a log jam in the stream. You threaten to reverse the flow and collapse The Universe, destroying our work, our fourteen trillionth try at this. Personally, my fourth try at it."

"What a fantastic story," Rold said. He snapped out of his trance. "If I believed you had survived a collapse of the Universe — four times no less — even if I believed that, how in the hell could our puny little culture effect either entropy or gravity! I can just see us corralling stars and planets, pushing them toward some Universal core; and of course the stars would just placidly obey as cattle. Please tell me another fairy tale!"

"Your insolence is understandable, but you must try to be reasonable. Your view of Time is so limited. I've lived several billion years. I can show you those memories. I can make you believe, but I want you to try to conceptualize it on your own. In another million years or so your culture will have turned the process around. You concentrate energy, matter, socio-networks. We have seen this pattern before. Technology is an attack on entropy. The complexity of the problem is the key to understanding it.

"Minerals, which are scattered and ever disintegrating, are mined and collected, then refined and used for manufacturing. Energy is concentrated, networked from one star system to another; conserved when possible. Material is transported from one star to another, and so on. The ramifications are subtle, but in another million years devastating.

"Your system of Scientists and Industrialists has accelerated the process. In the last few years, a thousand or so, you've managed to infect an entire galaxy. Certainly that's a small piece of real estate, but in a million years it'll be a thousand maybe two thousand galaxies. There are scientists right now who are about to stumble onto the principles of space folds. Another group — and this is the most damaging development — have finally completed the unified field theory by guessing at the relationship between entropy and gravity."

"Studies like those are considered alchemy these days," Rold said. "No one's come up with a closed mathematical system for either project."

"You're showing your prejudice. But this isn't a productive digression. Let me explain things this way: Natural Law is nothing but a roll of the dice. You've heard this saying? Yes. Well, imagine an infinite number of rolls of the dice. Certainly an infinite number of rolls should produce a run of sevens, say, oh, three hundred million times consecutively (just for the sake of picking a round number). Several generations of human beings would see this rolling of sevens enough to believe that the dice will always turn up seven. They can predict it absolutely. No human existed when the roll was not seven and probably no human will still be alive when it stops being seven. *I've* seen the dice roll many numbers other than seven."

Both were silent for a while. Rold listened to his own breathing. The bubble around his face caused an echo when he exhaled. He could smell his breath. It smelled of smoked meat. He smiled for a short time.

"You have my attention," he said.

"Good."

"Such a strange vocation you have. You're cosmological ecologists. Though it sounds more like a religion."

"If you want to call it that."

"You're lovers of decay rather than construction; you would prefer we destroy rather than build! This war should suit your purpose very well — especially if the Scientists and Industrialists destroy each other."

Rold struggled in his bindings. His instincts were to stand up as if he were sitting, because a horrible thought grabbed him by the lapels and jerked his body upward.

"Did you have anything to do with this war?" he accused. "Did you cause it to happen?" The anger in his words rang true even though it was a thought rather than an actual barking of his voice.

"Yes."

"Probably you did have something to do with it. But don't give yourselves too much credit. The existential nature of Humankind might just surprise that ancient ego of yours."

"We're counting on it! But calm your hurt pride."

"I have little left to hurt. I have only Yosana and our unborn child."

Both were silent again. Rold's breathing was hard and wheezy. He began calming himself but did not drop his new feelings of anger so that he might mask his fear.

"I have had a loss," Gwydmonia said.

A great blue, windy sea slid past them. Rold felt that they were flying slowly over it. He could smell the salt and hear the breakers in the distance where brown, rocky islands mottled the horizon.

"We had a great leader," she said. "His name was Pandodellock. He was very important among my people, a king. 'King of the fair folk' the islanders called him. There was a time when the Teton loved us — not so long ago. But then the demons came. It was so brief, just a wink. They came and saw little here they wanted. But they saw us and thought one of us would make a nice trophy.

"Look! There he is: Pandodellock. *Pandy.*"

Rold could see several living clouds. He could not distinguish one from the other.

"There, on the right," Gwydmonia said. "I'm showing you a memory — a painful one."

Rold tried to see what Gwydmonia was showing him, but his sensitivity was culturally biased so that he still only saw some anonymous living clouds floating over the islands.

"You spoke of demons," he said. "Are you talking about the cloud wars? Blikki told me some stories about cloud hunters and how they finally discovered a means of killing living clouds. It sounded like a myth. Are you not immortal? You're the closest thing to it that I can think of — if you're really as old as you say."

"No. We can be killed. Pandy was. And others. The Teton fought the demons, for we were powerless against them. The demons took the lifeless matter that was Pandy, immersed it in fluid and left to show the prize to their people in another galaxy. The Teton thought they had defeated them. Why spoil their self-image, ruin their confidence? We didn't tell them that the demons were barely bothered by their lances and arrows. But the Teton did annoy them enough to save a few of our lives.

"The Teton lost many lives in those wars. Many of them resented us because we didn't defend ourselves and seemed cold for their grief. The gay ceremonies and status of cloud riding suffered. And now Yosana is the last, and much of it is no longer understood. Your daughter has the potential for becoming a rider — if you allow it."

"If we all live that long."

"Yes. You must live. You have something to do. You'll be the one to make the decision at the correct moment. We don't know what or when, but there's a task we must perform in order to succeed, and you'll direct us."

"That's preposterous, of course. What do I have to do with it?"

"I don't know, yet. A time will come. For now you must return and stay alive."

"There's so much I don't understand."

"I'll say one more thing. You must give us something else, more than just your decision when the time comes — a gift. It will be difficult. It could mean your life — or someone else's dear to you. We're trying to discover which of you is the one. But we'll talk of that at a different time."

"It matters little if I'm dying now."

"I don't have time to explain. Here, let me show you something. This is a little gift for you."

The scene changed to the familiar alpine plateau where Rold had been traveling. They moved over it at a blurring speed then slowed to a stop. Down below, in a small glade was a camp — a camp for a single person. It appeared to be a warrior, a woman warrior, but she carried an energy blaster. So she could not be Teton! Who was this woman, with red dust caked to her face and hair, cuts and bruises and a cunning expression in her cold blue eyes?

"Tyler!" Rold was breathing heavily and shaking his head. "It can't be! But it must be. It is!"

"Yes. I've been watching her for days. She's grown up in a short time, Rold. She's no longer the child you knew. Her wound is healing now. She's quite healthy. And she has killed Zenians."

"I don't believe any of this. You're messing with my head again."

Rold found himself quickly back in his immobile world of clinging gelatin flesh. There was movement then an image appeared. Tyler was looking at Gwydmonia, making hand signals much like Yosana.

"Speak, Rold, and I'll provide your words to her."

He hesitated. He still did not fully believe that Tyler was actually outside there, speaking with the living cloud. But he decided to play along.

"Tyler, it's Rold," he said aloud. Gwydmonia showed him her lighted signals that were an interpretation of his words.

Tyler stepped back, her grimy face startled. Then her hands moved at a furious pace.

"Where are you, Rold?" Gwydmonia simulated Tyler's voice as she translated the signing.

"Within the living cloud. I'm doing what Yosana calls riding."

Tyler put her hands to her mouth. Tears muddied her face and a smile burst from her mouth.

"I've found you!" she said. "Finally. I thought you were killed by the nuclears."

"I thought you were killed by Rachel Meacom."

"I was saved. Gwydmonia has helped too. Oh, Rold, I missed you. I love you so much! Can you not come out?"

Gwydmonia now interrupted by talking to Tyler. She asked her to place her palm against her body so that they could meld. Tyler did so and felt the tingling again as Gwydmonia entered her body with her probing cilia.

"I'll mix her blood with yours, Rold," Gwydmonia said. "Perhaps it will be enough to thin the poison. Then I'll release you."

"I feel it," he said and felt himself strengthening.

In a moment Gwydmonia had pulled away from Tyler and deposited Rold on the ground, his naked body shivering.

"Rold!"

Tyler was upon him in a second. She kissed his head and put her arms around his shoulders. He stood slowly.

"I'm weak," he said. "But I can walk. We must find Yosana."

"I'm here, Rold. I'll help you."

"Oh, Tyler. Tyler. You've risen from the dead! I can't tell you . . ."

"Don't talk. Save your strength. Now, can you tell me which way to go? Where is Yosana?"

CHAPTER 16

Shades they seemed, the brother and sister;
Margona arrived in quiet solitude . . .

\- From "The Song of Margona"
  by Pitallela-Sim

Yosana watched the night pass without nodding a single time. Frank's arm seemed to be clean and already improving while Barbara's burns were becoming inflamed. She slept though; Yosana had given her an herb tea that helped her relax. But now the sun was rising and the camp began reviving. Pentat looked at Yosana, pain flooding his eyes. She sat, her body stiff, staring at the ground as she stirred the icy snow with a pine branch. Pentat turned, afraid to speak, afraid of his own anger at the abhorred living cloud. But hope still lingered and his heart stopped as he saw a living cloud moving toward the camp. Then another one floated over the valley and joined the first. And another and another, until there were a dozen minah-machacute all bunched together into something of a sphere just off the cliff.

Yosana jumped to her feet, dropping her stick, and ran to the edge of the cliff, stumbling on chipped rock debris close to the rounded drop of the granite dome. Pentat had to grab her before she plunged down the scree slope in her reckless run.

Pentat followed. Frank and Barbara stood at the edge watching.

Two people were climbing the hillside: a woman with a blaster strapped to her shoulder and a man she was helping, who was naked and pale.

Yosana and Pentat stood aghast.

"Ghosts!" Yosana said. "They're both dead."

"Mountain Bear?" Pentat called. "Is that you?"

"Yes," Rold called. "Come help. I don't think I can make it up."

"Well, sister," Pentat said in a low voice. "He lives. I wonder how the minah-machacute managed it. And who is the woman with him?"

"His dead sister: Tyler. This is not possible. It can't be true!"

Yosana shook her head. The sight of Rold, who should have died riding alone, and Tyler, whom she saw cut down outside of Minpana, here together shook her confidence in her sense of reality.

"Are you frightened, Yosana? Do you really think they're ghosts? Nonsense. That's Mountain Bear, in the flesh."

Pentat laughed at his own little joke as he carefully walked down the slope.

Yosana rushed by him, sliding in her hasty descent. She grabbed Rold and felt his chill. His body was blue and shivering as they stood in the wet snow. Bana had returned from the trail in time so see Pentat join Yosana in trying to warm Rold. He met them at the ridge as they finished the climb and threw a pitah blanket around Rold.

Yosana now took time to look at Tyler. She seemed strangely different. The bandages on Tyler's head were dirty and worn.

"We need to get you cleaned up," she said. "And change that dressing. I'm so glad to see you, Tyler. You don't know how much we've grieved for you."

Tyler joined Yosana and Rold in an embrace.

"I've thought of nothing else," Tyler said, "but finding Rold. I never thought to find you as well."

Yosana looked puzzled but did not question Tyler further.

"Hello, Tyler." Frank had been standing back, waiting for his turn.

"Frank! How . . ."

"I think we both have stories to tell," he said.

After some warm soup and the doctoring provided by Yosana, Tyler spoke of her rescuers and recovery from the blaster wound. Rold sat quietly and listened to this amazing tale, not quite believing it was his sister who was speaking. She has changed, he thought. The minah-machacute and the war . . .

Tyler decided to tell as little as possible about her contact with Gwydmonia. Yosana appreciated her reticence, but was determined to get her alone and question her further. She was not a *child-of-the-ride*. She should not have been able to communicate with Gwydmonia. But the most amazing event was Rold's ride! A man, alone, and he had survived! This story would certainly spread and stir questions in the minds of many Teton.

Yosana questioned him, but he refused to talk about his conversation with Gwydmonia. He seemed changed, moodier than normal. But his eyes still shined when looking at her, and especially when looking at Tyler; the miracle of her return awed them both.

But Rold was weak. Since coming to Salkinia he had lost his sister, mated within a living cloud, fought sickness, fought Zenians, ridden a living cloud alone and lived, and then recovered his sister. Enough to fatigue the strongest of Teton. Would he be able to stand up to the harsh winter to come? He had no idea what winter meant in these mountains. But he would soon find out.

Rold insisted on resting only a day; no one objected. Bana was sent ahead to delay the advanced party. Yosana found some clothes for Rold to wear, and by noon they were walking around ready to take to the trail. Frank, too, felt more fit and decided to walk the remainder of the trip. But Barbara was growing worse. She now had a fever and was even less coherent. She was strapped to the litter for traveling. Yosana worried whether she would live. But she had done all that she could, though she wondered if she would have done more if Barbara were Teton rather than the enemy.

Rold performed well on the hike, and the group made fifteen kilometers before sunset and found the main group of warriors. They had waiting per Bana's request along a black stream that rushed through the encroaching snow. The camp was below the alpine forest in foothills covered with low chaparral. Here the snow was thin but not yet melting even though the sun had shined all day. Fresh game was hunted, and a stew with the meat, some wild roots, and autumn berries was cooked. The hot meal was welcomed by all, and something of a celebration began — the first of many — honoring their victory and the success of the deception. Although Yosana missed her father, the jubilant warriors made her smile.

During the walk Tyler spoke little, only telling of her recovery and journey and the Zenians, Rold becoming quite impressed with his sister's heroics. He told her about the Library and the war and First Colony, and Blikki. He could hardly believe she was still alive and kept saying so.

Now at the evening gathering he was beginning to accept it, feeling happier then he had felt in months.

"Father would have loved this," Yosana said. Rold and she were sitting on a blanket with another one wrapped around them as they watched the dancing and singing Teton and the crackling fire below a black night sky.

"I can just imagine," Rold said. "I'm not a religious man; I have no beliefs of afterlife. But I do believe that a person's immortality lies in the memories of those who survive him. Blikki will live for as long as the Teton exist. He's here tonight — with you and me . . . and our baby."

Yosana put her hand across Rold's mouth.

"Not too loud," she said. "I'd like to wait a while before the whole world knows."

An uneventful trip took them home to the Library, the time flashing by at the cadence of the fleet pridda hooves. The crisis of infection of Barbara's burns passed in a single night, and by the time they approached the Library basin she was riding the pridda behind Pentat rather than on the litter. But she remained quiet — sulking and unhappy, except for a few derisive comments about the additional Teton warriors who escaped the bombing. Frank remained aloof and uncommonly quiet. Rold and Tyler could not get enough of each other, and Frank left them alone. He was happy that Rold was alive, and Tyler. For so long he had been told they were lost and probably dead. It felt good to watch Rold acting like a kid again: his love for Yosana was almost embarrassing and yet heartwarming to see.

The warriors began climbing the hill that hid the Library before noon. Scouts had trotted ahead the day before to herald the news of the bombing and to list the dead. As the sun was at its apex, Pentat strode to the top of the hill — to the same spot where he had stood when he had returned from the Minpana Hold. And again a massive reception awaited.

The sight of the Library itself, the tent villages, and the thousands of Teton elicited a long string of nonsensical exclamations from Frank that signified his positive amazement. But Barbara was dumbstruck. She slid from the pridda, pushed her way to a nook between two boulders that presented a clear vista and stared with an open mouth. She sat on one of the boulders as if her legs would not hold her, then in a panic bolted back down the hill. Yosana ran after her and grabbed her from behind. Barbara screamed for her release, but Yosana held her until she relaxed.

"We failed," Barbara said. "They failed." She laughed. "Rachel's head will explode. What a joke! She not only failed at destroying these people, but she didn't kill Simms — or even capture him. How many natives were at the bomb site?"

"None."

Barbara laughed again. "Beautiful!" she said. "If these people had weapons, if they worked with the Scientists, they could beat the Industrialist forces. You know that? Is that what's happening? Is that why you and Simms are here?"

She was hysterical for a moment. Yosana tried to calm her and sat beside her, holding her rigid, struggling body.

"The Whites brought this war to us," Rold said as he came upon them. He knelt beside them and touched Yosana's shoulder. She looked into his eyes and saw the change for the first time, though she realized it must have been happening all along. He was becoming Teton. Perhaps riding Gwydmonia hastened it. But the important thing was it was there, in his eyes, in the way he moved and talked. Even his Ameranglo had acquired a small accent. *I need you more than ever,* she thought. *I love you.*

"You talk as if you're one of them," Barbara said.

Yosana looked up and saw that the entire group was watching them and listening. Pentat had turned his back to the Library and was also listening to Rold. He turned his head upward and flung a whooping cry toward heaven — it was a cry of victory. Then he jumped onto his pony and charged down the hill toward the Library, his warriors following at a gallop. The villagers shook the earth with their roaring reception. Yosana, Barbara, Tyler and Rold still sat below the crest. They could not see the parade, but the sound reached them as thunder. Frank stood at the top and watched the decent of the warriors, still amazed, then he turned back down the hill to join Rold.

"Incredible," he said. "It's like stepping back into the past on O. E. I've never seen anything like it. Do you know that these people have outwitted the Industrialists, along with their technology? But who would have guessed there were so many? There must be close to . . ."

"A million," Rold said.

"Yes, but it'll do you no good," Barbara said. She stood and held her arms close around her chest. "Rachel will find you eventually."

"She won't be looking," Rold said.

A living cloud passed overhead, moving toward the Library. "Let's go down to the festivities," Rold said. "We want to show you the Library."

"We want to show you both," Yosana said as she gently took Tyler's arm and began walking up the hill. Barbara mounted Yosana's pridda and followed, resigned to her current predicament. Rold and Frank joined them, pulling their wary ponies behind them.

There was not the kind of celebration as the time of Rold's first arrival to the Library. A few warriors, mostly of the Eagle village, had followed Pentat and his small band to the steps of the Library, making joyous noises and inspiring others to join in. A full half of the city, though, was busy and seemed to pay little attention. Of course that also meant that the other half became thoroughly involved in the festivities, and as such made an impression on the newcomers. Music was started, and the smell of roasted meat and stewed vegetables mingled with the choking wood smoke of the campfires. The Master Librarian stood upon the steps embracing Pentat. Rold and Yosana watched them from the far end of the thoroughfare. They had lagged long enough to be half of a kilometer behind. To one side as they walked along the muddy street were a group of families wailing miserably. Yosana explained that they mourned the lost warriors who were related to them.

"Should we be joining them?" Rold asked.

"They have only just learned of their loss," she said. "And anyway, I don't believe in mourning — not public mourning. No matter how wretched I feel."

A wave of attention flowed from the steps back to Rold and Yosana. Everyone seemed to be staring and murmuring. Frank and Barbara cringed from it, thinking that one of them was the object of their stares. Yosana became self-conscious of her abdomen, knowing the strict morals of the Teton and worrying that her pregnancy had been revealed. The four of them stopped as a frightening silence swirled about the city. Rold looked into Pentat's eyes. He knew then that it was he that was commanding such notice. Then he saw the Master Librarian kneel. Everyone along the way began to kneel. The sound of knees thumping down on well-tamped earth filled the air. Rold could no longer stand still. He strode with a long, speedy gate, leaving the others behind until he was at the steps. Hands from the crowd reached out to touch him. They did not grasp nor pull, but gently brushed him with their fingertips. He felt like he had waded through a muddy swamp where reeds and hanging moss slid across his skin.

The Librarian stood and took his hand.

"Hello, Chaka," Rold said.

The old man smiled and nodded, keeping a steady grip on Rold's hand.

"You're not a ghost?" Chaka said.

"I don't think so."

"We've just heard of your experience: You rode the minah-machacute alone, a man, and returned alive."

"Yes."

"It is like you're a spirit walking on the earth."

Rold shrugged at the suggestion.

"Blikki is dead," he said. "I can hardly believe it."

"You describe a mystery we've all seen or felt. I'll miss my friend. Now turn around and acknowledge my people's awe. You're more than a hero to them: Pentat is their hero; you are their hope."

Rold turned and saw the blur of faces. He held out his hands as a broad greeting and received a cheer from the multitude that finally broke the spell of silence that was haunting the gathering. He turned to Pentat.

Pentat's stone face broke easily into a smile, and he grabbed Rold shoulder. A cheer arose from the middle of the city. Then, so quickly it surprised Rold, the crowd settled down and wandered back to their individual villages and chores.

"Well, I'm glad for that," Rold said as he watched the audience dwindle.

"There's much work to be done," Chaka said. "We can't celebrate every battle; heroes will have to take comfort in their own knowledge of their contributions in the future. Life can't stop for everyone. As you can see the snow is half way down the plateau. Soon it will cover our meadow. The Whites have destroyed many pitah. Every morsel of food must be preserved for the cold months because there's no fresh meat to hunt. And we must prepare for war. But . . . there'll be some time to relax soon, as in every winter when it's too cold to do anything else."

"The Whites will not relax," Rold said. "They'll discover our deception eventually and come looking for us."

"You haven't seen our winters, Mountain Bear," Pentat said. "No human, no machine could travel across the plateau or through the Spotted Valley once the snow is deep. By the time the Whites get suspicious of our plan (if they do), it'll be too late. We're protected here — and also trapped."

"But to be trapped in a library is not a bad thing," Rold said looking up at the building.

"Are these prisoners?" Chaka said looking at Barbara and Frank as they finally walked to the steps.

"She is," Pentat said, pointing to Barbara. "But he is not. This is Frank Diego, a friend of Mountain Bear, a man from Earth."

"You have an important name," Chaka said in English as he greeted Frank.

"And this is Mountain Bear's sister."

"The other one who has come back from the dead, I see. I'm afraid these events are taxing my already weary brain.

"And this prisoner? You've been hurt. Quickly, come inside where we can treat those burns. I take it you've kept these wounds clean, Yosana?"

"Of course," Yosana said. "She's much better today. Though her shock over seeing the winter gathering may have set her back."

"I'm 'set back' myself every time I walk outside and see this monstrosity," Chaka said peering out over the city. "Bana talked me into this. And now it's becoming more and more unmanageable. I'm certainly thankful you're here, Pentat. I'm getting too old for this. We've always been a peaceful community. We'll survive, though; we will survive."

He sighed and turned toward the entrance, a staff in hand. "Go with the librarians," Yosana said to Barbara. "We have our own lodge in the meadow. When your burns have been dressed tell someone to show you to the Eagle village; or I can come find you. Frank, you should also get that cut looked at."

Frank and Barbara followed the librarians into the huge structure. Pentat had slipped away to see his family, and Yosana and Rold slowly walked to their own lodge with Tyler following, both quietly relieved to be home and safe and clinging to each other for support. Yosana wept silently as she thought of her father. She waved away Rold's concerned expression and explained that she was all right and needed to cry occasionally — he should get used to it.

Tyler was silent.

The lodge was clean, and a fire in the stove was warming the room.

Tachina must have prepared the place for their arrival. A pot of stew was bubbling, filling the lodge with a glorious smell. They dropped to their knees on the fur rugs, exhausted.

"Am I staying with you here, Brother?" Tyler asked as she stood at the entrance.

"What a question," Yosana said. "Please. Stay with us."

"Of course," Rold said and held out his hand to take hers.

"I thank you. I must sleep."

Tyler's body was trembling with fatigue. She dropped to her knees then fell to a curled position and quickly lost consciousness.

Spring was getting underway at Collinsville; the mornings were cool and crisp, while the afternoons were warm and narcotic. A full meeting of the Committee had been called so that the military faction could make a state-of-the-war presentation to the political factions. The meeting was planned to take a week, but it had now been two, and a third was being discussed. It was the day before the week-end break that Ruth Poundstone arranged for an intelligence status report to be given. Malcolm Simms presided over the sessions each day, and this day was no exception, but his health was deteriorating, as all could see.

Ruth always put on a good show. She began in the morning with a review of territorial dominance, pointing out that the Industrialist wave had slowed to a standstill: The number and position of stellar systems held by each side had stabilized. Next she showed statistical models that predicted the Industrialist movements in the future using a handful of scenarios. The visual media was a holograph of the galaxy with green stars for the Industrialists, red for the Scientists, and white for unconquered stars. The models showed the time stepped movements, in three dimensions, of each contingent. The energy of the movement was predetermined; the only questions asked were tactics and overall strategy. The models were well received. Ruth explained that the input for the models was derived heavily from her intelligence network. She then revealed a new technological breakthrough that was aiding her efforts. It was a new method of transmitting long distance communications. She reveled in her reception as she explained the technique: It came from one of her own ideas about wave theory. The upshot was that it increased the transmission speed by a factor of three.

After a lunch break she began an unscheduled report. The Committee members were noisy and somewhat reluctant to pay attention after having a filling feast on the lawn in such fine spring weather. Ruth had to pound a gavel to quiet them. A holograph of an unfamiliar stellar system floated in the middle of the round room. Sixty-four Committee members had seats around it, and almost as many aids sat behind them. None could recognize the system.

"This is the Beldine System," Ruth said looking around the room. "Industrialist stronghold . . ."

A burst of gasps raced around the hall. Looks of smiling disbelief, of frowning dismay, and serious attention accompanied the gasps and murmurs. Ruth looked self-satisfied, though trying not to smile. This was the key to their victory, and she knew it — a triumph of secret intelligence.

Malcolm Simms stood up. For weeks now he had only sat quietly, allowing Ruth her moment of glory.

"Is that where my children are?" he asked as he pointed. All looked to Ruth.

"Yes, Malcolm," she said gravely. "Let me begin at the beginning." Malcolm sat down again, exhausted. "This planet here . . ." She pointed to Salkinia as it rotated around the Beldine sun. ". . . has an Earth-like support system. It's called Salkinia and until recently had conservation status with a small mining concession. But two years ago Industrialist Militia began building a base there. This has been planned for quite some time.

"My contacts followed leads from Caljunna, where Rold and Vivian Tyler were abducted. My personal concern for my old friend, our venerable comrade, Malcolm, prompted me to begin a search in earnest from the time of the terrorist abduction. This led us to Salkinia and our fantastic discovery of the enemy's primary base."

"And what of Malcolm's children?" one man asked.

"Yes, what about them?" another said.

"Patience," Ruth said. "Vivian Tyler was shot and killed by Militia trying to escape." Gasps spread around the room. Malcolm whitened. "Rold was imprisoned. But, he escaped with the help of some neo-primitive natives there. But, alas, the rebellious natives were such a nuisance to the Industrialists that they took steps to wipe them out. Some sort of tribal gathering was held by the natives. The Industrialists went in with a nuclear sweep, and . . ."

Pictures of the air strike now appeared in place of the Beldine System. Malcolm looked on in horror as the nuclear fireball ballooned in the Salkinian night sky.

"So," Ruth continued, "not only have they killed more innocent people, they have murdered Malcolm Simms' only children."

"Is there no chance he may have escaped or not been there in the first place?" Malcolm asked. All eyes turned to him; his voice sounded weak and unsure, quavering with age.

"He was reported to have been at the bombing sight," Ruth said. "In fact they claim to have destroyed ninety-nine percent of the native population.

They combed the surrounding area with Zenian troops. No survivors."

Malcolm coughed heavily. Ruth wondered what he knew. The news of his daughter's death was a shock, but he did not seem to accept Rold's demise. He stood quietly and walked out of the room.

The order of the hall was thoroughly upset. It took a long while for Ruth to regain their attention.

"What else could we have expected?" she said. "Rold Simms was lost long ago. The Industrialists never planned to keep him alive. But now . . . let us forge ahead. We have the information we need. In three months we'll be ready for a full-scale offensive. And now we know where to attack!"

A cheer arose as a grim sound. The thirst for blood had been revived by Ruth's news. As everyone calmed down, she made a more detailed presentation of the base's strength, in hardware and troops. Then she showed her enhanced plan for the offensive: ten thousand space destroyers, each capable of disintegrating a whole planet, to descend on Beldine.

After the session, which closed at almost midnight, Malcolm confronted Ruth in her chamber.

"Quite late for you, isn't it?" Ruth said looking up from her desk.

"I suppose. You . . . you took pleasure reporting my daughter's death, didn't you?"

"Is that what this is all about? Of course not. How could you think that? I'm very pleased with our discovery of the base. It could mean the end of the war. But I'm as saddened by the news as anyone — except you, I'm sure."

"I wish I could believe you, Ruth. And for a little while I'll convince myself that you're telling the truth, just so I can sleep at night. I believe that Rold is alive."

"Poor Malcolm. Denial is the first reaction at hearing such news, you know. It's quite common. But you must accept it and go on. We're in a war. Rold and Vivian Tyler were the first and most important casualties of the war. Their names will be remembered for years to come."

"That's little comfort, Ruth. I just want to return to O. E. I hate this network of death and destruction you've constructed."

"Perhaps you should go back. You need a rest. Let us manage this war. You don't need the grief."

"Perhaps you're right. If the whole galaxy is going up in smoke, I would rather be at home when it does."

"Well, August," Rachel said, "it seems that your job was rather easy." She was sitting on a window cushion sixteen storeys above Minpana gazing through the plate glass at the amber dots of light that defined the streets and hobbles of the city at night. The grid of lights was sharply bounded by the

Wall. All was dark beyond, up to the horizon where the only light came from the stars and moon. Rachel saw it as a symbol of their isolation; though if she were looking west the lights of the military complex there were visible to the far horizon, outshining the stars.

Colonel August stood in the middle of Rachel's apartment, holding a glass of wine she had poured him. He took a sip and waited for her to taste the wine from her glass.

"It was all very strange, if you ask me," he said. "How could there be no survivors?"

"Intelligence, planning. The sweep was effective. You had no refugees to round up because there were none."

"And no Simms to be found."

"Simms is dead!" Rachel's eyes tensed.

"Of course."

"That subject is closed. Now, give me a report. Tell me of your losses and anything interesting. Why were you out there for three weeks?"

"Well, first of all, the main loss occurred the night of the sweep. A company of Zenians was sent to control the perimeter around the bombing site and engaged in combat. This we know, but all were lost in the sweep. It seems they were drawn into the area and were destroyed along with the natives."

"A pity," she said smiling. "Go on. And please sit."

"I prefer to stand."

"Great Mother, man, relax. If you're going to drink my wine, sit down."

"Very well."

He took a stool that had been tucked under a small drink bar and pulled it more into the center of the room, then sat on it; though it looked like he was leaning on it more than sitting.

"After the bombing," he continued, "a wide search was made for survivors and extraneous settlements. None were found. A very large circle of destruction occurred from the blast. A great deal of seismic activity was set off which was far reaching."

"A good job, I must say. But what else were you doing out there? If there were no survivors . . ."

"At least half of the Zenians were searching in the mountains when a blizzard hit. We almost lost control of the bastards. They view snow and ice as we would molten lava. Several actually died. They were in such a panic that they fought among themselves and damaged their climate suits. It took several days to restore order and get them out of the muck. They were overjoyed to be back in the desert. I don't think they'll be much use to us in the mountains this winter."

"We won't need them in the mountains. The natives are destroyed. Even if a handful still live, how many could there be? But it's good information. I wondered how the Zenians would react. We'll have to add this to our strategy calculations so that no population centers are attacked in their winter cycles. Also, I think the climate suits should be improved.

"Damn it, though, I'm not very pleased this weakness has surfaced. It just means we'll have to depend on space weaponry more. Not to criticize my father, of course, but I never thought that a massive ground force was a necessary expenditure. Certainly there have been some successes; I'll not argue that.

"Well, anything else?"

"Oh yes, your friend, Barbara Jenkins. She's missing. A casualty of the sweep, most likely."

"That's a shame. Has her husband been informed?"

"Yes. He's asking for a transfer. Perhaps a viceroy position in another system. He has some influence."

"Not on this planet he doesn't. But, he can have it. Arrange it please."

August took a sip of his wine then walked to the window and sat beside Rachel.

"Things have certainly changed since we first came here," he said looking out over the city.

Rachel looked him up and down.

"Did I ask you to sit beside me?" she said. "Rather impertinent aren't you?"

"Oh? I just thought that since Simms was dead, perhaps you would finally forgive my past failure with him."

"Perhaps."

"It's going to be a long, cold winter."

Rachel laughed and returned her gaze to the city. It looked beautiful to her at night. It was such a contrast to its unromantic squalor of the daylight hours. How she wished to be gone from here. But here was where the work needed to be done. Here was where the power was — this dusty, savage planet.

She frowned as a black blob floated over the city blocking its view. Two, maybe three, living clouds were moving just outside her window. She stood and threw a switch that brought down shades covering the windows.

"Find me a way of exterminating those damned slunks," she screamed. Then she calmed down. "And perhaps the winter will not be quite so cold."

CHAPTER 17

Rold took the Rider, mother and wife
To the steps of the library to start their new life.

- From "The Song of Margona"
  by Pitallela-Sim

"And are we to wait here for months while Rachel Meacom destroys our world?"

Tyler was practically shouting. In the weeks that had passed since her arrival at the Library she had thrown herself into the Teton culture, becoming a woman warrior with the Eagle village. Rold was amazed in her transformation. Her body was becoming lean and sturdy. She kept her blonde hair short, and her blue eyes still shone when they met his. But she had lost her innocence — a sad but impressive change.

She was talking to Frank, who had spent his time roaming the Library, gobbling up books as fast as he could read them. They were walking along a muddy road, snowflakes falling in spirals on their shoulders, slowly dusting the road that had been cleared only yesterday.

"The last thing I heard was both sides were preparing for a large scale push in three to four months. You aren't missing a thing. Rold is right to have these natives preparing also."

"That's what you said two weeks ago. But I'm going crazy, Frank."

"You'll do more good here, I think, than getting yourself killed back in Minpana. Why don't you just relax and get involved with Rold's joining celebration."

"I know. Tachina has asked me to help. She's been marvelous, like a mother to me. I wonder what Father's doing right now. I wish there was some way to let him know we're all right, we're safe and alive."

"That'll be my job. Don't worry, Tyler."

Frank paused and looked at this tense young woman whom he had teased and played with when she was just a young girl.

"What is it?" she asked, smiling at his stare.

He shook his head. "You're all grown up. I miss that little girl who used to put live crabs in my bed."

"You were always mean to me."

"And you loved it!"

"Thanks."

"For what?"

"For bringing me down to earth. I guess I've got cabin fever already and the winter has hardly started. All right, I'll go see Tachina. I *am* happy for Rold. I assume this ritual is the same as a wedding?"

"Yeah. Do you understand it? They barely know each other."

"I understand it." And Tyler turned her gaze toward the southern mountains.

Both Rold and Yosana agreed that a huge celebration for their joining would be too extravagant, if not inappropriate. Rold had little means to provide for such a feast and preferred that the Teton not spend their stores. Blikki's absence was an unspoken reason for a small ceremony. So they asked Chaka to prepare the ritual and had Pentat, Tachina and their son, Chomata-te, Tyler, and Frank Diego to witness their bonding. The Teton word for marriage translated as joining or bonding — or *bondage*, which made Rold laugh a little when he thought about the implications of the idiom. Yosana was not very pleased when he explained his laughter.

In the many weeks before the wedding could be performed, the snow had descended to the meadow, which was now covered with a permanent coating of the fine, white ice crystals. The conical lodges poked up above drifts, splotches of snow sticking to them with smoke escaping the chimneys for acres around the colossal village. Library workers stayed busy every morning shoveling snow and scraping ice from the baked clay steps of the Library. On this morning they had to also drive away children who were using the steps as a bumpy ride for their sleds. Rold stopped and watched the librarians shaking their shovels at two boys as they jumped onto a toboggan. They laughed and screamed with each bounce and ended their ride overturned and deeply sunk in a drift of snow.

"Your mind is obviously not on our joining," Yosana said as she turned to see Rold stop several paces behind the others. They were on their way to a sacred spot at the edge of the meadow where the ceremony would take place. It was midmorning, and the sun was lighting a deep blue, cloudless sky from a very low perch just above the eastern plateau.

"It's a glorious morning," Rold said. Yosana's face glowed. Wisps of visible vapor escaped her mouth as she exhaled in the cold, dry air. A long, leather coat, decorated with colored beads, trimmed in a very large fur collar and lapel, sat on her shoulders. Her shining hair mingled with the fur of her collar.

Rold ran up to her, grabbed her hand, and pulled her at a run toward the foot of the steps where the two boys were cleaning the snow from their bottoms. "May we borrow this?" Rold asked as he lifted the toboggan by its leather cord. The boys shrugged, then one of them giggled.

Rold started running up the icy steps, pulling the toboggan behind him. Yosana stood still with her hands on her hips.

"Come on!" Rold shouted back at her. When he saw that she was standing firm, he raced back down and picked her up and threw her over his shoulder head first. She screamed and kicked.

"Put me down, you crazy White," she said. "You've lost your mind. We're supposed to be at the meadow lodge."

"Just hush," he said and in a few moments, and with some near slips, they were at the top.

The ceremonial party had stopped their journey and come back to the steps. Chaka was shaking his head. Pentat was smiling and shouting encouragement.

"That's Rold," Frank said. "He can't pass up a chance to kill himself."

"He's happy," Pentat said. "It's a beautiful day — a day for taking risks."

"Like trying to break your neck?" Frank said.

"Like joining woman," Pentat said and Tachina gave him a look.

"This is crazy," Yosana said as they positioned the toboggan.

One of the workers began shouting at them to get off the steps. He looked dismayed as he discovered that the two riders where adults. "What about the baby?" Yosana said. They were now sitting on the wooden board.

"It should be safe under all this padding," Rold said and patted her belly.

"Hey!" she said. "Watch your remarks about padding . . ."

They took off; Yosana screamed. She was in the front and was getting splattered with chunks of icy snow. Rold's ears were ringing from her screams. The ride was fast and less bumpy than he had expected. They landed in the same pile of snow as had the boys which broke their speed comfortably. They lay there in the snow laughing so hard they could not speak. Pentat and Frank helped them to their feet and all calmed down as they brushed the snow from their coats. Rold thanked the boys for the ride.

"We should let this stand as the ceremony," Pentat said. "It could become a tradition: sledding on the Library steps as a trial before joining."

"I just couldn't help myself," Rold said.

Chaka stood still shaking his head without a word. "Let's get these people joined before they kill themselves," Tachina said. "You should be thinking about your baby."

"I'm fine," Yosana said as she finished shaking the snow off her coat.

As they were about to leave the steps, Rold noticed how quiet Tyler was being. He went to her, hugged her firmly and smiled. She smiled back, and he returned to Yosana.

The procession began again, this time reaching the ceremonial lodge without interruption. The lodge was a giant cone made of weathered, wooden rails and sealed with mud. It was situated in a dale that was half-way circled by a thick stand of bare, hardwood trees which had smooth, purple bark pealing in places like paper. The plum color of the young thicket reflected on the snow causing it to display various shades of pink. Blue shadows on the snow from the trees crisscrossed the dale like icy fingers stretching to hold on to the earth as long as the sun was still low.

The group went inside the lodge where a small fire was already crackling in the center. An old woman was tending the fire; she placed some dried herbs that had been saved from the spring into the fire. The burning herbs filled the room with a sweet smell that reminded Rold of the desert where he had first set foot on Salkinia. It had only been a few months now, but it seemed longer. He felt he knew Yosana and Pentat well enough to have been a friend for years. And so much had happened in those few months.

Everyone sat around the fire except for Rold and Yosana. The woman from the Eagle village motioned them to begin circling the fire while holding hands. She sang a song and tapped a small drum as they slowly walked and looked into each other's eyes. Her voice was sweet and high with a constant trill. Most of the syllables were unrecognizable to Rold — some language from the Teton past he supposed. While she sang Pentat stood and chanted a prayer for the couple's happiness. He looked like a boy delighting in a game: his smile was so genuine.

> *A winter joining is full of smiles,*
> *Laughing children, music and sport,*
> *Great Mother of the Earth, as you rest,*
> *You give us this time to renew our love,*
> *Remember our ancestors,*
> *And enjoy our labors,*
> *Bless this woman and man*
> *As they know each other more each day,*
> *We thank you for this moment to share*
> *Ourselves, our souls, our love.*

As he sat Chaka stood and repeated the same prayer, though more seriously, with a monotone of ritual, then he too sat; all the while the woman sang.

She sprinkled water onto the fire. Steam pervaded the room as the drum stopped. All was silent. Then Yosana took Rold into her arms and held him with all her strength.

"You're my mate," she said. Her warm tears were wetting his face.

"Is that it?" he said.

"Not quite," shouted a man from outside the lodge.

Yosana and Rold walked outside pushing away the wool rug portal cover. The sun was now high enough to flood the dale with light, erasing the tree shadows. The rest of the wedding party followed, and all were blinded by the reflective snow for a moment. Then the scene came into focus and Rold saw Bana and several other Teton, men and women and children, waiting for them. Their attention was drawn down to their feet where a brilliant carpet of multi-colored flower petals littered the hard snow around the lodge. Also, the Teton had decorated themselves with feathers, beads, and flowers and were holding bundles of flowers, which were grown in the Library's greenhouses. All the cheery display was paled though by their smiles.

"You didn't think you could escape with such a pitiful ceremony, Mountain Bear," Bana said. "You have been joined with the daughter of Ah-Blikkinata la'Kunda, a great hero to our people. A celebration is required."

"But we felt . . ."

"There's no choice," Bana said.

At those words the women ran up and took Yosana by both hands, pulling her away. The men grabbed Rold and tossed him up where he sat on two men's shoulders as they trotted back to the Eagle village, a long way to carry such a large man but they managed. A trail of flower petals led them into the center circle where a fire was cooking the huge haunch of a pitah on a spit. The ground around the fire had been cleared of snow, the dirt tamped to concrete hardness. Furs of multiple size and color were spread around the circle with one particular pitah hide set close to the fire and bordered with flowers. It was on this rug that Rold was set, and soon Yosana was placed beside him.

"This haunch came from a pitah I killed myself," Bana said. "It's a gift from my village to yours, Pentat, in honor of this joining. Also I give this pridda to the wedded couple. On its back are some other gifts: leather, wool, coats, bowls and knives. So that you may begin your life with us as an equal, Mountain Bear and Yosana."

Rold started to thank him, but Yosana nudged his side and whispered: "The honor is Bana's for giving, not yours for receiving. Don't thank him; just accept it. He's being a little arrogant in making such a gift. You can see how impressed everyone is. But actually his village had better hunting than the Eagle village this summer, and this is his way of sharing while keeping face for Pentat."

Pentat stepped to the center and stood beside Bana and the pridda.

"I too have a gift," Pentat said. "I've brought bread to the feast. And I shall give to my new brother and my sister five pridda, so that they may begin a stable that will not be called lacking."

He walked around the fire then sat beside Rold. Mumbling ran quickly through the crowd. Bana nodded his head at Pentat and handed the reins of the pony to one of his warriors to take to the corral. He then sat beside Pentat signaling everyone else to sit.

"You're a rich man," Bana said. "You honor these young people, and you honor Blikki. You're a good son."

Music began and a dozen Teton began dancing around the fire. The music was beautiful, Rold thought, nothing like the clanging noise making of Pentat's triumphal procession on his return. The instruments were the same: drums, flutes, the long string instrument that required several people to play it. But the song was more controlled, more melodic. Rold looked closely at the string being stretched between the two poles and noticed that the poles were hollow, which accounted for the amplified sound. There was only one person stroking his bow across the string, and the deep pitched, somber tone blended well with the deep drum beats and high notes from the flutes. The dance was more a stylized drama. Both men and women participated, and he guessed that they were telling a story. But it was unfamiliar and too hard to decipher, so he asked Yosana to interpret.

"It's the story of Chomata-te and his wife — how they met and fell in love," she said.

Frank was sitting beside Rold, watching the dance with his hands on his knees. Above the din of the celebration, he tried to explain the dance.

"This leader, Chomata-te, had a lot of trouble with outlaw villages," he said.

"How do you know about all this?" Rold said.

"The Library," he said. "It's wonderful! Volumes of history. I've been spending hours there — not that you would notice.

"Anyway, Chomata-te and his village fought some outlaws, and he killed their chief. He felt so badly about the killing that he took a gift of food and ponies to the assaulted village. He met the daughter of the dead chief, his only living relative. She hated Chomata-te at first, but he soon won her over. She was alone in the world and found that Chomata-te was a good and brave man. Her name was *Bene-la*, but Chomata-te gave her a new name when they returned to his village: Pitallela, the explorer whose Old Earth name was like mine, Diego."

Rold put his hand on Yosana's belly and hugged her around her shoulders. He looked deep into her eyes.

"My Pitallela is in here," he said.

The baby wriggled, so energetically that Rold could feel it through Yosana's heavy coat.

"Yes," Yosana responded. "That'll be her name."

"So that in the next generation there will be a Pitallela and a Chomata-te," Pentat said smiling. "My boy, your girl. It'll be a terrible burden — these names. The names of our beginning."

"The names of a new beginning," Bana said as he squatted in front of them. He held two cups filled with warm beer for Rold and Yosana.

"So you even drink alcohol?" Frank said looking at Rold.

"It's not so bad," Rold said. "In moderation. You should try some, Frank. Join us, please."

"No, I don't think so," he said. "I plan on going back to my world — to Old Earth. I'm no Industrialist. I don't want to assume any habits now that I'll have to break then. If there is a 'then.' If my world will still be standing."

"Don't talk of war today, Diego," Bana said. "This is a celebration." Bana sat beside Frank and gave him a firm slap on the back, which made them both smile.

Tyler was beside Yosana and reached for the cup of beer that was to go to Frank.

"I'm not shy," she said and poured the golden liquid down her throat.

Bana looked at her admiringly and she smiled back.

Yosana sipped her beer and turned white. She put her hand to her forehead and breathed through her mouth.

"Rold?" she said. "I'm . . . going to be sick."

Rold took the cup from her and set it in the dirt. He took her in his arms and rocked her.

"The baby must not like beer."

For a moment she could taste the acid from her stomach in the back of her throat. Her head felt like it would explode as the vision of dancing Teton swirled in front of her eyes. A dull ache in her lower back caught her attention and then a sharp twist in her abdomen. The queasiness left quickly but her buttocks throbbed.

"I'm too far along to have the daily sickness," she said. The episode languished like a passing thunderstorm.

"I'm all right now," she said. "It passed. I guess I shouldn't drink anything."

"Are you sure you're all right?" Tachina said from behind her. She was sitting with little Chomata-te nursing under a heavy pitah blanket.

"I'm fine," Yosana said.

Barbara Jenkins walked up to the party dressed in Teton clothes. Her red hair had grown almost to her shoulders; she kept it braided as the Teton women did, though it was still quite short.

"Congratulations," she said. "I hope that you'll be very happy."

Since the bombing she had recovered her health living at the Library, with few scars from the burns. Her friendliness toward Yosana had puzzled everyone but was welcome, and her behavior was more relaxed with each passing day.

"Sit here, Barbara," Frank said as he patted the ground in front of him. She slowly dropped to her knees then sat.

"I hope I'm not intruding," she said.

"Of course not," Rold said. He could not stop himself from staring at her unusual hair. It had been years since he had seen such beautiful, red hair; the Industrialist class was primarily descended from the Oriental races who dominated industry on Old Earth, so most Industrialists had dark hair and eyes. And here among the dark Teton her hair was like a bright flame. She caught his stare and he self-consciously turned his eyes away.

"Is there something you want to say, Rold?" she asked. The question seemed out of place and irritating.

"Forgive me for staring," Rold said. "It's your hair. It's so beautiful. I keep thinking that you don't look like the same person that I traveled with on Blikki's transport. Why did you keep your head shaved then?"

"Oh, just a matter of fashion. Of course that's the least of my worries here — now that I'm a prisoner."

You'll not be welcome for long if you continue in that line, Rold thought.

"I've already been admonished for speaking of the war," Frank said. "Let's have some of that beer and listen to the music. When will the meat be ready?"

Rold looked at Frank with his eyebrows raised. He's actually taking a drink, Rold thought. A good friend; a good politician.

Frank took one sip of beer and spit and choked at the same time. Laughter exploded around the fire as Bana patted his back. Barbara downed her cup quickly, wiping her mouth with her sleeve. Bana filled it again.

"You've drunk before," he said.

"With me it's no pleasure but a necessity," she said.

The meat was finally cooked, and a couple of warriors began working at slicing thin strips and stacking them on wooden platters. A large pot had been set under the meat to catch drippings where a woman began mixing in vegetable pulp and herbs to make a sauce that was eventually poured over the meat on the platter.

Each person in the wedding party was handed a wide, shallow bowl. The warriors in charge of the meat then placed several slices in each bowl. A broken piece of malonta bread was placed on top and more beer was poured. Everyone ate in silence. Even the music stopped. The meat was tender and the bread was hot and fresh and full of nutty flavor. The beer tasted even better after eating the meat, which had soaked up the spicy gravy. The sun was low but the sky remained clear so that the cold from the mountains seemed less threatening. Rold felt good. His stomach was full; everything seemed calm. And he was going to be a father — such a strange thing to be happy about. But the feeling was like none he had ever experienced.

The music began again as bowls were retrieved and cleanup commenced. Another dance was started, this time consisting only of women.

Tyler rose and joined, not really knowing the steps but ready to try. She was smiling and laughed when she found herself out of step. Rold enjoyed watching her, thinking how she looked more like the old Tyler. Her laughter floated in the crisp air like the pealing of a bell.

"Don't look too closely at those girls," Yosana said.

"I only see you," Rold said.

"Corny," Frank said with a smile. "They sound like children in love."

"Yes," Barbara said. "It's hard to imagine what it must be like. I admit I married Daryl for money, for sex, for drugs. Never for love. He probably thinks I'm dead — and has forgotten me."

"No, I don't think so," Yosana said. "He wouldn't forget you."

Rold took advantage of the pause.

"What's the name of that stringed instrument?" he asked. "It has such a beautiful, full tone."

"It's a *fwalla*," Pentat said. "Come. Let me show you how it's played."

Pentat took the right pole, or rather tube, from the man who was holding it. This surprised Rold; he thought that Pentat would take the place of the bowman. But as he came closer and watched what Pentat was doing, he saw the secret of how the fwalla was played. The bow produced the vibration but the notes were changed by fingering holes on the tube. Each tube holder played harmonizing notes. Modulation was accomplished by changing the tension on the string. It produced a round, rich sound but a very eerie melody since the string was very sensitive and modulation occurred every few notes.

"Here, try," Pentat said. "The foot of the pole rests in the sand — like this. Then hold it against your stomach at an angle. These holes follow a chromatic scale. Remember to keep the thong stretched tightly."

Rold took his place. The other man stopped playing to allow Rold the chance to hear his own notes. Several of the wedding party paused to listen to Rold. The man stroking the string with his bow continued at a steady rate. Rold pressed one finger over a hole, then another and another. The scale was correct, so he attempted a simple melody he had learned as a child. The music vibrated through his body, making his belly itch, but the tone was delightful — and sounded rather good after having drunk several cups of beer. The other man easily found a harmony line after hearing the song only once. Together they played the fwalla well and a beautiful song emerged. The drummers joined in, then the pipes. They finished with a good-hearted, dramatic flourish, and all applauded. Rold bowed, generating laughter and a hug from Yosana as she jumped up and ran to him.

The sun was beginning to disappear behind a mountain peak; the little fires of the villages reflected amber against the snow covered, granite walls that surrounded the meadow. Rold and Yosana sat down with their friends while the party began to quiet and draw to a close. People were returning to their lodges, each saying good night to Rold and Yosana. A cold wind whipped at the fire in the circle.

"It was a wonderful day," Yosana said. "Thank you. Thank you, every-one."

"Yes, thank you," Rold said. "It's good to be with friends."

"Yes, we haven't seen you much lately," Frank said.

"He's been in training," Pentat said.

"Which reminds me," Rold said, "where have you been, Frank? Never mind, I know: the Library."

"Yes, well, I'm not much at hand-to-hand combat. But you remember, I was to be a spy for you."

"Are you still willing?" Bana said eagerly.

"Now wait," Tachina said. "Must we talk of war. That's all you ever talk about. Sooner or later the subject pops up like a persistent weed. Yes, yes, I know we're fighting a war. We must prepare. But this is supposed to be a celebration!"

"It's all right, Tachina," Yosana said. "Today was a great celebration. But it's not as if I were a blushing bride. Let them talk. We haven't all been together like this in a while."

"Well, I'm cold," Tachina said. "And Chomata-te needs to be in bed. We'll be in the lodge when you are finished, Pentat."

She then rose and walked silently to their lodge carrying her baby on her hip.

"She misses the hunt," Bana said.

"A wife with a child can't be a warrior," Pentat said. "To raise a child is more honorable than fighting the Enemy; I envy her. She shouldn't regret. She has been on hunts, but that's past. So it'll be with you, Yosana."

"Are you saying I should join her?" Yosana said. "That I should have no interest in your schemes?"

"Careful, Pentat," Rold said with a smile.

"You may stay," Pentat said with a very formal hand gesture.

"Damn right," she said.

"She's Blikki's daughter, all right," Bana said.

Frank had been patient through the family scene. His knowledge of the language was still weak. It was such a close knit group Rold had managed to join, and he wished to be home again. Though he would miss Rold, this was not the Rold he had known as a child — not quite. And this world of neo-primitives and vast wilderness was not for him.

"I guess I'm getting itchy feet," Frank said, "so, is there any chance a man could make it back to civilization across this snow? I can't very well do any intelligence-gathering from here."

"I thought we were 'trapped' — to use your word, Pentat," Barbara said. The beer had made her lazy all afternoon, but now she was very alert.

"There's a route used in emergencies, and only by volunteers, that leads to the western desert," Chaka said. "I'm not sure I approve of taking such risks right now. In a double moon there maybe a break in the snow; in a purple moon the ice will have thawed. Be patient."

"It'll take time to get established again," Frank said. "If I'm to do some good, I must leave soon. The trip itself, I would guess would take some time as well.

"I've seen the people of Minpana — the natives. They're virtually slaves to the Industrialists. An underground movement exists there that could be a great help. You have some Minpanese here at the Library who're ready to go with me."

"So, you've spoken to them already?" Chaka said. "What's your opinion, Pentat?"

"I would not send you through the snow, Diego," Pentat said. "Even though you're willing, you don't understand the dangers. I don't want to see Mountain Bear's friend die in the ice."

"I'm aware of the risks," Frank said. "But I can take care of myself. Besides, we'll be a sizeable company; twenty in all."

"You'll need a guide who knows where the caches are placed along the trail to the desert," Chaka said. "A young woman in my service has made the trip twice before."

"Then I'm going," Frank said. "I have to do something, and I'm not a soldier. Also, I'll get word to your father, Rold, that you and Tyler are alive. He should also know that he's going to be a grandfather."

"When will you leave?" Rold asked.

"In two days we should be ready."

"I can't stop you," Pentat said. "I'll pray for a safe trip — though there will be even worse dangers in the city when you arrive."

"I can handle it. I have before."

Chaka stood, slowly and with pain. He stretched out his crooked back and yawned.

"I must seek my bed, children," he said. "This has been a long day. May life be kind to you, Yosana, and you, Mountain Bear. We all pray for your happiness."

"Good night, Grandfather," Pentat said.

Rold stood as Chaka walked to the path that led to the Library. "We must go to our lodges as well," he said as he helped Yosana to her feet.

"We should all find our homes," Pentat said and the celebration finally came to an official end.

Frank walked Barbara back to the Library. Pentat and Bana left, speaking of training contests and preparations for the spring. Rold and Yosana strolled toward their lodge, arm-in-arm. Tyler followed pensively.

"I should find some place to stay," she said from behind them.

Yosana turned and smiled. "There's no tradition of honeymoons here, Tyler. You've stayed in our lodge, not just because we wanted you — and we do — but because it's the way the Teton live. You're a part of our family."

"Thank you. But I'm not Teton, and I feel like I'm intruding. I've seen that some of the warrior women among you have their own lodges. Is there not some way I can earn my own?"

"It's too late. In the spring maybe. Right now there aren't enough skins and no way to get more. Have I done something to make you feel unwelcome?"

"No, no. You've been wonderful. And Tachina, too. But she has her family; you two have yours. I'm the outsider."

Rold took Tyler's hand and pulled her into an embrace.

"I love you," he said. "You're not an outsider."

The sky was completely dark; tiny, wet snow flakes began floating down from clouds that had moved in after the sun went down. Inside the lodge a single, red coal still lived in the stove, keeping the tent bearable — just above freezing. Rold immediately stoked the fire with a handful of twigs and one fist- sized knot from an evergreen tree. He and Yosana undressed in the cold and then sank under the wool blankets where they cuddled for warmth. Tyler snuggled in her corner and used her talent for instant sleep to leave Rold and Yosana in a type of privacy.

For a while they were quiet, listening to the fire that crackled from sap dripping and exploding from the knot of wood. Rold and Yosana held each other closely, with a gentle rocking. Soon the rocking stirred other feelings and without talk they eased into the fragile exercise of love making. Yosana's skin tasted salty and her hair smelled of smoke. Rold liked tasting her whole body. Her round abdomen looked beautiful, perfect to him, and her face was warm and loving in the orange glow of the fire. The shadows of her nose and cheeks made her look older, but her skin was soft and delicious. They looked into each others eyes as they continued their slow rocking — and for a long time after.

This is what life is all about, Rold thought. *Now I finally understand. It's for these moments that we labor all our lives. This makes it all worth it.*

Finally they closed their eyes and slept — for the first time as husband and wife.

The smell of camp fires at dawn and the cold air invigorated Rold, stirred his energies so much that he paced as he talked. Frank was finally leaving after a week long delay. A fierce blizzard had blown for three days keeping the travel party sitting on their bottoms in the warmth of their lodges.

Several pridda were outfitted with packs and the travelers were dressed in furs and wearing snow shoes. Pentat and Rold were the only people there to see them off.

"I wish I could go with you," Rold said as he hugged Frank. The gesture seemed ludicrous since they were both so thickly wrapped in animal skins that they could not feel each other's embrace.

"You'll be there soon enough," Frank said. "I expect to see you and Pentat leading a triumphant parade of conquering heroes through one of those blasted city gates in two months time — or however many of these moon cycles, that is; I can't ever keep it straight."

"I wish you good luck," Pentat said.

"Thank you. You should get a message back from a runner in a month or less. I hope to get you as much information as I can. Also, I plan to alert the Scientists about this planet."

"They don't know?" Rold said.

"Maybe. I never made a communication while I was at Minpana because I had not yet found you. But they have their own people. I've suspected Ruth Poundstone had people following me. Now I know why, but it's too late to throw stones. So, perhaps they already know about the Beldine system and what the Industrialists are up to. I'll let them know of the Teton rebellion."

"Just don't get caught."

"I'll be careful."

As the impatient pridda were lined up and checked one last time, Barbara came running from the direction of the Library. She was out of breath when she arrived, so that she could barely speak.

"You can't leave without saying good-bye," she finally said.

Frank held her shoulders in his leather wrapped hands and kissed her forehead.

"Take care," he said.

She backed away without a word then bolted again, this time toward the villages.

"Is there something I should know?" Rold asked while Frank stared at the disappearing form of Barbara.

"She tried to talk me into taking her back," Frank said. "She could do a lot of damage. She could tell the Industrialists about our hoax and where to find the Library."

"Yes. I know. That's why I said no. Though, she was very persuasive."

"And you loved every minute of it."

"Maybe."

They hugged once more and the expedition was off. Rold and Pentat walked back into the mass of tents hoping to get a warm cup of tea from Yosana before joining the warriors at training. The villages were coming alive with children playing, people off to dump rubbish or gather fuel, and the line of wool workers on their way to the Library. Rold looked over his shoulder only once; Frank and his band of Minpanese were mere specks along an ascending trail that crossed a snowy hill.

"When the snow breaks," Pentat said, "Yosana will have your child. And soon after she'll have to say good-bye to you as we begin our attack of the Whites. That will be the hardest: to leave your wife and child."

"Yes, I know. I'm not looking forward to it."

"Nor I, Mountain Bear. But it's better to leave them here and fight than to have them mindlessly slaughtered by Whites. And don't think that there's any hope of avoiding such an end without fighting. Their foolish attempt at exterminating us at First Colony was not the only attack. Before you came more than thirty villages were wiped out. My own village narrowly escaped. It's only by luck that my Tachina survived. By luck, only, for certainly I had nothing to do with their rescue — the Whites had me captured before they started the raid.

"You've only seen a small sampling of their cruelty, Mountain Bear — discounting the fireworks of First Colony. Their evil lies in their lack of passion, lack of conscience. We're only a nuisance to them, and they want to destroy us!

"This is why your training is so important. You must learn discipline — something the Whites don't have; though they must think they do, but they don't really understand. And it's with this discipline — not our weapons or competence with them — that we'll find victory. I truly believe that, Mountain Bear, or I couldn't lead us into this war, for I would be leading us to our destruction. That's why I have confidence in you. Your discipline is good. Don't let Bana's chiding about your handling of a bow bother you. You're doing well. But he has to be hard on you."

"I'm ready. And Bana doesn't bother me. In another week, I'll challenge him to an archery contest."

A living cloud threw a slow moving shadow across the path and adjacent lodges as they continued walking. Rold was pleased to see that Pentat withheld his cursing. Finally they found Rold's lodge and made themselves tea; Yosana was absent. Then off they went, warmed by the tea in their stomachs, to the practice fields.

The work was demanding, but by dark Rold was smiling with accomplishment, though his body was tired and ached. He was met by Yosana outside their lodge. She looked upset; he ran to her immediately thinking of the baby. "What's wrong?" he said as they embraced. He said it quietly.

"Barbara's missing," she said.

"Are you sure? The Library is a big place . . ."

"I'm sure. At first I just thought she was running about so I didn't worry for a while. She was very upset about Frank leaving. I guess they had become close, drawn to each other, feeling so different from everyone else. You've been too busy to notice. Anyway, I suspected she might have followed Frank. We found a pridda missing from our corral and tracks along the trail."

"We have to go after her. She'll never make it alone."

"But it's dark, and Chaka would not send anyone in the dark. Tomorrow it'll be too late."

"It's already too late, Yosana," Pentat said as he joined them. "I just heard. She was spotted by a scout in the afternoon. But I regret that a winter storm has begun to the south of the Red Hills, and all passes are closed. If she holds up and sets a lodge, perhaps she'll survive. Or maybe she'll find Diego. For them I have no fear; they're well prepared for the snow.

"We should put her out of our minds. She has determined her own fate — whatever that may be. I won't risk anyone in a storm to save an enemy's life."

He turned and walked to his own home. Yosana held Rold's hand. They climbed into the lodge and spent a quiet, worrisome night, wakeful and solemn.

CHAPTER 18

A second rider came, but too late,
For in years to come, absence was persistent.

- From the recorded log of Chomata-te,
  Teton chief of the black times.

A wind was howling outside Rachel's apartment window. Although it was the middle of the day, the sky was dark, with visibility cut to a hundred meters by the blasting snow. The lights in her living room blinked off and on from power fluctuations until they went out and emergency chemical lights hissed on, giving the room a sour, gray-green tint.

She watched Colonel August approach on a security scanner moments before the blackout. He had to knock on her door since the intercom would not respond. Rachel manually pushed the sliding door into its slot to let him in.

"Can't you do anything about this weather?" she said half seriously.

He came in and struggled with closing the door.

"I barely made it off the elevator before the power went out," he said. "It wouldn't do to have a Militia officer caught between floors."

"Well, what is it? It must be something important to have braved this weather."

"I'm not sure how important it is, but Barbara Jenkins has been found."

"Alive or dead?"

"Alive."

"Is that possible?"

"It gets more incredible. She wandered into the city yesterday, dressed in native clothes, her feet little more than nubs after being eaten away by frost bite. She collapsed in the street and was taken to a Militia hospital where she was identified. She's in pretty bad shape, malnourished, various infections, frost bite. She moves in and out of delirium, mumbling about the natives."

"Will she live?"

"Oh, yes. Certainly."

Rachel left her desk and sat on some pillows in the middle of the room.

She swallowed a pill and drank some wine. August joined her, but at a distance.

"But why go out in this mess," she said pointing to the window, "to tell me this?"

"It's a bit fantastic. Laughable really. But I've seen her and heard her talking myself. She insists that the entire native population is still alive at some place called the 'Library.' And Simms is with them."

"She's mad, obviously." Rachel began twitching her foot nervously and downed her glass of wine then clumsily filled it again from a bottle she had in her robe pocket.

"What, did they use some magical transportation?" she said. "Or did they rise from the dead!"

"Speaking of rising from the dead: She also says that young woman, Simms' sister is alive and with him."

Rachel laughed.

"Well, there it is," she said. "She *is* mad. I saw to it that she was taken to the morgue myself."

"She also said there were at least three quarters of a million of them — more than half of those are warriors."

"And you're taking this seriously? Don't be so stupid, August. We have picture records, scans, computer constructed models of the city. The natives were there, and we wiped them out! She's sick, dreaming. Probably she ran into some stragglers your people couldn't find, or maybe lost Zenians. Or she hallucinated the whole thing. Just don't come back up here wasting my time with mad stories. Be prepared next time."

"There's some circumstantial evidence. Her clothes, her survival after all this time. And, I heard her; she couldn't have made it all up She mentioned someone else: Frank Diego."

Rachel's eyebrows rose slightly. She set aside her wine then left the room. When she returned she was wearing a snowsuit and was putting on thermal mittens.

"Well, let's go talk to her," she said.

"Are you sure you want to go out in this?"

"The Militia hospital is only fifteen minutes away. A half hour in this mess. I know Barbara. I think I can tell if she's gone mad or not. If her story's a lie you've gotten me out on a dreadful day, and it'll just add to the list of grievances I have against you. If it's the least bit true I should have you shot for you failures."

"I didn't plan the air strike."

"Watch yourself, August. You're playing out of your league."

"Well, it seems to me if your extermination attempt failed, and Simms is alive, your father, and the rest of the Industrialist board members, will perhaps re-think their decision to have a woman as commander of the Beldine base."

"You've just pushed me too far, August. Whatever the outcome, you're finished."

"We shall see."

She attempted to storm past him but was foiled by the stuck door. Seething, she slammed it open and strode down the hall with August behind her. They had to climb down stairs which doubled her estimate of the distance to the hospital. The slanted darts of snow and sleet stung her face, turning it bright red. But the exposed walk lasted only a few minutes since very little traffic interfered.

The hospital had power, of course, and the staff was accommodating if not patronizing in showing Rachel and August to Barbara's room. She was asleep in a room lit only by the violet light of a beam scanner that slowly traveled from head to toe in a tight spiral about her bed. Rachel commanded that the room lights come up and the scanner cease — and so it came about. Barbara forced her eyes open and saw Rachel leaning over her.

"Rachel?" she said. "Oh! A civilized face. Is it really you?"

"Yes, Barb," Rachel said. "I'm here. Did you think I wouldn't come visit you? It's a miracle you're alive."

"The Teton saved me . . . once. Kept me alive — gave me life. But I had to get back. The cold! It almost killed me, but I'm here; you're here."

"Yes, yes. And what about these Teton?"

"The natives, Pentat, Rold Simms, Yosana, and Tyler. They're all alive. They're in a big mountain meadow. The Library. Maybe a million. They plan to take Minpana in the spring. Spring is almost here."

"Now don't get excited."

Barbara held Rachel by her arms, gripping tightly with each wheezing breath.

"How could this be true?" Rachel said trying to pull loose. "You're just confused. You met some stragglers . . ."

"No. They were never there, Rachel — at that other place. It was a hoax, a decoy city. They knew you would bomb it. Rold predicted it. They have spies here in the city."

"Who! What spies? You must know."

Barbara hesitated.

"No," she croaked. "I don't know."

"Yes you do, goddamnit! You're lying."

"Perhaps she's just tired," August said. He was enjoying the scene.

"Yes," Rachel said as she stood and pried Barbara's hands from her arms.

"We'll let you rest."

She took August by the arm and pulled him to the door.

"Keep a guard on her," she said. "And find out where this Library is. We can destroy it as quickly as an empty city. And try to get some names. She knows something about those spies. Frank Diego is one of them; I'm sure of it."

"Then you believe her?"

"I'm forced to. And don't get any ideas, August. You'll do as I say. I don't want any of this to get out until after the bombs drop.

"These natives have been a nuisance since we arrived at this hell hole of a stellar system. We don't need any more interference now that we're ready to strike the Scientists.

"Everything seems to depend on the ice to melt. Well, I'll not wait for that to finally do away with these monkeys. Complete extermination, August. Destroy them."

An early thaw came to the Red Hills. The combination of a premature warmth and little snow for several weeks wiped the white ice from the hills, and the meadow of the Library was a carpet of green grass, though few flowers had yet opened. To the south and east the mountains around Minpana were still laden with snow; moisture from the southern sea combined with the cold air of the mountains and the snow continued there.

With this early spring came an early stirring in Yosana's womb. It was on a bright day while Rold and Tyler were out with a group of hunters looking for pitah on the grass sea. They had been away for three days. Tachina looked in on her each day, sharing talk and a midday meal. But today Yosana could not eat. Tachina found her huddled and whimpering, her blanket sopping wet. Her face was stained with dried tears, her hair matted.

"A moon early," Tachina said. "When did this start?"

Chomata-te crawled about the lodge touching everything, tugging at rugs and bowls and spoons, putting everything into his mouth. Yosana smiled at him as she calmed from her last contraction.

"He likes playing here," she said. "Soon he'll have a cousin to play with."

Tachina smiled as well and helped Yosana lie back on her bed of wool blankets.

"How long, Yosana?" she said.

"Oh, all night it seems. My girl's coming, isn't she?"

"Yes, dear. I must get Mahaisa. She's the only midwife in the village today."

"But you'll be here, too, won't you, Tachina?"

"Of course I will. But that Mountain Bear of yours — it's just like a man to be absent when his child is being born."

"Pentat couldn't help it in your case. You'd have to blame the Whites. And Rold thought it would be all right. I'm early."

"He should be here. Well, I'll be back quickly with Mahaisa. You rest."

Tachina wrapped Chomata-te in a blanket and strapped him to her back. He was almost too heavy for her now — and too wiggly. As she pushed aside the door flap, she was startled to see Rold at the entrance on his knees preparing to crawl in.

"Did I hear you say 'Mahaisa?'" he said. "Isn't she a midwife? It's too early."

"Tell that to the baby," Tachina said. "I must hurry. It's good you're here."

They passed each other through the door, and Rold scurried to Yosana's side.

"Is it true?" he said. "Could it be a false labor?"

"Oh, Rold! You're here. No, it's the real thing; my water broke, and I've had contractions all night. Our girl wants out."

"Then I'm glad there were no pitah and we hurried back."

"Better that there were pitah, Rold. I'm glad you're here, but we need fresh food. The stores at the Library are full of rancid meat and molded grain. Everyone was hoping this early spring would bring us some food. People are getting sick."

"I know; I know. It may look like spring here, but everywhere else it's still winter. There's snow on the rolling hills. Bana said the pitah are probably far to the south — close to the Industrialists (if they haven't killed them all yet). We'll have to wait a few more days, perhaps a month."

"There's fear that if we don't get fresh food soon there will be deaths, maybe children."

"Soon, sweetheart, soon."

Yosana cried out, first in unconnected words, then in one pure scream. She panted and squeezed Rold's hand until she finally relaxed.

"You're scaring me half to death," he said, wiping sweat from her face.

"Am I supposed to feel sorry for you?" she said. "Typical aristo. Pampered beyond belief. And you want me to go on pampering you. Well forget it. I'm lying here risking my life to give you a child, and *you're* scared."

She doubled up and held her scream until she could no longer and let it out. Tachina returned with a middle aged Teton woman with a round pretty face and slightly round body. She was very quiet as she went to work examining Yosana. She rubbed her cheek and brow as she felt her abdomen, nodding her head.

Tyler strolled to the lodge and immediately sensed what was going on. She crawled inside the crowded room.

"Oh, Yosana!" she said.

She looked at Rold with a smile and noticed his worried stare.

"Am I really that horrible?" Rold said quietly.

"What do you mean?" Tyler said.

"You should have heard the way she talked to me."

Tyler laughed in a sweet giggle, covering her mouth. She put her hand softly on Rold's arm.

"It's something that happens to a woman in labor," she said. "She loves you very much. Don't worry. You mustn't think of yourself right now. Think only of her, and the baby. They need you."

Rold went to Yosana's side again and took her hand. He kissed her and kept his face close to hers.

Tachina returned, this time without Chomata-te, carrying rolled scraps of fabric and a steaming pot.

Two more contractions passed, and Mahaisa said it was time to push. Yosana grunted and whimpered as Rold sat to her left and Tachina her right. They helped her to a squatting position, with Mahaisa ready to take the child. With one last push the baby burst out into the hands of Mahaisa along with a gush of diluted blood. Rold thought it looked like a cannon ball blast. The girl baby cried immediately, needing no help, and promptly squirted urine all over Mahaisa. Everyone laughed. Yosana laughed and cried. Mahaisa put the tiny child on Yosana's belly while she helped out the placenta and cut the cord with a small knife. She bound the cord back on itself with a short length of sinew and began washing the little girl and Yosana from the pot of water that Tachina had brought. The baby cried and kicked fiercely.

"Is she all right?" Yosana said breathlessly. "She's so small."

"A healthy child," Mahaisa said.

"Pitallela," Yosana said, "this is your father."

Rold stroked Pitallela's bright red face. His smile was genuine and seemingly permanent.

"My little 'lela," Yosana crooned. "How I love you so already. She has a grip on my heart. Thank you, Rold, for this moment. I've feared this all my life. But now I know the joy of it. I wouldn't change a thing."

Rold could not speak. He thought of Blikki, wishing, naturally, that he were here. He thought of his father, and especially now, his mother. This is something they should be sharing. But then he let the thoughts pass. For now there were only three people in the whole Universe.

They heard a commotion coming from the village as the sky darkened. Rold peeked out the door and saw a living cloud descending onto the village.

People were running around, wondering whether to be frightened or awed. It stopped just above the roofs of the lodges and spread itself in a circle covering the whole village.

Tyler joined him at the door.

"It's Gwydmonia," she said, and looked at the new mother and child.

Gwydmonia began her light flashing communication, which Rold better comprehended since practicing with Yosana.

"SHOW ME THE CHILD," she said.

"I'M NOT SURE . . ." Rold began his response, moving his hands about his body.

"SHE WILL BE FINE," Gwydmonia said. "BRING HER OUT, ROLD."

He scooted back in and looked at Yosana.

"She wants me to show her Pitallela."

"Absolutely not!" Tachina said. "You're not taking this baby from her mother."

"No, it's all right," Yosana said. "I'll join you, Rold, but you'll have to hold her. I'm not sure I'm strong enough to do both. And perhaps Tyler can help me?"

"Of course," Tyler said.

"Are you sure you can manage? After what you've been through . . ."

"Men!" Yosana said. "What do you know of what I've been through."

She began sitting up as Rold took his baby girl. Mahaisa had wrapped her in a soft, tanned skin. Rold crawled out carefully and stood with Pitallela in his arms. Tyler came out next and helped Yosana. Once outside Yosana grabbed Rold around his waist and tried standing but only managed a stoop. Gwydmonia signed a greeting and Yosana began signing and speaking aloud what Rold guessed was a ritual passage for such an occasion.

"The chain of riders is not broken," Yosana said. "I pledge her training here and now. As she was conceived so shall she live, riding the minah-machacute."

"THANK YOU, YOSANA," Gwydmonia said. "NOW LET ME SEE THIS NEW PITALLELA."

Rold held up the little bundle allowing the blanket to fall aside exposing her naked body. Gwydmonia produced a single, white light that shined on Pitallela's tiny body. Until this moment the baby had been crying, but as soon as she was immersed in the light of the minah-machacute she quieted and closed her eyes. The light abruptly stopped, and she began crying again. Rold returned her to his chest, wrapping her warmly.

"THANK YOU," Gwydmonia said and then quickly rose a hundred meters and disappeared.

"She was awakening the germ of wisdom that she planted at conception," Yosana said.

That seemed to be all the explanation needed, and the family climbed back into the lodge. Mahaisa had rolled up the soiled blankets and replaced them with fresh ones. As the sun began disappearing behind the mountains Tachina left to tend to her own family. But Mahaisa stayed the night helping Yosana with nursing — teaching both mother and daughter how it worked. Tyler watched in silence.

For two days Rold, Yosana, and Pitallela were together as one person. No one bothered Rold with training or hunting expeditions so he stayed with his wife and child, learning the routine, which, though clumsily at first, he adapted to quickly. Tyler, though, continued training and was successful on the hunt, bringing in several small prey for the Eagle village.

On the third day since the birth the village became excited with the news that Frank and his team had sent their first message. Though the message had not made it there yet, news of its coming was carried in by scouts. And late that day the messenger arrived. Pentat decided to collect the chiefs from the various villages — close to a thousand Teton — and meet in a large hall in the Library the next morning. Rold was invited, as he had been for the other few large meetings, but Yosana was not. She resented the exclusion, protesting to Pentat. He and his family had come to visit that evening, for the first time since the birth.

"I have a right to be there," she said.

The two families sat in a circle as Chomata-te stared at Pitallela, fascinated by her.

"What right?" Pentat said.

"I'm my father's only offspring. I'll speak for him now in all councils."

Pentat waved his hands and bowed his head.

"I'll not fight you," he said. "I just thought that now that you have an infant you would behave responsibly."

"Hah! I'll bring 'lela with me. And if she gets hungry, I'll feed her. She'll be no trouble. I'm going."

Rold smiled at Yosana, but Tachina was embarrassed and confused. After all, both Pentat and Rold will hear the message. Why does Yosana need to be present?

Someone scratched at the door flap, and Rold welcomed him in. He was a scout who had run an hour to speak to Pentat.

"Forgive me," he said, out of breath. "But I fear the message from Minpana may be too late."

"And who are you, scout?" Pentat asked. The scout was from another village but had been ordered to report emergencies directly to Pentat.

"Bizik, sir. I'm from the Greensnake village."

"Now, what is it that you have to tell us?"

"A flying machine of the Whites. Three hills west, with lamplight strong enough to brighten the ground in the dark. Only one, five trees high. Moving toward the Library but darting north and south as it sweeps east."

Just then the sound of jet engines could be heard very quietly. Yosana tried to hush Pitallela. She put her to her breast and rocked her.

"Gathering intelligence," Rold said. "Or perhaps searching for a downed aircraft."

"Did it pass the Spotted Valley?" Pentat asked.

"It circled the valley and stayed above the rim," Bizik said.

"Thank you for the warning," Pentat said. "I'll remember you to Himbla, your chief. Now, signal the village watchers to have all fires dowsed. We'll give them no light by which to find us. Go."

The man left. The whooshing roar of the jet came closer.

"It won't be soon enough," Rold said. "Infrared will show the whole gathering, camp fires or not. And sounds like it has a search light."

Each woman clutched her child close to her as if to protect it. Although it was a futile gesture, Rold smiled at Yosana's instinctual behavior. There was something about it being both futile and natural that made it seem so loving. He had faced death before — by accident and by choice. Before, he had little fear of death and violence, enjoying the challenge of it; now he had his first taste of fear because of his love for his child and his wife.

"Come, Mountain Bear, Tyler" Pentat said. "We must meet the enemy." Then he left the lodge.

After only a moment Pentat poked his head through the flap.

"Come and see," he said, with a peculiar scowl. "Everyone." Rold stepped out, helping both Tachina and Yosana. Tyler followed. Outside they looked up the gradual slope to the Library and saw that the lodges were slowly going dark closer and closer to the Library. But Pentat pointed to the sky. And as they looked they were all startled. Hundreds of living clouds were overhead, only visible by their occasional light flashes and the sheer blackness of their bodies at night. They were moving into a solid blanket above the meadow, stretching themselves until they sealed any space between them. The entire unit extended from the mountain above the Library to the Red Hills. The sound was muffled, but everyone could hear the jet crossing the night sky above the living clouds. Its search beam filtered through their bodies but was diffused enough not to illuminate the ground. A second, third, then a fourth jet flew overhead. Rold cringed at sensing the additional aircraft. But soon all was quiet. Pentat stood, looking up at the living clouds, and contemplated a curse. But he could not shout at them now. They had saved the Teton.

Rold took Tyler by her shoulders.

"What did you see when Gwydmonia connected with you that day in the mountains?" he asked.

She only stared into his eyes, all emotion draining from her face.

Everyone went to bed. Village watchers reported the living clouds stayed in place all through the night but disappeared by morning. The sound of jets had disappeared as well.

The near discovery by the Industrialists produced an atmosphere of anxiety among the chiefs assembled for council. Rold and Yosana arrived late to the domed hall, where men and women who were the leaders of their respective villages were assembled and cackling so loudly that Pitallela was frightened and screamed, though her scream could barely be heard. Chaka attempted a call to order which was not successful for a half hour. Rold led Yosana by the hand until they found Pentat and Bana sitting next to each other on felt pallets. Yosana spread a woven rug for them to sit on just as the room quieted. Rold looked around at the congregation of such diverse people — as different in appearance from one another as people from different planets.

There seemed to be a competition or show of pride involved in making an appearance at a large meeting such as this that he had overlooked in the past. Since his training began he had learned much about the different villages — enough to recognize regional cultures. There were the people of the plains and mountains such as Pentat and Bana, the southern jungle people, the desert people, the coastal fishers, and the Minpanese — or city people. There was essentially one language common to them all, though there were several dialects. The Minpanese dialect was the most like Caljunnese. The room had divided itself into regional groups. Rold was positive this had not been the case at other meetings he had attended. But there had not been such a large council since his arrival at the Library.

Chaka began the meeting.

"A delegation from the Alabrama River has asked to speak first," he said. "Please come up now so that we can receive the messenger."

Three men from the south, dressed in white cloth skirts, with very dark skin and round stomachs approached the center of the circular hall. The youngest of the three was to be the speaker.

"My name is Olama," he said. At first he seemed nervous, as all eyes were upon him, but quickly he set his jaw and stared back at the crowd, twisting the top of his body from left to right to see the eyes of the people around him. "Our villages are along the Alabrama River, many days south of here. We have something to say that we think others have thought but have kept silent.

"We came to the Library for the winter rest because we were asked by the Master, Chaka, and because others were coming. The winter is colder here than at our own home, but we don't wish to complain about the cold. The hunting has been bad, and our food is stale and running full of worms. But we don't wish to complain about the food either. We came, we saw the evil of the Whites, we have commiserated with our brother Teton, but it's time to go home.

"We didn't come to fight a war — as others did. The Whites have not come to our river. There are things more important than fighting skills and hatred. It's time for planting, and we're not at our fields! This is what's important: our fields, our homes — that have been neglected. I say to you, Pentat, we who live on the Alabrama will not fight."

A murmur that had begun in the middle of the speech grew now to a deafening jumble of heated shouting. Pentat raced to the place of speaking, with Rold standing up. The Alabrama delegation stood to the side but did not leave to be seated. Pentat raised his hands, and the room quieted immediately. A fire was in his eyes, and Rold wondered if anyone else knew what that fire might be.

"The Alabrama are a peaceful people. They farm the land and fish their river. They live in a lush forest that provides them with plenty to eat and warmth the year round. They don't have a taste for killing.

"What you still don't seem to understand, Olama, is that I hate killing as much as you, though you won't believe it. But the Whites have brought monsters in great numbers to our world to kill us. These monsters are humans without souls — a new enemy more fierce than the pitah. And they've brought their machines, their evil tools that almost destroyed us before at our ancient home.

"Olama, take your people home if that's your wish. And any other village, leave if you must. But first, all of you, listen to the information brought back from Minpana. The first step in defending your village from the enemy is to know the enemy."

Rold had remained standing, as had many others, quietly watching the assembly. There was a frown on every face. At first he wondered if this was just a small group, these Alabrama, but watching the crowd he could see there was a general confusion and many more outright detractors of Pentat. It was a shock. The Industrialists' probes of last night had obviously frightened a good many of the Teton.

Chaka settle the room after Pentat returned to his seat. There were no other speakers now to delay the entrance of the messenger. The reception was like a ceremony of sorts. It was an imitation of the arrival of a scout to a village. Even though the messenger had arrived the day before, he entered the room running and out of breath as if he had just run the entire distance from Minpana. Chaka invited him to the place of speaking where he knelt for a moment to steady his breath. He was a young man, dark and glistening with sweat. His face was streaked with a few scraggly whiskers. Scouts were trained to remember everything they saw and heard and to repeat it verbatim. Even though many could read and write, written messages were thought of as a burden on the trail. A message carried in one's head was less likely to be lost or stolen.

"Speak," Chaka said simply.

"My name is Yosma," the man said. "I was born in Minpana, but I was trained at the Library when I was young. This is what I've been told to reveal to you.

"First, the Whites have built a new city — on the north fork of the Alabrama River."

Gasps echoed against the ceiling. The southern villagers were wailing in dismay.

"It's a city for manufacturing weapons and flying machines," Yosma continued. "A few soldiers live there. And they have enslaved Minpanese to work in the factory. But mostly there are machines which look like people doing the work. They speak and walk, but they're machines.

"Another city has been made for the monster warriors in the Western Desert. The Whites built a thousand lodges that are each the size of the Library itself. The monsters can't live in our winter and must stay inside these giant lodges until the desert is warmed by the spring sun. There's still a trace of snow on the desert, though the sun is beginning to melt it and the wild flowers are trying to break through the sand.

"The suggestion of Diego is that the monsters, or the Zenians as he calls them, are hampered by the cold, and an attack before the air gets too warm could be the most successful strategy.

"In Minpana activity is growing as the Whites are making ready for an offworld battle with their other enemies, the Scientists. Every war machine possessed by the Whites has been brought to our world . . ."

A new round of hushed talk interrupted the messenger. The horror of so many machines was felt throughout the room. Rold sighed, and Yosana shivered. He held her closely, their eyes remaining on the speaker as he continued.

"Diego says that on our world, which they call Salkinia, and on Caljunna and its moons, the Whites have assembled all their space machines — space fighters and transports, even non-fighting transports. They have withdrawn them from other stars. They feel hidden here, safe."

"How many space machines are there?" a woman asked from the other side of the room. Yosma turned around to answer her directly.

"Eight hundred thousand," he said.

Disorder erupted, with shouts and people standing. Chaka worked very hard at calming the room. Even Rold stood. He found the news incredulous. Eight hundred thousand space transports, with weapons, gathered here in the Beldine system! Hope for the survival of the Teton — and the Scientists' force, which Rold imagined was meager at best — seemed as substantial as evaporating dew.

"There's more," Yosma said. "But you've already experienced what I'm about to report. The Whites are searching for the Library. They have their own spies and suspect that the bombing of First Colony wasn't entirely successful. The leader of the Whites is bent on our destruction.

"Diego will have another runner coming by now. I'm instructed to return with news from the Library. As I enter Minpana, the next messenger should be here.

"This is all I have to report. But before I leave I'll be at my family's lodge to answer any questions."

Yosma left, jogging out of the room. His role was that of a messenger, not a politician so he left the decision making to the chiefs.

Pentat went to the place of speaking again. He did not have the hopeless look on his face as many did.

"What we don't know," Pentat started, "is when the Whites will have their battle in the sky. I'll instruct Yosma to take this question back to Diego.

"When they're engaged in their own war, off of our world, we'll take Minpana back. It'll be ours once again."

A cheer came from a small group to Pentat's right. Negative shouts could be heard from the other side, such as: "For how long!" But slowly the cunning of the plan was absorbed by the majority of the chiefs.

"But when they return!" a detractor cried again.

"We'll have control of their bases," Pentat said. "We must be aggressive. We have nothing to lose, for it's all lost already. The White infection is growing faster each day. We have no choice."

"But the other cities? The Zenians!"

"We'll take Diego's suggestion and attack the desert lodges while the frost still clings to the grasses. What's a little cold to us? This is our home. The monsters are our only obstacle to taking Minpana. We've defeated a small army of them — even when we were outnumbered. If they're weak, we'll surely win. Who'll follow me?"

The air burst with noise as the assembly rose — even the detractors found their feet. Olama and his delegation stood and approached Pentat.

Olama went to him and hugged him. They both turned to face the circular assembly and held their fists in the air. A cheer went up that bounced back as a deep shrieking hum from the domed ceiling.

CHAPTER 19

*The Teton warriors, massed as they were, moved like a
colonial organism — unlike the proverbial "well oil
machine" of White armies. This "swarm" moved quickly
and efficiently across any terrain: a one time in
history marvel, unmatched by any military contingent
I've ever seen.*

- From "The Chronicles of Rold Simms"
  by Francisco Diego

Ruth Poundstone sat comfortably in a fabric hammock as she watched
the passing stars through the round window of her stateroom. Her cabin was
adjacent to the bridge of the space fighter transport. The bridge was an elongated bulge on the top of the log shaped carrier transport, which housed two
thousand small fighters. She had been awakened on the third watch so that
she could begin making plans. She was the only Committee member to join
the armada; the others remained at Newert awaiting their fate — good or bad.
There were three divisions of transports: two to enter Beldine from either
flank and the one assault division. Ruth chose the assault division for her
command position, as a show of leadership or probably as a quick end to her
labors — she was not sure. Intelligence reports were coming in with more
frequency. The closer they came to the confrontation the clearer their position became.

Her gaze was interrupted by a transmission that begged to be heard. She
waved her hand across a flat, circular panel which emitted a dozen beams of
light that terminated two centimeters from their source; they were as fine as
hair fibers. The panel looked like a coarse brush which she stroked to clean
her hand, but the effect was the acceptance of the transmission. A robed man
appeared, a Scientist soldier of middle-to-high rank, too blurred visually to
reveal his age or general appearance. But she knew the man and had expected
the message.

"Comrade Poundstone," he began. This was an online transmission so
that a conversation was possible, even though a significant response time

hampered the natural flow of language. "We have confirmed that the Industrialists have withdrawn all space travel vehicles to their Beldine bases, of which there are four: Salkinia, Caljunna, and its two moons, Roda and Sparrow. Three quarters of the old Industrial planets have only small numbers, using automated defense arrays. Weaponry, fighters, transports (personnel, weapon, and freight) have been collected at these frontier bases. There's only one conclusion . . ."

"They know we're coming," she said in her aged voice, its quaver matching the static soiled transmission.

She had cut off the speaker, but the officer soon heard her statement and remained quiet.

"Then we want to do it quickly," Ruth said. "They may be aware of our attack, but I would guess that we'll be there sooner than they expect. We'll try to get some fighters into the atmosphere on Salkinia, destroy the factories, cities. If we can get in quickly and hurt their nerve center, then we'll have a chance against their superior strength. Brain against brawn as they said in the ancient literature. We have had power for centuries because of it.

"Bring the clockwise flank division in behind the Beldine sun and send in a squadron of disguised fighters to Salkinia. We'll wait with the other two divisions in a star orbit about where we are now. We'll look like a comet to them this far out."

"Yes. And then?"

"Then we'll follow. And hope we'll survive this bloody game."
*

Pentat came scratching at Rold's lodge the next morning in the cold dark before dawn. Yosana and Rold were awake, drinking hot tea and preparing packs for their pridda. Tyler was already out and about, having prepared the night before. Rold held Yosana for a long time then picked up the sleeping Pitallela.

"I love you, little girl," he whispered. "I'm sorry for bringing you into this mess — you've barely seen the sun a handful of days. So small and so beautiful, like your mother. I have to admit you were pretty ugly your first day. I never knew babies were so ugly — but beautiful at the same time.

"If I live, we'll have a wonderful life together, you and I. Great friends. But if I die, at least you'll not feel the pain of it, you're so young. I love you. Sleep on this morning. I'll miss you."

His speech was labored by his passion. Yosana allowed a tear or two, watching Rold. Rold reluctantly handed the warm, sleeping Pitallela to Yosana. Pentat had stood outside the lodge, waiting patiently. He had also said goodbye to his family but was now steeled to the tragedy that was unfolding.

The two men left with quickened strides to saddle their mounts. They both wore leggings and vests of several layered, hard leather over soft leather shirts. The soft leather came from the belly of the pitah and the hard leather from its back. Pentat gave Rold a head band with a single feather and silver buttons all around. He wore no decoration himself, not even paint.

Rold found his favorite pony and secured his panniers to its rump and strapped a blanket to its back. He climbed on with confidence — which came from his constant companionship with the animal and also the fact that the pridda had shed its antlers in the deep winter and had only started growing spikes in the last few days. He rubbed the fuzzy knobs on the pridda's head affectionately and then turned him toward Pentat's corral where the two men met. They exchanged glances then walked their animals along a dark, muddy path to join the other silent warriors who were moving into position. There was no talking, but the ground rumbled under the thousands of hooves and human feet. The eastern horizon was turning pink, hailing the arrival of the sun. A mass of stars were still visible overhead, giving witness to the clarity of the sky. No ceremony was performed; everyone knew where they were to be. The warriors were divided into two groups; each numbered more than two hundred thousand. About half were mounted warriors, the other on foot. One group was to circle the Spotted Valley to the north and the other to the south. They could not move people through the Spotted Valley quickly enough. As it was, the detour would also hamper their speed, but not by much. They would be racing the weather — trying to reach the desert before the snow totally melted. Rold and Pentat would go with the southern group, which would have to camp and wait for the northern group to catch up. Bana was leading them.

By the time Rold and Pentat were at the lead, the sun had risen fully above the eastern mountain crest. With one hand signal the procession started. They rose above the meadow, climbing the Red Hills, destroying the land-scape with their numbers. Rold looked back and saw the thousands of riders moving slowly behind them and up the northern hillside, climbing up snow and ice covered cliffs. They looked like ants evacuating a disturbed anthill. In the center of each group were huge trains of pridda packed with provisions. It was an unusual device for the Teton, for they seldom carried community provisions. Each person or family was usually responsible for his or her own upkeep. But it was decided that with such a large group there were certain efficiencies attained by this method of pooling provisions. Though many saw it as an effect of the Whites on their lives — to break with tradition, to follow the White ways. But everyone had his own weapons, though stores of the specially tipped arrows were also on the pridda trains.

"Six weeks may be optimistic," Rold said. "You've never had to manage such a large party before."

"That is our advantage, Mountain Bear," Pentat said. "I don't need to manage it. We're still a collection of villages, and each chief will take care of his own. And that will be your job. If I'm to be the chief of chiefs, who will be chief of the Eagles? You, my friend."

"Me! I've come to fight not to lead."

"We've all come to fight, but I need you to lead my village. You know everyone. They respect you. Lampa will help you; he knows you the best. If I give an order to the chiefs, I need you to carry it out with our own village. You will be what we sometimes call a battle chief — someone who assumes the lead on the field."

"I'll do my best."

Tyler had been listening as she rode behind the two men. She was an experienced rider, like Rold: on horses. Rold had given her one of the ponies he had received at the joining banquet. She took to the pridda even faster than Rold. And now she loped behind him. She kept silent and turned her thoughts to the coming battles — and other events to come.

The solemnity of the departure was replaced by songs and story telling as the day worn on, and continued for hours as the monotonous plodding of the mounted army moved onward. By dusk the southern army had crossed into the grass covered basin where Rold had first ridden Gwydmonia with Yosana. Melting snow had dribbled into the basin in the form of small streams that dampened the ground and the cold air. Rold wished he had Yosana beside him.

The warriors brought no tents since the night air would stay above freezing. They simply wrapped themselves in heavy furs, ate cold rations and tried to sleep. Rold took first watch for the Eagle village — as he had seen Pentat do many times. As the moon set in the middle of the night, he woke Lampa's son to take second watch. The night was quiet and cold, and it was hard for him to relax. Tyler found him, having trained herself to wake with the change of watch.

"Hello," she whispered.

She made her bed beside him. He had already set his robe and was lying on his back, hands behind his head, his eyes on the wavering stars.

"Thank you," he said, not quite in a whisper but a low, husky monotone.

"For what?"

"For being here. For being alive — though I fear I'm going to lose you all over again in this damn war."

"I love you too."

"You've changed."

"So have you."

"I know. But you — I thought you had grown up so much when I saw you that day at the Caljunna space port. But now! What happened out there? With the Zenians? With Gwydmonia?"

"The path was hard and long. *Salla te'madda poh-yah, poh-yah te'madda sal.* 'Time becomes space; space becomes time.' We must choose when the time has come."

Rold looked at this person whom he did not recognize anymore.

"I guess you got the adventure you were looking for when you came to visit me, eh?"

She smiled at him, now silent.

Rold turned on his side. Finally they slept.

A dream crept into Rold's cold body of his love making with Yosana suspended inside the hulking Gwydmonia. He seemed to be watching himself with Yosana from some distance. Gwydmonia's flesh looked cold to Rold-the-observer, but it felt warm and comforting to the cloud-riding-Rold. Then Yosana was no longer Yosana but a beautiful woman with white hair and white gown that billowed about her slender body as if being blown by a breeze. The sexual encounter became hot and sweaty, passion setting fire to blood and muscles. Rold shook his head, feeling guilty watching himself with another woman. The woman turned her head and looked at Rold-the-observer and smiled, then laughed. She quickly changed back into Yosana. Rold woke just before dawn and found himself aroused. He ached to relieve himself but felt trapped amid the thousands of people with no privacy to be found.

Tyler was already up. Always a step ahead, he thought. He rose and wandered to where the pridda had been hobbled, a wide arroyo drenched in mud. He slid down to the sticky, trampled bottom and emptied his bladder against a dirt wall. Feeling better he searched until he found his mount and began the day as many of the other warriors had.

For twenty-two days this was the routine, as the army of pridda riders and infantry scratched a wide trail across the grass sea until they dropped into an arid basin that was the Western Desert. Here they made camp to wait for the northern army. They chose a canyon that fell a hundred meters below the flat plain. The entire southern army was thus hidden from surface surveillance. In the days they had traveled, not a single Militia jet had passed overhead. Rold worried about reconnaissance flights at ten, twenty, thirty thousand meters — the Teton would not notice those jets — but so far, there had been no overt signs of discovery.

Scouts were out trying to make contact with the northern army when a Militia patrol was spotted. It seemed that the Teton were still invisible to the Industrialists, however, and Pentat wanted to keep it that way until the northern army rendezvoused. Camp fires were forbidden, and absolute quiet was maintained for two days. But as it would happen a small party of Militia in land rovers were exploring the canyon on the fourth day. Frost appeared each morning on the grasses of the plain, but the canyon was warmer, and the Industrialists were hoping to move the Zenians from their solar canopies to an open area to begin exercises.

The land rovers followed the small, muddy stream that had formed the wide canyon. It twisted and turned and was fed by small tributaries. Hardwood trees, naked except for the barely discernible buds that encrusted their branches, lined the river bed. As the Militia turned a corner they could not believe what they saw: thousands of Teton warriors. Immediately, several rows of warriors were crouched with arrows strung, then behind them were mounted warriors with shields and lances. The rovers attempted to turn around, getting stuck in the mud and tangled in the tree roots. Pentat dropped his hand, and arrows flew; warriors sprinted to the wallowing vehicles. There were five rovers, and at least twenty arrows passed through each. Three of the machines stopped and quieted as all life seemed to seep out of them, but two were limping along and escaped back around the bend. Pentat sent twenty riders to follow. They chased the land rovers down the jagged canyon floor, never getting close enough to throw their arrows.

The canyon widened, and the two vehicles raced behind lines of more Militia ground vehicles, armed with energy weapons. The small rovers looked like scared puppies searching for their mother's teats. There were at least a hundred of the mobile energy cannons and a thousand Zenians moving up the canyon. The Teton riders saw their mistake and pulled up. They had little knowledge of this technology and waited to test the range of the Industrialist weapons. One cannon fired an energy blast that was shaped like a cone and killed three of the Teton instantly; they seemed to melt into the sand along with their pridda. One Teton turned to get back to the army to warn them, and a narrow beam of energy, as thin as a needle, cut through his chest; he slumped, falling from his mount. The other Teton pulled out bows and arrows, realizing their futility against these numbers but willing to fight. The Industrialists accepted their superiority and began moving toward the Teton without firing. The mobile cannons moved easily a meter above the ground; the Zenians kept up with them on foot with amazing speed and stamina.

As they drew closer a shadow formed along the eastern edge of the canyon; the warriors glanced up at the rim and smiled at the source of the shadow: lining the rim as far as they could see, from north to south, were mounted Teton warriors with drawn arrows pointing downward onto the approaching Industrialists. It was the northern army; it had just arrived and heard the energy blasts. From their elevated position they were able to throw their arrows a great distance, onto the vehicles below, and the Zenians. It was like rain hitting parched earth. The specially-tipped arrows penetrated the armored vehicles easily and cut down the Zenians, two for every one arrow, severing arms and legs and destroying weapons. The ground rumbled, and boulders fell from the canyon walls, partially burying the Militia force. A few energy blasts, misaimed, added to the geological destruction.

The pridda of the Teton held steady through the tremor, and only dust reached them. The noise of the quick battle was all the warning Pentat needed, and the rest of his army was down the canyon, but only in time to see the remaining few Zenians fleeing. Pentat considered no strategy in his pursuit; he simply moved to the front with little care or seeming knowledge of traditional behavior of army commanders. Rold led the Eagle warriors with old feelings of revenge, his blood sloshing like icy water within him.

Two groups of mounted warriors from Bana's army descended the canyon wall in what seemed like seconds. The slope was steep and dusty. They met the Zenians ahead of Pentat's main body, routing them mercilessly. But some Militia fire did get through and tore into the Teton, felling a dozen riders.

Pentat slowed as he reached the devastation of the Militia vehicles and the smear of blood and flesh of the Zenians. Warriors from the villages of the dead Teton retrieved their effects then with purposeful haste, built pyres, disregarding the order for no fire — the Industrialists now knew they were there, though they must have seemed as ghosts risen from the ashes of First Colony. Other warriors began picking through the rocks and bodies and broken machines of the Industrialists. Rold halted the Eagles. All were mounted, and he rode up to Pentat who was surveying the wreckage. Bana was leading the northern army south to find the canyon entrance, which would take all afternoon. "Well, they know we're here, that we exist," Rold said.

He then saw a face that seemed like a dream. A woman warrior was being lifted from the mass of bodies, her arm bleeding. He shook his head and she was gone, apparently taken by her village warriors into the thick of Teton trying to move back to the main body. She looked so much like Yosana; but, of course, the Teton women had similar features. He must have been mistaken.

Pentat was staring in the same direction, then he turned back to Rold.

"Yes," he said. "And we need to know where they've gone. Organize scouts to trail them, unseen, and find their base camp. They'll be back with more of their monster warriors since we could not cut them off."

Rold looked around. The sight of the grim destruction caused his mouth to stretch into a hard grin.

"Our losses were very small considering their weapons," he said. "We were very lucky."

"But this . . ." Pentat gestured to the smoking scene. He paused with quivering emotion. He was trying to see the whole mess in one glance, but it was too great. "Such a slaughter. We don't slaughter pitah like this. Why must we fight this way?"

"We're at war," Rold said. "The Zenians are not a pleasant race. They have unimaginable strength that comes from their madness, and the only way to stop them is to do battle. We've encountered them twice, and each time we've been lucky. This wasn't a real battle, not face to face. They were out numbered here in this canyon. But soon they'll be back, as you said, and if the reports are accurate, there are a hundred times as many of them as there are of us."

"Let's move out of this canyon. It served its purpose –hiding us until Bana could get here, but we're no longer hidden. I fear we'd be caught like these poor devils were if we stay.

"Quickly. Send word to Bana not to enter. We'll join him on the plain."

Rold turned his pony and ran him back to the Eagles. He took Lampa with him to the rear of the army, deciding to tell Bana himself of Pentat's order. Galloping, with a clear corridor open to them through the throng, it still took better than an hour to reach the front of the northern army. Rold recognized Bana immediately. It was surprising, considering the number of people crowded about, but Bana was Bana. He had yellow grass attached to his breast plate, back, and shoulders, as he had the first time Rold saw him rising from the grassy hills to the north. They greeted, and Bana signaled a stop to the march. A wave of mimicked orders radiated through the army, slowing their progress until finally they all stopped.

"I fear we wasted a few arrows back there," Bana said grinning. Rold appreciated his easy speech after being with Pentat for almost a month.

"Enough, I'd say. Effective at least," Rold said.

"Masterful timing, yes?"

They both smiled at Bana's pride.

"Soon your head band will be too small for you," Rold said. "Ah! What an insult. Well, I'll let it pass. Now, what's the word, Mountain Bear?"

"Pentat wants to leave the canyon. He feels we could be trapped down here. He's going to turn his army formation inside-out and follow you eastward a bit onto the plain. Also, scouts are needed to watch the Whites and see where they are, where they're going."

"They're going to Minpana."

"So you've had reports. So soon?"

"The machines are moving. But those crazy Zenians are still here in the desert. And they're moving toward us or to the south of us. It's not clear.

But, yes, we need new information — especially since we've been seen."

The two men pulled their pridda side-by-side and walked them up a grade to the plain and looked about. The mass of warriors deep in the canyon was beginning to move their way. Across the canyon, far to the western horizon, they could see a line of dust.

"It'll be morning before they can reach us," Bana said, shading his eyes as he peered at the tiny evidence of the approaching Zenians. "Tomorrow we'll be truly tested."

Bana smiled and slapped Rold on the back.

"There's this odd woman in my army who has been a real trouble maker the last few days," Bana said.

Rold frowned, fearing what Bana was about to tell him.

Bana saw the grown and laughed. "Do you know this woman? Well, she has become the chief of the Shihayah village."

"What!"

"Their chief was old and got sick two days from the Library. We hadn't even made it across the mountains. He was taken back, and his daughter relinquished her rule to this crazy woman, who has done nothing but try to tell me what to do for the last two weeks."

Rold was shaking his head, worried about little Pitallela, surprised Yosana would risk so much just to be in battle.

"Where is she," he asked.

"Close by. She's been wounded, but she's all right. Ask for the Shihayah village. And help me get this rabble turned around as you go."

Rold sent Lampa back to the Eagle warriors to lead them out of the canyon. He knew Pentat would question why he was not there, but right now he wanted to see Yosana.

Messengers were recognizable by a red feather that each wore in a down position behind the left ear. Rold explained the move onto the plain to each one he passed and also asked for the Shihayahs. With surprisingly little confusion the mob was turned and began moving eastward, and quickly Rold found the village and saw his wife sitting proudly upon her pridda.

"I have a message for your chief," Rold shouted.

Yosana was riding at the front of the village, her arm wrapped with bandages and in a sling. There were at least twenty riders between Rold and her.

"I'm the chief," she shouted before seeing who he was. She gave an order, Rold could not hear, to the Shihayah warriors then turned her mount and rode to Rold's side. They grabbed each other, Yosana wincing from the pain.

Rold looked at her arm, taking it gently.

"It's not bad," she said. "Just a few stitches."

Rold had a pleading look, impatient but not angry.

"I couldn't help it," she said. "Sakamat, the chief, was an old friend. He caught a chill and had to go back. They wanted me as their leader in this battle. What could I say?"

They rode slowly with the flow of the thousands of dusty warriors, telling of their days on the trail and little else. Rold feeling powerless with this head-strong woman.

After a while he felt responsibility tugging on his shirttail.

"Pentat will be fit to be tied when he hears," he said. "I'm not quite sure how I feel right now myself. I must go back now."

"I know. We'll find each other in camp."

Rold turned and fought the unrelenting current of warriors moving out of the canyon, traveling in the opposite direction of the hoard. It was now all one giant mass of weary Teton and pridda, as the two armies merged on their way up the gradual canyon exit. He was able to find Pentat before dark, who was with the Eagles.

"You've been talking to Bana a long time," Pentat said. Rold moved in beside him, joining the trudge. A cold moisture that instantly turned to frost on the prickly grasses blew in from the north as the sun escaped into the flat horizon behind them.

"He has some information?" Pentat said.

"Yes. The Militia are moving most of their equipment to Minpana. But the Zenians are still in the desert."

"This I know. You can see their silhouette against the setting sun."

"Bana thinks they'll be here by morning."

"Yes. Did you speak to anyone else?"

Rold looked at him suspiciously. Pentat frowned.

"You know!" Rold said.

"I've known Yosana much longer than you, Mountain Bear. I know the whole story, so you don't have to repeat it. I learned of her charge down the canyon wall and her wound. I'll accept her generous help and courage, and let's hope for Pitallela's sake, if not for our own, she survives the battle. We'll not all survive."

Pentat, now sullen, spurred his pridda to take him to the front. Rold stayed with his new charge to organize the camp. The whole army finally stopped with the rising of The moon. Camp was prepared and fires were allowed. It was decided that everyone should have a hot meal. They were no longer hiding.Pentat rode around to each camp, conferring with its chief on the strategy for the morning.

Tyler sought out Rold as everyone settled for the first watch.

"Did you see Yosana?" she asked

"How did you know?"

She simply smiled and placed her hand on his shoulder.

Second watch fell to Rold. He could see a long, thin line of lights to the west but little movement, only the twinkling of the amber dots. He watched the sky, ablaze with stars. Why had they not sent fighter jets? They were too close to Minpana to use nuclear bombs, that he knew, but a great deal of damage could be done from the sky. And the Teton could not fight back, not with arrows.

When relieved he slept for only a couple of hours. Predawn brought no warnings, no screaming or drums pounding, but the gentle calling of the morning watchers waking the camp as they had done now for days. Rold saw Lampa riding into camp. He had been at a scouting position all night.

"No word?" Rold said.

"They have skirted us in the night," Lampa said jumping from his mount. "It looks like all are headed for Minpana. They moved very fast to be ahead of us this morning, a half day by our speed. We couldn't have cut them off; we're too slow for them. And our pursuit will be slow as well. No battle today."

Everyone's emotions were raw by sunlight. Not that fighting would be so welcome, but the anticipation was nauseating. Quickly they were on the move, heading southeast. Minpana was only two days away at their current pace. Pentat ordered camp that night, seeing no need to march without rest. No fires were lit, however, and all was quiet. The talk was positive: many were saying the Whites were afraid, running scared. Rold knew, and Pentat, that there was a reason for the pull back to Minpana and the avoidance of the Teton. Minpana with its walls and fire power would make a better battle ground for the Industrialists, fewer losses and a clearer victory.

Pentat called a meeting of the chiefs which congregated in the center of the camp, the Teton chiefs sitting in a circle. The lights of Minpana reflected in the evening mist, which the Teton could see as a dim glowing in the eastern sky.

It was colder now that they were closer to the mountains. Patches of snow still littered the ground. Rold felt a pang in his chest when he recognized the camps orientation: they were only meters from the mining port that Yosana and Blikki had used to bring him to this world. He thought of the trip in the Industrialist hovercraft that took him to his prison cell. It was warmer then; he could still remember the sweet smell of the desert grasses and the impressive sight of the Minpana Wall. He thought of Rachel Meacom, the way she looked that day — smug and menacing when she cut down Tyler. His heart ached when he remembered his emotions of that moment. And he remembered his realization of the meaning of her plot. It has come to this, he thought. I wonder if she's in there.

Rold sat beside Yosana as they listened to Pentat's directions, bringing Rold back from his daydreaming.

"It'll take a concentration of arrows to unhinge Desertgate," Pentat said. "If it can be brought down, that will be our victory. The Minpanese will revolt the moment we enter the city. But first we must get through the Zenians. And that will be our true test. It may take days, or only hours."

"Why haven't they attacked us?" one chief asked. "We're so close, and they have their weapons."

"We have information now that the Whites are busy preparing for their other enemy: Mountain Bear's people. Diego got word out of the city. He sent three messengers; only one made it into camp alive. The Whites are beginning a war in the sky. They see us as only a bother." He paused and looked around the circle. "It's their mistake."

Everyone nodded and grunted approval of his statement.

"We'll begin tomorrow," Pentat said and adjourned the meeting.

The circle broke, as the chiefs ambled toward their villages.

"There's another reason why I've made you chief, Mountain Bear," Pentat said. "In our quest for a pain dream I did see something, though I held it from you. I saw what you did not. I saw my death. I fear I will not be coming back. You'll take care of Tachina for me, won't you? And Chomata-te? He should be educated at the Library — if the Library still stands."

"As I'm sure you would take care of Pitallela for us," Rold said. "If we don't make it. But don't force your death to happen just because you dreamed it."

"Look around, Mountain Bear. Tell me this isn't what you dreamed."

"Yes," Rold said. "What is to come in the next few days may very well resemble what I dreamed on that damned, cold rock. I've already thought of that. And it's very eerie, but you didn't die in my dream."

"Our dreams are not whole alone. Only together do they tell a complete story. I'm as Achilles at the Scaean gates."

"Let the dream happen," Rold said, looking only at Pentat. "Don't make it happen. All right? We'll see what it means."

With that the group broke up, each going to find some rest, though little sleep would be had this night. There was no more chance of reprieve from battle; the Teton were going to attack.

After midnight the Teton were moving. Pentat had decided to attack before the sun was visible, using the Zenians' fear of darkness and cold to his advantage. It would take some hours to reach the Zenian camp.

The Zenians were corralled under acres of fabric canopies, illuminated with electric lights which burned all night. On their home planet they lived in total sunshine for periods of five to seven years — the rotation of their planet was so slow. Their species had no concept of sleep but rather hibernation at their dark cycles. So this night was as day to them. With the Industrialists technology, light was not a problem; and with the proper environment suits, the cold was also not a problem. But the combination of cold and dark still made them uneasy. They would not initiate an attack themselves without the sunlight.

The Teton charged the glowing campsite, without a single moment of rest from their march, throwing arrows into the pacing mass of alien soldiers. A chilling clamor of wails and screams came from the Zenian camp. Pentat had his warriors surround them, though not in a total circle, for the Zenians were backed up against the Minpana Wall. Energy blasts escaped the tents randomly. Teton warriors were going down. But much damage was wrought on the Zenians. Rold was sweating, even though the air was freezing. He strung his arrows and let them fly sparingly, with deliberation. He would occasionally peer along the line of mounted Teton looking for Yosana but never found her among the faceless warriors. Tyler fought bravely with his Eagle warriors. After each personal battle they would find each others eyes and smile as they confirmed they were both still alive.

And then the sun rose. Slowly at first and then with incredible speed and vigor, with inhuman cries, the Zenians left their camp to plow into the Teton. The Teton shields were effective against the energy weapons of the Zenians, though several blasts would topple a warrior, and many went down. And many dropped to the ground, locked in physical battles with the giant Zenians, the monsters frustrated with how little damage their weapons made.

Tyler fearlessly waded into the forest of howling monsters. From the back of a pridda she was the height of the giants she fought. She threw arrows in rapid succession, felling the beasts in circles about her. But once the hoard was upon her she found she was not strong enough to fight them in hand combat. One grabbed her and she found herself flung into the air almost ten meters and came crashing down among her Teton cohorts. Shaking away her dizziness, she arose, without her mount, and did as many of the warriors had done now in close quarters: she began slicing into the Zenians with the exposed point of a treated arrow. Blood gushed and splattered the participants, lubricating the violent clash.

The magical arrows of the Teton were devastating. The aliens were being pushed back. But then the Militia turned cannons from the top of the wall down on the battle. The conical spray of searing energy emitted by the cannons wiped across the rear ranks of the Teton, melting a tenth of the entire army to puddles of hydrocarbons. Fighting stopped as the horror struck them, and then the cannons blasted along the front line, with little care of whether Teton or Zenians were killed. Rold screamed at the sight, spurring his pridda and running to find Tyler, whom he could no longer see.

This was not a weapon they could fight. The cannons simply blew away the Teton shields, and they were too high up for any arrow to reach with the strongest of bows.

Rold was knocked from his pridda by the concussion of an explosion; his mount was crushed in the tumble. Fearing the next blast, he ran desperately, jumping over bodies, stepping in fleshy goo. The cannons fired again, but upward not downward on the battle. A space fighter swept down from the sky over the battle, its wings almost scraping the tall Minpana Wall, as it evaded the cannon blasts. It was a Scientist fighter! Rold shook his head, trying to understand what was happening. But then in a flash, the fighter shot three blasts: one hitting the Zenian camp and the other two striking the cannons on the Wall. Huge, black smoking holes gaped from the top of the wall, looking like giant bites in its rim. The fighter made another pass and blasted the Zenians once more then the last cannon before it retreated. The Teton were cheering though Rold could barely hear them over the ringing in his deafened ears. A burning, pungent smell reached him as smoke engulfed the wall and the camp.

He was frantic. He walked like a drunken man, trying to gather his warriors and was caught from behind by a Zenian. They tumbled to the ground. The beast actually sank its teeth into Rold's shoulder. He found his hunting knife at his side and cut the Zenian's throat, only slicing the skin. It released its grip and Rold plunged the blade into its abdomen. As the dying Zenian rolled to its back, Rold saw the pouch and knew it was a female. Two nude infants — fetuses? he wasn't sure what to call them — crawled from the pouch with closed eyes, squeaking and grunting. With a labored sigh Rold wiped his stinking knife and returned it to its scabbard. He ran from the corpse, angry and appalled at the alien scene. Looking toward the gate, he saw that the Teton had made their way to the foot of it through the path that the fighter had blasted. Pentat was there directing an elite corp of archers as they cut through the hinges with their arrows.

Rold ran to the gate. He still had his shield, which he had to use along the way as blasts came whizzing at him, but his bow was lost. His heart was in his throat when he saw Yosana fighting her way to the gate with a handful of the Shihayah warriors behind her. Just as he reached her, Desertgate began creaking and slowly falling toward the battle. Warriors on pridda scurried out of the way as it crashed, dust billowing to the heights of the wall.

As water breaches a broken damn, the mass of Teton warriors flooded the fallen gate with renewed strength. Rold was swept along with them, as was Yosana. He shouted to her; she saw him, finally, but they could not reach each other. Through the gate he could see widespread destruction, probably caused by the Scientist fighters. After entering he stepped to the side and climbed atop an overturned vehicle to improve his vision. Yosana saw him and started toward him, pushing through the army. He looked through the gate, back toward the desert, and saw surviving Zenians escaping into the cracks and crevices of the red sandstone bluffs. The Teton had been a match for them, more so than he would have imagined. And now the Teton were inside — a liberating army. But how much of a match were they for the Industrialists, with their technology? Yosana reached him and dismounted. Rold climbed down from his perch. They looked at each other at arm's length for a moment then their bodies melded into each other's. They turned and saw the invading hoard of Teton streaming down the city streets, looking for a war. Regretfully they ended their moment of comfort and followed the race, joining the spoilers on their spree.

CHAPTER 20

*The shining miracle of Margona's birth
Stands in the hearts of us all.*

- From "The Song of Margona"
  by Pitallela-Sim

Resistance came — but too late. The Militia that were stationed in the city actually had none of the large hardware that Rold expected. The cannons at the gates were the only serious defense. But the Industrialists were not giving up. They had concentrated in the modern ward of the city and found themselves surrounded by the Teton.

Rold felt helpless without a bow; but during an organized charge against a street barricade, he swung a handful of arrows about as many had done, slicing through metal, brick, flesh and bone. Once through the main line of Militia, the ward was easily invaded — though Teton were falling, and it tore at Rold to see the dead bodies dropping right and left. He had managed to catch up to his warriors; many had lost their mounts. But Tyler was nowhere to be seen.

In the fray a Militiaman was waving both his arms madly, surrendering; many had been taken. In fact, by twilight much organization had crystallized, and the Teton were setting up prisoner corrals, infirmaries; and food was being prepared, mostly on one of the large, green parks.

Rold wiped the burning soot from his face and realized the man who was surrendering was Frank. He ran to him, grabbed him around the waist and lifted him up off the ground.

"Frank!" he shouted. "We're here."

"And what an entrance!" Frank said as Rold let him down.

"The Teton have what they wanted," he continued. "Their planet back. But it's not over yet, Rold."

"It's been hard and fast. We've lost several warriors; hundreds, I guess. Too many. But I was thinking: it's been too easy, really. Even with all our losses. The city is practically abandoned. We got through the Zenians, but only with the help of a Scientist fighter. That was luck. I thought we were finished, and we would have been. Then it came out of nowhere. But the city . . . so few are here. The Scientists: they must be in the stellar system."

"That's where the big show is, Rold. Except for this section of the city, all the Industrialists are up there."

Frank pointed at the darkening sky. The air was clear, and the stars were exceedingly bright. But then Rold realized what he was seeing. Those were not stars: they were fighters, transports. The real battle was in space! As the rays of the now hidden sun faded, and the sky became darker, the scene in the sky became all too clear. Thousands of transports were doing battle, so thick that they could be seen from Salkinia. Occasionally one of the bright dots would flash then darken, or one would slip from the sky and streak through the atmosphere like a meteor, burning into ash. As Rold watched, he saw that the flashes and burning streaks were happening all over the dark canvas of the night.

"We have an excellent view down here," Frank said. "An amazing bit of luck, don't you think? That this continent is rotated in such a position as to face the battle, and with the sun to the back of the planet so that the fighters are visible; it's just amazing."

"It's magical and horrible at the same time. Thousands, millions, of people killing each other. You can't see their faces, but you know they're dying. How many?"

"The Industrialists have pulled together almost all their transports, from every system. With the Scientists up there the battle probably accounts for two thirds of the space transports in the whole galaxy. Spectacular."

"Armageddon. Why am I not up there? If it's not stopped there be nothing left! Horrible."

"Yes, well, certainly not a paradigm of subtle strategy — on either side. But I'm afraid the Industrialists are the more powerful. When they've destroyed our fleet they'll be down here to take this planet back."

Rold's neck grew stiff from looking at the sky, but he could not turn his eyes from the terrible scene.

"Frank!" Yosana shouted. She ran to him and threw a joyous embrace around him.

"What in the world are you doing here!" Frank said. "Is everything all right? The baby . . ."

"Everything went well," Yosana said. "I had a little girl. She's with the Eagle village. I couldn't stay behind."

"Well, it's good to see you alive. Both of you. And Tyler?"

"I saw her before the breach of the gate," Rold said. "After that, many of the warriors were separated. I have most of my warriors here in the ward. I don't know where she is."

Frank put his hand on Rold's shoulder.

"I'm sure she's fine."

Yosana nodded.

"I came to tell my wandering husband there's still a battle being pitched in the Industrialist ward. There are a few Militia still loose in the city, we think, hiding in alleys or ruins. Bana's warriors are trying to round them up. Pentat needs us with him. I know where he is. Hopefully Tyler will be there."

"It's all happened so fast," Rold said. "I sent Lampa to find Pentat. I guess he found you first."

Tyler itched from the sticky blood that clung to her arms and neck. At first she was sickened by the individual combat that the Zenians seemed to prefer, but she soon developed a strength she did not know she had and waded through the giants, refusing to be crushed.

When the gate had fallen she lost sight of Rold. She saw him lose his pony, but by then all hell had broken lose. Literally, she thought, since these Zenians resembled demons of Old Earth lore. Several times she received support from the still mounted Eagle warriors around her, and they cheered her on as she slew each enemy that attacked.

Once inside the city she was swept up in the ravaging horde, a battle frenzy propelling her deep into the city. Eventually the movement slowed as everyone found that little resistance existed. She looked around and saw no familiar faces: she was no longer with the Eagle warriors. Finding a grass covered strip in the median of the wide boulevard, she dropped to her knees, exhausted, and closed her eyes until she dozed in the warm late afternoon sun, sleeping into the twilight.

The street in which Rold stood had become peaceful with the darkness. It sparkled from the electric lights of the buildings and torches of the Teton reflecting on its damp pavement — damp from weather and blood. Energy blasts and the cries of warriors had diminished to only a few crackling echoes from other parts of the city. Rold thought of the maddening sound of the battle earlier then he looked up at the silent devastation that was taking place in the sky.

At least up there death was somewhat antiseptic, he thought. The smell of dead bodies in the city had become nauseating, and the clean up was slow. This was a part of war about which he knew little or nothing. In stories of wars — which were always written as propaganda, either for or against some political construct — collecting of the dead was seldom mentioned. No images were put forth in those stories that could prepare someone for the reality. Rold returned his gaze to the clean sky, trying to avoid the reality.

"Is my father up there?" he asked.

"No," Frank said. "He's at Old Earth. I got word to him. He knows you're alive. And I told him about Tyler — and Yosana."

"Thank you," Rold said.

The three walked, with Yosana in the lead and the Eagles following, for more than an hour before reaching Pentat's position. The Teton were spread about the city in strategic locations, but the largest group was here on a green with a single, small adobe hut in the center. A group of Militia were bunched behind barricades toward the eastern entrance to the park. Energy blasts were raining on the Teton, the booming was deafening and the heat and smoke Rold's nose and eyes.

"The prison: Minpana Hold," he said. "An elevator takes you to it from that building. Interesting that Pentat would pick this spot for his command camp."

"Not so odd," Lampa said as he greeted them.

"Have the pridda been fed?" Rold asked.

"Yes," Lampa said. "Only a few were lost. Now get with us under cover. We need your leadership, Mountain Bear. Pentat is missing."

Rold nodded grimly.

"Have you seen Tyler?" he asked.

"No, Mountain Bear. She came through the gate with us, but then she was lost. Her . . . she . . . has not been seen."

Rold immediately began barking orders as he, Yosana, and Frank moved in among the shielded Teton. With this new direction the Teton hurled arrows at the source of the energy blasts, silencing the hissing explosions. But only for a moment. Blasts began again, but fewer than before.

A commotion came from one of the streets where a crowd of Teton approached the camp. Leading them was a warrior who carried another man in his arms. The warrior was Pentat; Rold stood, with his stomach in knots, waiting for him. Pentat came to them, seeing Rold, and placed the man on the ground. It was Bana.

"No!" Rold screamed. Frank hurried to his side. Yosana was on the ground, taking the dead man's hand in hers.

"He's gone," Pentat said.

Yosana sniffed back invisible tears, her face down; Frank was shaking as he stared at Bana's blackened face. Rold felt an anger well up inside him. His manic desire for revenge was awakened. He looked up and was startled to see the whole sky white with massive explosions. His anger turned to a hatred of war and the evil, ignorant nature of human beings that allowed it to happen, that promoted it. He had been a part of it; he had no room for shame, only anger.

Pentat looked tired. He was much more sad than angry. Although the day had been successful, the payment for the victory was harsh. Life seemed empty at that moment.

A living cloud moved overhead blocking the fireworks in the dark dome of the sky and muffling the Militia blasts. Rold's pain, his anger, now reached up to the living cloud, knowing that the human lives lost in this war somehow could be blamed on these seemingly innocuous creatures.

"I don't understand how they do that," Frank said. Everyone had their eyes on the living cloud, their thoughts temporarily diverted from Bana. "Just floating around up there like that. Don't they respect the principle of gravity?"

Rold laughed, in a way that worried Yosana and his friends. They were not laughing.

"They're trying to defy gravity with a very profound, widespread effort," Rold said. His words made no sense to the others, but suddenly it was all clear to him. This was what he was meant to do.

Confirming his thoughts, the living cloud descended until it was just above their heads. The Teton were awed and frightened. Pentat did not seem to care. Yosana spoke first — with the minah-machacute sign language.

"Is it you, Gwydmonia?" Yosana said aloud and with her hands.

"YES, YOSANA," Gwydmonia answered with very precise, tiny lights in a tight circle just above Yosana.

"Why are you here?" Yosana said.

"ROLD KNOWS."

Yosana looked at him. He seemed different. She sensed the power of him in the same way she had when they went cloud riding together.

"What did it say?" Frank asked.

"She wants to talk to Rold," she said with inflections that made her statement weak and almost a question.

"DON'T BE UPSET, YOSANA," Gwydmonia said, her lights attracting Yosana's attention. "ROLD IS THE ONLY ONE WHO CAN SOLVE THIS PUZZLE. HE MUST PRONOUNCE IT, OR THE CONTINUUM WILL BE DISRUPTED."

"I understand — or, I don't really understand, but it's all right."

"WELL, ROLD?" Gwydmonia said with her lights.

Rold threw his pointing hand up at the silent space battle, violently, as if he were trying to jerk his arm out of his shoulder.

"YES," Gwydmonia said. "QUICK AND CLEAN. WE COULD WIPE OUT THE WHOLE BUNCH. YOUR TECHNOLOGY WOULD CRUMBLE WITH SUCH A LOSS. THE END RESULT: ISOLATION. PERFECT SOLUTION. PERFECT."

Rold screamed one, long unintelligible bellow that echoed against the buildings surrounding the green. He was standing unprotected, and a thin beam of red energy cleanly sliced through his forearm. The blood that oozed from the wound sizzled and turned into steam from the heat of the blast.

Yosana clutched at Rold's arm, then ensnared his waist. He jerked at the pain but pushed it out of his mind as if it were only a bee sting.

Yosana was the only other person there who understood the conversation, finally realized the scope of what was happening, though the details were still so mysterious. She found a shield and tried to protect Rold while he stood in reckless defiance of the Militia blasts.

"How can a living being as advanced, old and wise, at the same time be so stupid!" Rold shouted. "I can't think of another word to call you in this sign language."

He sighed, trying to pull up some hidden strength — if he could only find it.

"THEN WHAT?" Gwydmonia said.

"I don't know. But why do you always assume destruction is the only course?"

"TELL US WHAT TO DO. YOU WILL DESTROY EACH OTHER ANYWAY IF LEFT TO YOURSELVES."

"Pull them apart. Force them to disengage. Don't worry about a permanent solution right now. Just stop that!" He pointed up again.

"YES! BRILLIANT! BUT, ROLD, WE NEED SOMETHING IN RETURN. IF WE ARE TO STOP THIS WAR, YOU MUST GIVE US SOMETHING."

"What? What can I give you?"

"TYLER."

He looked at the massive, undulating creature, puzzled and angry.

"I don't understand, but I'm not sure I want to."

"IT HAS BEEN SEEN THAT ONE OF US WILL EXPIRE, DIE, IN THE COMING ERA. A NEW LIVING CLOUD MUST BE BORN. TYLER HAS THAT COMPONENT NECESSARY TO BECOME ONE OF US. EARLY IN YOUR HISTORY WE SPENT SOME TIME WITH THE ANCIENT HUMANS ON YOUR HOME PLANET. SOME HUMANS WHO STILL LIVE ON EARTH CARRY A GENE THAT WE GAVE TO YOUR RACE. TYLER IS ONE."

At first the thought was too obscure, too unconnected to anything in Rold's notions of reality. He pondered this request, this concept of metamorphosis, then he reacted, putting aside the issue of consequences.

"Tyler's an adult. I'm only her brother. I can't 'give' you my sister. She's not a slave to be bartered."

"NO, SHE IS NOT. BUT SHE IS AFRAID. YOU CAN HELP HER MAKE THE DECISION."

Rold paused again, considering carefully what he was about to say.

"One life to save millions?" he said.

"YES. BUT DO NOT THINK OF HER AS GIVING UP HER LIFE. SHE WILL LIVE WHAT WOULD BE AN ETERNITY TO YOU."

"If she has this capacity, then I must also. Why not take me?"

"WOULD YOU BE WILLING?"

Rold looked at Yosana. She was openly crying — something she rarely did. Her eyes were locked with his. She did not understand all that Gwydmonia wanted, or why, but she knew that her whole world was teetering. And all the while, the park was being inundated with deadly streaks of energy.

"Yes," Rold said aloud then signed.

"A GREAT SACRIFICE. BUT NO, ROLD. YOU DO NOT HAVE THE DISPOSITION: YOU HAVE A SPARK BUT NOT THE FULL FIRE WITHIN YOU. YOU MUST CONVINCE TYLER."

"But I don't think I could lose her again!"

"YOU MUST IF YOU WISH TO STOP THE SLAUGHTER AROUND YOU."

"No. Forget it. We'll take our chances with the outcome of the battle. I'll not be a party to your abduction of my sister. You can't intimidate me."

"I'll need no convincing." It was a new voice, a hoarse deep voice of a woman.

The warrior pushed her way through the crowd that had gathered to watch the conversation between Rold and the living cloud.

"Tyler," Rold said.

He left Yosana and took both of Tyler's hands. They were grimy where dust had clung to drying blood. Her face was marked with burns and a long scratch from temple to chin that was dotted with beads of blood. Her cold blue eyes peered through swollen lids, her mouth set in a tight frown.

"It is my destiny," she said. Her voice was about to disappear.

"No," Rold said. "I can't let you . . ."

"I was drawn here, Rold, to this star, for more than a visit. The process has already begun. I'm ready to take the final step."

"I won't let you!"

"You can't stop me."

She signaled to Gwydmonia her acceptance.

Just then the Militia made a last mad dash toward the Teton. The ground erupted into dust around them. The Teton gathered at Pentat's command and let loose thousands of arrows at the pitiful band. Not a single Militia was left alive. The silence was startling.

Tyler had stood her ground, paying little attention to fight.

"And now you'll stop this war?" she asked, looking up at the living cloud.

"CONSIDER IT DONE!" Gwydmonia said. "I WILL BE BACK, TYLER." And she disappeared, leaving a swish of cold air lifting debris all around the camp.

"What is she going to do?" Rold said frantically.

"The right thing," Tyler said and she found a place on the grass to sit.

Dust swirled high into the dark night sky. The valley floor rumbled, the surrounding hills echoing the groans and creeks of the stubborn spheres. The bronze balls of the Spotted Valley were rising for the last time. Above were a handful of living clouds. The spheres rose, one by one, to follow the minah-machacute as sheep, lining up singly. Occasionally two would bump on their way into the dark sky, emitting electrical sparks and clanging loudly. In a short time the valley was free of them, for the first time in a million years.

High above the atmosphere of Salkinia the spheres congregated, herded by the living clouds. They bunched together, looking like grapes, then formed a single, giant sphere. Energy burst forth and the sphere collapsed into a pin whole in the fabric of space.

As Rold watched the space battle, still wondering how many would die, a circular black shadow appeared in the middle of the speckled sky. He thought perhaps it was a cloud, or a living cloud, very high up, blotting a piece of the sky. It grew, keeping its shape. Peering at it, Rold felt his gaze disappearing into it as if it were a well where no light entered. He guessed what it was even before the first signs of the extraordinary event began. The dots of light, which must have been space transports closest to the shadow, zipped into it with such speed that Rold calculated they were approaching super lumina in their acceleration. Several dots streaked across the sky toward the shadow, disappearing into its blackness. Another went and then another, from further away. Then the show truly began: the space transports were falling into the shadow from all over the sky, leaving dazzling trails behind them. The shadow took on the appearance of an eclipsed sun with narrow, white rays as its aurora. The sky was white again; not from the battle but from the flashing trails of shooting stars.

The Teton were cheering as though it were a fireworks display in honor of their victory. Rold, though, was horrified and saw the disappearance of the transports as murder.

Then a rumbling came. The earth rolled under their feet, throwing everyone to the ground. Another quake shot through the city, and buildings cracked, debris tumbling down. The last, stray dots of light in the sky flew into the black maelstrom of plasma that had grown to fill half of the sky. The shadow erupted into a flash of light that made the night seem as day. Then the sky was dark, with stars twinkling, seeming faint compared to the battle that was there only moments before.

The tremors slowed, then stopped. Pentat was quickly around the camp checking on everyone's condition. He found Yosana and Rold holding each other, sitting on the ground. He knelt beside them, took Yosana by her hand and drew her into his arms. He patted her back and motioned Rold to join the embrace.

Gwydmonia returned. Rold was full of anger and questions. He stood on wobbly legs.

"What have you done!" he shouted without signing. Then, frustrated with the clumsiness of the hand communications, he forced himself to ask his question so that she could understand.

"DID YOU NOT THINK IT WAS BEAUTIFUL?" she said.

"Have you destroyed them then, after all? How could you!"

"THE HUMANS ARE ALL ALIVE."

Rold nodded his head, a tired look of acceptance with little understanding coming upon his face. He preferred to believe her, to think that he had not been a part of the destruction of millions of lives. Though to be a savior of those lives was just as taxing.

"Do you understand this?" Yosana said, looking at Rold.

He snorted. "The war is over. That's all we need to understand — except, what's to happen to Tyler."

"HER TIME WILL COME. GOOD-BYE."

Gwydmonia slowly rose into the invisible night. Rold felt tired but was too restless to settle down as yet; it was all too much to absorb. With the excitement over, the camp broke into a quiet rumble, people wondering whether to relax. Rold took first watch, but this time Yosana kept him company — and Frank. Tyler kept to herself. Rold already felt he had lost her. He was not sure he had actually ever accepted that she was still alive.

Yosana told Frank all about Pitallela, which took until late in the night. She and Rold pleaded with him to stay on Salkinia, but Frank insisted that if he could find a transport that had not been destroyed by the Teton, he would return to Old Earth. Finally, the next watch began, and the three found a place to rest. They actually slept.

In the morning the Teton went about the city in an effort to clean up after the battle of the day before. Both Rold and Frank were disturbed by the

Teton's constant need to destroy machinery. Most of them felt that the evil of the Whites was locked up in their technology and went about smashing machines as a type of exorcism. Rold had seen such behavior before and tried to understand. To Frank's horror, he finally joined in the attack of the defenseless machines, reluctantly at first, then with determination as he smashed the weapons of war that he came across with his warriors.

Later that morning, he, Frank, Yosana, and Tyler left the warriors and walked to find the command center in the Industrialist ward. If there was any trace of the remaining forces, an indication may be there. Frank knew his way among the glass buildings and smoothly paved streets. Last night's quake, though, had wrecked the complexion of the neighborhood. Glass was scattered along the streets, dropped from high above, and the pavement was cracked and buckled. Frank took them over the uneven, jumbled road to the far end of the city, close to the wall. The nerve center of the Industrialist operation was below ground, under a tall building built of golden metal and green glass. But the entrance was blocked by huge chunks of pavement and fallen debris.

"We'll need help moving this stuff," Rold said as he hopped around the piles of brick and glass, trying to see a way in.

They were startled by an energy blast — there had been no sound of weapons for hours. A second blast exploded upon impact next to Rold. He jumped and turned, then saw in the middle of the street two Industrialist Militia: they were women. Frank and Tyler were at the end of the block, too far for Rold or Yosana to reach. The Militia saw them and kept sweeping a weapon back and forth between Rold and Yosana, Frank and Tyler.

"*Barbara?*" Yosana said.

Rold recognized her also, and then the other person came into focus: Rachel Meacom. She was badly hurt, her leg ripped open and limp, her face burned, but it was she. And she was holding Barbara Jenkins tightly as if she were hostage.

"And so you *are* alive, Rold Simms," Rachel said. Her voice was hoarse; it sounded as though her lungs were full of fluid. "As Barbara claimed. You're inhuman, you bastard. I wish I had never . . . met you, heard of you. You've ruined our beautiful world, our whole society. Are you proud of what you've accomplished? You and those slunks, those bags of shit? Human kind has been set back thousands of years."

"Your war would have wrought worse," he said.

Tyler notched an arrow.

"Stop!" Rachel said. "Or Barbara will kill Rold, or I her." She had a hand weapon at Barbara's neck. Barbara held a larger weapon, steadied between her arm and chest. "So, you too live, Vivian Tyler. Phantoms both!"

"I am no longer Vivian Tyler," Tyler said. Her voice was that of a stranger.

Rold was taken aback but remained focused on Rachel.

"Please, Rachel," Rold said starting toward her with his hands open and reaching.

"Stop!" she screamed. "My father was in the battle. Where's he now, Rold? What did those monsters do? I watched from a viewer that was linked to his transport. It was like a hole, a deep chasm. I could see it; I could see my father. I watched as his ship was pulled out-of-control into the depths of it — then the leviathan swallowed the fleet; all was blank.

"The funny thing is: Ruth Poundstone had surrendered. We had won. Your weak Scientists were beaten. But she left too. Through the hole.

"August is dead. Everyone is dead. Except for you, of course. But now you'll die. Finally! God, if you had just died before, or if you had stayed in that prison cell, how different everything would be. I blame myself. I underestimated your real importance. I thought I had invented your importance to the game, but you were a part of it already."

Now Tyler lifted her bow above her head, lowering it slowly until she sighted Rachel.

"I'm telling you, stay back!" Rachel said. "Now you die, Rold Simms. You stupid little prig. How is it that you've brought us to this end? Have you thought at all about what has happened? The gravity of it?"

Rold laughed; in this moment, with death facing him, he laughed.

"What a bastard. Millions of people — gone. Like they never existed. My father! Gone, and you laugh!"

"And did you cry over the attempted genocide of the Teton!" Rold said. "Or cutting down my sister in cold blood!" Anger flashed in his eyes and raged in the timbre of his voice. Yosana was captivated by his manner — proud, and frightened. She wanted to go to him, but she stood ready.

Rachel pressed her weapon against Barbara's neck until her head bent forward, but her eyes stayed on Rold.

"Kill him!" she said. "As you were supposed to do before. Now, obey me."

Barbara did not speak at first. She aimed her black weapon at Rold.

"Why can't you do your own dirty work, Rachel?" Rold said. His taunt was in desperation. He swallowed as his stomach quivered.

The sound of people approaching startled everyone. Rachel's madness became acute, her own desperation peaking.

"Now!" she screamed and pressed harder against Barbara's neck.

"Forgive me," Barbara said, defeated. She looked at Frank; their eyes met, then she forced her head up and looked at Rold.

She fired the weapon, and in that instant Frank fired his, hitting her in the chest. Tyler threw her arrow and cleanly stole the life from Rachel. In the same moment, with no one seeing except Rold, Yosana leapt and shielded Rold. Barbara's shot hit her in the lower abdomen, knocking her into Rold and tumbling them both to the ground.

Pentat had come with a handful of warriors and had just reached the confrontation when Barbara fired. He was on top of Yosana and Rold immediately. The two women Industrialists were allowed to drop where they stood, though Frank gave Barbara one last look as she lay dying. Rold was unhurt but splattered with blood. He pushed everyone back, away from Yosana, screaming his orders. She lay on the ground still conscious, but with a seared hole in her middle. She tried to speak, coughing blood between each word.

"Rold . . . Pitallela," she said, looking into Rold's eyes. "I love you . . ."

She had a violent seizure then lay limp, death taking hold.

Rold screamed, when he thought he could scream no more. His screams brought fear to those around him — even Pentat who was feeling his pain. But he could not get close enough to help him. Yosana's head was in Rold's lap, and he kept stroking her hair as he finally calmed.

Gwydmonia came, floating up the street, between the buildings. Other living clouds came as well, much higher up. A crowd was forming around the street as word got out that Yosana was dead, the news racing quickly from person to person.

Rold looked up with little energy left in him to ridicule the living clouds, to blame them for this, but it occurred to him that he would trade the ending of the war for Yosana's life if things could be turned around. So instead of cursing, he stood calmly and spoke to Gwydmonia.

"Why did this have to happen?" he said, though he knew she had no answer.

"WE CAN NOT INTERFERE IN SOMETHING THAT WAS MEANT TO BE," Gwydmonia said.

Rold laughed, shaking his head. "How insipid that sounds. You've done nothing else but *interfere*. What about the war?"

"WHAT WE DID HAD TO HAPPEN, WAS MEANT TO HAPPEN."

"To lose a rider, the last rider, does that not upset the balance?"

Gwydmonia did not respond. No lights flashed for several minutes. Then she descended, pushing her hulking mass down onto the street.

"STAND BACK," she signed finally.

Everyone moved so as not to be crushed. Rold and Pentat stood together as they watched Gwydmonia take up Yosana's body. Several warriors angrily rushed toward her, but Rold held them back. No one knew what her intentions were, but Rold had little strength left to question her.

Gwydmonia's body lifted and began to shutter. Several living clouds congregated above her until the sky was dark. In an instant she fell to the street, collapsing to the thinness of a man's height. Yosana's naked body rolled from her as a log down a hill, all the way to Rold's feet. Rold knelt beside her and saw that the burned hole in her stomach was totally healed, and she was breathing! Rold shed hot tears over her, and Yosana opened her eyes. She was too weak to speak but was alert. Pentat examined her and nodded. Rold stood to thank Gwydmonia, to praise the miracle; then he saw at what cost it had occurred. She was shrinking, shriveling up as a slug being dehydrated by the summer sun. He made signs trying to get her to speak.

"How can I say thank you?" he said. "Why? Why did you do this? How did you do it? It's like a fairy tale."

"MY GIFT TO YOU, ROLD. I FELT YOUR PAIN."

"I REGRET," Gwydmonia continued, "I WILL NOT HAVE THE PLEASURE OF TAKING PITALLELA RIDING."

"I didn't ask you to kill yourself," Rold said. "It's too great a burden."

"IT WAS MY CHOICE," she said. "I'M GOING TO JOIN MY PANDODELLOCK. I FEAR, THOUGH, I MAY HAVE UNDONE EVERYTHING WE HAVE TRIED TO ACCOMPLISH. PERHAPS TYLER WILL MEND THIS BREACH."

She made a great shutter and burst open her shell along its top. Fluid spilled out in small rivulets, soaking into the street, as if the hard pavement were sand. Yosana was now sitting, staring in wonder, moisture in her eyes. But Rold's eyes were dry.

Tyler approached the lifeless hulk and pressed her hand into one of the rifts. The living cloud flesh curled about her like a cloak until her entire body was covered. Gwydmonia's shell shrank until what had been the giant form of the living cloud was barely a tenth its original size. Tyler could still be seen through the milky membrane.

Rold leapt to her side. Yosana reached to hold him back, but he pulled away.

Sparks of light burst about the surface of the new symbiotic entity, obscuring Tyler's form. Words formed from the lights: "I AM MARGONA, ONCE A QUEEN AMONG YOUR PEOPLE."

"And what of Tyler?" Yosana asked. Rold could not speak.

"I WAS TYLER FOR ONLY A MOMENT IN TIME, NOW I AM SET FREE. IN TIME I WILL KNOW HER HISTORY AND WILL SHOW HER TO YOU AGAIN. SHE STILL LIVES. BUT FOR NOW I MUST TAKE MY COMPANIONS, THOSE YOU CALL MINAH-MACHACUTE, TO THE PLACE OF BIRTHS. FAREWELL."

From the sparkling wet ground arose this new creature, not quite a living cloud, but no longer human either. Other living clouds surrounded it, seemingly to help it make its first steps. Among the flock floated a ghost: the image of a beautiful, white lady, with white hair, wearing a white gown. She gestured a farewell with her delicate hand, then rose above the multitude until all that Rold could see was the blue spring sky of Salkinia — a sky with birds and warm sunshine and stillness. An eagle circled silently in the high draft above them.

Rold held Yosana close to him, and as he gazed through his tears, he wondered if anyone else could see the beautiful lady. But he knew it was not important. He had seen her; that was all that mattered.

Welcome to the world of Domhan Books! Domhan, pronounced DOW-ann, is the Irish word for universe. Our vision is to provide readers with high-quality hardcover, paperback and electronic books in a variety of genres from writers all over the world.

ORDERING INFORMATION

All Domhan paper books may be ordered from Barnes and Noble, barnesandnoble.com, Amazon, Borders, and other fine booksellers using the ISBN. They are distributed worldwide by Ingram Book Group, 1 Ingram Blvd., La Vergne, Tennessee 37086 (615) 793-5000. Most titles are also available electronically in a variety of formats through Galaxy Library at www.galaxylibrary.com. Rocket *eBook*™ editions are available on-line at barnesand noble.com, Powell's, and other booksellers. Please visit our website for previews, reviews, and further details on our titles: www.domhanbooks.com. Domhan Books, 9511 Shore Road, Suite 514, Brooklyn, New York 11209 U.S.A.

ACTION AND ADVENTURE

Paladin - Barry Nugent 1-58345-365-2 192 pp. $12.95

Princess Yasmin must go on a quest for a mythical crown, the only thing that can prevent civil war erupting in the exotic land of Primera. Along the way she meets her favorite adventure author Barnaby Jackson, and the sparks really start to fly. This is a taut action novel reminiscent of the Indiana Jones series of films.

Yala - Don Clark 1-58345-561-2 180 pp. $12.95

In the no man's land between the U.S. and Mexico in 1896, a Chinese clan stakes a claim to a new territory. Two Texas Rangers decide to end their law officer careers and go to New China in order to raise the bankroll needed to start a ranch. Hank and his younger sidekick, Luke, soon meet Yala, a condemned and notorious Chinese criminal: a female assassin.

CHRISTIAN FICTION

The Gospel According to Condo Don - Fred Dungan 1-58345-004-1 216 pp. $12.95

This is an account of the Second Coming as witnessed by a homeless alcoholic. While loosely modeled on the initial books of the New Testament (Matthew, Mark, Luke and John), it interjects humor into the classic story and presents it in a more readily understood contemporary format. Thus,

Mary becomes Marva, a poor 16- year-old girl from Central Los Angeles, an evil televangelist takes the place of the money changers at the temple, and our bureaucracy is substituted for that of Rome's.

The Way Found - Nina J. Lechiara 1-58345-017-3 472 pp. $20.00
1532-1558
Matteo and Gianna search for love and truth in university studies, religion and philosophy, from Padua and Venice to Egypt and Arabia. They find it unexpectedly in Yahshua, in the one place they have never looked, the Scriptures. They learn both the truth and the meaning of love and marriage, and become shining examples of Yahvah's way.

<u>FANTASY</u>
The Druid's Woman - Shanna Murchison 1-58345-245-1 120 pp. $10
In this novel of Ireland, Davnat encounters Parthalann, a mysterious druid who trains her up to be his helper and consort. But despite all the powers she is given, their Fates have already been decreed....

The Wizard Woman - Shanna Murchison 1-58345-020-3 204 pp. hardcover $18.95; 1-58345-018-1 paper $12.95
Ireland 1169
The great Celtic myth of the Wheel of Fate is played out against the backdrop of the first Norman invasion of Ireland in 1169. Dairinn is made the wizard's woman, chosen by the gods to be the wife of the handsome but mysterious Senan. Through him she discovers her own innate powers, and the truth behind her family history. She must bargain with the Morrigan, the goddess of death, if she is ever to achieve happiness with the man she loves. But how high a price will she have to pay for Senan's life?

The Wings of Love - Karen L. Williams 1-58345-466-7 180 pp. $12.95
There is no room in Sean MacDonagh's life for imagination. But when he finds himself having the same dreams over and again, he has to do something, and quickly. The last thing he considers as good therapy is a trip to Northern Ireland to see his estranged family. Then again, getting away from the hustle and bustle of New York City might be just what he needs to clear his mind of the mysterious woman who begins to haunt his whole life.
Treyanna, Faerie princess, rebelling against an arranged marriage, travels through time to win her freedom. Completely opposite to Sean in every way, the time they spend together brings them all they are missing in their lives. But can Sean learn to live with Treyanna's mystical powers, or will he flee from her-and his own insecurities and failings?

HISTORICAL FICTION

The Wildest Heart - Jacinta Carey 1-58345-041-6 224 pp. $12.95
Rebecca Whitaker is struggling to keep her family ranch from foreclosure by trading with the Indians, working in a saloon, and breeding horses. Enter the mysterious Walker Pritchard, claiming he wishes to stay with Reb to leave the memories of the Civil War behind and learn about the ways of the west. They fall in love, but can Reb trust Walker? What are his real motives for coming to the Bar T, and how did he know there would be gold in those hills? Reb must fight to save him and her ranch, before everything she loves is destroyed by the men from Walker's mysterious past.

Natchez - Deb Crockett   1-58345-008-4 180 pp. $12.95
Welcome to Natchez, home to whores, gamblers, and anyone out to make a fast buck, no matter what the cost...
The untimely death of lovely young Rebecca Bennett's father forces the feisty girl from Savannah to live by her wits. Alone, penniless, and seemingly betrayed by the only man she has ever truly loved, she struggles to stay alive and fulfill her dream: to buy her beloved Oliver's plantation and have a home of her own, even though he is miles away. But though she tries to live honestly through hard work, she makes powerful enemies. Can she ever find happiness, safety, love, and the people responsible for her father's death and her ruin?

The Summer Stars - Alan Fisk 1-58345-549-3 202 pp. $12.95
Britain's oldest poems were composed in the sixth century by the bard Talicsin. Many legends have been told about he of the "shining brow," but in this novel he tells his own story. Taliesin's travels take him through turbulent times as Britain tries to cope with the disappearance of Roman civilization, and the increasing threat of the Saxon invaders.

Scars Upon Her Heart - Sorcha MacMurrough 1-58345-011-4 232 pp. $12.95
Lady Vevina Joyce and her brother Wilfred are forced to flee Ireland after being falsely accused of treason. On the road with Wellington's army, they meet an unexpected ally in the enigmatic Major Stewart Fitzgerald. Side by side they fight with their comrades in some of the most bitter battles of the Napoleonic Wars. Can Vevina clear her name, protect those she loves, and stop the Grand Army from taking over the whole of Europe in a bold and daring move engineered by the person responsible for her family's disgrace? Is Stewart really all that he seems? Appearances can be deceptive....

Destiny Lies Waiting - Diana Rubino 1-58345-078-5 hardcover 208 pp. $18.50;
1-58345-451-9 paper $12.95
Volume One of *The Yorkist Saga*
Beautiful orphaned Denys has been bought up a member of the Woodville family, now in power thanks to her aunt Elizabeth, wife of the new Yorkist king Edward IV. Unwilling to become a pawn in her aunt's bid for power, she decides to seek the truth about her family and identity.
Valentine Starbury, loyal ally to young Richard, Duke of Gloucester, the King's brother, agrees to woo Denys in order to save his friend from Elizabeth Woodville's plan for Richard and Denys to wed. He unexpectedly falls in love with her, thus earning the enmity of the queen. The secrets both uncover will have dangerous consequences for Denys and Valentine, and the whole of England itself.

Thy Name is Love - Diana Rubino 1-58345-079-3 hardcover 212 pp. $18.50;
1-58345-392-X paper $12.95
Volume Two of *The Yorkist Saga*
The story first begun in *Destiny Lies Waiting* continues in this second volume. Denys Starbury and her husband Valentine are thrust into the world of power politics as one by one the royal family is eliminated, until only one man can contend for the throne, Richard, Duke of Gloucester. Denys continues to search for her lost family, but she finds only a trail of murder and destruction. She also seeks the love of Valentine. In a world of shifting allegiances, how can she ever bring herself to trust him?

The Jewels of Warwick - Diana Rubino 1-58345-080-7 hardcover 236 pp. $18.50; 1-58345-413-6 paper $12.95
Volume Three of *The Yorkist Saga*
In this sequel to *Thy Name is Love*, the saga of the Yorkist royal family continues. The "Jewels" are two sisters, Topaz and Amethyst Plantagenet. They are descendants of Richard III, who lost his life and kingdom to Henry Tudor, future father of Henry VIII.
Topaz always felt she was the rightful queen, and would have been, had her father been crowned as Richard's heir. But life holds many strange twists of fate....

Crown of Destiny - Diana Rubino 1-58345-081-5 hardcover 204 pp. $18.50;

1-58345-456-X paper $12.95
Volume Four of *The Yorkist Saga*
In this sequel to *The Jewels of Warwick*, Topaz's rebellion against Henry VIII
gets under way, throwing England into civil war and chaos. Amethyst is forced
to choose between remaining loyal to her sister, or losing the only two men
she has ever loved: the king, and her sister's husband Matthew....

I Love You Because - Diana Rubino 1-58345-082-3 hardcover 264 pp.
$18.50;
1-58345-423-3 paper 264 pp. $12.95
Vita Caputo meets handsome Irish cop Tom McGlory at the scene of a crime.
This fateful encounter has consequences for both their families as they must
struggle together to end the corruption in turn-of-the-century New York City
politics before more crimes are committed and more lives are lost.

An Experience in Four Movements - Lidmila Sovakova 1-58345-002-5
124 pp. $10
This is a historical puzzle situated in the seventeenth century. Its pieces re-
construct the infatuation of a Poet with a Princess, culminating in the death of
the Poet, and the retreat of the Princess within the walls of a monastery.

<u>**IRISH INTEREST**</u>
Call Home the Heart - Sorcha MacMurrough 1-58345-072-6 hardcover
244 pp. $18.95; 1-58345-394-6 paper $12.95
Young widow Muireann Graham Caldwell is left destitute by her dissolute
husband, Augustine, killed in a shooting accident on their honeymoon. Faced
with a choice between returning to her stifling parents in Scotland or taking a
chance on running her own estate, Muireann finds an ally in the broodingly
handsome Lochlainn Roche. He has secrets of his own to keep. As the Potato
Famine rages across Ireland, can Muireann save her new home Barnakilla?
Can she and her estate manager ever have a future together? Does he even
love her? Or has he been using her all along?

The Faithful Heart - Sorcha MacMurrough 1-58345-023-8 204 pp. $12.95
Who has murdered Morgana Maguire's brother, poisoned her father, and stolen most of her clan's ships? These are just a few of the pressing questions
Morgana must find answers to if she and her one true love Ruairc MacMahon
are ever to find happiness in each other's arms. Set against the backdrop of
Renaissance power politics during the reign of Henry VIII, Morgana and Ruairc
must fight not only to win each other, but also to protect all of Ireland from
civil war and foreign invasion.

The Fire's Centre - Sorcha MacMurrough 1-58345-025-4 264 pp. $12.95
Riona Connolly is willing to do anything to save her family from starvation
during the Potato Famine. So when she meets the handsome Dr. Lucien
Woulfe, who offers her post at his clinic, it seems a dream come true. But
their growing attraction is forbidden in the straight-laced society of Victorian
Dublin. Riona and Lucien must walk through the fire's centre to secure their
happiness before it is destroyed by the evil Dr. O'Carroll and the vagaries of
Fate.

**The Hart and the Harp - Sorcha MacMurrough 1-58345-030-0 288 pp.
$12.95**
Ireland, 1149
Shive MacDermot and Tiernan O'Hara agree to wed to end a five-year feud
between their clans. Though an unlikely alliance at first, Shive begins to fall
in love with her new husband. She soon realises the murderer of her brother
is a member of her own clan. How can she win Tiernan's love and prove to
him she is not the enemy? Shive undertakes an epic struggle to save her lands
and Tiernan's from the ambitious Muireadach O'Rourke, determined to kill
anyone who opposes his bid to become high-king of all Ireland. Will she
prove worthy of Tiernan, or will he believe all of the vicious lies about her
supposed love for another, and become her enemy himself?

Hunger for Love - Sorcha MacMurrough 1-58345-005-X 244 pp. $12.95
Ireland and Canada, 1847
Emer Nugent and her family are evicted from their home at the height of the
Potato Famine in Ireland. Forced to emigrate to Canada, they endure a har-
rowing journey on board a coffin ship bound for Grosse Ile. Emer, working
as a cabin boy to help her family's financial situation, meets the enigmatic
Dalton Randolph, the ship's only gentleman passenger, who is not all that he
seems. They fall in love, but darker forces are at work against them. Emer's
duty to her family forces the lovers to separate. Will they ever be able to
overcome the obstacles in their path to true love? This incredible saga of love,
adventure and intrigue continues in the second volume *The Hungry Heart*.

**The Hungry Heart - Sorcha MacMurrough   1-58345-006-8 232 pp.
$12.95**
Canada and Ireland 1847-1849
Emer Nugent leaves her lover Dalton Randall to search for her family in the
hell of the Grosse Ile quarantine station. The land of opportunity is nearly the
death of them all. Dalton is deceived by his father into thinking Emer is

dead, and is about to marry the daughter of a business rival when he meets Emer again. Outraged that his plans for keeping the two apart have failed, Dalton's father has Emer arrested on false charges and transported back to Ireland.

But the Ireland she returns to is on the brink of civil war. Emer finds herself unwittingly embroiled in the 1848 rebellion, and is put on trial for her life. Dalton must travel half way across the world to try to save her before it is too late. This incredible saga of love and adventure begins with the first volume, *Hunger for Love.*

The Sea of Love - Sorcha Mac Murrough 1-58345-032-7 6 hardcover 148 pp. $15.95; 1-58345-033-5 paper $10
Ireland 1546
Wrongfully accused of murder, Aidanna O'Flaherty's only ally against her evil brother-in-law Donal is the dashing English-bred aristocrat Declan Burke. Saving him from certain death, they fall in love, only to be separated when Declan is falsely accused of treason. Languishing in the Tower, Declan is powerless to assist his beloved Aidanna as she undertakes an epic struggle to expose her enemy and save her family and friends. She must race against time to prevent all she loves from being swept aside in a thunderous tide of foreign invasion....

LITERARY/MAINSTREAM FICTION
The Nestucca Retreat - M. Lee Locke 1-58345-009-2 216 pp. $12.95
J. Cunningham Raleigh died in an Oregon rain storm — struck by lightning while playing an electric guitar on a river dock. A mediocre rock musician who never quite left the Sixties, Ham Raleigh was an intimate part of a long-standing triangle. Millie and Jake Prince, a forty-something couple, were Ham's best friends. He was a part of Jake's life from childhood and Millie's since college. He was an intruder in their marriage and also the glue that kept them together. Millie and Jake drift apart after Ham's death, though continue to struggle with staying together, still using Ham as a crutch. Ham's death does not really cause this distancing but reveals the existing rift between them, one that has been ever widening for years. At the ceremony Millie, Jake and Ham's ex-wives hold to say goodbye to Ham, an unexpected visitor turns up who will change their lives forever.....

Eclipse Over Lake Tanganyika - Albert Russo 1-58345-057-2 hardcover 208 pp. $18.95; 1-58345-058-0 paper $12.95
A novel of Rwanda on the eve of its independence.
In this novel of Africa, Russo offers us a wide range of fascinating characters,

their hopes, desires, dreams and aspirations, as they struggle against themselves and a rapidly changing society.

Mixed Blood - Albert Russo 1-58345-050-5 hardcover 212 pp. $18.95; 1-58345-051-3 paper $12.95
A moving novel set in the Belgian Congo on the eve of Independence.
Leopold, an orphan of 'mixed blood,' is adopted by a lonely American who tries to fit in with his adopted society. Leopold's new mother is the indomitable Mama Malkia, who has a fascinating story of her own to tell.

Falling in Love - Lidmila Sovakova 1-58345-039-4 hardcover 184 pp. $18.95;
1-58345-289-3 paper $12.95
Volume One of *The Jazz Saga*
Set in Prague, this is a poignant tale of love, loss, and the search for happiness of a young girl growing up in turbulent times.

Like a Bubble in a Glass of Champagne - Lidmila Sovakova 1-58345-290-7 hard-cover 164 pp. $16.95; 1-58345-040-8 paper $10
Volume Two of *The Jazz Saga*
Irene's adventures in Prague, begun in the novel *Falling in Love*, continue in this moving novel as she must struggle to find happiness with the very different men in her life.

The Sophisticated Lady - Lidmila Sovakova 1-58345-059-9 hardcover 148 pp. $16.95; 1-58345-291-5 paper $10
Volume Three of *The Jazz Saga*
Irene, growing up in Prague, thought she had it all, and could keep it all. In love with and loved by four very different men, one by one they have been stripped away from her, leaving only Leo, the man she has finally wed. Now her family are stripped from her one by one. Can she maintain the façade of the happily married and blushing young bride? Or is she set on her path of self-destruction?

The Frosted Mirrors - Lidmila Sovakova 1-58345-286-9 160 pp. $10
Volume One of *The Gray Saga*
This is the story of Rinaldo, a young boy who adores his mother and will do anything for her approval. But she is oblivious to all else except the creative muse which drives her poetry, and her cat. The story is also of a painter who is doomed to fall in love with them both.

The Scarlet Maze - Lidmila Sovakova 1-58345-287-7 192 pp. $10
Volume Two of *The Gray Saga*
The story of Rinaldo and his mother, started in *The Frosted Mirrors*, continues in this moving novel. The passionate triangle continues, defying even death, as the three lovers struggle to hold on to each other, even in the face of overwhelming odds.

The Eye of Medusa - Lidmila Sovakova 1-58345-288-5 172 pp. $10
Volume Three of *The Gray Saga*
The sequel to *The Frosted Mirrors* and *The Scarlet Maze*, this novel continues the saga of Rinaldo and his mother, and their search for happiness, which is often at odds with the creative muse that drives them. It also furthers the tale of the painter Christopher Gray, and his struggle to win both their loves.

LITERARY CRITICISM
The Playmaker: A Study Guide - S. McNally 1-58345-412-8 124 pp. $10.00
A study guide to the book now currently on various examination syllabi. It contains notes on each chapter, sample essays and questions, historical background, and biographical information about the author and his works.

MYSTERY
St. John's Baptism - William Babula 1-58345-496-9 260 pp. $12.95
In this first of the Jeremiah St. John series, the hero is summoned to a meeting by Rick Silverman, one of San Francisco's most prominent drug attorneys. St. John knows Silverman's unsavory clientele and so docs not think anything of the invitation—that is until he finds Silverman dead.

According to St. John - William Babula 1-58345-521-9 240 pp. $12.95
In this second St. John adventure, St. John's friend Denise is supposed to be in Frisco appearing in a new production of *Macbeth* with legendary actress Amanda Cole. They arrive at the theater only to discover that Amanda has been murdered and Denise is the prime suspect. St. John soon learns that everyone involved is playing a role. By the time they track down the killer, St. John and his intrepid colleagues uncover some horrifying secrets from the past, and the mind-boggling motive.

St. John and the Seven Veils - William Babula 1-58345-506-X 208 pp. $12.95
In this third mystery in the popular series, St John and his two partners Mickey and Chief Moses are hired to track down a serial killer by a woman claiming

to be the killer's mother! Three men have been brutally murdered, but they are without any apparent connection until St. John stumbles across one through a seemingly unrelated case. From the Seven Veils Brothel in Reno to a hide-out in Northern California, St John is hot on the trail, crossing paths with a famous televangelist, prominent military man, high-powered doctor, and a complete madman.

St. John's Bestiary - William Babula 1-58345-511-6 264 pp. $12.95
St. John should never have taken this fourth case. But he just couldn't help it—Professor Krift's story of his eight stolen cats strikes a sympathetic chord. After rescuing the victims from a ruthless gang of animal rights activists, the CFAF, he is caught catnapping as the CFAF kidnap the professor's daughter. Suddenly the morgue is filling up, and not just with strangers. St. John's new love Ollie is killed, and he determines to stop at nothing until her murder is avenged. The tangled case drags him through every racket going: money laundering, dope pushing, porno, prostitution, and very nearly drags him six foot under.

St. John's Bread - William Babula 1-58345-516-7 hardcover 180 pp. $18.95;
1-58345-516-7 paper $12.95
In this fifth volume of the series, St. John and his two intrepid partners get caught up in a tangle of missing children's cases after he and Mickey rescue a baby about to be kidnapped in a public park. Mickey tries to tell him that he needs the "bread" to pay for his brand new Victorian stately home which houses him and their detective agency, but this case comes with a higher price tag than any of them are willing to pay.

The Fox and the Puma - Barbara Sohmers 1-58345-486-1 156 pp. $10
This is the first novel in the popular Fred and Maggy Renard series.
When a nude, partly-devoured body is found near a popular beach on an island off the southern coast of France, the small community erupts into panic. Old hatreds and sins begin to surface, and many more ugly secrets will be revealed…

The Fox and the Pussycat - Barbara Sohmers 1-58345-491-8 160 pp. $10
In the second of her Fred and Maggy Renard adventures, the intrepid pair become embroiled in the raunchy underground world of Paris in an effort to track down the killer of her friend Marie-Claude.

POETRY

Cold Moon: The Erotic Haiku of Gabriel Rosenstock 1-58345-042-4 108 pp. $12.95

This is a bilingual book in English and Irish from one of the foremost poets in both languages. Complete with powerful illustrations, this is a must for anyone who loves poetry, elegant books, and all things Irish.

A Portrait of the Artist as an Abominable Snowman - Gabriel Rosenstock 1-58345-124-2 108 pp. $12.95

Another fine collection of poetry in English and Irish from this stunning voice in the world of verse.

SCIENCE FICTION

The Event - Gregory Farnum 1-58345-553-1 176 pp. $12.95

This is a fast-paced technothriller. Prendyk and his girlfriend Jennifer are dragged into a dark world of government conspiracy. "The Event" will have far-reaching consequences for all of mankind.

ROMANCES

Campaign for Love - Michaela Brennan 1-58345-285-0 144 pp. $10

Tired of being hassled over her gorgeous looks, Suzanna Sills dresses down to get a wonderful new job in a top-notch ad agency. She soon regrets her frumpy appearance when she has to work with the gorgeous Quentin Pierce. Quentin hasn't failed to notice that his hottest new star has more to her than meets the eye. But office intrigues get them both into a spin. Can they avoid losing the biggest ad campaign the company has ever seen, and learn to trust one another?

The Right Code - Sharon Holmes 1-58345-448-9 $12.95

Jonathan C. Evans is mocked as a computer nerd who lives by logic. Jasmine Banks is the only one who sees Jon differently. She grows determined to make this man realize that logic has nothing to do with a relationship between a man and a woman. But she gets more than she bargains for as the real JC Evans is revealed...

The Picture of Bliss - Jacqui Jerome 1-58345-268-0 168 pp. $10

Just when Candice Edwards thinks she has escaped from her past, she is propelled into a nightmarish encounter with her ex-fiancé. Can she trust the secretive and mercurial designer Lochlainn Alexander, or is he part of the whole plot to ruin her career?

Heart's Desire - Sorcha MacMurrough   1-58345-031-9 160 pp. $10
Nurse Sinead Thomas rescues the hospital's handsome architect Austin Riordan from a life-threatening situation. She accepts his offer to be his private nurse over the Christmas holidays, but gets more than she bargained for as they grow ever closer. A young widow, she never wants to go through the torment of being in love again. But Austin is nothing if not persistent. Can they fight the demons from her past, to secure their hearts' desire?

Star Attraction - Sorcha MacMurrough   1-58345-037-8 168 pp. $10
Zaira Darcy literally bumps into the man of her dreams in an elevator. Dashing Brad Clarke, Hollywood's hottest new director, working alongside her in New York, is everything she could want in a man, and more. But the secrets from her past, and the double life she leads, threaten to destroy any chance of happiness the two might have. Zaira must lock horns with her ex-husband Jonathan one last time to save Brad's life, even if it means sacrificing her own.

Love's Sweet Song - Annabelle Stevens 1-58345-275-3 132 pp. $10
Angelica Castle Murray loses everything in a tragic accident: husband, daughter, and very nearly her life. But in the aftermath of his disaster, she must not only struggle to regain her health, but to come to terms with the fact that ever since her ex-fiancé Winston broke up with her seven years before, she has been living a lie. Winston Murray has never stopped loving Angelica, even when she was married to his brother. Her old life is now in shambles; but how can he tell her that her life with Oliver has been a big lie?

The Art of Love - Evelyn Trimborn 1-58345-001-7 164 pp. $10
Struggling Dublin artist Shannon Butler gives a hugely successful show. Enter her estranged adopted brother Marius Winters, hell-bent on revenge. He accuses her of robbing him of his share of their dead father's estate. Thrown together by circumstances, they try to make up for the mistakes of the past. Despite all their differences, they grow ever closer. But Marius' lying ex-wife threatens any chance of happiness they might have. How can Shannon prevent her new-found love from leaving her forever?

Castles in the Air - Evelyn Trimborn 1-58345-019-X 168 pp. $10
Poverty-stricken aristocrat Alanna Lacy is at her wits' end. Enter property developer Bran Ryan, who offers her a way out of her desperate financial situation— marry him! Faced with her father's disapproval, and Bran's spiteful ex-fiancée, can they build a future together, or will all their dreams go up in smoke?

Forbidden Fantasy - Evelyn Trimborn 1-58345-256-7 124 pp. $10
Rose Gray is one of America's top romance writers. So why is it she can't
ever seem to meet Mr. Right? Luke Byrnes changes all that when he bursts
into her life unexpectedly. Will it be "Happily Ever After" Or "The End"?

Heedless Hearts - Evelyn Trimborn 1-58345-251-6 132 pp. $10
Inexperienced housekeeper Marielle gets more than she bargains for when
she takes a post at the house of architect Tristan Fitzmaurice. Sparks fly from
the moment they meet, but all too soon, she can feel herself being drawn to
him irresistibly. But how can she love him, when he is about to be married to
another? But the heart is heedless when it comes to love.

Design for Love - Shirley Wolford 1-58345-594-9 $10
Beautiful interior decorator Ann Seymour gets the chance to prove herself
more than capable of running her family's design works when she runs into
the enigmatic Adam Frazier, a swashbuckling hunk who has lived abroad for
many years and returned home to Orange County. She has a job to do, but can
she ever learn to control her feelings whenever they meet?

THRILLERS
The Delaney Escape - Brent Kroetch 1-58345-021-1 264 pp. $12.95
Ex-CIA agent turned IRA man Noel Delaney plans to escape from Leavenworth
prison.
Guy Morgan, an ex-agent trained by Delaney, is determined to track his old
mentor down. He teams up with his long-time love, Karly Widman of British
Intelligence, to trace Delaney's movements to Ireland. But the trap springs.
Who is the hunter, and who the prey?

**Ghost From the Past - Sorcha MacMurrough 1-58345-029-7 180 pp.
$12.95**
Biochemist Clarissa Vincent's fiancé Julian Simmons was killed in a terrible
explosion five years ago. Or was he? Taking a new job in Portland, Oregon,
Clarissa sees a man at the airport who could be Julian's double, and is suddenly propelled into a nightmarish world of espionage and intrigue. She
must struggle to save her family and the man she has always loved from the
ruthless people who will stop at nothing to achieve world domination.

In From the Cold - Carolyn Stone 1-58345-007-6 224 pp. $12.95
Cambridge scientist Sophie Ruskin is dragged into a world of espionage and
intrigue when her father, a Russian defector, vanishes. Adrian Vaughan, handsome, enigmatic, but haunted by his past, is assigned to train her as a spy to

win her father's freedom, or destroy his work before his kidnappers can create the ultimate weapon. But Adrian's fate soon lies in Sophie's hands, as she travels two continents to save his life, win his love, and fight for the freedom of the oppressed, war-torn Russian Republic of Chechnya.

Mutual Attraction - Diana Waldhuber 1-58345-382-2 148 pp. $10
Journalist Jordan Taylor's dream job turns out to be a nightmare when she meets the cool, suave, Ashford Blackard. Each presents an irresistible challenge for the other—but what will the fateful consequences of their game of cat and mouse be?

Spin Me a Web - Shirley K. Wolford 1-58345-598-1 $12.95
Caitlin Cameron, amateur sleuth and feature writer for *Antique Autos Magazine*, challenges her readers to find the thief who stole four priceless antique sports cars. Her life is threatened unless she stops her column. But she's stubborn and has other ideas. She asks Rick Falconer, world-class tennis ace, and new owner of the romantic pre-war, hand-made, antique sports car, *the Princess Eula*, to help trap the thief by using his car as bait.
Rick is appalled at her request and refuses. But then the car is stolen and Rick becomes the main suspect. Both must work together to find the real thief, and uncover a conspiracy which threatens their blossoming love for one another.

ORDERING INFORMATION

All Domhan paper books may be ordered from Barnes and Noble, barnesandnoble.com, Amazon, Borders, and other fine booksellers using the ISBN. They are distributed worldwide by Ingram Book Group, 1 Ingram Blvd., La Vergne, TN 37086, 615 793-5000.
Most titles are also available electronically in a variety of formats through Galaxy Library at www.galaxylibrary.com. Rocket *e*Book editions are available on-line at barnesandnoble.com, Powell's, and other fine booksellers. Please visit our website for previews, reviews, and further details on our titles: www.domhanbooks.com
Domhan Books, 9511 Shore Road, Suite 514, Brooklyn, NY 11209